# PRIVATE
# PLEASURES

*Also by JoAnn Ross*

*Secret Sins*

JoAnn Ross

# PRIVATE PLEASURES

St. Martin's Press    New York

Design by Tanya M. Pérez

Library of Congress Cataloging-in-Publication Data

Ross, JoAnn
        Private pleasures / JoAnn Ross.
                p.   cm.
        ISBN 0-312-07762-9
        I. Title.
   PS3568.O843485P75   1992
   813'.54—dc20                                                                    92-3603
                                                                                   CIP


First Edition: May 1992

10 9 8 7 6 5 4 3 2 1

*To Jay and Patrick—my good fortune*

# *Prologue*

1986
*Seriphos, Greece*

Even from a distance, Jade recognized him immediately.

He was standing on the white cliff, overlooking a stretch of golden sand studded with models, a photographer, assistants, and a gaggle of local fishermen who'd returned from a morning's fishing to discover their beach inhabited by Sirens.

His eyes were hidden by the opaque lenses of his aviator sunglasses, but his mouth was set in a firm, forbidding line that was a distinct contrast to the devastating smile she remembered. Which was just as well. She'd gotten her fill of Roarke Gallagher's smile years ago.

Try as she might, Jade could not hide her distress at Roarke's unexpected appearance. There was turmoil in her heart and her stomach; her movements, normally fluid, turned stiff and jerky.

"Christ, Jade," Brian Devlin, the Irish photographer she had worked with on numerous occasions, complained, "That grimace belongs on a bleedin' corpse." He thrust his camera at his harried assistant, barked for, and instantly received, two small plastic bottles.

Cursing under his breath in the colorful Irish brogue that Jade had always found endearing, Brian yanked off his sneakers and waded into the lacy surf. The rumbles of an approaching afternoon thunderstorm threatened ominously in the sky overhead.

"You're supposed to be selling swimsuits, darlin' girl," he scolded as he sprayed Jade's voluptuous body first with coconut oil, then water.

The droplets beaded up on her gleaming skin like sequins. "Not funeral plots."

Unlike most redheads, Jade didn't sunburn. Her flesh, revealed by a gold mesh bikini that would have gotten her arrested in all forty-eight contiguous states, gleamed with warm gold and caramel tones.

"I don't know what's bothering you, Jade," Brian said, "but I do know damn well that *Vogue* won't be thrilled at the prospect of keeping an entire crew on location an extra day just because their cover model can't get her act together."

He was right. Jade reminded herself that she was a professional. She was not permitted pimples, premenstrual weight gain, moods, or any problems that might interfere with a shoot. "I'm sorry, Brian. It's the weather. Storms make me nervous," she explained with an apologetic smile. "But I'm fine now."

"That's me darlin' girl," he said, with the air of a man who expected no other answer, as he expertly tousled her russet hair. The magnificent halo, tinted copper by the afternoon sun, was a wild gypsy tangle over her bare shoulders. "Let's give it another try, shall we? Before that storm hits."

Frowning up at the sky, he waded back to the beach and retrieved his camera. "Try bending over, Jade."

The irritation was gone from his voice, replaced by the low, seductive brogue designed to make Jade feel as if she were the most beautiful, most desirable woman in the world. Which, if the glowing story in last month's *Newsweek* was any indication, she just might be.

"That's it," he coaxed huskily. "Splash a little. . . . Terrific. Come toward me. . . . That's dynamite, darling', you remind me of glorious Venus risin' on her shell. . . . Now give me one of your man-meltin' smiles."

Although she was looking at the camera, Jade could feel Roarke's intense gaze as she tried to obey the photographer's command.

Devlin dropped to his knees on the damp sand. "Come on, darlin', you can do better than that," he complained. "Think sex."

That was, unfortunately, all too easy. All Jade had to do was think of Roarke. And remember how his strong hands used to make her body come alive, how his mouth once warmed her flesh.

Turning her back, she looked over her shoulder straight into the unblinking lens of the camera, then licked her lips, wetting the bronze Chanel gel that the makeup girl had applied. Her cat-green eyes, emphasized with gold shadow and khol liner, flashed with invitations, each one more suggestive than the last. The seductive look was one the world had come to know well.

The instant the now-famous issue of French *Elle* with her face on the cover had hit the newsstands, Jade had been declared the "New Face of the Decade."

On a list that included British model-turned-actress Rachel Ward, *Harper's Bazaar* named her one of the most beautiful women in America. The readers of *Penthouse* voted her the woman they'd most like to be stranded with on a desert island, while in a poll conducted by *Seventeen* magazine, Jade was named the woman most admired by its youthful female readership.

Her agent, Nina Grace, kept her booked months in advance; in the four years she'd been in the business, Jade had gone on nearly eight hundred shoots and was earning much more than the hundred thousand dollars a year Nina had initially predicted.

But it was never enough. Because somehow, her ambition had become a relentless force, whipping at her, driving her to greater and greater success. Wants, needs, a burning desire for revenge had all metamorphosed into a continual hungering for wealth.

Raindrops the size of silver dollars began to fall, canceling work for the day. As she slipped into a hooded terry-cloth robe, Jade risked a glance at the cliff where Roarke had been standing.

She was relieved to see that the rock was deserted. While the rest of the crew strolled off in the direction of a tavern down the beach, Jade—considered a quintessential loner by everyone who had ever worked with her—climbed the narrow path to the hotel. As she made her way up the cliff, she decided that perhaps the man who had been watching her with such unwavering intensity had not been Roarke at all. Her imagination had been playing tricks on her.

She had almost convinced herself of that when she turned a corner and suddenly found Roarke blocking the narrow cliff path. She was forced to stop directly in front of him.

"Hello, Roarke," she greeted him with a great deal more calm than she was feeling.

If Jade was appalled at whatever impish fates had caused her to run into Roarke, here, miles from home, he seemed no more pleased to see her. He'd taken off the sunglasses, allowing her to read the censure in his gaze. The past six years had added character rather than age to his features; he was, regrettably, as handsome as ever, and wore the inevitable jeans with an elegant flair many men of Jade's acquaintance could never achieve in black tie.

"Hello, Cassie." His mouth twisted in a mock smile. "Or should I call you Jade?"

She stiffened her backbone, pulling herself up to her full height of six feet. Even so, she had to look up at him. "Actually, you don't have to call me anything. Since we have nothing to say to one another."

He caught her arm as she tried to pass him. "Christ," he murmured, more to himself than to her, "you are even more beautiful than your photographs. I wouldn't have believed it possible."

As he subjected her to a slow once-over, Roarke's contemptuous gaze softened. Suddenly, he reminded her of the man who once, in another lifetime, had been the sun around which her entire young world had revolved.

Jade was looking up into a pair of blue eyes that were every bit as compelling and dangerous as she remembered. The gleam of masculine admiration in Roarke's gaze shouldn't make her feel so good. But it did.

She raised her chin and gave him a cool, direct look, as if by doing so she could nullify the subliminal sparks. "Let me go."

"I'll let you go when I'm damn well ready to. And not one minute before." He leaned down until his face was on a level with hers. "You know, you're dead wrong about us not having anything to say to one another, Cassie. Don't you think you at least owe me an explanation after all these years?"

"*I* owe *you* an explanation?" Jade restrained her temper. "You really are unbelievable, Roarke Gallagher!"

"So are you." If he was disturbed by the animosity in her voice, Roarke didn't reveal it. "Unbelievably lovely."

His steamy look, one she remembered all too well, threatened to melt her resentment. Before she could tell him to go straight to hell where he belonged with the rest of his treacherous family, he'd pushed her hood back, and his fingers had slid into her hair and held her unwilling gaze to his.

"Damnit, I don't want to fight with you, Cassie." His thumbs began expertly massaging the knot of tension centered at the back of her neck. "Have dinner with me," he murmured huskily. "We'll eat a little moussaka, share a bottle of ouzo, and over some baklava so flaky that it'll practically melt in that ridiculously sexy mouth of yours, you can explain why you disappeared from my life without a single word of good-bye."

His voice had changed from its earlier sarcastic pitch to pure silk; his breath, warm and minty, whispered across her lips. "Then afterward, we can go back to my room, open the shutters to let the night in, and be unbelievable together. Just like old times."

How could he think it was that easy? Was he actually arrogant enough to believe that he could abandon her for years, then expect her to fall into his lap like a ripe plum? Remembering a time when she would have agreed to anything Roarke Gallagher might have suggested strengthened Jade's determination to refuse him now.

"Sorry." Her frigid voice told him that she wasn't at all. "I have other plans."

Annoyance was building up in his eyes again. "With your photographer friend, perhaps?"

"That's none of your business." She jerked away, moving treacherously close to the edge of the cliff. Pebbles loosened beneath her sandals and went skittering down the rocks to the beach. Her right foot met empty space.

Grabbing her, Roarke pulled her against him and his hands began to stroke her back. Jade wasn't sure who took the next step, she or Roarke. Perhaps they took it together. She only knew that while she was distracted by his hands, Roarke's mouth settled on hers.

She stiffened instantly. Her hands pressed against his chest to push him away, but Roarke didn't stop. The tip of his tongue flicked across her tightly set lips as he tasted, without pressure, without hurry. He was kissing her as if it were his perfect right, his mouth exactly as Jade remembered. Warm and sure and thrilling.

Jade knew she should leave.

Now.

She should.

She didn't.

She could feel her strength, her resentment, her thoughts, all draining away. The steel gray clouds overhead rumbled; Jade thought it was the sound of her blood pounding in her head. Steeped in a thick, liquid pleasure, she could find no will to resist. For the first time in her memory, her mind went absolutely blank.

Even as Jade tried to tell herself that this wasn't what she wanted, her fingers clung to his shirt. Caught up in emotions even older than the forces that had formed the cliff on which they stood, she wrapped her arms around him, as if they belonged there.

Her head fell back, inviting him to take more. The breeze cooling her face was tinged with the tang of the sea. His lips created an ache that once felt could never be forgotten.

"You may have changed your name, and where and how you live," he said against her mouth. "You may wear the latest designer fashions instead of faded jeans, and jet around the world with the Concorde crowd. But some things never change, Cassie. Like the way your lips still melt against mine."

His words, low and dark, seemed to sear her lips. "And the way my body remembers every soft curve and sweet hollow of yours." His hand moved down her back, past her waist, then lower still, slipping beneath the short hem of the robe.

"No!" A deeply ingrained survival instinct made her draw her breath in sharply.

"It's over," she insisted, stepping back from an emotional cliff far more frightening than the rocky one she'd almost fallen over.

"Is it?"

"I'm not the same naive girl I once was." She dragged a hand through her wet and tangled hair, struggling for calm. "I've made my own life, Roarke. And it's a good life. I have an exciting career, more money than I ever dreamed of, friends—"

"And lovers? Do you have more rich, exciting lovers than you ever dreamed of, Cassie?"

Something in his tone made her tremble. "You have no right to ask me that."

"You still have a great many questions to answer," Roarke said, ignoring the defiance in her voice. "I've been waiting a long time for the answers."

Jade was grateful for Roarke's anger. If he were gentle again, if he showed her even the smallest scrap of tenderness, she might crumble. "You'll just have to go on waiting."

His arm slid around Jade before she could make her escape. "Running away again, Cassie?" he inquired mildly. "I don't recall you being such a coward."

"I'm not a coward," she flared. "And I didn't run away. I left!"

"You ran," he corrected. "Just like you're running now."

"Go to hell." Prying his fingers from her waist, she brushed past him and began walking as fast as she could up to the village.

By the time she reached her hotel room, panic was racing through her system like amphetamine. In her room, Jade's hands shook as she closed the blue shutters to keep out the dreaded storm and Roarke.

Electricity ignited the sky; thunder rumbled like cannon fire. Storms always filled her with an edgy fear. It was on a night just like this . . .

"No." Jade shook her head, denying the images that the storm had stirred in some dark corner of her mind. She'd put that night behind her, locking it away in a deep, unapproachable place inside her.

How many times had she prided herself on her ability to shake off her past? Ten times a day? A hundred? Yet despite all her self-congratulations, it had taken only one brief meeting with Roarke Gallagher—one foolish, reckless kiss—to dredge up those old feelings of fear and hatred.

Shivering, she went into the bathroom and began to vigorously rub her hair dry with a fluffy white towel. But as she stared at her reflection in the full-length mirror, Jade did not see the woman who'd become the darling of the international modeling set; instead, she saw the old Cassie.

Cassie McBride. A girl who'd been called white trash by every man in Gallagher City who'd wanted her. And Lord knows, they all had. But she'd escaped their leers, their knowing winks, their grasping hands. Just as she had escaped Gallagher City, Oklahoma—or thought she had. . . .

# One

Jade was still Cassie McBride when she first met Roarke Gallagher. It had all started one sunny spring morning when she was trying to wake up her mother, who had a hangover.

"Damnit, I told you to leave me alone!" Belle McBride jerked the blanket over her head and rolled toward the wall.

"I can't, Mamma," thirteen-year-old Cassie insisted. "You know Miss Lillian hates it when you're late for work."

Although Cassie sympathized with her mother's condition, her tolerance was at a low ebb. It was only seven o'clock, yet she was already showered and dressed, had done the laundry, and had cleaned up the overflowing ashtrays and empty bottles Belle and her friends had left scattered about the night before.

She'd also searched the trailer for hidden bottles in the kitchen cupboards, the clothes hamper, the toilet tank, the wastebasket under the kitchen sink. The daily routine was a lot like hunting for colored eggs on Easter morning, not that Cassie had ever experienced that particular American tradition. Holidays were a bad time for Belle.

"Come on, Mama," Cassie coaxed. "Shelby Gallagher's birthday barbecue is today, remember? You told me that Miss Lillian wanted you to come in early to help get things ready."

"I'm not goin' to work."

"Mama!"

Dragging her hands through her thick russet hair, Cassie closed her eyes and prayed for strength. There were times when dealing with her mother was a lot like trying to discipline a recalcitrant two-year-old. Hollering never worked, and if you tried to put your foot down, she'd only become more obstinate, just for spite.

Taking care of her mother was nothing new to Cassie. Sometime back—she could barely remember when—their roles had switched. She had become the mother and Belle the rebellious, mixed-up daughter. What Cassie had never taken time to realize was that playing the role of the responsible adult brought a much needed stability to her life.

Muttering a curse, Belle tossed off the blanket, crawled out of bed like a zombie, and disappeared into the bathroom. Cassie waited, secure in the knowledge that she'd searched every square inch of the cramped lavatory only an hour ago. If Belle had hidden any alcohol in there, she would have had to have stuffed it into the toothpaste tube. There was the sound of running water, a toilet flushing. Finally Belle reappeared.

"You're gonna have to call Miss Lillian for me, Cassie," she said, pulling a long, slim cigarette out of a crumpled pack on the dresser. "Tell her I can't come to work today." Her hands shook as she struck a match, then chased the tip of the cigarette. "Tell her I'm sick."

"But, Mama, Miss Lillian's been planning this barbecue for months. The kids at school say Quinlan Gallagher invited everybody in the county."

Belle smoked and looked at Cassie. "I didn't get any invitation. Did you?"

"No, but—"

"Then he sure as hell didn't invite everybody, did he?" Belle took a deep drag on the cigarette. "Besides, baby, I really am havin' one of my sick spells. So be a good girl and do your mama this one little favor, okay? You can call on the pay phone down at the fillin' station."

Her mother had been having these sick spells for as long as Cassie could remember. And for just as long, Cassie had been making excuses for her. Lies, excuses, secrets . . . all were as common as air.

Cassie worried that if Belle didn't show up at the Gallagher mansion, where she'd been working as a maid for only three weeks, she'd be fired. Again. Something they couldn't afford. Her mother's medical bills this past winter had used up their savings and they were in debt not only to the doctor but to the grocer and the landlord as well. If Belle lost this latest job, they'd have to go back on relief. And in this part of the world, "going on county" was about as low as a person could go.

"Maybe if you had a little tea." She held out the cracked earthenware mug. "I fixed it with extra sugar, just the way you like. It'll settle your stomach."

"It's gonna take a helluva lot more than that pukey tea to fix what ails me." Plopping back down onto the bed, Belle puffed angrily on the cigarette. "And if you think I'm gonna spend my day, sick as I am, being bossed around by that muscle-bound Nazi housekeeper, bowin' and scrapin' to the likes of stuck-up Miss Lillian and that spoiled rich bitch Shelby Gallagher, you've got another think comin', missy. I'm not going. And that's final."

Cassie realized that she'd run into the brick wall of her mother's intransigence. Belle's bad spells came and went in cycles. They were worse at the end of the month, when the overdue bills covered with fluorescent red stickers came flooding in. Cassie had learned to lay low during these periods.

"All right," she said on a frustrated sigh. "You win."

"That's my baby girl." Belle smiled in a way that suggested that having gotten her way, she could afford to be a little generous. "You'd better go make that call right away, Cassie," she said. "Before Miss Lillian starts havin' cats."

"I'm not gonna call, Mama. Not today."

Belle's hazel eyes narrowed dangerously. "But you said—"

"I'll just have to go in your place."

"That's a damn good idea, Cassie," Belle acknowledged as Cassie went into the bathroom to change into the uniform Miss Lillian insisted all her maids wear. "In fact, I don't know why I didn't think of it myself."

The uniform was much more revealing than the loose blouses and jeans Cassie usually wore. She felt just like a bean about to burst its pod. She'd become more conscious of her body over the past months, acutely aware of its growing curves. Every morning she measured herself against the previous day's mark on the doorjamb, terrified that she'd grown even taller during her sleep. As for her breasts, which had seemed to pop out overnight, she'd taken to walking bunched over in a vain attempt to keep people—particularly the men of Gallagher City—from noticing them.

Tugging ineffectively at the too-short black skirt, she came out of the bathroom and slowly turned around. "What do you think?" she asked her mother worriedly. "Is it too bad?"

Belle exhaled a stream of smoke and eyed her daughter through the thin blue cloud. "You're growin' up, baby. Shelby Gallagher better be prepared to take a back seat at her own party, 'cause there won't be a man there who'll be able to keep his eyes off you."

She lit another cigarette from the smoldering end of the first. "Now you'd better hustle your butt over to the Gallagher's before Miss Lillian finds somebody else to take my place."

Cassie's eyes held small seeds of concern. "Are you sure you'll be all right?"

"I'll be just fine." Belle waved her away. "Promise."

Taking one last nervous tug on the skirt, Cassie shrugged into the shabby black coat she'd bought secondhand from the Salvation Army thrift shop and left the trailer.

Gallagher City was actually two towns, divided by the railroad tracks. The rich—Gallagher Oil and Gas Company executives—lived in large white houses tastefully set back from the street behind neatly clipped green hedges on the north side, while the poor—roustabouts, rough-necks, wranglers—were relegated to trailers and rundown rental houses with weedy lawns, slumped stoops, sagging shutters, and unpainted clapboards on the south. Cassie and Belle's trailer was located on the south side, next to the Santa Fe switching yards.

After waiting for a locomotive to switch tracks so she could continue down the gravel road, Cassie headed out to the highway to thumb a ride. Although she knew hitchhiking was risky, it wasn't as if she had a whole lot of other choices. She turned down rides from three consecutive good old boys with the requisite gun racks behind the front seat of their pickup trucks, the Confederate flag on the rear window, and danger in their eyes and was beginning to worry that she'd never get to the Gallagher ranch on time when a beige Buick station wagon pulled up beside her. One glance at the kindly round face assured her that she had nothing to fear from the middle-aged Bible salesman.

The salesman let her off at the turnoff to the Gallagher Ranch just as Quinlan Gallagher galloped his palomino across a vast pasture where shaggy brown bison grazed and oil rigs pumped endlessly. The fifty-year-old man was built like one of his outlaw Brahma bulls. And was every bit as single-minded.

Cassie knew the catechism of the Gallagher family, of course. Every-one in Gallagher County knew how Padraic Gallagher, orphaned by the potato famine in 1847, had joined the hundreds of thousands of Irish emigrants bound for America. He made his way to Texas, where he signed on as a scout for the Texas Rangers.

After serving in the Confederate Army during the War Between the

States, Padraic took the monies gained from selling treasures looted from abandoned southern mansions and began buying up what was then known as Indian Territory. By 1902 he was shipping more cattle to Kansas City than any man in the territory. Encouraged by an oil strike in Bartlesville, he decided to seek the black gold, and one rainy November afternoon in 1903, a gusher hit in the middle of his south pasture, causing a stampede of cattle who'd been peacefully grazing nearby.

The boom was on.

The Gallagher family owned Gallagher County. Literally. They owned all of the land (including mineral rights) and the majority of the buildings—the mercantile, the courthouse, the jail, most all the houses, including the trailer that Cassie and Belle rented from Gallagher Realty.

Quinlan Gallagher and his family not only provided the town with its primary source of income, they also supplied the lion's share of gossip. Everybody knew that even before his son Roarke was born, Quinlan had decided that his boy would be the first president of the United States from Oklahoma. Unfortunately, the scuttlebutt was that Roarke had no interest in politics. Even worse, he wasn't the least bit interested in oil. Or ranching.

"Can you believe it?" Mrs. Dawson, who ran the cash register at the Rexall drugstore had asked Cassie just last week. "Why, I stopped in at the Feed and Grain this morning and Jeb Martin told me that old man Gallagher near had a stroke when Roarke called from that fancy eastern college and told him that he was plannin' to become an architect."

"What the boy wants don't make no never-mind," Ben Dawson, who worked as the store pharmacist, harrumphed, counting out the rumpled bills Cassie had given him in exchange for Belle's prescription. "You know as well as I do that by the time Roarke graduates Yale, Quinlan will have turned him around. He's gonna come back home, marry Lacey Young, go to work for Gallagher Oil and Gas, then run for Congress, just like his daddy's always planned."

Although she didn't know Roarke personally, Cassie agreed with Ben. Tales of Quinlan Gallagher's temper were legion. It was a foolish man—or woman—who dared to cross him.

Walking up the long road, Cassie wondered, as she so often did, how it was that two families who'd begun the same way had turned out so differently.

The McBrides had escaped the potato famine the same as Padraic Gallagher; it was even possible that they'd shared steerage space on the same boat bound for America. Unfortunately, her family seemed to be lacking in the Irish luck so enjoyed by the Gallaghers. After generations of barely scraping by, the McBrides seemed destined to failure.

Something Cassie was determined to change.

Despite her mother's drinking problem, despite her daddy being just another oil-rig worker who'd deserted Belle long before Cassie was born, Cassie knew that she was meant for a better, richer life.

But not in Gallagher City. Or even Oklahoma City or Tulsa. Unlike the rest of her family, she wasn't about to waste her life away in the Oklahoma oil patch.

"I *will* make it out," Cassie muttered. She was approaching the Gallagher mansion—a vast marble pillared Georgian manor house set on a rise of velvety green lawn. "I'm not going to give up like my Mama."

How many times had her mother told her about her youthful plan for escaping the fate of her poor Dust Bowl parents? At least a hundred, maybe even a thousand. Belle was going to be a famous country and western star; she'd dreamed of performing "San Antonio Rose" at Cain's, Tulsa's Timeless Honky-Tonk. After conquering Tulsa, she'd take Nashville by storm.

Although she left home at fifteen, Belle never made it to Nashville. Nor did she make it to Tulsa. Actually, Belle managed to get a few singing gigs from time to time, but she never really made it out of Gallagher City.

"I'm not going to end up like her," Cassie vowed. "I'm not going to be stuck here in boring old Gallagher City, with nothing to do but drink and feel sorry for myself."

When she pressed the gold button located beside the tall oak front doors, a rousing electronic chorus of Rodgers and Hammerstein's "Oklahoma" sounded from inside the house.

The door opened and a man dressed in a dark suit stared down his pointed nose at Cassie. "Deliveries at the kitchen door."

"But—"

"Don't you understand the Queen's English?" he huffed. "I told you to go around to the kitchen."

After pointing to the left side of the house, he shut the door, leaving Cassie stranded on the portico. He might be dressed up like some fancy, citified gentleman, she thought furiously, but the Gallagher butler had all the manners of a junkyard dog.

Pushing down her anger, she turned back down the curving red driveway, went a long, long way around the corner of the house to where a small, neat sign stated: DELIVERIES ACCEPTED 7 A.M. TO 11 A.M. ALL OTHERS MUST BE ARRANGED FOR IN ADVANCE.

Cassie knocked. The door was opened by a large, hatchet-faced woman whose grim expression was no more inviting than the butler's had been.

"Good morning, ma'am." Cassie flashed her most ingratiating smile. "I'm Cassie McBride, Belle McBride's daughter, and—"

"Where is Belle? She is late."

From her thick, guttural tone and rigid demeanor, Cassie realized that this overbearing woman was the Gallagher's housekeeper, Helga. The one Belle called the Nazi. "I know, ma'am. But, you see, Mama took sick this morning—"

"It is more likely that she is *betrunken.*"

Cassie didn't need a German dictionary to understand the woman's meaning. Was there anyone in town who didn't know about Belle's drinking?

"Oh no, ma'am," she insisted earnestly, "she's really sicker than a dog. But you needn't worry, 'cause she sent me in her place."

"*Unmöglich.* Impossible," Helga translated gruffly for Cassie's benefit. "You are too young for such work. And tell your lazy drunkard mother that she is fired." Point made, the housekeeper slammed the door in Cassie's face.

Angry tears welled in Cassie's eyes; she resolutely blinked them away. She began pounding furiously on the kitchen door and finally, just when she thought her knuckles were going to be skinned all the way to the bone, the woman flung open the door.

"Go away!"

Cassie was beginning to understand why Belle hated working here. But Cassie didn't care whether or not Belle enjoyed herself. Because they needed the money. Desperately.

"I need to talk to Miss Lillian." Miss Lillian Gallagher, Quinlan Gallagher's older sister, had been mistress of the Gallagher mansion ever since Quinlan's wife left Oklahoma shortly after giving birth to her third child, Shelby, thirteen years earlier.

"Miss Lillian is busy. You will leave now. Or I will call the sheriff."

Although Cassie was tall, Helga was taller. And she outweighed Cassie by a good fifty pounds. Secretly intimidated, Cassie held her ground. "I'm not leavin' till I talk with Miss Lillian."

Helga shrugged her muscular shoulders. "It is your choice. I am calling the *polizei.* You go now, or you go to jail."

She began to slam the door shut again, but this time Cassie was quicker. Putting her foot between the door and the jamb, she shoved with all her might. Not having expected physical resistance, Helga was caught off guard, and by the time she'd realized Cassie's intentions, Cassie was inside the house. She took off looking for Miss Lillian, the disagreeable Helga on her heels.

The dining room adjoining the kitchen literally took Cassie's breath away. It was as big as a ballroom in those old MGM musicals Cassie loved to watch on "The Late Show." Winged, chubby-cheeked angels smiled down from a fresco that took up most of the ceiling; in the center of the room a massive crystal and gold chandelier hovered over a mahogany table large enough to comfortably seat eighteen.

Crystal shimmered from behind the diamond-cut upper doors on the breakfront, gold-rimmed china gleamed from the open shelves. The walls were ablaze with gilt-framed paintings; a blood red Persian rug, the kind a sultan would have been proud to walk on, spread lushly underfoot.

"Law," Cassie whispered. She stared around the richly appointed room, her mission momentarily forgotten. "It's like out of a movie."

A harsh male voice shattered the suspended moment. "What in the bloody hell are you doing in here?"

Cassie spun around and found herself face to face with the butler. When Helga came up behind her, Cassie understood the saying about being between a rock and a hard place. Things were getting worse by the minute, but she couldn't give up without a fight.

"I have to talk to Miss Lillian. It's important."

"I told the girl I was going to call the sheriff," the housekeeper informed the butler. "But before I could get to the telephone, she forced her way into the house."

Something that almost resembled a twinkle flashed in the butler's stern brown eyes. "You actually got past Helga?"

"She caught me by surprise," Helga insisted gruffly.

"I've always been strong for my age," Cassie explained. "I can do my mama's work, even if I am only thir—uh, fifteen," she lied, deftly tacking two years onto her age.

"The girl's mother is a drunkard." Helga kept her eyes pinned on Cassie as if she expected her to abscond with the silver. "And everyone knows that apples do not fall far from the trees. I am going to call the *polizei.*"

At that moment, a small delicate woman, dressed in a discreet gray silk dress, entered the room. Her silver hair was gathered into a simple chignon at the nape of her neck and pearls, set in antique gold, glowed warmly at her ears. A rose cameo, surrounded by tiny natural pearls, nestled in the white lace at the throat of her dress.

"Grayson, Helga, whatever is all this commotion about?"

The butler cleared his throat. "This young woman wishes to speak with you, ma'am."

Miss Lillian greeted Cassie with a warm smile. "Why, hello. We've met before, haven't we?"

Cassie nodded. "Yes, ma'am. I'm Cassie McBride, Belle's daughter. I spent last summer workin' the fountain down at the Rexall drugstore."

Miss Lillian nodded. "Of course. I remember now, I was driving back from Oklahoma City when the air conditioner in my car went out on the hottest day of the year. I stopped into the drugstore for something to drink and you made me the best chocolate soda I've ever had."

For Cassie, praise was an unknown thing. Color drifted into her cheeks. "Thank you, ma'am. That's right nice of you to say."

"It's the truth," Miss Lillian said simply. "Now, what can I do for you?"

Cassie explained that her mother was ill. "She wanted to come in this morning, but the doctor said she had to stay in bed."

"He did, did he?"

"He surely did, ma'am. You can call him and ask him yourself, if you don't believe me." Cassie's green eyes were wide and guileless.

Miss Lillian's gaze narrowed slightly. "You wouldn't lie to me, would you, Cassie?"

Cassie shook her red head emphatically. "Oh, no, ma'am. It's the truth, I swear. Why, after the doctor left, Mama tried to get dressed against his orders, but her fever's so high—nearly one hundred and three—" Cassie improvised quickly, "that she got real dizzy and near passed out before I could get her back to bed."

Her words were coming so fast that she was running out of air. She took a deep breath. "But you see, she was so worried about all the work you needed her to do for Miss Shelby's birthday barbecue, I wasn't sure I could keep her down like the doctor ordered, so I promised that if she'd only stay abed, where she belonged, I'd come in her place."

Cassie crossed the fingers of both hands behind her back. "So, here I am. Ready to work."

Miss Lillian looked up at the butler. "Grayson," she said, fingering the cameo at her throat, "Belle was scheduled to work in the kitchen, wasn't she?"

"Yes, ma'am."

It took Miss Lillian exactly twenty seconds to make up her mind. Twenty seconds that, to Cassie, seemed an eternity. "Helga will show you what to do." Business concluded, she turned and left the dining room.

Relief flowed over Cassie in waves. A relief that was to be short-lived.

"You come with me now," Helga grunted, shaking her head in disgust.

"Helga's bark is worse than her bite," Grayson offered in an undertone. His thin lips curved in a brief, reassuring smile.

As she followed the grim-faced Helga into the kitchen, Cassie found scant comfort in the butler's words.

# *Two*

No stranger to hard work, Cassie soon realized that Helga was doing her best to make her quit. No job was too dirty, no task too menial. But all day, Cassie just continued to do as ordered without murmuring a word.

Oklahoma society began arriving for the party late in the afternoon, and soon the large circular driveway was bumper to bumper with Cadillacs, Mercedes-Benzes, Jaguars, Rolls Royces, Chevy Blazers, and four-wheel-drive pickup trucks. Several of the trucks boasted oil-patch bumper-sticker slogans—DRIVE EIGHTY, FREEZE A YANKEE was one of the more popular.

The invitations had stated casual dress, which in this lofty stratum of oil-patch society meant Neiman Marcus western chic. Urban cowgirls made head-turning entrances in supple leather dresses studded with turquoise, rhinestones, and sequins. Diamonds, emeralds, sapphires, and rubies from Van Cleef and Arpels twinkled from ears, wrists, fingers.

Viewing the dazzling jewels these oil-baron wives and daughters had adorned themselves with, Cassie thought that a great many dinosaurs had had to die to provide such a glittering display of wealth.

Although the men were more casually dressed in Levis and western-cut, snap-front shirts, their expensive hand-sewn boots had been fashioned from such exotic skins as caribou, lizard, and crocodile. The value of the hammered silver belt buckles, bolo ties, and concho hatbands alone could have rivaled the entire treasury of many third world countries.

As for the food, Quinlan Gallagher's idea of casual turned out to be a mammoth feast: Hot, buttered ears of corn, barbecued beans glazed with molasses, trays of crumbly yellow corn bread laced with hot jalapeño peppers, enormous bowls of crispy cole slaw, and a slew of spicy Mexican favorites, intended to carry out the fiesta theme of the party, were spread out on tables set up at intervals across a sprawling backyard that Cassie decided must be at least as big as Founders Park.

Bartenders mixed margaritas, poured pitchers of beer, and handed out bourbon and branch water, while cooks, wearing red-and-white checked aprons that matched the tablecloths, barbecued mountains of thick prime beef steaks and ribs.

Mariachis with wide sombreros and colorfully striped serapes strolled across the velvety lawn, strumming guitars and crooning Mexican ballads. Sawdust had been scattered over the tennis court, allowing guests to dance to the enthusiastic sounds of a country swing band, while across the vast yard, beside a sparkling turquoise pool built in the shape of a cowboy boot, Willie Nelson entertained with songs of hard days and harder nights, cruel, two-timing women, and whiskey.

To Cassie, observing the elaborate barbeque was like getting an insider's glimpse of paradise. She'd never had a birthday party. Not knowing what shape Belle would be in by three o'clock in the afternoon, she had never even dared bring friends home after school. Once, when she was eight, she had coaxed Belle into allowing her to have a slumber party during Christmas vacation. That was the night Belle, who'd promised not to drink, had fallen into the Christmas tree. It was also the last time Cassie had invited anyone home.

The sun had gone down, but the fairy lights strewn through every tree on the grounds twinkled like a million tiny stars in the clear night sky. Candles flickered on the red-and-white draped tables and floated serenely atop the darkened swimming pool, and the heaters that had been set up to ward off the night chill glowed with a deep red warmth.

Cassie was returning to the party after having replenished the silver canape tray for the third time when Trace Gallagher, Shelby's sixteen-year-old brother, suddenly stepped in front of her.

"I've been watching you, Cassie. You're a real hard worker. In fact, I haven't seen you even stop to catch your breath all evening. Don't you think it's time you took a little break?"

"I can't. Helga will accuse me of slacking off."

Trace tilted his black Stetson back and grinned at her from beneath the brim. "But you don't work for Helga," he pointed out. "Since you're earning Gallagher money, honey bun, I'd say you work for us Gallaghers."

"Try telling that to Helga." When Trace moved a little closer, Cassie purposely pushed the tray toward him in an attempt to force him to keep his distance. "Would you like something?"

"Well, sugar, I'd say that depends on what you're offering." His breath, as he leaned toward her, was warm and stank of beer.

Cassie pretended not to understand his insinuation. "Well, we have tacos and burritos and guacamole, and—"

"Now you know that wasn't what I was talkin' about, Cassie." His gaze lingered on her breasts, then moved slowly down her legs before returning to her face.

Yes. She knew exactly what Trace was talking about. She also knew it was time to leave. "I'd better get back to work." When she turned away, Trace captured her wrist in his hand.

She paled at his touch. "Please, Trace," she said quietly, not wanting to draw any attention to them that might get her fired.

His grin reminded Cassie of a wolf curling its lips back to show its teeth. "Please, no?" His thumb stroked the soft skin at the inside of her wrist. "Or please, yes?"

Fear mixed with anger twisted her stomach in half. Trying to remember how desperately she needed this job, Cassie forced down her pride and allowed a soft, plaintive tone to creep into her voice. "Please, no."

"I guess I'll just have to change your mind." Pulling her into the shadows of a towering cottonwood tree, he reached his free hand toward the soft swell of her breast.

Just when Cassie was afraid that she was going to be forced to dump her tray of canapes right onto Trace Gallagher's fancy armadillo-skin boots, a deep voice sounded at her ear.

"I wouldn't try it, Trace."

The hand that had been inches away from Cassie's flesh dropped instantly to Trace's side.

"Cassie and I were just talking," Trace insisted gruffly, as Roarke Gallagher came up to them. The antagonism between the two brothers was so palpable that Cassie felt as if she could reach out and touch it.

"Then you won't mind if I have a word with Cassie here, will you, little brother?"

Not waiting for an answer, Roarke took the tray from Cassie, placed it on a nearby table, cupped her elbow in his hand, and led her to a private corner of the garden. When she looked up at him, Cassie realized that she'd never met anyone who exuded such sheer physical confidence as Roarke Gallagher.

He took a large white handkerchief from his pocket. "I thought you might want to tuck this into the neckline of your dress." His tone was surprisingly gentle for such a large man. "That crowd is going to get a bit more rambunctious as the evening wears on, Cassie. No point in waving a red flag in front of a bunch of drunken bulls."

Cassie's flesh burned as the damning blush—the bane of all red-heads—rose on her chest and face. "Thank you." Lowering her eyes, she accepted the handkerchief and stuffed it into the V-neck of the dress. "For the handkerchief and most especially for . . . well, you know . . ." Cassie didn't want to admit how badly Trace had frightened her. She'd seen that dangerous look in men's eyes too many times lately.

Roarke appeared to be amused by the way Cassie averted her eyes. "If my hell-raiser brother gives you any more trouble, just let me know."

If there was one thing Cassie figured would probably get her fired on the spot, it would be initiating a fight between Quinlan Gallagher's two sons. "Thanks for the offer. But I can take care of myself just fine."

"I've no doubt of that, Cassie. But Trace can be a real handful. Look up *carouse* in the dictionary, and you'll find my little brother's picture. So if he bothers you, come to me."

His smile was so warm and reassuring that Cassie wished she could spend the rest of the night just basking in it. "Trace isn't really all that bad, Cassie," Roarke assured her, not really believing his words but feeling that family honor, drilled into him from childhood, required him to say them. Actually, he thought his brother had the personality of a wild dog. "It's just that when he gets a few beers in him, he can't tell a little girl from a fully grown woman."

Reaching out, Roarke adjusted the handkerchief more suitably. When his fingers brushed against her skin, Cassie drew in a deep breath. "There." He nodded his satisfaction. "That should keep you out of trouble for a while." His gaze moved down her long legs. "Unfortunately, I don't have any way to lengthen that skirt."

"Perhaps I should crawl around on my knees."

His smile was kind, sympathetic without being pitying. "Don't ever be ashamed of your height, Cassie. Or your figure." When he ruffled her thick red hair in a friendly, fraternal way, an unfamiliar excitement gripped Cassie's stomach. "You're going to be one of the world's great beauties, Cassie McBride. And when you have all the world at your feet, I hope you won't forget I'm the one who first predicted it."

Forget it? She knew she'd never forget a thing about tonight. When he continued to smile down at her, Cassie went suddenly mute. She couldn't have spoken if her life depended on it. Fortunately, she was saved from answering by Shelby, who was standing on the edge of the patio, impatiently calling Roarke.

"Duty calls."

Cassie watched him join his sister and wished that she were a grown woman. A rich, sleek beautiful woman who could attract a man like Roarke Gallagher. A woman like Lacey Young.

The Young family raised horses on the adjoining ranch and the word around Gallagher County was that Roarke's relationship with Lacey was a great deal more than neighborly. Cassie wondered if the rumors about Roarke's planning to marry Lacey and join the two properties were true.

To Cassie, Lacey Young appeared to have it all; she was both beautiful and rich. Tonight she was wearing a red silk western shirt, a skintight pair of black leather jeans, and so much Joy she seemed to have bathed in it. She'd left the top four buttons of the blouse unbuttoned, the better to display the five-karat ruby nestled between her firm, tanned breasts. Matching rubies blazed from her ears; the thick blue-black hair that hung straight down the middle of her back shone like ebony.

Later, standing beneath a shower of fireworks that lit up the sky, Cassie watched Lacey draw Roarke off into a dark corner. Their heated kiss lasted for what seemed like a lifetime. Still in the shadows, Cassie watched Roarke's wide hands move up and down Lacey's silk-clad back and experienced a sudden, unexpected jolt of jealousy.

Why was it that some women had so much? While others had so little? Wasn't it enough that God had made Lacey Young rich and beautiful? Did He have to toss in Roarke Gallagher for good measure? Maybe Belle was right after all. Maybe God only put a rug under people like the McBrides so he could jerk it out from under their feet.

Roarke and Lacey disappeared into the house. Breathing a soft, painful little sigh, Cassie returned to work.

Several hours later, when Cassie was in the kitchen, immersed in soap-suds up to her elbows, Miss Lillian entered the room. Helga, who'd been sitting at the table sipping a glass of schnapps, leaped to her feet and began vigorously scrubbing the ceramic tile counters.

"Your performance was quite exemplary, Cassie dear," Miss Lillian said.

Cassie ducked her head. "Thank you, ma'am."

"I was wondering if you'd like to work here on a permanent basis." If she heard Helga's irritated grunt, Miss Lillian chose to ignore it.

Hope instantly rose in Cassie's green eyes, replaced just as quickly by regret. "I'm sorry, ma'am, but much as I appreciate your offer, I can't quit school."

Although she still didn't know exactly what she was going to do with her life, Cassie was smart enough to realize that schooling was the key. Belle's hardscrabble life proved exactly how hard it was to make it without a decent education.

"Well, of course I hadn't intended for you to drop out of school," Miss Lillian said. "I'd thought you could work after school and all day Saturday. Then, once summer vacation begins, you could work full time."

"I'd love to come to work here, ma'am."

"Fine." Miss Lillian's satisfied nod suggested that she'd never expected any other outcome. "Now, as to your salary . . ."

The figure she offered was ridiculously low. Cassie had been making five cents more an hour working as a maid at the Rose Rock Motel. But then she thought about spending her days in such a beautiful setting, surrounded by so many treasures—antique furnishings, brilliant oil paintings, misty watercolors, gleaming marble sculptures, solid gold flatware, and shimmering crystal. Why, it would be like spending her days in a palace!

"That'll be just fine, ma'am."

"Good." For the first time since entering the kitchen, Miss Lillian acknowledged the housekeeper's sullen presence. "I trust this will be all right with you, Helga?"

"Ja," Helga muttered unenthusiastically. "We will train the girl to be a good worker."

"I'm sure you will." Turning back to Cassie, she said, "Roarke is in the library with his father. When you're finished cleaning up, Cassie, he'll drive you home."

The idea of being alone in a car with Roarke Gallagher was as terrifying as it was thrilling. "That's right nice of you, ma'am, but I can get home by myself."

"Nonsense. We can't have you walking all the way back to town on that lonely road in the dark."

"I could call my mama." Cassie knew the chances of finding Belle at home were slim to none. The chances that she'd be willing—let alone sober enough—to drive all the way out to the ranch to pick Cassie up were even less. But Miss Lillian didn't have to know that.

"But I thought Belle was ill."

Cassie had been so immersed in her work, she'd forgotten all about that damned lie. "Maybe she's feelin' better by now," she improvised quickly. This time Helga's grunt was a great deal more audible.

"If Belle had a high fever this morning, she has no business getting out of bed," Miss Lillian insisted. "Besides, you're not imposing on Roarke, Cassie. As a matter of fact, he was the one who suggested driving you home in the first place." Matters settled to her satisfaction, Miss Lillian swept from the room in a billowy cloud of pearl gray chiffon.

Cassie passed the library on her way back to the kitchen with a tray of dirty glasses. When she heard shouting, she paused, listening to Quinlan loudly accuse Roarke of making him the laughingstock of the entire county. Recalling the conversation at the drugstore with Ben and Edna Dawson, Cassie guessed that the argument was about Roarke's continued refusal to bow to his father's not inconsiderable will. And although she didn't dare dawdle, she did notice that Roarke wasn't yelling back.

She was scouring out the stainless steel sinks when Roarke strode into the kitchen. The look on his tightly set face reminded her of a gusher about to blow sky high.

"Ready to go?" he asked abruptly, his tone devoid of its earlier warmth. His face was so taut and sharp it looked as if it had been carved with one of Helga's kitchen knives.

She cast a nervous, questioning glance toward Helga.

"Ja, go," Helga said, waving her away. "Tomorrow you learn about real work."

With that threat ringing ominously in her ears, Cassie followed Roarke outside to the back of the house, where his sporty forest green MG was parked in the five-car garage.

Roarke didn't say a word as the car ate up the miles between the ranch and Gallagher City. But he didn't need to speak to reveal his anger; the air in the car seemed to vibrate with ill humor. Finally, Cassie couldn't stand it any longer.

"I really appreciate this," she offered quietly.

Roarke shrugged. "It's no trouble. Besides, I wanted to get out of the house."

"Don't you have to take Lacey home?" she asked. She hadn't seen the woman since the fireworks.

"I already did. She left earlier. She has to get up early for a horse show tomorrow morning."

"Oh. . . I love your car." Her soft voice could hardly be heard over the Muddy Waters blues playing on the eight-track tape deck Roarke had installed in the dashboard of the MG.

"That's funny. Most girls around here complain that it's like riding around in a sardine can. They'd just as soon I drive it only as far as the nearest junk pile and then go out and buy a new Cadillac."

"A big white one, with steerhorns on the front?" Cassie asked. "And a horn that plays the Sooners' fight song? Like your daddy's?"

Roarke laughed at that. A deep, rich sound that made her feel funny in the pit of her stomach—fluttery. "I don't think that's quite what they had in mind." Reaching across the space between them, he patted her arm. Cassie imagined she could feel the heat of his hand through her coat when he touched her. "Thank you, Cassie."

Five minutes earlier, Roarke had been filled with seething irritation. Any lingering pleasure from his and Lacey's earlier lovemaking had disintegrated the moment he'd returned to the house and found his father prepared to do battle over his refusal to go into politics. The old man was like a damned pit bull; he just wouldn't let go.

"For what?" Her throat was tight, making words an effort.

"For making me laugh." He shook his head. "I can't remember the last time I found anything to laugh about around that house."

The conversation was getting too personal. Besides, Cassie knew she didn't have any advice to give a man as smart as Roarke. He'd been valedictorian of Gallagher High School and she'd read in the Gallagher City *Gazette* that he routinely made the dean's list at Yale.

"You have a beautiful home," she said.

Moonlight flooded the interior of the car, casting the rigid planes of Roarke's face in sharp relief. From the tight set of his jaw, Cassie realized she'd said the wrong thing.

"It's a beautiful house," he corrected. "But a house is not necessarily a home."

Cassie, more than anyone, knew that. Afraid of saying anything that might darken his mood even further, she fell silent, content to watch the shadows streak by the window.

Muddy Waters gave way to the equally bluesy John Lee Hooker, who in turn gave way to a plaintive Billie Holiday singing about her man treating her bad. That particular song reminded Cassie uncomfortably of Belle, but she didn't want to think about her mama. Not tonight.

Instead, for a change, she was going to enjoy the brief, stolen pleasure of being alone with Roarke Gallagher in his racy European sports car.

Cassie began to feel almost like Cinderella, returning home from the ball in her transformed pumpkin coach with the handsome prince. Her romantic fantasy lasted until they reached the railroad yards. Then it shattered into a million crystalline pieces, replaced by gritty reality.

"You can just let me off here," she said, a few blocks away from the trailer.

Roarke took one look at the flickering fire marking the hobo jungle at the far end of the switching yard and shook his head.

"Not on a bet. You can give me directions, or we can drive around all night."

"Really, I used to walk home alone every night from the Rose Rock." Directing her gaze out the passenger window, she pretended a sudden interest in a boxcar parked on a siding. "It's okay, Roarke, really."

Stopping the car, Roarke cupped her chin in his fingers, gently turned her head, and lifted her downcast eyes to his. "We don't choose our parents, Cassie," he said. "You can't help it that your mama drinks too much any more than I can help it that my father is . . ." *an arrogant, power-hungry, opinionated son of a bitch,* he considered grimly.

". . . my father," he finished up, not willing to reveal his still fresh wounds to this little girl. Even if she did make him laugh. "I understand how you feel, honey, but embarrassment is not worth losing your life over."

His warm gaze and gentle touch made that strange fluttering start up again in her stomach. "Go two more blocks, then turn right at the corner," she whispered. "It's the second trailer on the left."

He smiled. "That's better." Releasing his light hold on her, he shifted into first and drove across the tracks, through the dark, mean streets. When they reached her trailer, Cassie breathed a deep sigh of relief. The Fury was gone; Belle wasn't home to ruin things.

Before Cassie could say thanks for the ride, Roarke was out of the car. When he opened the passenger door for her, Cassie felt just like a movie star. Like Ali McGraw.

Her feet didn't touch the ground all the way to the door. Wrapped in a soft mantle of pleasure, Cassie was only vaguely aware of Roarke saying good night. She entered the darkened trailer and stood at the window, basking in the lingering warmth of his smile long after the glow of the MG's tail lights had disappeared around the corner.

Then, wrapping her arms around herself, she began dancing dreamily around the room, swaying to soft music only she could hear. Somewhere in the distance, the lonely, three-tone wail of a locomotive whistle swelled and faded, leaving behind a strange, empty kind of sadness that settled over her, banishing her earlier pleasure.

# Three

Although the work was hard and her salary was below minimum wage, Cassie enjoyed her job at the Gallagher mansion. To exchange the wretchedness of the rundown trailer for the splendor of such a house fed her ambition for a richer, better life. It was her first inside view of life on the other side of the tracks and she loved it. Cassie watched and listened; she took note of Miss Lillian's gestures, her mannerisms, her choice in clothes, soaking up everything like an eager sponge.

Miss Lillian didn't hesitate to show her approval of Cassie's love of beautiful things. Under her employer's tutelage, Cassie learned that the enormous painting of waterlilies in the double-height entrance hall, the one that never failed to take her breath away, the one she could look at forever, was painted by Monet.

The life-size portraits hanging on the red leather walls of the library were Sargents, and the chair in the corner of Miss Lillian's dressing room was not just any old piece of furniture, but a 1770 Philadelphia carved mahogany armchair which her benefactor had purchased at auction for a mind-boggling two hundred thousand dollars. Every Saturday morning Cassie would dust the intricate carvings and marvel at its beauty. If there were times when she considered that this single piece of furniture cost more than Belle could ever make in a lifetime of waiting tables, she pushed the errant thought away.

She loved setting the dinner table with the hand-painted, translucent china that Miss Lillian told her was from Dresden. The delicate edges of the plates and saucers were rimmed with a latticework of real gold that shone on the damask linen like a king's ransom in the gleaming light from Miss Lillian's silver candelabrum. The matchstick-stemmed crystal—a dramatic pattern of diamonds and rosettes that created dancing rainbows when she held it up to the summer sun shining through the kitchen window—was Waterford, from Ireland.

"It's called the Emerald Isle," Miss Lillian had told Cassie one day while instructing her on how to set the table properly with the glistening goblets and wine and champagne glasses. "It's such a beautiful country, Cassie, with mountains that are forty shades of green."

"I reckon that's why they call it the Emerald Isle," Cassie decided.

Miss Lillian smiled. "I believe you're right, dear. You'd love it there. Why, there are beaches and cliffs and wildflowers like carpets and hundreds of old stone churches. I swear, the first time I visited, I hated the idea of coming back to Oklahoma."

"You've been there?" Cassie's expression would have held no less awe if Miss Lillian had told her that she'd visited the moon with the astronauts. "To Ireland?"

"Padraic Gallagher came from the Waterford area," Miss Lillian explained. "It's a Viking town on the River Suir. Out in the country, there are some crumbling ruins that are alleged to be the castle Gallagher."

"A real live castle?"

"It's just a pile of stones, now." Miss Lillian smiled. "But it's always nice to visit the family roots."

At the thought of roots, Cassie—offspring of a one-night stand between a tool pusher with wanderlust and an alcoholic failed country and western singer—experienced a sharp, painful stab of envy.

As the days and weeks went by, Cassie began to feel as if she were existing in two separate worlds. Her life at the mansion was light-years away from the one she was forced to share with her mother. Once school had recessed for the summer, she began to spend more and more time at the ranch. When she slept, she dreamed the impossible dream of someday living in a house just like Miss Lillian's. But when she woke up, she'd be right back in the smoky darkness of the cramped trailer with Belle.

Despite all their wealth and privilege, it soon became obvious that the Gallaghers were not the ideal family they pretended to be. Trace didn't try to hide his jealousy of Roarke's favored status as the eldest son.

Instead, he spent nearly every night in Oklahoma City, getting rip-roaring drunk. Each morning, as she'd scrub the evidence of last night's binge from the porcelain rim of Trace's toilet, Cassie wondered bleakly if God had decreed cleaning up after drunks to be her life's work.

Although everyone in the county knew that Roarke was his father's favorite son, it would have been difficult to believe. From what Cassie could tell, Roarke continued to ignore his father's carefully constructed plan for his life. Unaccustomed to having his law questioned, Quinlan became more furious with each passing day.

The atmosphere in the house grew increasingly tense as Quinlan and Roarke alternated between shouting matches and icy silence. The only person unaffected by the battle of wills was Miss Lillian. She blithely went through her day, oblivious to the stormy atmosphere that had settled over the family, and Cassie realized that the older woman had the unique ability to shut out anything that didn't interest her. And it became readily apparent that the only thing that interested her was Quinlan Gallagher's house. Cassie gradually came to understand that the house was Miss Lillian's baby—the child the unmarried woman never had.

Having observed Roarke surreptitiously over the two past months, Cassie realized that he was not going to give in to his father's demands, which meant that he was bound to leave, something Cassie dreaded.

Cassie loved Roarke—she loved looking at him, she loved listening to him talk, she loved his tall, muscular body. In fact, everything about Roarke Gallagher filled her with indefinable yearnings. She thought of him endlessly, she dreamed wonderful, impossible dreams. During that long hot summer, Roarke became the center of Cassie's entire young universe.

One day as she was in the library, dusting the tops of the leather-bound books, Quinlan stormed in, followed by Roarke. Although she could practically see steam coming from the older man's ears, Cassie felt as if the temperature in the room had dropped a good fifty degrees.

"That'll be all, Cassie," Quinlan instructed gruffly.

Cassie didn't need to be told twice. "Yessir." She hurried from the room, but not before darting a glance Roarke's way. His stony face could have been carved onto the side of Mount Rushmore.

She was in the front parlor, polishing a Sheraton side table, when she heard the front door slam. Going to the window, Cassie saw Roarke march out to his car. A moment later, the MG disappeared in a rooster tail of dust.

The news spread through the house like wildfire. Miss Lillian remained composed as always, her only complaint being that with Roarke leaving, there would be an uneven number at tonight's dinner party. Shelby, furious at her father for banishing Roarke, and even madder at Roarke for pushing their father to such extremes, locked herself in her bedroom and proceeded to spend the day pouting. Trace, true to form, picked up a buxom sixteen-year-old carhop at Lennie's Burger Shack and drove down to Indian Lake where he drank his way through half a case of Lone Star beer, celebrating his good fortune.

Roarke returned during Miss Lillian's dinner party, coming in the back door like one of the servants or a Fuller Brush salesman from town. Cassie, who'd been watching for him out the kitchen window, was the only one besides Helga to realize he was in the house. He went up to his room and came down later with his luggage.

Afraid that Roarke was going to leave forever, Cassie screwed up every ounce of courage she possessed and went out to the garage just as he was packing the last of his things into his MG.

"Do you really have to go?" she asked. An enormous lump was rising in her throat; Cassie had to work to push the words past it.

"I'm afraid so."

"But summer's not over yet."

"It is for me. I've got to find a job, Cassie. You, of all people, should know how that is."

"But you're rich."

"Correction. My father's rich. Since I just got disinherited for sticking to my guns, I'm as flat broke as a wildcatter who just brought in a string of dusters."

Cassie stared at him, attempting to imagine Roarke living in the wretched poverty that was part of her life with Belle. "You could marry Lacey. She's rich."

Roarke threw back his head and laughed. "I'd forgotten how good you can make me feel, Cassie McBride." He touched her arm. "And for the record, I'm not going to marry Lacey."

The declaration made her heart swell so that Cassie thought it was going to burst right through her chest. "Really?"

"Really." He gave the contents of the car one last perusal. "Well, I'd better be hitting the road."

Cassie saw her chance slipping away. Taking a deep breath, she blurted out, "I love you, Roarke."

"What?" Obviously startled by her breathless admission, he turned back toward her.

"I said, I love you. I've always loved you. And I know I'm not old enough yet to get married, and I'm not as beautiful or rich or smart like Lacey, but I'd make a right good wife, if you'd only be willin' to wait for me, Roarke."

Now that she'd opened up the floodgates, the words came tripping out, practically stumbling over one another. "I'd cook for you and clean your house and have your babies and I'd never, ever complain if you came home late, and—"

"Cassie." Roarke pressed his fingers against her lips. "You're a lovely, sweet girl."

Hope was a hummingbird, fluttering inside her heart. "You really think so?"

"Of course. And I'm flattered by your feelings."

Cassie's young heart soared. "Then you'll wait for me?"

"Honey bun, it's just not that simple. You're only thirteen."

"I was fourteen last week. And everyone says I'm mature for my age. Why, just ask your Aunt Lillian."

Roarke stifled his smile. "Fourteen is still too young to be thinking about love and marriage, Cassie," he said gently. "You'll have plenty of time for that once you grow up."

Bending down, he gave her a quick, brotherly kiss on the cheek. "When the proper time comes, Cassie McBride, you are going to make some lucky guy a terrific wife." His eyes were warm with affection. "Just give it time, sugar."

With that he climbed into his MG and backed out of the garage, leaving Cassie alone. She stood in the driveway, watching until Roarke had disappeared from sight and the red Oklahoma dust had settled. Then, devastated, she ran home to the trailer she shared with Belle and wept into her pillow, yearning for a womanhood that seemed years beyond her reach.

When Belle arrived back at the trailer at two-thirty in the morning, Cassie, who was finally all cried out, did something she hadn't done for years. Hoping for some faint scrap of condolence, she confided in her mother.

"Hell, Cassie," Belle asked, pulling her red dress over her head, "what did you expect? It's a basic law of nature. Eagles fly with other eagles, they don't nest with mud hens." Dressed in only her yellow rayon slip, she sat down on the edge of the bed and lit a cigarette.

Cassie, who remembered what Miss Lillian had told her about the Gallagher family roots, didn't answer.

"And no Gallagher would ever fall in love with a McBride," Belle continued. "Oh, they might screw one. In fact, Quinlan and I had some good times back in the old days, which is why I know that Gallagher men are incapable of falling in love." She scowled furiously at some long-ago memory. "And they damn well ain't going to marry outside their own circle. You'll see, once the dust settles, Roarke is gonna do what his daddy wants."

"But he said he wasn't going to marry Lacey," Cassie protested.

Belle eyed her through a stream of blue smoke. "I know how you're feeling, Cassie," she said, her tone revealing an uncharacteristic sympathy. "I once bought the same line from Roarke Gallagher's son-of-a-bitch father."

The thought of Belle and Quinlan together was a revelation. One Cassie would have to think about later. "But Roarke's nothing like his daddy."

Belle exhaled a long-suffering sigh. "Look here, girl, even if you could get Roarke interested, if Quinlan ever suspected his precious son was foolin' around with a townie, he'd run you out of Gallagher County on a rail. But you're right about one thing," she allowed as she ground out her cigarette. "Roarke probably ain't gonna marry Lacey. Hell, the only reason the old bastard allowed Roarke to go to Yale in the first place was so he can marry one of them rich Yankee girls whose people came over on the Mayflower.

"Quinlan Gallagher is a millionaire. Probably even a goddamn billionaire," Belle corrected grimly. "He can buy anything he wants, Cassie, including the presidency, for Roarke. But the one thing the old man has never been able to buy is class, which is why Roarke'll end up marrying it instead."

Point made, Belle reached over and turned out the light. "Now, you'd better get to sleep, Cassie. You wouldn't want to show up late for work and disappoint Miss Lillian."

Cassie didn't miss the acid tinge in her mother's tone. Although Belle had been quick to accept the money Cassie was earning at the ranch, it had become increasingly apparent that she was jealous of Cassie's growing relationship with Lillian Gallagher. Sensing Belle's feelings, Cassie never expressed the pleasure she received from taking care of the lovely art objects Miss Lillian had collected, nor the discussions she'd had with her about them.

Belle's life had never been easy, a fact she hadn't hesitated to tell her daughter time and time again. Having been Belle's scapegoat for years,

Cassie had learned to keep her rare and infrequent pleasures private, rather than risk her mother's lethal tongue spoiling them.

After all, Cassie thought, as the long hot months of July and August evolved into a warm Indian summer, everyone had their private pleasures. Miss Lillian had her treasures, Quinlan exulted in controlling everyone and everything around him, Shelby had her clothes, Trace his sports car and his wild friends. Even Belle had her alcohol and her men.

As for Cassie—she had those wonderful, magical hours spent at the Gallagher mansion.

Cassie's second summer at the ranch mellowed into a clear, crisp autumn, which in turn gave way to a cold, difficult winter. Icy rains froze first to sleet, then turned to snow that lay wet and heavy over the land. On those occasions when drifting snow banks made the road to the ranch impassable, Cassie was forced to remain at the mansion. But instead of finding such overnight visits a hardship, she reveled in them. On these occasions, life was almost perfect.

Lying on a linen sheet so silky she felt as if she were sleeping in the bed of a princess, Cassie would close her eyes and pretend that she was the mistress of the beautiful home and this was the bedroom she shared with her husband and soon Roarke would walk in that door and all her dreams would be complete.

But it seemed that Roarke would never return home. A second Christmas came and went without a sign of him, then New Year's, then Easter. And although Quinlan pretended not to care, Cassie noticed that Roarke's father grew increasingly querulous as each new holiday approached.

Roarke wasn't the only son causing Quinlan grief. Trace grew wilder with each passing day, making his father explode with predictable regularity. Cassie, who'd learned at an early age to stay out of the way when Belle was drunk, did her best to avoid Roarke's younger brother. Not that her efforts were always successful. He began to seek her out—in the pantry, the garage, the library. One afternoon he cornered her in Miss Lillian's dressing room. Fortunately, Shelby's unexpected early return from a shopping trip to Dallas allowed Cassie to escape his amorous clutches.

Although Trace's aggression had frightened her, alone in the trailer later that night, Cassie stood naked in front of the bathroom mirror and ran her hands over the path Trace's had taken, imagining what it would feel like to have Roarke touch her that way. Her rosy nipples tightened in response, and she felt a distant tug between her legs.

Cassie knew that what she was doing was probably the kind of sin that could cause her to burn in hellfire for all time. But that didn't stop her from picturing Roarke's face as she parted the coppery nest of hair with her fingers. When she touched herself there, in that secret, forbidden place, she felt a hot dart of guilty pleasure.

Cassie had been working at the house for two years when Miss Lillian called her into the formal sitting room that served as her office. Cassie's first thought was that something had happened to Belle. Her second, and just as terrifying, thought was that she was going to be fired.

"Come in, dear," Miss Lillian said.

Cassie twisted ice-cold hands together behind her back. "Is something the matter?"

"Why no, dear." Miss Lillian appeared surprised by Cassie's trembling tone. "I think what I have to say will please you."

Cassie kept silent, waiting.

The older woman folded her hands on the top of her Queen Anne desk. The mahogany gleamed from the lemon oil Cassie had spent hours painstakingly rubbing into the wood.

"I've been watching you, Cassie, and I've come to the conclusion that your talents are being wasted on housework. Especially when you have such a lovely hand. You'd be a perfect choice for handling my correspondence."

"You want me to be your secretary?"

"My private secretary," Miss Lillian agreed. "I'm afraid, what with oil prices being down at the moment, and household expenses rising the way they are"—she gestured with obvious irritation at the lettuce-green pages of the household ledgers in front of her—"I can't offer you a raise. But I promise that you'll find the position rewarding."

Cassie still didn't understand exactly what was expected of her, but she had the feeling that if she didn't snap this opportunity up right now, she might never get another chance.

"I'd be right honored to be your secretary, Miss Lillian."

"Then we have an agreement?"

"Yes, ma'am."

Miss Lillian nodded. "Fine. You can begin by taking care of these thank you notes for Shelby's birthday presents. All the names, addresses, and gifts are on this list. I'd like the notes to go out in tomorrow's mail at the latest. Lord knows it's been too long as it is," she added. Her pursed lips suggested her disapproval of Shelby's attitude about compiling the list.

"What about the laundry, Miss Lillian?"

"The laundry?"

"I was just about to put it away."

"Well, do that," Miss Lillian decided. "Then you can start on the notes." Satisfied, she returned to her ledgers.

Cassie was in Shelby's room, putting away the laundry, when Shelby practically skipped into the room. "Guess what?"

Cassie glanced up. "What?"

"I just finished talking to Roarke."

"He called? Here?"

"Well, it is his home, Cassie."

"I know, but—"

"He told me that he would have hung up if Dad had answered," Shelby allowed. "Anyway, he had the best news! He just beat out more than three hundred applicants for a summer internship at a really famous New York architectural firm!"

The news of Roarke's success brought mixed emotions. The part of Cassie who had her own reasons for wanting to escape Gallagher City was thrilled for him. But there was another, very strong part that was crushed to learn that he wouldn't be returning to the ranch.

"So I guess this means he won't be coming home," she said her thoughts aloud.

"Honestly, Cassie," Shelby chided, "the way you keep mooning over my older brother is downright embarrassing."

Cassie turned away, damning the hot flush that rose in her cheeks. "I'm not moonin' over anybody."

Shelby plopped herself down on the white eyelet comforter covering her canopied bed. "Of course you are," she drawled, watching Cassie carefully fold one of the half slips purchased last month from Saks in Dallas. "Not that I blame you. Roarke's a real hunk, better lookin' even than Warren Beatty or Robert Redford."

"I hadn't really noticed," Cassie said, embarrassed. Even talking about him with Shelby made her blood hum in a way that was anything but comforting.

Forcing down what she feared were forbidden thoughts, she ran her hand over the flowered silk slip, enjoying the cool feel of it against her hand, trying to imagine what it would feel like against her body. What would he say, she wondered, unable to keep her mind from wandering—always, dangerously—back to Roarke. What would he do, if he did come home and she sneaked into his room one dark and lonely night, wearing one of Shelby's frothy confections?

"Either you're telling one whopper of a fib, Cassie, or you are blind, girl."

Shelby's remarks jerked Cassie from her turbulent reverie. When she refused to answer, Shelby went over to her dressing table and picked up a tube of lipstick. "Next time you're dustin' that old painting of Padraic Gallagher that hangs over the library fireplace, take a good look," she advised, coloring her parted lips a petal soft pink. "It's obvious that Roarke's gorgeous, wavy black hair and wicked blue eyes come straight from the old thief's gene pool. . . .

"Ugh. Too wishy-washy." Eyeing her reflection with distaste, Shelby wiped the pastel shade off her lips with a tissue. "And my brother's knife-edged cheekbones, which I would personally do murder for, come from our great grandmother, who was one-eighth Cherokee. But, of course, our family never mentions that," she confided, searching through the numerous gold tubes. Cassie thought that Shelby had enough cosmetics and perfume bottles on that dressing table to open her own department store.

It hadn't taken Cassie long to learn that Quinlan Gallagher's only daughter was like all the other oilmen's daughters—spoiled rich girls who thought nothing of taking their daddy's Lear jet to Dallas for a shopping spree.

"So I can certainly understand how you feel, Cassie. But if I were you, I'd quit hoping for somethin' that isn't going to happen," Shelby advised as she applied a daring crimson. "Because Roarke isn't comin' back home. . . .

"This red is too dark," she decided. "I can't imagine what made me buy it."

Cassie put the slip away in the top drawer, atop a rose-scented sachet. Until she'd begun working at the ranch, Cassie had never realized that one girl could have so much underwear. The contents of Shelby's lingerie drawer reminded her of a spring garden.

"He isn't?" she asked with a nonchalance she was a long, long way from feeling.

"Isn't what?" Shelby tried a frosted fuchsia shade next, blotted her lips with a tissue, then sat back and admired the results.

"Coming back to the ranch."

"Of course not." With a look of concentration on her brow, Shelby began to apply a matching polish to her toenails. "After all, you've been working here long enough to realize that the rift between Daddy and my big brother has been widening since Daddy finally realized that Roarke was serious about building skyscrapers instead of a political career. Of course Roarke's always known his own mind, and in his own way he's even more ambitious than Daddy. . . . Why, I recall one of his teachers, back in high school, calling him a shark."

"A shark?" In all of Cassie's romantic daydreams, she'd never thought of Roarke as coldblooded.

"Because he's always hungry," Shelby explained. "And always moving forward. Personally, I've always believed that description suits Roarke to a T."

She wiggled her painted toes. "What do you think? Doesn't this color match my new sundress perfectly?"

Her mind still on Roarke, Cassie murmured a vague agreement.

# *Four*

Cassie was in the library, painstakingly typing out an updated inventory of paintings for the insurance man, when her employer entered.

"I believe you're out of school next week for spring vacation."

"Yes, ma'am."

"Have you made any plans?"

"Plans?"

"Are you and your mother going away? Shelby, Trace, and Quinlan are going to St. Thomas," she said, as if that would help Cassie understand her meaning.

She and Belle, take a trip just for pleasure? The idea was beyond Cassie's wildest comprehension. "No, ma'am. We're not going anywhere."

Miss Lillian didn't try to hide her satisfaction. "Good. Then you'll be free to go to New York."

"New York?" Cassie couldn't believe it.

"Sotheby's is having an auction of carved gemstones I want to attend. I thought, since you've shown a marvelous appreciation of art and antiques, that you'd enjoy accompanying me."

It was as if Christmas had suddenly come early. "Really?" Cassie asked, still not quite trusting her good fortune. "You really want me to go to New York City. With you?"

"That's right. Unless you think your mother would object."

Cassie's heart sank. Of course her mother would object. In fact, if Belle even got wind of the fact that Cassie was trotting off to New York City, as carefree as a jaybird, she'd show up at the Gallagher ranch and make one helluva scene.

Refusing to give up the chance of a lifetime, Cassie decided to do whatever it took to keep Belle from finding out about the trip. Lord knows, she'd lied *for* her mother enough times, she doubted that she'd go to hell for lying *to* her.

"Oh, my mama won't mind," she said, as if her firm, confident tone could make it true. "Law, Miss Lillian, I don't know how to thank you."

"It's enough that you're pleased, Cassie dear." Miss Lillian smiled at Cassie's honest enthusiasm. "Now, here are our airline tickets and a book I'd advise that you read before our trip."

Cassie took the red, white, and blue airline folder and the large book entitled *Cameo Appearances.*

"It details the history of cameos," Miss Lillian explained when Cassie began leafing through the book's beautifully illustrated pages. "I'm hoping to purchase at least one and you'll enjoy the auction more if you understand what's being sold."

She handed Cassie another, smaller text. "And this is the catalogue." A longtime Sotheby's customer, Miss Lillian received the catalogues by mail. Cassie had watched her pore over the glossy pages for hours. "Why don't you study it and see if there's anything you think we should buy."

"Me?" It came out a startled squeak.

"You have a talent for recognizing beautiful things, Cassie. It's time we began honing that talent. Although most of the pieces are too ostentatious for my personal taste, as I said, they are offering a very nice collection of cameos."

Her hand fingered the gold-rimmed ivory cameo adorning the throat of her lavender silk blouse. "I've already marked the ones I'm particularly interested in. Perhaps you'll discover something I've overlooked."

"Yes, ma'am." It was all too much. Cassie's mind was whirling, making coherent thought impossible. She stood staring at the catalogue long after Miss Lillian had left the room.

Cassie set to work with a fervor, devouring the text and glossy pictures of the book Miss Lillian had given her, learning that the sculpture-in-miniature art of cameos dated back to remote antiquity. She learned that it was the Sumerians of southern Mesopotamia who'd first engraved flat gemstones in intaglio for use as signet stones. The Egyptians, carrying the idea a step further, carved the rounded side of a cabochon in the form of a scarab, engraving the flat side with a seal or amuletic inscription. These stylized representations of the common dung beetle—revered symbol of Khepera, god of the morning sun—were mounted as pendants or worn as rings.

By the late fifth and sixth centuries B.C., Greek artisans had abandoned the unappealing dung beetle and began engraving the flat surface of a single-color hard stone while leaving the rounded surface *en cabochon.*

The art of gem carving changed drastically when Alexander the Great's campaigns made available a stunning stream of multicolored stone from the orient: Arabian sardonyx banded in gray and violet brown, Indian sardonyx with warm cream and brown tones, and myriad types of banded, massive quartz.

Engravers soon discovered that these new stones, with their bands of contrasting colors, were ideal for a new form—carvings of relief designs on a contrasting ground. It was then—between the end of the fourth century B.C. and the beginning of the third—when true cameos first appeared.

They were, Cassie read, among the first of the truly useless man-made objects, created solely to be admired. And as she studied the marvelous photographs depicting stones from the Hellenistic period in Greece, through the days of the Roman Empire, the Middle Ages, the Renaissance, the Victorian Age (called fussy ladies in shell by many modern dealers), up to the present, Cassie decided that the delicate artwork definitely deserved to be admired.

Although Cassie knew she could never consider herself an expert after reading a single book, as the time for her trip to New York approached, she did at least feel confident that she understood what Miss Lillian was looking for. Which is why, when one pale green stone in particular caught her eye, Cassie wondered if she had the nerve to bring it to her employer's attention.

She also wondered—with a great deal less confidence—what she was going to do about her mother.

Cassie had determined at a young age that whenever the fates dallied with a McBride, the luck they'd bestow would usually be the bad kind. So it came as such a surprise when Belle suddenly announced, two days before Cassie was scheduled to leave for New York, that she'd landed a singing gig in Tulsa and didn't know when she'd be back. Cassie, who'd been struggling to come up with a lie she thought her mother—an

accomplished prevaricator herself—would believe, nearly wept with relief.

Miss Lillian and Cassie arrived at their hotel in New York late at night.
Central Park, swathed in deep purple shadows, was surrounded by the
glittering lights of the city.

"You must be hungry," Miss Lillian said as Cassie roamed the spacious suite of the Pierre, in awe of the period furniture, the antique satin
draperies, the decadent marble bathroom. "You didn't eat on the
plane."

Cassie had been too excited to do more than push her chicken around
on her plate. "I'm fine," she assured her employer.

"Nonsense. A young girl needs her strength." Miss Lillian handed
Cassie a leather-bound folder. "Order anything you like."

When Cassie stared uncomprehendingly at the room service menu,
Miss Lillian said, "Just call down and order your dinner, dear, then sign
the ticket when the waiter arrives.

"I'm going to take a long hot bath. I swear, airline travel gets more
unpleasant every year. All those crying babies and young people in jeans
and T-shirts. Why, I remember when ladies wore suits and white gloves
while traveling." She sighed and gave Cassie a slight, self-deprecating
smile. "Old age must be catching up with me."

"You're not old."

"I knew I was smart to bring you, Cassie," Miss Lillian responded.
"You always say exactly the right thing."

Never having stayed in a hotel, Cassie found room service to be an
exceptional treat. She stared at the white linen tablecloth, the fine,
gold-rimmed china, the fragrant red rose in its crystal vase. All that for
a club sandwich and a Coke. New York truly was amazing.

Although she was dying to explore the city, Cassie's first morning in
Manhattan was spent at Sotheby's. But if she was disappointed about
having to put off her sightseeing, the minute she stepped inside the York
Avenue auction house, Cassie changed her mind.

The auction of exquisitely carved gemstones was certainly more discreet than the raucous annual cattle sales held in Gallagher City, but the
atmosphere was still absolutely electric. Cassie noticed that the bigger the
bid, the more imperceptible the nod.

She watched, spellbound, as a dapper man sporting a pencil-thin
mustache kept the bidding moving at a frantic pace. A lighted board
behind the auctioneer kept track of the bidding. When Miss Lillian

explained that the currencies displayed were dollars, Swiss francs, French francs, British pound sterling, German marks, and Japanese yen, Cassie, who'd never met a foreigner, knew that a new world was being opened up to her.

The sale began with the relatively less expensive items: an amazingly lifelike agate rabbit cravat pin, a broach featuring an amiable gold gorilla peering out from between a pair of carved green tourmaline stalks, a trio of carved rock crystal eggs adorned with diamonds, and a bracelet that linked seven separate cameos depicting different birds carved in high relief on pink coral and moonstone. Cassie remembered from her reading that such bracelets were popular in the Victorian era.

The bidding continued briskly, the momentum of the pace designed to excite the buyers, to carry them along with the thrill of the chase. No one was allowed to catch a breath as both the prices and the elaborate detail of workmanship escalated.

A beehive carved from black jade, adorned with pavé canary diamond bees went to a paunchy, balding man in the first row; after a heated battle, a diamond falcon with eighteen-karat-gold feathers studded with rubies and emeralds went to a white-robed Saudi Arabian prince surrounded by dark-suited Bedouin bodyguards. Minutes later, the same tall, austere-looking man purchased a royal jasper dragon so fierce it breathed flames of gold.

A dazzling necklace of rhododendron created from pink tourmaline entwined with green tourmaline leaves, and pistils accented with pink diamonds, was sold to a bone-thin matron dressed in an ivory silk morning suit adorned with her day jewels.

A jasper terrier, carved by Fabergé for England's Queen Alexandra (sister of the Dowager Empress of Russia, widow of Czar Alexander III, the dapper auctioneer reminded the bidders) was sold to an anonymous telephone bidder. As were a quartz pig and an aventurine quartz shire horse, also created by Fabergé as part of the Sandringham farm animal collection commissioned by King Edward VII.

From the mind-boggling prices the auctioneer was receiving Cassie realized that she was in the presence of the wealthiest people in the world. But they'd ceded their mighty collective power to the man behind the mahogany podium, the man who could determine winner from loser by the crack of his gavel.

At that moment, Cassie knew what she was going to do with her life. Someday, she'd be the one standing at the front of this room—or one exactly like it—auctioning off glorious treasures to elegantly dressed men and women for whom money was no object.

Cassie was dizzy with excitement when they finally left the auction. Miss Lillian had arranged to have her purchases—a pair of nineteenth-century Italian earrings with female profiles carved in pink lava; a nineteenth-century French broach with rose-cut diamonds, pearls, and a black emerald band surrounding a classical helmeted head in sardonyx; and a stunning sixteenth-century portrait of Mary Stuart carved in minute detail from a nearly translucent piece of green Burmese jadeite—delivered to her hotel, where she'd left orders with the manager to have them put in the safe. It had been the most exhilarating two and a half hours of Cassie's life.

"I take it you enjoyed yourself, Cassie." Miss Lillian gave Cassie a fond look as they sat in the back of a limousine slowly making its way through the almost impenetrable traffic.

"It was amazing!" The word didn't begin to describe how Cassie was feeling, but it was as close as her whirling mind could come.

"I know exactly how you feel." She patted Cassie's hand. "And I can't thank you enough for discovering the Mary Stuart broach. I don't know how I overlooked it."

It had taken all her nerve to point out the jadeite broach. In the catalogue, the cameo had appeared lovely, but the real broach, an exquisitely carved piece of jewelry, had been one of the most beautiful things Cassie had ever seen. The translucent green stone seemed to glow with life.

"There are many more colors to jade than the green you admire so, Cassie," Miss Lillian said after the girl had tried to explain her attraction to the unique cameo to her benefactor. "It's an amazingly versatile stone. In fact, now that I think of it, I recall an ancient Chinese myth about jade, telling how when man was stumbling over the earth, beset by all sorts of wild beasts, the storm god took pity on him and forged a rainbow into jade axes and tossed them to earth for man to discover.

"The legend claims that's the reason jade appears in all the hues of the rainbow. It's also why it's often referred to as the Stone of Heaven."

The stone of heaven. Cassie could not have come up with a more perfect name if she'd tried. Although she'd always found Miss Lillian's possessions remarkable and had admired them for both their beauty and their value, that single jade cameo was the first treasure she'd ever seen that had emotionally moved her.

"I know you've got your heart set on sightseeing, Cassie," Miss

Lillian said, "but I thought we'd have lunch at the Russian Tea Room first."

"What a wonderful idea!" Impulsively, Cassie flung her arms around Miss Lillian's shoulders and hugged her.

"Gracious." Miss Lillian straightened her feathered hat and smoothed the wrinkles from this season's Chanel suit. "If you are capable of generating such enthusiasm over a mere lunch, I'm almost afraid to tell you that Roarke will be eating with us."

"Roarke?" Cassie stared, afraid to believe. "But—"

"I know. My brother had forbidden the family to speak to him. But Roarke is my nephew. And if anyone had asked my opinion—" anyone meaning Quinlan, Cassie determined—"I would have said that the boy had every right to follow his own star."

Roarke. She was going to have lunch with the man who'd played a starring role in her romantic fantasies for the past four years!

On more than one occasion, after Cassie had probed in what she had hoped was a casual manner for news of Roarke, Shelby had accused her of being obsessed with her brother. Although Cassie had steadfastly denied such claim, she did take the time to look the word *obsession* up in the dictionary. When she read the definition—the domination of one's thoughts or feelings by a persistent idea, image, or desire—she realized that Shelby was right.

The shiny brass revolving doors of the Russian Tea Room reminded Cassie of a time machine. The moment she entered the restaurant and viewed the spectacular confusion of paintings, fresh flowers, and gleaming samovars, she felt as if she'd been whisked back to the days of the czars. When her wide eyes drank in the ever-present Christmas decorations, Cassie felt as if she were experiencing the holiday in April.

If she was excited by the voluptuous scene, Cassie felt her heart treble its beat when a tall, dark-haired man rose from one of the half-circular red booths to greet them. The maturity stamped onto his rugged features made him even more handsome than ever, she decided, watching Roarke greet his aunt with a kiss on the cheek. His black hair had been stylishly trimmed a little shorter than she remembered it, but his eyes were still the same electric blue. When those vivid eyes settled on Cassie, she began to glow.

"I knew it," he murmured, forsaking a more conventional greeting.

"Knew what?"

"That you'd grow up to be a beauty."

Cassie had felt underdressed compared to the other women in the restaurant. What she didn't realize was that in a season when every woman seemed to be yet another Annie Hall clone, the unadorned white blouse and slim black skirt emphasized her natural beauty. Embarrassed by the compliment, Cassie ducked her head and murmured a soft "thank you."

Roarke waited until his aunt and Cassie were seated in the booth before reclaiming his place beside Cassie. When his thigh accidentally brushed against her leg, she felt an almost electric jolt. Something alien and wonderful shimmered through her.

"So, how are you ladies enjoying New York?" he asked.

"Cassie hasn't had an opportunity to experience very much of the city," Miss Lillian divulged. "We only arrived last night. And of course we had the auction this morning."

"Ah yes, the auction." Roarke nodded. "Tribal rites of the rich and powerful. So, how did it go?"

"Not as well as it might have." When Miss Lillian's lips drew into a thin line, Cassie knew she was remembering the tall silent Arab who'd outbid her for a rare four-hundred-year-old cameo depicting Cleopatra and her asp fashioned in banded agate, gold, and enamel.

"Still, we did manage to acquire a lovely pair of earrings and a French helmet broach and an absolutely stunning sixteenth-century Burmese jadeite cameo portrait of Mary Stuart, thanks to Cassie." She patted Cassie's hand. "I don't know how, but I'd completely overlooked the piece in the catalogue. Fortunately, Cassie brought it to my attention."

"I hadn't realized you were an jewelry aficionado, Cassie," Roarke said.

"Cassie's a quick learner," Miss Lillian said. "Collecting has its own secret language. Cassie was born to speak that language."

Cassie, embarrassed by both her employer's words of praise and the way Roarke was looking at her, as if seeing her for the first time, blushed and began to fiddle nervously with her cutlery.

Lunch passed in a blur as hustling waiters dressed in red Russian tunics delivered the unfamiliar taste sensations. Although Miss Lillian ordered the chicken salad, Cassie allowed Roarke to coax her into trying several of the house specialties.

The meal began with little pancakes—blini, Roarke called them—topped with sour cream and caviar. Although she pretended to enjoy the appetizer, Cassie secretly decided that caviar must be an acquired taste. Next came bowls of hot borsch, which Cassie was surprised to enjoy.

Her favorite dish, hands down, was a plump meat dumpling with dill in broth.

"Your timing is perfect," Roarke said when Cassie declared it delicious. "They serve Palmeny Siberian only on Wednesday."

*Palmeny Siberian.* The name was as foreign as everything else about this magical day. Cassie couldn't remember ever being so happy.

"So how do you like the Pierre, Cassie?" Roarke asked.

"Oh, I love it," Cassie breathed. "It's like living in a palace."

Cassie was stunned when Roarke threw back his head and laughed. "I'd almost forgotten how much fun you are, Cassie McBride."

Confused by his surprising response, Cassie stared uncomprehendingly from Roarke to Miss Lillian and back to Roarke again.

"My nephew, the admittedly brilliant big-city architect, has always insisted that the Pierre was designed for travelers who think Marie Antoinette had all the right decorating ideas," Miss Lillian said stiffly.

From the reluctant smile in the elderly woman's eyes, Cassie realized that this was a long-running joke between aunt and nephew. "Well, I think the hotel's beautiful," she said loyally.

As the lunch continued, Cassie tried to drink in everything about the restaurant, so she could recall it in vivid detail once she returned to Oklahoma. But her attention kept swinging back to Roarke.

When he described the building his design firm had recently unveiled—a forty-two story pink granite tower, patterned at each corner to create the illusion of tall classical columns, built for a Japanese bank—her gaze riveted on the ebony hair gracing the back of his wrists as he sketched the building on the back of a business card.

"I know it's heresy in my business to say anything against Philip Johnson," he said, "and I'll be the first to admit that the old glass boxes of corporate America were boring—but at least they were reasonably unobtrusive.

"I have this bad feeling that before the next decade is over, Johnson and Robert Venturi—who are admittedly brilliant—will have spawned a whole lot of postmodernist clones who'll erect aggressively ugly, monstrous buildings all over the country. Like a bad dream. Hell, a nightmare.

"I can't help wondering if, when Venturi argued for messy vitality and turned Mies van der Rohe's dictum about less being more on its head by insisting that less is a bore, he knew what he was doing."

Roarke scowled as if he were envisioning a landscape cluttered with corporate headquarters posing as Victorian mansions, Renaissance palaces, and neoclassical villas. "No one can deny that the modernist movement is responsible for its own downfall, for having failed to respond to human needs and scale. But from what I can tell, a lot of these postmodernists are nothing but nihilists who, since they lack the talent to add new ideas to the design vocabulary, are forced to vandalize the styles of other periods."

That he cared deeply about his work was obvious. All during his impassioned monologue, Cassie nodded enthusiastically, without understanding a single word he said. She was too busy watching the attractive lines fan out from his smiling blue eyes.

Miss Lillian turned to Cassie. "If my nephew had his way, he'd tear down every historical building in the city and replace them with red steel and glass block." Her indulgent smile took the sting out of her words. "I knew your father made a mistake when he bought you that erector set instead of the Lincoln Logs I suggested."

"I'm not in favor of getting rid of the past," Roarke protested. "But architecture is supposed to start your blood pumping. I'm sure those old buildings spoke to the people of their day, but this is a new era. We're standing right on the brink of the nineteen eighties, not the eighteen eighties or the seventeen eighties. And architecture should reflect who we are now, not who we were."

Cassie, who'd always considered Quinlan Gallagher's marble-pillared Georgian mansion to be the most beautiful house in the world, couldn't understand Roarke's views on tossing out the old in favor of the new, but she wasn't about to risk offending him by uttering a single word of argument.

"That's enough lecturing for today," he said with a self-deprecating grin. "Sorry, ladies, sometimes I just feel like a salmon trying to make its way upstream, fighting against the tide every step of the way. But I didn't mean to take my frustrations out on you." His grin widened and his eyes warmed. "How about some dessert?"

As if the day weren't magical enough, after lunch Roarke informed them he'd taken the remainder of the day off in order to take them sightseeing. When Miss Lillian declined, claiming fatigue, Cassie's heart plummeted, but she'd never been one to turn her back on her duty.

"That's right nice of you, Roarke," she said, "but we'd better be getting back to the hotel."

"Don't be silly," Miss Lillian said. "Just because I'm turning into an old lady is no reason you shouldn't have a good time. I'll simply take the limousine back to the hotel."

They exited the restaurant together. Roarke opened the door of the limo for his aunt, then bending down, kissed her smooth cheek. "Thank you."

In that brief moment, Cassie suddenly understood how isolated Roarke must feel, being banished from his family, and her heart went out to him. She wondered if he sometimes, late at night, felt as lonely as she always did.

She was given no time to dwell on that surprising thought as Roarke took her on a whirlwind tour of the city. To Cassie, who'd never been out of Oklahoma, Manhattan might as well have been Baghdad. She struggled to see everything at once, but it was like trying to look at the world through a kaleidoscope. The colorful views kept shifting, changing.

She oohed and aahed over the Woolworth Building's lavish entrance, insisted on going all the way up to the eighty-sixth-floor observation deck of the Empire State Building, and giggled as the wind whipped her hair into a brilliant copper tangle. Back down on the ground again, she drank in the sight of the public library, guarded by an immense pair of marble lions, and marveled over Park Avenue's limestone and brick buildings and the bright red and yellow tulips adorning the boulevard's islands.

And there was the amazing mix of people: Hasidic Jews on "Diamond Row," Korean greengrocers, vendors on every corner, tidal waves of tourists and businessmen crowding the streets, white-faced mimes in Central Park, old men sailing their boats on the park's pond.

Day turned to evening, then to night, and although Roarke told Cassie that he'd take her anywhere she wanted for dinner, she couldn't bear the idea of wasting any more time than necessary eating. Besides, she assured him, her guidebook insisted that no trip to New York was complete without a Nathan's hot dog. Although Roarke protested treating her to such plebian fare, Cassie found the salty hot dog, on the slightly stale roll, with chili on the side, to be ambrosia.

The miraculous day ended with a ride through the dark of Central Park in a horse-drawn hansom cab whose driver was dressed like a character out of *Black Beauty*.

"I haven't properly thanked you for my graduation present," Roarke said.

Cassie had saved her money for months to pay for the engraved silver mechanical pencil set. "You wrote me that letter." She still had it, hidden beneath her panties and bras in the top drawer of her bureau.

"Letters aren't the same as thanking you in person."

"But coming back home would've probably set your pa off somethin' awful."

"You're right there, sugar," Roarke agreed grimly. He leaned his head back against the seat and sighed. "He refuses to understand," he muttered, more to himself than to Cassie. "For as long as I can remember, I've wanted to design important buildings, like the ones designed by Frank Lloyd Wright, I. M. Pei, or Philip Johnson. Buildings that'll bear my name the way a Picasso or a van Gogh painting bears the artist's signature. What I want, I guess, is to leave my footprints in the sand."

"You will," Cassie insisted with the fervor of a zealot. She was flooded with emotions, some of which were almost maternal. She wanted to soothe the pain created by his estrangement with his family, she wanted to heal his wounds, she wanted to battle all his enemies. There wasn't anything she wouldn't do for this man she'd loved for so long.

"I just know that you're going to build skyscraper office buildings and hotels, Roarke, and when I'm rich and famous, I'm going to stay in one of your hotels and tell everyone that I know the architect. Personally."

He turned his head and looked at her, his eyes smiling warmly in the moonlight. "I must be a world-class dolt, complaining about my family problems when I'm with such a beautiful girl." He took hold of her hand. "You really have grown up, Cassie."

When he linked their fingers together, Cassie went mute. How was it that other boys' touches made her cringe, but Roarke's felt so impossibly right?

"A girl as pretty as you must have guys waiting in line to take you out."

How could Cassie explain that Belle's less than pristine reputation had resulted in her being viewed by the population of Gallagher City as a younger version of her mother? Hardly a week went by when some grinning boy with teenage lust in his eyes didn't invite her to one of the weekend beer bashes held outside of town. Cassie always refused, painfully aware that there were two kinds of girls. The first kind got invited to basketball games, to movies at the Bijou, to the spring prom at the country club. The others, girls with a reputation, girls like her, got taken to beer bashes that turned into drunken petting parties.

Determined to enjoy herself for this single incredible day, Cassie pushed the depressing thought away. "I'm too busy to have much time for dating, what with school and my job and all."

"I can certainly appreciate that. When I was at Yale, I held down two jobs. I worked three days a week as a construction laborer and six nights a week and all day Sunday as a janitor in an office building, so I could pay for my classes."

"You were a janitor?"

"Hey, nobody ever said that independence came easy." He reached down and adjusted the blanket that had begun to slip off her knees. When his fingers brushed against her leg, Cassie's blood hummed. "So tell me, Cassie, what do you want out of life? What are your dreams?"

"I'm coming back here, to New York City," she said. "And become rich and famous." Her eyes glittered with steely determination. "I'm going to have a closet full of fancy clothes and fur coats and jewels. Diamonds and emeralds and rubies redder than an Oklahoma sunset. And a dog," she said, continuing to compile her list. For years Cassie had begged for a pet. For years Belle had refused.

"One of those fluffy white poodles like all the rich society ladies and movie stars have. And I'll take him for walks up and down Fifth Avenue, him in his diamond collar and me in my diamond rings and bracelets."

Cassie was relieved when Roarke didn't laugh at her admittedly fanciful dreams. Instead, he merely said, "Good for you. Have you come up with a plan?"

It was as if a dam had suddenly burst. Cassie talked practically nonstop, telling him about the plan that had been born from her exhilarating experience this morning at Sotheby's.

"And I want to learn a lot more about jade," she said. "Did you know it's called the stone of heaven?"

Roarke smiled. "No, I didn't know that."

"Well, it is." She went on to explain about the legend Miss Lillian had told her earlier that afternoon.

To Cassie's delight, Roarke took her seriously, and after instructing the driver to take another turn around the park, he even offered helpful suggestions. Eager acolyte that she was, Cassie hung on every word.

"You're going to make it, Cassie McBride," Roarke said as they stood outside the door of the hotel suite at the end of the evening. His arms were looped lightly around her waist, his expression, as he looked down into her uplifted face, was tenderly encouraging.

"One of these years, when you get a little more experience under your belt, you're going to take this city by storm. And when you do, I'm going to be proud of you."

Seventeen-year-old Cassie, embroiled in the throes of young love, took his words to be the promise of a future together. And when he ducked his head and kissed her—a real kiss, right on the lips, light, brief, but devastatingly wonderful—she was sure that her love was no longer one-sided.

As soon as she returned to Gallagher City, Cassie began studying in earnest. She pored over the catalogues Miss Lillian received from Sotheby's, Christie's, and Bentley's, a smaller, but no less prestigious New York auction house. Twice a month on her day off, after cleaning and cooking for Belle, Cassie hitchhiked into Oklahoma City, where she ensconced herself in the fine arts section of the library and didn't budge until the overhead lights blinked at the end of the day, signaling the library's closing. Then, after checking out the maximum number of books on art and antiques allowed, Cassie would trudge back home carrying them.

Realizing that she would never get a job in the art world if she sounded like some dirt-poor Okie, she spent every evening listening to the radio. Eschewing the ubiquitous country and western music, she tuned to the public broadcast FM station and, determined to rid her voice of its harsh Oklahoma twang, stayed awake late into the night repeating the announcer's smooth round tones over and over again.

One day, walking home from the ranch, Cassie saw a poster of Manhattan's skyline at night in the window of Ginny's Hallmark store. She took the poster home in its cardboard tube and hung it on her wall, where the gleaming art deco dome of the Chrysler Building was the last thing she saw before falling to sleep for two glorious weeks until Belle got drunk and ripped it up.

"Goddamnit, Cassie McBride," Belle hollered loud enough to be heard all the way down to Tops Cafe, "when are you gonna grow up and realize that a no-account nobody like you can't never make it out of Gallagher City? You're stuck here, girl, just like the rest of us. So you might as well save yourself a lot of grief by puttin' those damn fool ideas out of your head."

Cassie refused to listen. She kept the dream of New York in the forefront of her mind, where it gleamed bright and magical like the Emerald City of Oz.

And although Miss Lillian professed concern that Cassie was looking tired, Cassie didn't care that her intense study was causing her to forgo sleep. Having finally found a way to get out of Gallagher City, she wanted to make certain that she was well prepared for her future.

A glorious, shining future that would include Roarke Gallagher.

# *Five*

*June 1980*

Quinlan Gallagher's heart attack occurred during a heated confrontation with a rival oil man and immediately sent the household into a state of chaos. Although the doctors assured Miss Lillian that Quinlan would be back in the saddle—both figuratively and literally—in two months, they also told her that during that time her brother would need to avoid stressful situations. And while Gallagher Gas and Oil's senior executives were capable of running the company during their CEO's recuperation, Quinlan insisted that Roarke take his place at the helm.

Having graduated from Gallagher City High School, Cassie was working at the Gallagher mansion for the summer before moving to Tulsa, to begin her freshman year at Oral Roberts University. Miss Lillian, a lifelong Methodist and supporter of the former tent preacher and faith healer, had arranged for her to receive a full scholarship to the private liberal arts college. When she had learned the news, Cassie had been overwhelmed by her employer's generosity.

Cassie knew that she should feel sorry about Quinlan's heart attack; after all, the man did pay her salary, even if Miss Lillian was the one who wrote out the checks. But try as she might, Cassie could not be sorry about anything that would bring Roarke back to the ranch.

Cassie had learned from Shelby that Roarke was working in Paris, after winning a coveted assignment with François Guimard, the famed French architect who'd been awarded a contract to design a cultural center.

Shelby had also said that the center would be the largest of its kind in the world, encompassing two art museums, a theater, and a concert hall.

Roarke was not surprised to find that little had changed during his prolonged absence. Except Cassie. The promise she'd possessed at seventeen had, a year later, definitely been fulfilled. She was tall—just under six feet—with the body of a Valkyrie. Her Oklahoma twang had been mysteriously replaced by a lushly melodic tone.

During the five years she'd worked for Miss Lillian, Cassie's youthful crush on Roarke had escalated into a hunger like nothing she'd ever known. The fact that her body ached whenever he was near her made that painfully evident. Not only that, Roarke also represented her way out of Oklahoma.

Although she was excited about going to college, Cassie was pragmatic enough to realize that Oral Roberts University was known more for its nationally ranked basketball teams and Prayer Tower—a two-hundred-foot structure in the shape of a cross topped off with a crown of thorns—than its academics. A degree from the small Oklahoma college wouldn't pull much weight with the New York auction world.

But Roarke, despite his Oklahoma roots, was beginning to garner some small measure of fame. People were beginning to know his name; he was frequently mentioned in articles written about the young new breed of city builders, and although not all the writers agreed with his views, everyone considered him intriguing. Even more intent than ever to buck the rising tide of postmodernism, he was a maverick in an occupation that thrived on imitation.

Such recognition made Roarke a rising star. And Cassie knew that as such, he could open doors to everything she had ever dreamed of: wealth, fame, respectability.

Cassie's spirit was bolstered by the knowledge that she did not appear to be alone in her feelings. On those rare occasions when Roarke would let his guard down, she'd catch him looking at her and realized that as much as he might pretend otherwise, Roarke no longer considered her a child.

Telling herself that nothing—or no one—worth having ever came easily, she set about seducing Roarke with the same determination she'd learned to tell the difference between a Renoir and a Monet.

If Roarke was working in the library, she'd find it necessary to retrieve a book for Miss Lillian, pretending surprise to find him there. If he went to the kitchen in search of a cool drink, she would be there, ostensibly dying for a glass of water. There was no escaping her. But try as she might, Roarke did not respond to her feminine lures. Finally, a frustrated Cassie was forced to conclude that she simply could not compete with the sophisticated women of Paris.

Two weeks after Roarke's return, Cassie discovered exactly how wrong she'd been. She was alone in the house; Roarke was out riding, Shelby and Trace were in Dallas with friends, and Miss Lillian had taken Quinlan into Oklahoma City for his doctor's appointment. The rain had begun shortly after they'd left; by noon it had turned to hail and the sky was nearly as dark as midnight.

Undisturbed by the building storm, Cassie was working in the library. When she'd first begun work at the ranch, she'd hated the library. Whenever she'd had to dust the leather-bound books, she'd felt as if Quinlan Gallagher's hunting trophies on the leather-covered walls— stag, elk, mountain lion, moose, big-horned sheep—were watching her through unblinking marble eyes. Eventually, however, with the exception of a huge mounted kodiak bear standing eternal guard in the corner, she'd learned to ignore them.

Suddenly, a window shattered. A wind with the force of a locomotive blew the papers off Quinlan's desk, and hail was driven into the room to melt on the steer-hide rugs. No stranger to tornadoes, Cassie ran out of the room, heading for the storm cellar in the basement. She'd just reached the door to the stairwell when Roarke came running up to her.

"Where the hell have you been?" he demanded in a voice close to a shout. His black hair was wet, his eyes were deep and black and furious.

"In the library."

"I've been looking all over the damned house for you." Grabbing hold of her arm, he dragged her down the stairs.

The storm cellar was made of reinforced concrete masonry; a reinforced concrete ceiling separated it from the rest of the house. Since Gallagher City was located in Tornado Alley, the room was furnished with cots and supplied with blankets, candles, canned food, bottled water, and a portable radio. Although Cassie knew that she was safe down there, she couldn't help remembering the time when a tornado had picked up the mobile homes on either side of her and Belle's and dumped them one hundred yards away, in the middle of the railroad tracks. Miraculously, their trailer had gone untouched.

Roarke lighted three fat candles and placed them on the floor beside where Cassie was sitting on one of the blankets, and tuned the radio to the emergency broadcast station, which was warning residents to seek shelter. A supercell generated over the western part of the state had created several twisters, one of which had already flattened a barn, a church, and a school north of Oklahoma City.

As Roarke sat down beside her, Cassie smelled rain, leather, and saddle soap. The blend was more stirring than the most expensive male colognes. "It'll be all right," he assured her. "You'll be all right."

"I'm not frightened."

"But you're trembling. Are you cold?" As if on impulse, he ran his knuckles in a slow, warm sweep up her cheek.

"No," she whispered. "I think I'm burning up." Lifting her hand, Cassie ran her own fingers over the strong bones of his face, over the taut skin darkened to the hue of mahogany by the strong Oklahoma sun.

The storm brewing in his dark eyes rivaled the one outside. His irises deepened until they were nearly as dark as the pupils. Her lips parted. She drew in a deep breath and held it, waiting.

They had only to move. A slight shifting of their heads and their lips would meet.

Roarke was not a man to act on impulse. He always analyzed every line on a blueprint, weighed the pros and cons of any move he made. There had never been an aspect of his life or his work that hadn't been carefully planned in advance. Until now.

His hands moved to her waist, whether to push her away or pull her closer, Roarke could not quite decide. "This is a mistake," he said.

"How can anything that feels so right be a mistake?" Cassie asked. "I've been dreaming of this," she whispered. "Wicked, wonderful dreams, dreams of you touching me. Me touching you."

"A helluva mistake," he repeated. Then, with a low curse, he covered her mouth with his.

The intensity rocked them both. This was no gentle first kiss. There was no slow, smoldering warmth. The passion ignited instantly, causing a hot, urgent flow of desire. Roarke's mouth craved passion; in response, sweet passion flowed from Cassie into him. His hands, running up and down her arms, sought submission; she melted quickly into the heated kiss, her body following her reckless heart, offering herself unconditionally.

As his mouth ravaged hers, as his hands stoked hidden fires burning deep within her, Cassie knew that nothing would ever be the same again. Needs welled up inside her—there were years of emptiness waiting to be filled. She was starved for more, she was desperate to learn the erotic secrets her body had been hungering for ever since Roarke's return.

Roarke knew those secrets. She'd seen it in his eyes, dark and dangerous and tempting.

The bodice of her cotton sundress fell to her waist, revealing her full, firm breasts. When she heard him catch his breath, she felt a thrill of womanly pride.

The touch of his fingers on her bare flesh warmed her. The dark hand at her breast caressed, fondled, tormented. Desire sang its clear high notes in her blood. Cassie began unbuttoning his shirt, but inexperience made her fingers clumsy. She concentrated on manipulating the buttons through the narrow holes as if it were the most important task on earth. Finally, she managed to push it off his shoulders.

"Glory be," she breathed, slipping back into the accent of her roots. "You're beautiful, Roarke." Cassie ran her palms tentatively at first, then possessively, down his chest, over his rigid stomach. When her fingers slipped beneath the low-slung waistband of his jeans, Roarke's control snapped.

"God help me. I give up." Pulling her down on the blanket, he unzipped the dress and pulled it down her long legs. Her white nylon bikini panties followed.

Then, as if he had all the time in the world, his mouth coaxed, tempted, beguiled. His hands touched, stroked, aroused. Her flesh was hot and smooth and damp under his lips; she trembled under his touch. Her hair was like nothing he'd ever touched. There were handfuls of it, carrying her scent.

It was torment. It was heaven. No longer the one in control, Cassie surrendered to him mindlessly. She was drifting on a rising sea of sparks, boneless, pliant under his increasingly devastating touch. Her soft sighs became moans. She heard herself whisper his name as his mouth lingered at her nipple. When his tongue made a long, wet swath across the aching fullness of her breasts, a strangled sound of pleasure escaped her parted lips.

The ripe scent of passion filled the air. She was on fire. Heat like nothing she'd ever known, or imagined, was building inside her. And outside. The air practically sparked with it. Cassie had never known that a man and a woman could share something so dark, so incendiary. So dangerous. And even as the flames threatened to engulf her, she wanted more. Much, much more. Outside, the vicious, spinning wind roared like a jet engine, a million bees. Caught up in a passion-filled storm of her own, Cassie couldn't hear it.

In the smoky haze surrounding her mind, Cassie realized with an erotic start that the rest of Roarke's clothes were gone, whipped away, perhaps by the heated, rising winds. Hot flesh to hot flesh, mouth to mouth, they moved together, driving each other to the brink of sanity. And beyond.

When he touched her, really touched her, inside, Cassie called out his name in a half moan, half cry.

He drew his fingers back. "Am I hurting you?"

"Oh, no," she answered on a soft, thready tone. "It—it feels good."

"It's supposed to." He brushed a soft, reassuring kiss against her lips and continued the intimate caress.

For the first time in her life, Cassie was totally, amazingly aware of her body—every nerve, every pulse, every pore. Dizzy from the scent, the touch, the taste of him, Cassie clung to Roarke, thinking that passion couldn't possibly get any stronger than this. Or pleasure more intense.

As his teeth nibbled at the flaming skin inside her thighs, she suppressed a muffled cry. His warm breath teased her. And then, dear Lord almighty, he was kissing her *there*.

Torn between forbidden pleasures and shame, Cassie stiffened. Unperturbed, Roarke's soothing words gradually transcended her shock and his never-ceasing, caressing touch convinced her that maybe nice people really did do this wonderfully wicked thing.

His mouth was hard and hot and hungry, creating pinpoints of painful pleasure. Drunk with the glory of it, she whispered his name, over and over, like a prayer.

Flames funneled through her, from his mouth to that exquisite pleasure/pain center between her legs. Seeking relief, she twisted her fingers in his hair and pressed his head closer. Her gleaming thighs trembled in helpless spasms.

She wanted him to stop. She wanted him never to stop. Roarke's tongue flickered over moist hot flesh, bringing her to the brink of a perilous peak, but before she could go tumbling over the edge, he retreated, only to begin again.

Her breath grew shallow, her skin sensitized as that heat gathered, knotted, then exploded, the building flame turning into a sudden flash that raced outward to her fingertips. Weak, limp, stunned, she was still trying to catch her breath when she looked up to see Roarke poised over her, every muscle taut. Her arms and legs wrapped around him, enveloping him like warm silk, drawing him in.

Cassie gave up her innocence with a soft cry and then she was moving against him, urging him on, racing with him, higher and higher to a place where there was only lightning and thunder. And blinding heat.

Much, much later, they emerged from the storm cellar to discover that although the trees in the yards had been stripped of their leaves and Miss Lillian's brand-new Cadillac Seville had been flattened like an empty can, the house had miraculously escaped damage. Cassie set to work cleaning up the library while Roarke worked in the yard, and by the time the family had returned the next morning, everything appeared to be as close to normal as possible.

For the next six weeks, Cassie and Roarke made love whenever and wherever the opportunity arose. Like every romantic young girl in love, Cassie dreamed of marriage. Not for her, though, the neat frame house with a white picket fence and spacious backyard large enough for a used-brick barbecue and an elm tree from which dangled a black tire swing.

Cassie's dreams were not of a suburban paradise. Nor did she dream of usurping her employer's place as lady of the Gallagher manor. She and Roarke would have a much more exciting life in New York City. Where they would live on Park Avenue, in an apartment with a distinguished-looking doorman who would wear a royal blue uniform with fringed gold epaulets.

She would work at Sotheby's while Roarke would have his own architectural firm. On Madison or Park Avenue. Cassie vacillated continuously on this minor point. Wherever his office, he would design towering glass buildings destined to become focal points of the Manhattan skyline. When they weren't being seen at all the "in" clubs, their luxurious, antique-filled home would be a mecca for all the Beautiful People.

They'd have two children: a boy with curly black hair and devilish blue eyes that would make Cassie forgive him anything, and a red-haired girl who'd grow up realizing that there were exciting places for women in this brave new world. Every night, before going out, she'd tuck her darling children into bed and read them a story, something she'd once desperately wanted her own mother to do. Needless to say, Belle never had.

On weekends, the family would embark on adventures: visits to museums, the Rockettes' Christmas show at Radio City Music Hall, ice skating on the Rockefeller Center rink, afternoon excursions on the Staten Island ferry. That was the wonderful thing about New York,

Cassie considered blissfully—you never ran out of exciting things to do.

Her life with Roarke was going to be absolutely, positively wonderful. Better than wonderful, Cassie thought as she helped Miss Lillian address the invitations for Quinlan's first barbecue of the season. It was going to be perfect.

Since there wasn't a politician in Oklahoma foolish enough to ignore a summons from Quinlan Gallagher, all the state's heavy hitters—the governor, the secretary of state, the attorney general, the chief justice of the Oklahoma Supreme Court, as well as numerous other state representatives and political party honchos—arrived at the barbecue to celebrate Quinlan Gallagher's return to health.

After a devastating summer drought, Hurricane Allen, howling its way across the Gulf of Mexico, had brought thunderstorms inland to Oklahoma, forcing the party indoors.

All conversation centered around business: the new gas pipeline in Alaska, the Interior Department lifting its moratorium on tar-sand leasing in Utah, drilling platforms off the coast. Rumors of an impending war between Iran and Iraq had sent countries supplied by the two Middle East giants scrambling for new sources. This increased demand, along with the recent decontrol of oil prices, sent costs spiraling upward. Seven years ago the spot market price per barrel of crude had been $2.40; having already passed $30, analysts were predicting that it would soon hit $40. Such welcome news precipitated the most hectic drilling action in twenty-five years.

During this long, hot, profitable summer, the men's wives were also engrossed in the oil business as everyone debated who shot J.R. on TV's "Dallas."

Cassie, who'd been drafted into service when one of the kitchen maids came down with a sudden case of flu, watched Quinlan greet his guests with an enthusiasm that seconded the doctor's opinion that the oil baron was well enough to return to work. Which meant, she realized bleakly, that Roarke would soon be returning to Paris.

She was in the kitchen, helping Helga with the food, when Roarke suddenly pushed through the swinging doors. "I need to talk to you," he said abruptly.

Embarrassed to have Roarke see her looking so disheveled, Cassie pushed back the damp strands of hair from her forehead. "I have to work." She glanced nervously at Helga. Six years working under the same roof had not lessened her fear of the stoic German housekeeper.

"You go," Helga surprised her by saying. "But do not stay away very long. We have much work to do."

Roarke took Cassie by the elbow and led her outside, into the shadows of an elm tree. "I have to go back to Paris."

"I know." He had told her all about his work. He'd even given her his address so she could write to him after he'd gone. And although she would never deny him anything that gave him so much obvious pleasure, Cassie had been dreading his leaving the entire time that they'd been lovers. "When?"

"Tonight."

The moment had finally come. Feeling as if she'd been hit in the stomach, Cassie sucked in a deep breath. "So soon?"

"I don't really have any choice. But I promise to write as soon as I settle things in Paris."

"Settle what things?"

"I have to go back to France and try to get my job back." His dark scowl gave Cassie an unsettling idea of what Quinlan must have looked like as a young man.

"You lost your job? But why? What happened?"

"My father got me pulled off the project."

Cassie knew that Quinlan Gallagher's power was enormous in Gallagher City. He even had considerable clout throughout the state. But surely his influence couldn't extend all the way to France.

"You'd be surprised what my father can do when he puts his mind to it," Roarke responded when she voiced her doubts. "Everyone knows that the old man is infamous for his Machiavellian machinations. I've come to expect them. But this time the extent of his betrayal has gone beyond anything even I could have imagined.

"There are tribes," he said through gritted teeth, "where, when a man dies, his heart is eaten by his eldest son, so his memory will live on. My father's heart, such as it is, would make a very meager meal."

"But you're important to the project," Cassie protested, unnerved by the cold, implacable hatred in his voice. "You were chosen from hundreds of applicants. Surely Mr. Guimard wouldn't want to lose you."

"I'm not irreplaceable, Cassie. Hell, the brutal truth is that I'm more of an intern on this project—a kind of glorified draftsman. And even if Guimard had wanted to keep me on, Dad managed to assuage his disappointment by informing him that Gallagher Oil and Gas was looking for a world-class architect to design their new Saudi Arabian headquarters building."

"Your father admitted to buying him off?" Even Cassie, who'd grown up with Belle's self-indulgent behavior, could not imagine one family member betraying another so wickedly. She decided that this was a shining example of the Golden Rule—he who has the gold, rules.

"Of course he did. When I confronted him, the old man simply shrugged, lit one of those damn cigars the doctors have forbidden him to smoke, and told me that every man had his price." Roarke's expression was fierce. "Even me."

Cassie lifted her palm to his cheek and felt the muscle tense. "He was wrong," she whispered.

"He was wrong," Roarke agreed grimly. "I'm going to shake this damn red Oklahoma dust from my boots once and for all."

He kissed her then, his lips claiming hers with an intensity that took her breath away. His searing mouth molded hers to the shape he preferred, his hands skimmed over her body, inciting a tremble of desire. Feeling as if her heart were being ripped out of her, Cassie clung to him.

Roarke reached under her skirt, his hands tugging at her panties, his fingers probing her dampening flesh. Knees shaking, Cassie lifted the black skirt over her thighs, pulled the white cotton panties the rest of the way down, and stepped out of them.

Then, her eyes gleaming in the filtered moonlight, she unzipped his jeans and freed his tumescent penis. "Make love to me, Roarke. Now. So I'll have something to remember."

With a muffled groan, Roarke pulled her to him. His fingers dug into her waist as he pressed her against the trunk of the tree and surged into her. Their coupling was fast and hot, possessing none of the leisurely tenderness of the other times. But that did not make it any less shattering.

"God, I'm going to miss you," he said, when it was over.

Cassie's head was spinning too fast for her to pick up on the naked surprise in his voice. "I'll miss you, too," she managed weakly, determinedly blinking back tears that would betray the intensity of her feelings.

Roarke stepped back so they were no longer touching, but realized that he wasn't quite ready to break contact. "I'll call as soon as I know what's happening." He ran his thumb along her cheek in a warm, slow sweep. "We can talk dirty over the phone."

Cassie was grateful for the darkness that hid her blush, and she whispered, sadly, "Have a good flight."

"It damn well should be a great flight." He touched her hair. "Because I'm going to spend it dreaming of making love with you."

He kissed her one last time, a brief, fiery flare that left Cassie shaken. And then he was gone.

A week after Roarke's departure, a recovered Quinlan, Shelby, and Miss Lillian debarked on a vacation cruise to the Caribbean. Trace, who had taken a job at Gallagher Gas and Oil after dropping out of Oklahoma State University, was inspecting the company's oil platforms off the coast of Louisiana.

Although Helga and Grayson were away on their annual vacations, Cassie, at Miss Lillian's request, was at the house, cataloguing the extensive collection of first edition books.

Cassie reveled in having the house to herself. Although she knew it was wrong, she roamed the rooms as if she owned them, eating frozen pizza off Royal Dalton china, drinking Tab from Baccarat goblets, lying on Roarke's bed in the middle of the afternoon. Life would be perfect if it weren't for her uncharacteristically queasy stomach. Cassie wondered if she had finally caught the flu that had attacked the rest of the household staff while Roarke was still home.

One night, when Gallagher City was in the grip of another thunderstorm that kept her from returning home, Cassie took a luxurious bubble bath in Shelby's sunken pink marble tub. Afterward, clad only in panties and a bra, she was drawn to the room-size closet, unable to resist the lure of Shelby's new fox coat. She was standing in front of the mirror, admiring the way the lush red fur set off her hair, when Trace appeared in the doorway.

"Hot damn, you're lookin' good," he drawled. He was leaning nonchalantly against the doorjamb, his arms crossed. From the way he was swaying slightly, Cassie knew he'd been drinking.

"What are you doing here?" she asked as the thunder boomed outside. The room lit with a bright, unearthly glow of lightning.

"It's my house."

"But you weren't due back for two more days."

"I finished up early. Besides, if I'd come back when I was supposed to, I'd have missed seein' how purty you look in my sister's coat." The dangerous sheen in his blue eyes—eyes that resembled Roarke's, but without the warmth—sent out storm warnings. Anxious to leave, Cassie tried to slip by him.

Trace grabbed her arm. "Jus' one minute," he said, slurring his words. "I been thinking about us, Cassie. A lot."

His strong fingers were digging painfully into her arm. "There isn't any *us.*"

His fingers tightened. "Now, that's jus' what I was thinkin'. And you know what I decided?"

"What?"

"That it's about time you and me got to know each other better." He was breathing hard.

"In your dreams, cowboy."

"I've already been that route, sugar. But it isn't exactly the same, if you know what I mean." He ran his hand down her throat. "Didn't my big brother tell you that he and I were brought up to share?" He pulled the fur coat off and stared at her breasts.

"Don't touch me."

His breath surrounded her in a dank cloud of stale nicotine and bourbon. "Now, Cassie, you know you don't mean that."

"I do." Her arm swung up, but he caught it. She tried to twist away, but he yanked her arm behind her back with such force that she was afraid he was going to break it.

"Go ahead. Try to get away. I like it when a woman fights." His frightening grin sent ice skimming down her spine. "It adds spice to things." He held her with one hand, while the other grasped painfully at her breast.

"Let me go!" Panic made her rash. She jerked her arm free and struck out at him, her fingernails leaving a scarlet trail down his face.

Trace's stinging backhand caught Cassie's face with whipping force, almost knocking her off her feet. Before she could fall, he jerked her against him.

"We can do this the easy way," Trace warned, his liquored breath hot against her face. "Or the hard way. It's up to you." His face was so close to hers she thought she'd suffocate from the smell of the whiskey. He scooped her up, carried her across the room and threw her onto Shelby's bed.

Then, as if he'd done such things many times before, Trace roughly stripped Cassie of her cotton bra and panties and used them to tie her wrists to the brass headboard.

"Damned if you're not gonna have to be taught some manners, Cassie McBride."

He unbuttoned his shirt and tossed it onto the floor. As he looked down at her, his eyes reminded Cassie of a mad dog. His body, huge in the lamplight, cast an enormous shadow as he leaned over her.

The sinewy muscles were rigid in his arms and Cassie found that trying to fight against his superior strength was useless. But she was damned if she was going to do anything that might give him enjoyment.

Directing her gaze to a spot over his shoulder, Cassie lay like a stone statue. When his cruel fingers began to probe obscenely into her, she removed her mind and heart from her body.

"Damnit," he growled menacingly, "quit acting like some frigid fuckin' virgin."

She might be down. But Cassie wasn't out. Not yet. "Go to hell."

"If I do," he growled, "I'm taking you with me, bitch."

Sweat was dripping off his forehead and from under his armpits, landing in little droplets on her icy flesh, the smell darkly feral. She closed her eyes, willing herself to some other, saner place. The storm moaned at the window. Heavy raindrops like stones pounded on the roof.

His hand struck the side of her face with a crack, and Cassie's eyes flew open. "Wouldn't want you to miss anything," he said with a cruel smile.

Kicking off his boots, he stood to undo his silver trophy buckle and drop his rain-soaked Levis, then his white briefs, allowing his thick purplish penis to spring free. There was another rumble of thunder and—on top of it—a powerful flash of lightning. Instantly, every light in the house went out. Trace cursed.

Cassie had almost wiggled free when his hot, sweating body crashed down onto hers, threatening to crush all the air out of her lungs. Before she could catch her breath, he rammed into her. Lightning washed the room in a brief stuttering glow, like strobe lights, adding a surrealistic atmosphere to the terror. As he pounded into her again and again, blessed darkness swooped down on her like a bird of prey, spreading its black wings over her eyes.

And then it was over. Trace lay sprawled on top of her, his brutal penis limp and flaccid between her thighs.

"You're going to be sorry." Cassie said on a low, flat tone.

"Are you threatening me?" Trace asked, his bleary eyes staring at her in disbelief.

"It's not a threat. It's a promise." Her quiet voice was edged with contemptuous fury. "If you think just because you're a high and mighty Gallagher you can get away with rape, you're crazy. I'm going to call the sheriff."

Trace slapped her. Hard. Hard enough to bring tears to her eyes, but

Cassie refused to utter a sound. "You're a slut," he growled, "just like your mama." His fist whirled over her head and into the wall, missing her by the merest fraction of an inch. Cassie didn't flinch.

Trace cursed, then grabbed her hair and pulled her face to his. "You even think of calling the law and you'll be thrown out of here on your ass so quick you won't know what's happening," he warned. "There isn't a man in town who'll believe this was rape," he said. "Everyone knows that McBride broads are easy. I'll just say that after a summer of screwing my big brother, you decided to go looking for a real man." He laughed as he untied her wrists. Then he picked up his clothes and strode from the room. Cassie lay on the bed, frozen to the spot, listening to the sound of his boots on the stairs. Once she was sure he was gone, she curled into a ball and began to shake.

The storm passed. The shadows of night had given way to the shimmering gray light of dawn when Cassie finally returned home to the trailer. Relieved to find Belle gone, she went into the bathroom and threw up in the toilet.

As she stood under the pelting hot water of the shower, Cassie felt like a horse that had been rode hard and put away wet. She felt, she thought wearily, like Belle.

She rubbed her flesh until it was raw, first with the threadbare washcloth and then, when she still didn't feel clean, with her toothbrush. But no amount of scrubbing could wash away the horror of what had happened to her.

# $Six$

Two days after the rape, and one day after the Gallagher family had returned from their cruise, Cassie was at the pharmacy, picking up a prescription for her mother, when the county sheriff, Walter Lockley, stepped in front of her.

A former Gallagher City High School linebacker, Sheriff Lockley was a man whose considerable bulk had turned to flab, but that didn't stop him from liking a good fight. Tales of his brutality—all in the name of law and order—were legion.

Normally, a jurisdiction the size of Gallagher County would need only a single constable. But since oil workers were known to get rowdy on payday, Gallagher Gas and Oil paid for the three-officer force. Such outlay of funds allowed Quinlan Gallagher absolute control over the county that bore his name, and everyone knew Lockley was a man bought and paid for by Quinlan Gallagher.

Cassie didn't understand the sheriff. He told her that several ivory and jade figurines were missing from a glass case in the Gallagher library. It was terrible, but what did it have to do with her?

"Simple," Lockley said. "The lock wasn't broken, missy. And since Miss Lillian and you are the only people with access to the case, this here is an open-and-shut case of grand larceny."

The shock went through Cassie like a seismic jolt. He couldn't mean it. This had to be some some sort of cruel joke. When Lockley whipped out a pair of steel handcuffs, locking them so they cut into her wrists, she realized that it was all too real.

Cassie was terrified. All the movies she'd ever seen about women in prison flashed through her mind. After having her photograph taken, she was fingerprinted, then forced to undress while a woman deputy searched her for contraband. When the rubber-glove-clad finger probed deeply into her vagina, Cassie felt a degrading urge to urinate. She cried out when that same finger thrust into her anus with more force than was necessary.

"Shut up," the woman demanded. She shoved a bar of soap that smelled like disinfectant into Cassie's hand. "Go in the shower and scrub yourself down. And don't forget your hair. If I find any lice, I'll have to shave it off." Her cruel smile suggested that she'd love doing exactly that. Terrified, Cassie washed as ordered, silent tears mixing with the water that streamed down her face.

The painful ordeal finally over, she was given a drab gray dress with the words "Gallagher County Jail" stenciled across the back. When the heavy, barred cell door clanged shut, Cassie knew that it was a sound she'd never forget.

The sweltering claustrophobic cell made the shabby trailer Cassie shared with Belle seem like a palace in comparison. A single forty-watt bulb jutted from a porcelain socket in the yellowed, smoke-stained ceiling. The rusty sink was water-stained and the toilet looked as though it hadn't been cleaned in months. Perhaps years. The unpainted block walls were covered with the ragged graffitti of scrawled initials, phone numbers, declarations of love, and the predictable obscenities.

A dinner of pork and beans was delivered by the grim-faced matron at six o'clock. Cassie left it untouched. Three hours later, the dim light went out and Cassie was left alone in an unfamiliar darkness that smelled of sweat and urine. She lay on the stained single mattress, her arms stiff at her sides, and wondered if this nightmare would ever end.

To Cassie's dismay, Miss Lillian refused to see her. Her only response was a note claiming to be shocked, appalled, and gravely hurt that Cassie could have betrayed the family after all they'd done for her.

Desperate, Cassie wrote to Roarke at the address he'd given her in Paris, certain that he'd return to Gallagher City and convince his father that she was incapable of such a crime. But although she sent three separate letters, she received no answer.

In a rare show of motherly concern, Belle visited Cassie in jail, bringing with her Mike Bridger, a lawyer who'd agreed to take on Cassie's case. The attorney was wearing an expensive, fawn-colored western-cut suit and a bark brown Stetson. Lizard boots with silver-embossed toes gleamed from beneath the cuff of his trousers.

"I don't have any money for a lawyer," Cassie told him.

"Don't you worry about a thing, Cassie. I'm taking your case *pro bono*. That's no charge," he explained. A man in his midthirties, Mike Bridger was good-looking in a blond, all-American way, with a light, cinnamonlike dusting of freckles across his pug nose that made him look almost too young to have passed the bar. It was, Cassie decided, the face of a man she could trust.

"Why would you want to go up against Quinlan Gallagher?" she asked.

"You ever read about a fella named Don Quixote?"

Cassie nodded, grateful for the Gallagher's extensive library. "Yes."

"Well, let's just say that every once in a while I enjoy tilting at windmills. Besides, I believe you're innocent."

"Really?" How she'd needed to hear someone—anyone—say those words!

"Really." Mike smiled at her across the small table, his brown eyes warmly reassuring.

Cassie had never been one to hand over control of her life to anyone, but Mike Bridger was a pillar of strength during the next five days. She didn't know what she would have done without him. So when he arrived one morning to discuss final strategies, she was appalled to hear him recommend that she plead guilty.

"What? But I thought you said you believed me."

"I do." Mike reached out and took Cassie's hand in his. "Quinlan Gallagher is after blood on this one, Cassie. He's telling everyone in town who'll listen that you're just like a sly, chicken-stealing dog. That after he took you into his home out of the goodness of his heart, you betrayed his trust."

"But I didn't!"

"I know that. And you know that." His thumb soothingly stroked the inside of her palm. "But I'm afraid that the chances of finding twelve jurors who'd stand up in public against Quinlan Gallagher in his own county are slim to none."

"But I'm innocent," she protested in a soft voice that was little more than a whisper.

"Sometimes that's not enough. Look, I know the judge who'll be hearing your case. He's an honest man, known for his leniency. Since you're young and pretty, and this is your first offense, if you plead guilty, you'll get off with probation."

"And if I don't plead guilty?"

His expression was grave. "If you insist on going to trial, Cassie, you can count on ending up in the state prison."

Cassie dragged her hands through her unwashed hair, shaken by what he was suggesting. Her gut told her that he was wrong, that she should fight for her freedom, that she shouldn't let Quinlan Gallagher bulldoze her. But her head kept reminding her that she was a novice when it came to the law. If her own attorney was advising her to plead guilty, then perhaps that's what she should do.

"I have to think about this." Her thoughts were in such a muddle; she just couldn't make a decision.

Mike nodded. "Fine. I think that's a good idea." He gathered up his papers without a word of argument and returned them to his black alligator briefcase. "Your arraignment isn't until tomorrow morning; I'll come by early and you can give me your decision then."

He paused in the doorway and looked deep into her pale face, as if testing the emotional weather brewing there. "It's going to be all right, Cassie," he assured her quietly. "All you have to do is trust me. Do you think you can do that?"

"Of course I trust you," she said, meaning it.

He flashed her one of his million-watt grins. "Then we'll do just fine, sugar. You can count on it."

Despite Mike's encouraging words, Cassie hated the idea of pleading guilty to something she hadn't done. Her pride was a fierce thing; it was all she had left. For most of the night, her mind whirled in a fever of indecision. Then finally, just before dawn, she fell into a light, troubled sleep.

Belle did not understand Cassie's dilemma. "You need to do what your lawyer says," she insisted before the hearing. "He knows what's best."

"But I didn't steal those figurines. Doesn't that count for anything?" she asked, confused and exhausted.

"All that counts around here is Quinlan Gallagher," Belle countered. "That man's above the law. Don't tell me you've forgotten the way he managed to cover up his part in that oil rig fire six years ago? A lot of innocent people died in that fire, girl. But Quinlan Gallagher got away scot-free."

"What does that have to do with me?"

Belle shot her daughter a look of pure disgust. "Gallagher doesn't just own all the land hereabouts, Cassie, he owns the people, too. If you're smart, you'll take your lawyer's advice, then get as far away from this hell-hole town as you can go."

She pulled a rumpled red-and-white cigarette pack from her purse. "At least this proves I was right about the Gallaghers not accepting you," she said acidly as she lit a cigarette. "Kin's kin. And the only kin you've got in this world is me. You might want to remember that the next time you get an urge to act so high and mighty, girl."

Although Cassie couldn't quite dispel her doubts, she decided that for once in her life, Belle had a point. Quinlan Gallagher's power was enormous; who was she to think she could go against such a man? Five minutes after telling Mike her decision to plead guilty, she was standing in front of the judge. The very same judge who, Mike had assured her, would be sympathetic to her plight. So why couldn't she read any sympathy in his stern gaze?

She stood in front of the high judicial bench, her eyes directed straight ahead, her ice-cold hands clasped in front of her. As the judge listened impassively to her lawyer, Cassie felt a rising anxiety just behind her sternum. Her complexion was unnaturally gray and her lips were pressed together so tightly they were white. Perspiration slid down her sides.

Finally, it was the judge's turn to speak. At first his voice sounded as if it were coming from a long distance away, but when his words finally sank in, Cassie reeled, feeling the shock as keenly as she would a slap from a cold hand.

Five years on the county farm? Horrified, she turned toward Mike, her wide, frightened eyes begging for an explanation.

But her attorney, a man she had trusted, a man whose advice she had taken against every instinct she had possessed, ultimately showed his true colors. His handsome face went politely blank, as if he were emotionally removing himself. Then, without a word, he turned and left Cassie standing alone. And abandoned.

Dinner was beans and rice. Again. Just as it had been for the three weeks Cassie had been incarcerated in the Gallagher County Jail, awaiting transfer to the County Work Farm. Cassie stared at the unappetizing meal for a long time. Then her stomach clenched and she vomited.

When the painful stomach spasms and nausea continued for days, Sheriff Lockley finally relented and called in a doctor. Cassie was lying on her dingy bunk, her arm over her eyes to shut out the sunlight filtering in through the high window, when she heard the unmistakable sound of a key turning in the metal lock.

When she saw who was standing just inside her cell, black bag clutched in his hand, Cassie groaned. Everyone knew that Dr. Ralph Watkins was a drunk. His license had been withdrawn from Oklahoma hospitals after losing three malpractice suits in a year.

Having spent so many years with Belle, Cassie immediately recognized the signs of a man coming off a bender. There were food stains on his tie and the armpits of his wrinkled white short-sleeved shirt were yellow and crusted with perspiration. His red-rimmed eyes were watery, his complexion was the color of library paste, and his hands, as he held the stethoscope against her bare chest, shook. The stench of whiskey surrounded him like a rancid cloud.

"Don't you worry none, gal." He painstakingly filled a syringe from a small glass vial. "This here megadose of antibiotic will fix you up just fine."

The shot burned, but Cassie decided that it was a small price to pay for ridding herself of such a debilitating nausea. The only problem was that it didn't work. When Cassie was still ill ten days later, Dr. Watkins returned. This time his eyes were clearer and his hands steadier.

"Hell, little lady," he drawled after examining her. "The only thing wrong with you is that you're gonna be a mama."

Cassie was stunned by the doctor's diagnosis. Roarke had always been so insistent on protection. Except that first time in the storm cellar.

"It only takes once," Dr. Watkins said knowingly when Cassie tried to convince him that he must be wrong. But the timing was right because he said that she was more than two months along.

"Didn't you get a little suspicious when you missed your monthlies?" he asked her.

Cassie's head was spinning. She felt as if she was going to be sick again. "I've never been very regular," she said. "I've missed a lot of periods, but that didn't mean I was pregnant."

"Well, you're sure as shootin' pregnant now," Dr. Watkins said as he packed up his little black bag.

If Cassie was surprised, the news of her condition hit the Gallagher home like a bomb. The subsequent fallout was immediate. After a consultation in the judge's chambers with Mike Bridger, Cassie learned that she was to be released from jail with the caveat that she leave the state.

"But Roarke's and my baby will be Quinlan Gallagher's first grand-child," Cassie protested.

Mike Bridger reached into his briefcase and pulled out a sheaf of papers. "Mr. Gallagher has obtained these affidavits from eight separate men, all who claim to have had sex with you during the time in question."

"That's a lie!" Cassie's cheeks flamed red as she scanned the papers, her heart lurching as she read the names of boys with whom she'd refused to go to those drinking parties in the past. "This is all a damn lie! Trace stole those figurines," she said, as comprehension finally dawned. "He did it to make sure nobody would believe me if I tried to charge him with rape!" How could she have been so stupid not to think that he wouldn't have done something—anything—to protect himself.

Bridger snatched the papers from her trembling fingers and locked them away. "Those are sworn statements."

Cassie noticed that he didn't look surprised at her accusation against Trace and realized that she was fighting a losing battle. "They're still lies."

"Look, Cassie," he said, "there isn't anything left for you here. So why don't you just take advantage of Gallagher's generosity and begin a new life somewhere else?"

"I don't believe that even Quinlan Gallagher has the power to run his enemies out of the entire state of Oklahoma."

His eyes turned hard. "As your attorney, I wouldn't advise putting him to the test."

After the way he'd turned on her, convincing her to plead guilty to a crime she had not committed, Cassie knew that Mike was not really her attorney at all, but Quinlan Gallagher's. But she also realized that she'd be a fool not to heed his warning.

Besides, she assured herself after she was finally freed, once Roarke learned about their baby, he'd return from Paris and set things straight. He'd never believe the horrid lies that Quinlan was telling about her.

Belle was not so optimistic. "There's only one thing to do. Get an abortion. Lucky for you they're legal now."

"I'd never get rid of Roarke's baby!"

"Life's hard enough without having a kid to drag you down. You're not the first woman to let a man fuck up your dreams, Cassie. No point in making a bad situation worse."

Cassie had heard it all before.

Belle had been eighteen years old and was working at a honky-tonk outside Stillwater when she met a tool pusher with eyes greener than any eyes had the right to be and a blazing red beard. From the way Cassie had always heard it, when the sensual lips nestled amidst all that red hair smiled up at her, Belle had fallen in love.

She didn't make it back to work for three days. Three passionate days and nights spent in an incendiary world of burning flesh and hot tangled sheets. Six weeks later, the doctor confirmed what Belle had already suspected. She was pregnant. There was, of course, the option of an illegal abortion. But Belle had known a cocktail waitress who'd nearly bled to death after a driller-turned-back-alley-abortionist had carved up her insides. Terrified of suffering the same fate, Belle was stuck.

"Babies are a helluva long way from the sweet-smelling, docile, powdered cherubs they're made out to be in all those sappy TV commercials," she warned now. "And believe me, girl, they work like man repellent.

"Bein' without a man is damn hard on a woman, Cassie. Just you wait and see. You don't have any idea what it's like, havin' to take care of a youngun all by yourself. Always worryin' about where the next meal is coming from. Never havin' any money to buy a pretty new dress, feeling old and haggard before your time."

"Roarke will marry me. We'll raise our baby together."

"And I suppose he's gonna carry you and your bastard off on his white horse?" Belle lit a cigarette and blew out a frustrated breath of smoke. "When are you gonna get it through your stubborn head that Roarke Gallagher ain't no knight in shining armor come to rescue the pregnant maiden in distress? The boy ain't comin' back, Cassie. Leastwise not for you."

"But he said—"

"It don't matter what a man says when he's in bed, Cassie. Like the Conway Twitty song, that's only make-believe."

Emotion flooded through Cassie as she suddenly, for the first time in her life, understood her mother's lifelong pain. Flinging her arms around Belle, Cassie began to cry. "When I'm rich and famous, I'll come back for you, Mama."

"Sure you will, baby," Belle agreed, her flat tone saying otherwise.

If Quinlan Gallagher expected Cassie to slink away like a wet cat, he was wrong. Yet another one of his famous weekend barbecues was in progress when Cassie arrived at the ranch. She stormed out to the terrace, where she found him surrounded by a group of laughing cigar-smoking men. They seemed totally isolated from the grinding poverty that existed only a few miles away. What right did these people have to live like this? Cassie wondered bitterly. What made them so special? *Money.*

"You and I need to talk," Cassie said into the sudden silence that greeted her arrival.

Quinlan waved his hand, as if brushing away a pesky fly. "We have nothing to discuss."

"The hell we don't!" Cassie spat out. "What about you putting me in jail?"

"You put yourself there when you stole Miss Lillian's figurines," he said coldly. "And after all she did for you." He shook his head. "I should have realized that your kind doesn't understand gratitude. My daddy always told me that you can't make a champion hunting dog out of a mangy mongrel."

A ripple of nervous laughter went through the crowd. Cassie stared defiantly back at Quinlan, her sweeping gaze taking in his powerful guests. Hate coalesced into a hard ball in her chest. "You know I didn't steal anything. But that's not what I'm here about."

"Oh?" His plunging brows and frightening scowl reminded Cassie of a mean jack-o'-lantern.

"I came to tell you that you can pay all the men in Oklahoma to lie about going to bed with me and it isn't going to change a thing." She pressed her hands against her stomach, as if shielding her child from Quinlan's glare. "This will still be Roarke's baby."

"You're a lying whore!" he roared. He turned toward the two off-duty deputies who were standing at the edge of the terrace, their hands resting lightly on their holsters. "Get this piece of trash out of here."

They grabbed Cassie by the arms, prepared to drag her from the terrace, when Quinlan held up a hand. "Wait." His fingers tightened painfully on her chin as he held her defiant glare to his own blistering one. "I'm warning you, girl," he said in a low tone that conveyed more of a threat than the loudest shout. "If you have any idea about coming back here with your bastard brat and trying to get money from me, you'd better forget it right now. If you know what's good for you."

Cassie's green eyes were fierce above her flushed cheeks. To think she'd wanted her baby to be a part of this family. No price would be too high to protect her child from these people.

"The last thing I want to do is to inflict another Gallagher on the world," she shot back. "I'm going to get rid of this baby," she cried. "So it won't grow up as sick and twisted as you!"

She was still shouting heated threats over her shoulder as the deputies dragged her through the house and down the front portico to their waiting police car. Throwing her into the back seat, they drove her to the Gallagher City bus depot.

There was one thing this debacle with Quinlan Gallagher had proven once and for all, Cassie decided as the Greyhound bus pulled out of the station headed for New York City. It was that money was power. Money ruled the world. She was going to become so rich and powerful that no one would ever be able to hurt her—or her baby—again.

# Seven

Manhattan was shimmering in a haze of Indian summer heat as Cassie diligently made the rounds of the auction houses, galleries, and museums looking for work. She had been in New York for three weeks, and she soon learned that the same individuals who had praised her for her knowledge when she was with Miss Lillian now looked through her as if she were invisible.

Whenever she had visited Manhattan with Miss Lillian, their transportation was usually a limousine or the occasional taxi. Now she was faced with the maze of turnstiles, staircases, platforms, and trains of the New York subway system. Cassie hated the subway; it made her feel as if she were going down into a concrete tomb.

On this particular morning, people were jammed into the cars, and at first she thought that the man behind her was pressing against her only because of the close space. But when he began rotating his pelvis against her bottom, a shock of disgust curled through her. She tried to move away, but he pressed even closer, his erection stabbing through her thin cotton skirt. Her stomach roiled. Glaring at the blank-faced man over her shoulder, she left the train two stops before her intended one.

Bentley's was on Park Avenue, down the street from its longtime competitor, Christie's. It was situated between the blue-green glass and steel Lever House, which, she remembered Roarke saying, had been considered avant-garde when it was first built in the fifties, and the

Mercedes-Benz showroom, a building designed by Frank Lloyd Wright. The auction house's imposing granite facade and royal blue awnings had been designed to blend in with a neighborhood of buildings that were over one hundred years old.

Cassie had been there several times with Miss Lillian, and the effusive Reginald Bentley—managing partner of the auction house—had always praised her knowledge of antiques. So Bentley's was the first place Cassie had tackled when she arrived, but with no success. Now, unable to find work anywhere else, she'd returned for another try.

Taking a deep breath, Cassie gave the doorman a smile brimming with a confidence she was a long way from feeling, walked past the embossed copper door he'd opened for her, and entered the reception area.

"It'd like to see Mr. Bentley," she told the impossibly slim blond woman sitting behind what Cassie recognized to be a leather-topped mahogany George III partner's desk. Last year she'd attended an auction here with Miss Lillian and seen a similar desk go for thirteen thousand dollars.

The receptionist put down the novel she'd been reading with a sigh. "Whom may I say is calling?" she asked, her smooth round tones devoid of welcome or enthusiasm.

"Cassie McBride. I'm a friend of Miss Lillian Gallagher's." It might be stretching the truth, but she was getting desperate.

The woman lifted a disbelieving blond brow at that, but gestured toward a tapestried mid-Georgian library armchair that was sitting against the red lacquered wall. "Take a seat. I'll see if Mr. Bentley is in."

Three minutes later, the receptionist returned. "I'm sorry, but Mr. Bentley has a very busy schedule. If you'd like to make an appointment," she opened the leather-bound book and ran a pink tinted nail down the page, "he'll be able to see you on Thursday, October twenty-fifth, at two o'clock."

By then she'd be sleeping on the streets. "I can't wait that long. Did you mention Miss Lillian Gallagher? She's a very good customer."

"I informed Mr. Bentley that you were a friend of Miss Gallagher's," the woman answered, not bothering to conceal her obvious disbelief, "but he really can't be disturbed. By anyone."

"But it's an emergency," Cassie insisted.

"I'm sorry," the woman repeated, not bothering to try to sound as if she meant it. "October twenty-fifth is the very best I can do."

"I'll wait for him," Cassie decided.

"It's up to you," she receptionist said with an uncaring shrug of her silk-clad shoulders. "But I wouldn't hold my breath," she advised before returning to her novel.

The hours crawled by, Cassie's stomach becoming more rebellious with each passing moment. She sat in the chair, purse clutched in her lap, watching the stream of clients come and go.

The morning passed and Cassie was still waiting when three women, carbon copies of the woman behind the desk, came from the back rooms into the reception hall. They were all tall and slim and, Cassie could tell, rich. Their blond hair had been swept up, society girl–style, a look recently popularized by the Ford sisters.

Two of them were clad in the same type of chic, understated suit the receptionist was wearing. The third was wearing a flowered silk dress that reminded Cassie of the blooms in Miss Lillian's rose garden. Their presence filled the room with a heady blend of Chanel No. 5, Je Reviens, and Dioressence.

They were arguing with good-natured laughter about where to eat lunch—La Caravelle, the pool room at the Four Seasons, or the Palm Court at the Plaza. Eventually, the lobster salad at the Plaza won out. They left in a cloud of expensive fragrance, not bothering to even toss a glance Cassie's way.

It didn't surprise her. Watching these women, who reeked of money and breeding, Cassie realized how ordinary she appeared. Her plain white blouse and beige skirt were more suitable to waiting tables than selling dazzling treasures to the world's wealthiest people.

She'd come to New York with such high hopes, clutching her dream tightly to her breast. Despite the odds, she'd never allowed herself even to consider that she might fail. After all, she'd come such a long way since that day she put on her mama's uniform and went to work for the Gallaghers.

But now, faced with the reality of her competition, Cassie realized how very far she still had to go. It didn't matter how smart she was, how hard she had worked and was still willing to work, or how much she'd taught herself about the world of art and antiques: The lines separating her from these privileged, well-born women were as clear and indelible as the Santa Fe railroad tracks that had separated the mobile home she and Belle had lived in from the Gallagher's mansion. And it was painfully obvious that in the antiques business, pedigree counted.

Nearly two hours later, the women returned, in even better spirits than when they'd left. Continuing to ignore Cassie, they returned to work.

Cassie was still sitting in the same chair late that afternoon when Reginald Bentley walked a customer to the front door.

Before he could return to his inner sanctum, she jumped up and said, "Mr. Bentley, may I talk to you?"

"You again." He looked at Cassie's best Ship 'N Shore blouse and cotton skirt with overt disapproval. "I've already told you, young woman, you are dismally unqualified."

"You didn't think that when I helped talk Miss Lillian into that Louis XVI console you were trying to push," Cassie retorted.

Reginald Bentley was properly British from the top of his homburg to the gleaming toes of his hand-lasted shoes. Cassie had never seen him in anything but pinstriped gray trousers and a neatly pressed morning coat.

She'd also never experienced his remote, coolly British disdain. Normally, he fell all over himself to bring Miss Lillian a Wedgwood plate of cucumber sandwiches and cup of perfectly brewed English Breakfast tea. Today, however, he was making Cassie feel about as welcome as a swarm of mosquitoes at a Fourth of July barbecue. Once again, she was being given a humbling lesson on the power of money.

"Miss Lillian has always had excellent taste," he sniffed, waving a dismissive hand. "Now, if you don't mind, I have a great deal of work to do—"

"Wait!" Cassie grabbed his arm. "I'll do anything, uncrate merchandise, clean, polish, run errands." Her pale face was set and strained. "How can you know I haven't any talent when you won't give me a chance?"

He glanced down at his sleeve, glaring at her hand as if it were some type of vile insect. "Young woman," he said with restrained irritation, "if you do not leave these premises immediately, I will be forced to telephone the authorities."

"You wouldn't do that. Not just because I asked you for a job."

He folded his arms across the front of his morning coat and scowled down his long, pointed nose at her. "I wouldn't advise you to put the matter to the test."

The remaining color drained from her face. Swallowing the bile that rose in her throat, she dropped her hand to her side and managed to walk, with an amazing amount of dignity for someone whose life was falling down around her, across the oriental carpet and out the door.

Shaken, and with no specific destination in mind, Cassie began to walk. She'd gone only a few blocks when a late-afternoon cloudburst stormed across town, the downpour giving a licoricelike sheen to the wet pavement. Seeking respite from the pelting rain, Cassie ducked into the Museum of Modern Art.

She was drenched to the skin. Exhaustion, nerves, fear, and an empty stomach caused her morning sickness to return with a vengeance. Rushing into the restroom, she knelt on the tile floor, retching until her throat burned.

She gripped the porcelain bowl as if it could keep her from sliding off the edge of the earth. Her hard-earned nest egg, saved during five years of working for the Gallaghers was nearly gone; Roarke hadn't answered the letter that she'd mailed the day after arriving in New York, telling him what had happened and where she was; she was sick, pregnant, unemployed, and frightened. Even Cinderella had a fairy godmother to pull her out of the ashes.

"So where the hell is mine?" Cassie groaned.

As if conjured up by her tumultuous imagination, someone knocked on the steel door. "Are you all right?" a female voice called in to her.

"I'm fine," Cassie lied. Her stomach clenched in another spasm. She retched two more times, but there was no vomiting. Only the deep dry heaves of exhaustion.

The woman remained unconvinced. "You need help."

Cassie didn't answer. Instead, she leaned back against the door and shut her eyes against the weakening waves of vertigo.

"If you don't come out, so I can see for myself that you're really all right, I'm going to get help," the woman warned.

Realizing that this well-meaning busybody was not going to go away, Cassie swore softly under her breath. Struggling to her feet, it took her trembling hands two tries to unlatch the door. Finally, she managed to struggle out of the stall.

The woman's unblinking eyes—a vivid, blue—observed Cassie from behind the oversize lenses of her black-framed glasses. "You're not at all well," she corrected, taking in Cassie's pallor. "Is there someone I can call to take you home?"

"There isn't anyone." Making her way on rubbery legs to the row of sinks, Cassie ran some water into her palm, swirled it around in her mouth, and, conscious of the woman's unwavering gaze, spit it back into the sink.

"Surely you have family."

"No." Cassie splashed some cold water on her face, feeling somewhat revived. Shaking off her self-pity, she reminded herself that no one had forced her to have this baby. Whining about it certainly wouldn't get her anywhere. "There's no one."

"Well, *now* there is." The woman handed her a paper towel.

"Really, I don't need any help."

"Don't be silly. Everyone needs a little help from time to time. But I suppose I can understand why you'd be reluctant to go off with a stranger in this city." She held out her hand. "My name is Nina. Nina Grace."

Cassie recognized the name immediately. Nina Grace had been a famous international model in the sixties. With long blond hair, pale lips, and legs that went on forever, Amazing Grace, as she was called, had been touted as the American answer to Jean Shrimpton.

She'd retired to marry a Greek shipping magnate, Cassie remembered, and when she was widowed a brief eighteen months later, the former model returned to the United States with all that shipping money and opened her own modeling agency.

Even now, although the woman had to be in her midforties, she was still stunning. Her blond hair had been swept into a chignon at the nape of her neck, revealing the unmistakable cheekbones of a former cover girl. Elegantly clad, despite temperatures in the eighties and a humidity just as high, she wore a slender black Halston dress. Her long shapely legs were clad in black hose, and on her feet were a pair of black Charles Jourdan pumps.

Feeling unbearably disheveled, Cassie wiped her damp palms on her skirt before shaking the woman's outstretched hand. "I'm Cassie McBride."

Nina Grace nodded approvingly. "There. Now we're no longer strangers, so you can come with me." Ignoring Cassie's protest, she propelled her out the restroom door and through the lobby.

Even as Cassie continued to insist that she could take care of herself, fear and hunger and dread roiled in her stomach like acid. White splotches danced in front of her eyes. Folding onto the floor, she surrendered to the darkness.

"This really isn't necessary," Cassie insisted as the Yellow cab inched its way through the snarl of midday traffic. "I'm fine."

"Of course you are. That's why you fainted."

"I was only out a second. You said so yourself."

"A second or an hour, a fainting spell is dangerous." Nina's eyes drifted to Cassie's still flat stomach. "Especially in your condition."

"I didn't realize I showed." Cassie had been hoping to find a job first, then cautiously spring the news of her pregnancy once she'd proven herself.

"You don't. Actually, it was an educated guess."

"I don't want to talk about it."

"Fine," Nina said agreeably. Leaning back against the cracked vinyl upholstery, she crossed her long legs.

Cassie was grateful when Nina seemed disinclined toward conversation. Although she no longer felt like throwing up, little white dots continued to dance in front of her eyes.

"Why don't you lean your head back," Nina suggested mildly, as if reading her mind. "And close your eyes. It should help."

Cassie did as instructed. By the time the taxi pulled up in front of her building, the dizziness had passed.

Nina Grace didn't bother to conceal her distaste for Cassie's cramped, dark room. The only furniture was a single bed and a scarred bureau that was missing handles on two of its three drawers.

"These walls look as if they haven't been painted since the McKinley administration," Nina said. She glared at the grimy window that looked out at a neighboring brick wall. A three-inch-long roach skittered from beneath the narrow bed, disappearing behind the bureau.

"And the view definitely leaves something to be desired." Leaving the room, she headed down the hall, her high heels making staccato tappings on the chipped linoleum floor. "Well, one thing's for certain," she said after a brief, disgusted glance at the communal bathroom, "you certainly can't stay here."

"It's not that bad," Cassie countered defensively, refusing to admit that she'd been appalled when she'd first viewed the room in the ramshackle SRO. "Besides, it's cheap."

"It's also filthy. And dangerous. Or are you going to tell me that those refugees from the sixties don't scare the hell out of you?"

Actually, Cassie lived in constant terror of the long-haired, unkempt bearded men who seemed to have taken up residence in the dark and narrow hallway. But so far, they'd been either too stoned or too drunk to make a move.

"I can take care of myself."

"But you have your baby to consider. And this is no place for a child."

Before Cassie could respond that she certainly wasn't going to be living here that long, Nina surprised her again. "You're coming home with me."

Cassie's arguments proved as ineffectual as they'd been at the museum, and before she knew what was happening, she found herself back in the taxi, on the way to Nina's home. During the ride she explained all about Miss Lillian and her trips to New York and her hopes that she'd be able to get a job in the art world. She said nothing about Roarke and was relieved when Nina didn't ask about her baby's father.

Cassie had thought that during her years at the Gallagher mansion, she'd grown accustomed to wealth. But Nina Grace's vast penthouse apartment on Fifth Avenue, with its grandly proportioned rooms, eighteen-foot ceilings, graceful staircase, and Fourcade fabric walls adorned with gilt-framed portraits of somebody's ancestors, resplendent in their dark suits and gold watch chains, left her speechless. It was all too much.

"I can't stay here."

"Of course you can. I run Grace Model Management," she told Cassie. "My girls all stay here when they first come to town." Before Cassie could point out that she wasn't one of her girls, Nina said, "Why don't you rest while I make some tea to settle your stomach. It's cook's day off, but I'm sure I can find some biscuits. Then we'll talk about your future."

"Really—"

"Sit down. And stop worrying. We'll find you a wonderful job."

With that tempting promise she was gone, leaving Cassie to sink down onto a red velvet Victorian chaise longue and consider her options. As her gaze took in the art nouveau marble and bronze bowl, the Napoleon III neoclassical bust, the Gothic revival candlesticks, and the nineteenth-century Chinese bronze horse, Cassie realized that compared to Nina Grace, Miss Lillian was an amateur collector. It was obvious that her hostess spent a great deal of time and even more money at the auction houses. Perhaps Nina really could help her get a job.

Looking out over the restful greenery of Central Park, Cassie began to relax for the first time in months.

Later, over cups of Imperial Darjeeling tea, Nina's intense blue eyes were riveted on Cassie's face, studying its features in detail. "You really are beautiful," she said finally.

"Thank you," Cassie murmured, wondering if she was ever going to outgrow her hated response of blushing.

"Don't thank me. Thank your parents. And all those other relatives who contributed to your gene pool. I should sign you before someone from the competition snatches you up."

"Sign me? As a model?" Cassie McBride, a model? Girls who grew up on the wrong side of the tracks in Gallagher City, Oklahoma, didn't become high-fashion models. The idea was ridiculous.

"Of course." Nina spread a generous layer of raspberry preserves atop a freshly baked scone. "You are incredible-looking. But, although I never thought I'd hear myself saying it, you are also much too thin." She added a dollop of Devonshire cream and handed the plate to Cassie.

Cassie had never tasted anything as wonderful as the rich, currant-studded little biscuit covered with preserves and thick cream. "I don't look anything like a model," she protested, when she'd finished chewing. "Models are blond, blue-eyed American girls-next-door like Shelley Hack and Christie Brinkley."

"That's just the point." Nina plucked a stack of fashion magazines from a Duncan Phyfe table. "California beaches are overrun with that kind of girl, they're a dime a dozen. Look at this," she said, tossing a back issue of French *Vogue* onto Cassie's lap. "Not an beach bunny in the bunch. That stunning brunette cover girl, by the way, is one of my models."

Cassie thumbed through the magazine, noting that Nina was right about the lack of American-looking models gracing the slick pages. But that didn't mean she could make it.

"I've built a reputation for my agency by going against the norm," Nina said, as if sensing Cassie's silent argument. "After you have your baby, we'll have some photos taken. Stick with me kid, and I'll make you a star." She laughed.

The idea, as intriguing as it was, was too preposterous. Besides, Cassie had a dream. One she wasn't about to let go of, even if every gallery owner and auction house in town were currently refusing to hire her.

"I still need to find a job," Cassie said quietly, but firmly.

"I'm sure I can find something for you in the art world. In the meantime, how would you like to come to work for me?"

"For you?"

"Six weeks ago I had the world's most efficient receptionist. Then she decided to stay home and play house with her new baby. I've been through five employment agencies in the past month alone. Please say you'll save me."

Even as she accepted Nina's offer, Cassie knew that it was Nina Grace who was saving her. And her baby.

The offices of Grace Model Management were located in the striking office building at 9 West 57th Street next to Bergdorf's. As she entered the elegant fifty-story building with its sloping, tinted-glass-curtain exterior walls and travertine marble edges, Cassie decided that Roarke would probably approve its unique design.

Brilliant abstracts in primary colors adorned the stark white walls of Nina Grace's reception area. Interspersed with them were glossy covers of *Mademoiselle, Vogue, Harper's Bazaar, Glamour,* and *Cosmopolitan.* A gleaming black lacquer desk sat upon thick, muted pewter carpeting.

Gaunt-faced fashion plates—an astonishing beautiful brunette clad in a red leather mini, an androgynous redhead wearing a pair of skintight, stone-washed jeans tucked into high cuffed boots and a white cotton shirt studded with turquoise cabochons, and a stunning black woman whose hair had been wound into beaded braids that fell to her shoulders—had claimed three of the lipstick-red chairs. One look at the women and Cassie decided that Nina's comment about her someday becoming a model had merely been meant to make her feel better after a horrendous day.

Cassie remained a reluctant guest in Nina's home for eight weeks. Whenever she'd protest that she was taking advantage of her new friend's hospitality, Nina's answer was always the same.

"With five bedrooms and six bathrooms, we've more than enough room. Besides, you're not the only one staying here."

That was certainly true. The parade of models came and went with such frequency that Cassie had given up keeping track of them. At the moment, Nina was providing shelter for a stunning black South African woman, a tall Norwegian blonde who, since she was only thirteen, required a tutor to finish high school, and a French redhead who complained incessantly that American men knew nothing of chivalry.

"But I'm not earning you the money the others are," Cassie protested. She'd been amazed to learn that the redhead had made more than one hundred thousand dollars last year alone.

"Not yet," Nina replied calmly, reminding Cassie of their earlier conversation.

Before long Cassie had reorganized the entire filing system, designed a more efficient billing system for bookings, and memorized the telephone numbers of nearly every model, photographer, magazine style director, and maitre d' of any importance in the city.

Professing that things had never run smoother, Nina promoted to her office manager. The subsequent raise in salary allowed Cassie to sublet a rent-controlled apartment from one of Nina's models, who had gone to work in Paris for a year.

Nina hovered over Cassie like a mother hen. She took her to a renowned obstetrician on Park Avenue and served as her coach at Lamaze class, sitting inelegantly on the hospital auditorium floor, helping Cassie huff and puff her way through the exercises. At first Cassie was embarrassed to be the only woman at the class without a husband, but her desire to do everything to have the healthiest baby possible eventually overcame her self-consciousness.

Even before Cassie's belly had swelled enough to require it, Nina took her shopping. After one four-hour spree, they staggered home under the weight of shopping bags filled with a maternity wardrobe suitable for a princess.

Then they started in on baby clothes.

"What do you think?" Nina asked, holding up a yellow crocheted sweater that looked as if it had been designed to fit a doll. "Isn't it adorable? And see, it's got a matching hat."

Cassie's eyes widened as she took in the price tag. "I could buy a dozen sweaters for this price."

"A dozen sweaters in Gallagher City," Nina corrected. "This is Manhattan and I refuse to have my godchild going out in public looking like some orphaned waif."

Brushing aside Cassie's complaints, Nina made her way through the store like Sherman burning his way through Georgia, gathering up booties, sacque sets, kimonos, tiny white undershirts, blankets, more sweaters, lawn gowns hand-embroidered at the hems, stretchie sleepwear, numerous pairs of infant socks, and bunting for those brisk walks in the park. By the time she handed the clerk her credit card, Cassie had enough baby clothes for quintuplets.

But Nina wasn't finished. On one memorable February afternoon, she practically emptied out F.A.O. Schwarz, turning Cassie's apartment bedroom into a dream nursery.

It was the first time in her life that Cassie had ever been pampered and as much as she wished she could relax and enjoy it, she couldn't help feeling as if her life was on hold. Her dream was out there, hovering enticingly just beyond reach. Perhaps, once her baby was born, she would be able to grasp it.

Although Nina had tried her best, all the galleries continued to insist that Cassie was not properly trained. Cassie had begun to despair of ever getting work in her chosen field when one evening Nina stopped by her apartment with a stack of papers she dropped into Cassie's lap. Or where Cassie's lap had once been.

"What are these?" Cassie asked. She was sitting in the rocking chair in the nursery. Before Nina had arrived, she'd been arranging the menagerie of stuffed animals on the glossy white shelves, walking around the room, spinning the gaily colored mobile that hung over the maple crib Nina had bought, refolding all the infant clothes, imagining how it would be when her baby came.

"Brochures for NYU. The Gallatin Division is tailor-made for you, Cassie—it allows flexible hours, course freedom, and the ability to develop your own major." Her smile revealed a woman more than a little pleased with herself. "One of these days, sooner than you think, all those prissy antiques snobs will be crawling all over each other to hire you."

Cassie leafed through the course brochures, feeling a surge of excitement as she checked the varied course listings. "I'll enroll after the baby's born."

In the meantime, she would continue to pore over the wealth of books on art and antiques at the Fifth Avenue library. The first time she'd been inside the imposing Beaux-Arts-style building, Cassie had realized that the entire Gallagher City library wouldn't even take up one tiny corner.

Her green eyes filled with gratitude. "I don't know how to thank you."

"You don't have to. Hell, Cassie, we all have to have a little help from time to time. One of these days remind me to tell you what a mess my life was in when a scout for Eileen Ford plucked me out of that diner in Forks, Washington, where I was serving burgers and greasy fries to a bunch of loggers and fishermen. Eileen brought me to her place here in the city and taught me everything I know.

"She saved my life, Cassie," Nina said with atypical gravity. "So the way I look at it, the best way to pay back such a debt is to help someone else." Her smile returned. "And you're it, kiddo, so you might as well get used to it. Because you're stuck with me—What's wrong?" Nina asked suddenly, when she saw Cassie's eyes widen.

"It moved." Taking hold of Nina's hand, she held it tight against her swollen abdomen where a tiny foot was kicking away.

"Oh, my God," Nina breathed with shared awe. "You really are going to have a baby."

For the first time, Cassie found herself thinking of her unborn child as a gift and not a burden. "Yes." Her face blossomed into a huge grin. "I am."

\*   \*   \*

March roared in like a lion. In order to banish lingering winter blues and Cassie's heartburn, swollen ankles, and insomnia, Nina insisted that they treat themselves to a girl's day on the town. Makeovers at Bloomingdale's, lunch at the Palm Court, followed by a matinee performance of *Dreamgirls,* a glittering hit musical based on the Supremes.

Cassie perched uncomfortably on the high stool in the cosmetics department of Bloomingdale's while the impeccably made-up Helena Rubinstein saleswoman brushed "Golden Khaki" shadow over her eyelid.

"Metallics are hot this year," the woman said, eyeing her handiwork with approval. "With your eyes, dear, the effect is dynamite." She glanced over at Nina, who was nearby, spritzing Dioressence onto the inside of her wrist. "Doesn't she look exactly like Cat Woman?"

"Exactly."

Cassie pressed her hand against her back, which had been aching all morning. "I feel more like an elephant than a cat," Cassie complained, looking down at her protruding stomach and swollen ankles. There were times, and this was one of them, when Cassie thought she would never look like herself again. "Or a beached whale." This was all a waste of time; makeup wasn't going to help her feel any more attractive.

The hard stool made the base of her spine ache and she had to cross her legs—no easy task—to suppress a sudden, urgent need to go to the bathroom. As the woman began applying a bold sweep of copper to her cheekbones, Cassie felt a trickling of moisture between her crossed thighs. Then a gush. Mortified, she stared down at the spreading puddle of amniotic fluid beneath the stool.

"Nina?"

"Mmmm?" Nina asked absently. Picking up a frosted bottle of L'Air du Temps from a nearby counter, she sniffed appreciatively.

A fist was gripping at Cassie's abdomen, twisting it viciously. She paled as the first wave of pain swept over her. "I think we'd better skip the matinee."

# Eight

The afternoon seemed endless. Cassie's body was soaked with sweat and although she was able to doze a little between contractions, as the day turned to evening, then to night, she grew exhausted. Nina remained by her side.

"Relax," Nina soothed as she massaged Cassie's swollen abdomen. "Remember what you learned in class." She gave Cassie a chip of ice to suck on. "Don't fight the pain. Go with the flow."

Cassie tried to do what she'd learned in class, to picture the contraction as an ocean wave, gathering, breaking, subsiding. But as the hours dragged on, Cassie was discovering that wasn't nearly as easy as it had sounded in class.

Every so often, the doctor and the nurses would return, their hands probing her abdomen, between her legs. The worried frown on the doctor's brow was definitely not encouraging. Finally, she was taken downstairs to the X-ray department—contracting and breathing all the way—to have pelvic photographs taken.

"I'm not going to die, am I?" Cassie asked raggedly, after she'd been returned to her room.

"Of course not." The doctor had gray hair, a kind face, and an aura of supreme confidence. He was not a man accustomed to failure, she told herself. He was not a man who would let her baby die.

He patted her belly in a paternalistic manner that Cassie had neither the strength nor the energy to protest.

"The good news is that you're nine centimeters dilated, Cassie," he said. "Only one more to go. The bad news is that the baby is in a breech position. If it doesn't turn soon, we'll have to schedule a caesarean."

"Oh, you can't do that," Nina argued. "The scar would ruin her modeling career."

The obstetrician gave her a withering look. "My concern is for the child," he said. "And her mother's physical welfare."

"Of course," Nina agreed quickly. After he'd gone, she began rubbing Cassie's belly with renewed vigor. "Come on, kiddo," she urged. "Let's get this show on the road so your mommy can become rich and famous."

Cassie bit her lip, refusing to scream as one contraction became two, then three, then four. Amazingly, soon after Nina's encouragement, the baby turned with a force that was visible to all in the room. Declaring her properly dilated, the doctor had Cassie moved quickly to the delivery room where, after she'd been transferred to the delivery table, her abdomen and legs were draped and her feet were placed into towel-padded stirrups.

Nina stood beside her head, timing her contractions, coaxing her on her breathing, telling her when the doctor wanted her to push. Cassie was more exhausted than she'd ever been in her life; sweat beaded on her brow, above her lip, ran in rivulets down her side beneath the white cotton hospital gown.

"Here we go," the doctor called out. "Your baby's crowning, Cassie. Come on, push a little harder. That's it! We've got the eyes, the nose— keep pushing—we've got the mouth. Bingo." Cassie watched in the overhead mirror as her baby came into the world.

Finally, twenty-eight long hours after Cassie's water had first broken in the cosmetics department of Bloomingdales, Amy Tara McBride was born. Cassie held her breath, waiting for the baby's cry. When the ragged whimper turned into a full, healthy wail, Cassie and Nina hugged each other and cried.

The doctor cut the cord and the nurse quickly bathed the infant girl in warm water, clearing her nose and mouth of mucus. Cassie thought her baby's strident cry to be the most beautiful sound she'd ever heard.

The nurse placed Cassie's daughter into her arms. "Here you are, Mommy."

*Mommy.* Was there a more wonderful word in all the universe? It was a miracle, Cassie thought as she gazed down into her daughter's scrunched-up pink face. All the pain had vanished; even the memory was swiftly fading away like smoke. She ran her finger over her daughter's satiny cheek and played with the soft fuzz of ebony hair. When the baby opened her bright blue eyes and seemed to be looking right into her mother's adoring gaze, Cassie fell in love.

Cassie was in seventh heaven; having Amy was like having a living, breathing doll to play with, even if that doll did bear a startling resemblance to her father.

At first, frightened and alone, Cassie had been devastated when Roarke had not answered any of her letters. But gradually she'd come to the unhappy conclusion that Belle had been right about the Gallaghers never accepting her into their family.

Roarke's refusal to acknowledge his child was a terrible disappointment—she'd thought him to be a better man than his father—but having overcome so many other obstacles in her life, Cassie decided that she'd just have to be both mother and father to her beautiful daughter. If only she could stop having nightmares about Quinlan Gallagher chasing her and trying to snatch her child from her arms.

She returned to work six weeks after Amy's birth, crying as she left her daughter for the first time in the care of a Dutch au pair. Although the young woman's references were impeccable, Cassie couldn't help thinking that no one could take care of her daughter as well as she.

"You are definitely a walking advertisement for motherhood," Nina remarked one June Saturday afternoon. They'd returned from taking Amy for a walk, and now Cassie was bathing her in a plastic tub placed in the kitchen sink. "I swear, you're absolutely blooming. I'd love to get that face on film."

"Please," Cassie said, laughing as Amy splashed water all over the front of her T-shirt. "Don't start in on my modeling again."

"I'm going to keep after you until you break down and listen."

"Even if I could be a model, I know better than anyone how much traveling is involved," Cassie argued. "I don't want to leave Amy." Slapping the water with her tiny hands, Amy babbled happy gibberish, as if seconding Cassie's statement.

Nina shrugged, knowing when she was licked. "Hey, it's your life," she said. "Perhaps we should get the kid into the business. Lord knows she's cute enough and behaves like an absolute angel."

At three months Cassie's daughter was beautiful, chubby and healthy, with pink cheeks, black curls, bright, inquisitive blue eyes—her father's eyes—and a smile capable of melting the coldest of hearts. "Amy isn't going to be a model."

"Why not? When it would help you get some of that money you're always talking about wanting?"

"I don't want to take a chance on anyone finding out about her," Cassie insisted.

Despite the way Quinlan had run her out of town, despite Roarke's cruel rejection, Cassie could not get the threat of the Gallaghers' power and money out of her mind. If for some reason they changed their mind and wanted her baby, Cassie knew she wouldn't stand a chance. Quinlan Gallagher always got what he wanted; her deep-seated fear was that someday he would want Amy.

All her life, Cassie had longed for someone to love her. First her mother, then Roarke. Now she had Amy, who loved her unconditionally. As she loved her daughter. In fact, there were times when Cassie felt so much love for Amy that she was surprised her heart didn't burst. What had she ever done in her life, she'd wonder, to deserve such a treasure?

"Don't you think you're being a little paranoid?" Nina asked. "None of the Gallaghers, Amy's father included, showed any interest in your pregnancy."

Cassie almost wished she hadn't, in a moment of weakness, told Nina everything. She toweled Amy dry, and sprinkled her fat little tummy and pink bottom with sweet-smelling talcum powder. Amy smiled up at her mother, eyes crossed, chubby hand reaching for the plastic powder dispenser.

"I'm not taking any chances," Cassie said in a tone that brooked no argument.

Determined to be a perfect mother, Cassie constantly referred to her well-worn copy of Penelope Leach's book, *Babyhood*. The British psychologist was being touted as having replaced Dr. Spock as the standard reference for child rearing, and Cassie treated her writings with the same reverence Miss Lillian had treated the gospels.

She was pleased when her baby seemed to be not only right on schedule but actually ahead of the curve. Amy rolled over a full two weeks before her fourth-month birthday and held her dark head up soon after that. Before she was five months old, she started to sit up—albeit only for a few seconds—and began to drool, a sign that her first tooth was not far away.

When Amy was six months old, the model whose apartment Cassie had been subletting returned from Paris and Cassie moved to a larger, two-bedroom apartment. That same week she finally fulfilled her long-delayed dream of continuing her education and enrolled at NYU.

Nina took Cassie out to dinner to celebrate, and afterward they returned to the apartment for coffee and slivers of decadently rich chocolate raspberry cheesecake Nina had picked up at The Market, the gourmet's heaven inside B. Altman's on Fifth Avenue.

Years later, Cassie would remember every detail of that night. It was the night that the peaceful pleasure of her life was rocked violently and irrevocably.

Never tiring of looking at her baby, Cassie had brought Amy's hand-carved cradle into the combination kitchen/dining area. She was spooning the dark brown grounds into the coffee maker when she dropped the nearly empty can of coffee. The sound of metal striking the floor reverberated around the kitchen, but her daughter continued to sleep, her pink fist shoved happily into her rosebud mouth.

Cassie felt a chill of fear. Afraid of what she was thinking, she crouched down behind the cradle and banged two pot lids together, like the crash of cymbals. Amy didn't flinch.

Exchanging a look with Nina, Cassie turned on the radio, twisting the dial until she came to Kool and the Gang belting out "Celebration." She increased the volume until the glasses began vibrating on the open shelves. She looked at Amy. Nothing. Absolutely nothing.

Nina left the room. A moment later she returned and switched off the radio. "I brought you something."

Cassie looked at the brief pamphlet, entitled "Pediatric Audiology," then up at Nina. Her eyes were glazed like a victim of shell shock. "You can't think that Amy's . . ." Her voice trailed off; she couldn't make herself say the word, afraid that if she voiced her fear out loud, it might become true.

"Deaf?" Nina supplied. "I don't know, Cassie, but to tell you the truth, I've suspected something was wrong for a while. But I kept telling myself that I didn't know anything about babies. Perhaps the stories about them crying all the time were exaggerated. Or perhaps Amy really was the best little girl in the world. Or—"

"You're wrong." Cassie thought back to a group of deaf children she'd seen playing in the park. She remembered their broadly exaggerated movements and facial expressions, the tugging, pulling, prodding, the sounds that resembled noises more than speech. Amy wasn't like that.

"I hope I am. But it won't hurt to get her tested."

"I can't afford specialists. Besides, it's not necessary."

"I can afford all the specialists you need." When Cassie looked inclined to argue, Nina's jaw firmed. "In case you've forgotten, Amy's my godchild," she said. "So I'm damn well going to pay for any medical bills and you're damn well going to put aside your stupid Okie pride long enough to do what's right for your child."

She'd just said the magic words. Of course Cassie wanted the best for her child. She decided to agree to the testing, if only to prove Nina wrong.

Cassie ran her finger down the side of Amy's petal-soft cheek. The baby stirred, then woke, treating her mother to a sweet smile. When she began to coo happily and reached out her arms, Cassie picked her up, sick with worry even as she told herself that Amy wasn't deaf. She wouldn't let her be.

And so began a pilgrimage from one doctor to another. When asked if anyone in her family had suffered from hearing loss, Cassie said that although she knew nothing about her father, she'd never heard of deafness in Belle's side of the family.

"And Amy's father?" Dr. Harriet Greene asked.

"Her father's dead."

That was a lie; only this morning, while sitting out in the waiting room, she'd been absently flipping through the pages of a *Time* magazine and had seen Roarke's face smiling out at her. Cassie learned that he'd moved back to the States, was now living in San Francisco, and had recently won a design contest for a theater complex in that city.

"Excuse me?" Cassie suddenly realized the doctor was talking to her. Her mind had been on the photograph of the sleek blonde seen with Roarke exiting the Golden Gate Theater. The caption beside the photo had revealed the woman to be Philippa Hamilton, divorced daughter of Richard Hamilton, CEO of Hamilton Construction, a worldwide construction company based in San Francisco. Ms. Hamilton was, according to *Time*, Roarke Gallagher's "frequent companion."

"Is there any deafness in Amy's father's family?" the doctor repeated.

"No," Cassie answered, certain that she would have heard rumors if any of Gallagher City's first family had been deaf.

The questions went on to cover her prenatal health—no rubella, no Rh incompatibility, no premature birth. She told about her early devastating bout of nausea, describing the antibiotics she'd been given (leaving out the fact that she'd been in jail at the time), and her long labor.

No, Amy had experienced no loud noises near her ear, no blows to the head, nor had she suffered any illness. She was, Cassie insisted, and Nina confirmed, a remarkably healthy infant.

"She babbled constantly from the day she was born," Cassie argued, as if that fact would disprove what the doctor was suggesting. "Doesn't that mean she was repeating sounds?"

"It's normal for all babies to babble for the first six months," Dr. Greene told Cassie gently. Of all the doctors who had examined Amy, Cassie felt the most comfortable with the grandmotherly Dr. Greene. "Hearing-impaired babies suffer from an absence of auditory feedback, so eventually, vocal play ceases. When the baby becomes silent, the mother begins to notice its lack of response to sounds."

Cassie's face grew paler. "I have noticed that she's gotten awfully quiet lately," she admitted reluctantly. "But sometimes, when I make a noise behind her, she turns around." She didn't add that she'd been testing Amy almost continuously since that terrifying first night.

"And you, of course, reward her with a smile."

"Well, I suppose I'm relieved when she responds, but I wouldn't actually call it a reward."

"You daughter is obviously a very bright child."

"She's ahead of the curve," Cassie related with motherly pride.

"The point is, Ms. McBride," Dr. Greene said in a kind but firm voice, "there's a chance that Amy is seeing you with her peripheral vision and has learned that if she turns around, Mommy will give her a smile."

Cassie couldn't answer. The idea was too terrifying.

"So, what do we do now?" Nina asked.

"We'll do some basic diagnostic assessment," Dr. Greene said. "Along with impedance audiometry—a test to detect problems in the middle ear."

"How can you possibly test a child Amy's age?" Cassie asked.

"Tests can be modified for children of any age, even Amy's," the doctor assured her. "In addition, I'd like to do an ABR to assess Amy's brainstem response to auditory stimuli. ABR testing has proven particularly helpful in evaluating the hearing of infants." She took off her dark-framed glasses. "It is, unfortunately, quite expensive."

"Money's no problem," Nina answered immediately, ignoring Cassie's sharp look. "Do whatever you have to do."

The doctor nodded. "Fine." She smiled at Cassie, a smile that was meant to be encouraging. "I know this all seems catastrophic, but children born with hearing deficiencies can do remarkably well, so long as the problem is caught early. As you've done."

Cassie looked at her limp hair. She couldn't remember the last time she'd washed it; all her energies these past weeks had been directed toward Amy. "It's my fault, isn't it?"

Dr. Greene turned brisk. "According to your obstetrician's records, you took excellent care of yourself during the prenatal period. Still, Amy's birth took a long time, which sometimes results in hearing problems. There is also a chance that the antibiotics you received during your first trimester may have played a part in Amy's problem, but we'll never know that for certain.

"Approximately five out of every thousand babies are born with or develop a significant hearing loss. Amy's is certainly not an isolated problem. Nor should you take any guilt upon yourself."

She rose from her chair, came from behind her desk, and took Cassie's trembling hands in hers. "This isn't the dark ages, dear. Whatever the final diagnosis, your daughter will be able to lead a full, productive, happy life."

If only she could believe that, Cassie thought later that night as she sat in the exquisite nursery and rocked her baby in her arms, crooning a lullaby she now knew Amy couldn't hear. If only she could stop blaming herself.

A week later, Cassie sat in the suede chair in front of the doctor's desk, staring at the framed diplomas on the wall, her ice-cold hands clasped together tightly in her lap. All the tests had been completed, it was now time to hear the verdict. She was almost paralyzed with fear; dread engulfed her.

As she waited for Dr. Greene to finish making a notation in Amy's file, Cassie realized when she had felt this way before. It was the day she had stood before the judge. That day, she had been sentenced to the County Work Farm. Praying to a God that she wasn't even sure she believed in, Cassie begged for a happier outcome for her daughter.

"Cassie." Dr. Greene took off her glasses and folded her hands on top of the thick manila folder. "I'm afraid I have bad news for you." Her grave expression caused Cassie's terror to increase.

When Cassie didn't—couldn't—speak, the doctor continued. "Our suspicions were correct. Amy has a severe hearing loss of unknown origin."

Was there some law of nature that had her paying for every happiness with unhappiness? Twenty years of living had taught Cassie to expect the worst. But that didn't stop her heart from lurching, or her blood from turning to ice. She stared at the doctor for a long moment, trying to sort out the words that were an incomprehensible buzz in her ears.

Thoughts tumbled around in her mind: Would Amy never hear her mother's voice, go on a date, attend a prom, have a sweet-sixteen party, share a first kiss, get married in a flowing white dress and veil, have children? It didn't matter that Cassie herself had never attended a prom, been given a sixteenth birthday party, or married. She'd always expected her daughter to have a richer, fuller life than the one she'd experienced.

"Are you sure?" she managed, desperation making her voice tremble. "Maybe someone made a mistake. It happens all the time, maybe you have the wrong test results, perhaps someone in the lab read the names wrong. . . ."

"All the consulting physicians agree with the diagnosis, Cassie," Dr. Greene said gently. "There's no mistake."

"But you can help her, right?" Cassie asked hopefully. "Surely there's some medicine you can give her. Or an operation."

"Amy's hearing loss is sensor-neural," the doctor answered. "That means that the sound can reach her inner ear, but it can't reach the brain. I'm afraid that such damage is irreversible."

Cassie slumped in the chair and dragged her hands down her face. This couldn't be happening. It was all a terrible nightmare and soon she'd wake up and Amy would be babbling all sorts of happy baby gibberish and they'd both laugh at how silly Mommy's dream had been.

"It's not as bad as it sounds," Dr. Greene assured Cassie. "With hearing aids, Amy will be able to hear things like thunder, a telephone ringing, an auto horn, a radio turned louder than normal, and probably even raised voices."

"Will she ever be able to talk?" Cassie asked the question she'd been afraid to think for weeks. From deep down inside she felt the tears welling; resolutely, she blinked them away.

The doctor smiled gently, as if to soften the blow she'd already inflicted. "While I can't guarantee that she will, the optimum time for learning language is the first three years. There is also evidence that the ability to hear some sound—which Amy possesses—helps provide a foundation for learning language. Thanks to your early intervention, it's not impossible to expect that she'll learn to speak.

"Although," the doctor added as a caveat, "you must understand that hearing children begin to notice fractional differences in sound as soon as they are born. Deaf children, on the other hand, can't differentiate. So, since all sounds are the same to Amy, she doesn't have a clear auditory image of words, which means that she will need a great deal of training.

"She will have to learn to recognize minute differences in the length and intonation and pattern of words, at the same time that they are nothing but blurred distortions of sound. And even then, as she learns to mimic those sounds, she will undoubtedly have the most trouble discriminating consonants."

That would definitely have given her trouble back in Oklahoma, Cassie thought with bitter irony, where most people had trouble enunciating consonants. But what was life without language? If Amy didn't learn to communicate, she'd be forced to withdraw from a confusing world into a meaningless silent existence. Cassie was not about to allow that to happen. It was merely an inconvenience, she assured herself. All right, a major inconvenience. But she would overcome it, the same as she had overcome all the other problems in her life.

"I taught myself to speak correctly," she said, thinking back on all those long lonely nights spent listening to the radio. "I can teach Amy."

"I know you mean well, dear," Dr. Greene said kindly, "and a mother's love and help will be very important to Amy. But my recommendation, both as a physician and a mother, would be to place your daughter in a special boarding home, where she can receive the proper care from professionals."

Cassie's jaw jutted forward. "I am not putting my daughter away in an institution." The very idea was reprehensible; she would not participate in stigmatizing her child.

"Placing Amy in an environment where she can learn to cope in what might otherwise be a frightening, unintelligible world is no sign of your failure as a parent," Dr. Greene assured Cassie. "I can recommend several fine ones."

How could she explain that her guilt was already almost too much to bear? "I can do whatever's necessary," Cassie insisted. "I'll learn how to help my daughter."

Since survival had always been paramount in Cassie's mind, it terrified her that her daughter might not be able to learn the most rudimentary skills needed to survive. Horrible images of Amy getting hit as she crossed a street because she couldn't hear a car horn, or the siren of a speeding ambulance, of Amy dying in an apartment fire because she couldn't hear the alarm, raced through Cassie's mind like scenes from some late-night horror movie.

It was a mother's responsibility to protect a daughter. It was her duty to ensure that Amy would grow up strong and self-sufficient, able to buffet any storms that life might send her way. Her own rocky life had taught Cassie at an early age that there were always storms.

# Nine

Cassie hovered over Amy like a mother bear protecting her cub. She quit her job with Nina, signing on instead with an employment agency that got her a job typing insurance policy endorsements at night. She was able to work at home; if she typed most of the night, this would allow her to spend her days with her daughter. If sleep became a precious, almost unknown thing, Cassie didn't care. Having taken the burdens of Amy's deafness squarely upon her own exhausted shoulders, she refused to complain. She had learned from watching her own mother how destructive self-pity could be and refused to give into it.

After a second attempt to make an ear mold that fit her tiny ear, Amy was fitted with dual hearing aids. At first, Cassie hated taking Amy outside for her morning and afternoon walks. She felt as if the fawn-colored aids were some kind of sign to the world that she'd been a bad or neglectful mother. She also feared the prejudices imprinted by society—prejudices she realized uncomfortably that she had shared—that caused the hearing world to regard the deaf as somehow inferior.

Refusing to let her own ignorance be a barrier to her daughter's growth, Cassie scoured the library for books about deaf children, appalled that there were so few. And those that she could find seemed designed for physicians, written in medical jargon that made about as much sense to her as Amy's infant babbling.

She bombarded her baby with sound—the vacuum cleaner, water

running, the radio, banging pots and pans behind Amy, then in front of her—in the belief that the more sounds Amy learned to recognize, the wider her knowledge of her environment would be. Along with the constant noise, Cassie talked incessantly, hour after hour, hoping that her words would be imprinted on Amy's memory, helping her come one step closer to understanding the meaning of each word, and eventually to using it herself.

It seemed like a logical plan. But as the days and months went on, Cassie saw no indication that Amy understood a single word she had said. It wrenched Cassie's heart to see her darling girl smiling up at her so innocently, oblivious to the lessons she was desperately trying to impart.

"You need to get professional help," Nina said late one afternoon. She'd stopped by with an enormous stuffed giraffe for Amy and a ballotin of Godiva chocolates for Cassie.

"I'm not putting a one-year-old child in a home," Cassie insisted, as she had every time Nina had brought it up over the past six months. What she wouldn't—couldn't—admit was that she'd let her guilt about Amy's deafness override her common sense.

The hearing aid on Amy's right ear whistled. "I'm her mother, damnit," Cassie said as she turned it down. Exhaustion and worry had her temper hanging by a thread. "I'm the only one who understands what she wants and needs. I'm the only one who can help her."

"That's why she's making so much progress," Nina said dryly. When Cassie's face crumbled, Nina put her arm around her. "I'm sorry if that sounds harsh, honey, but someone has to make you listen to reason. You keep insisting that you're the only one who can help Amy, but you have to face the fact that the child is nearly a year old. And despite you running yourself into the ground for the past six months, she hasn't shown any real signs of improvement."

Exhausted and demoralized, Cassie covered her face with her hands, unwilling to face her friend's sympathetic gaze, unwilling to face the truth. "I love her," she sobbed.

"I know," Nina murmured, stroking Cassie's head in an attempt to soothe her pain. "So love her enough to give her the skills to live her own life."

Tears filled her eyes. "You're right," she agreed with a deep, ragged sigh. "I'll go talk with Dr. Greene."

Cassie, who still found the idea of putting her daughter in a home an anathema, was relieved when the doctor offered an alternative solution.

"There's a very good audiology clinic at Columbia," she said. "If Amy could receive therapy three times a week, I'm sure she'd make progress. Of course you'll also need someone to work with Amy—and you—at home." She took off her glasses and toyed with the mock tortoiseshell frames. "As luck would have it, my former nurse is looking for employment."

"A nurse?"

"Oh, Edith Campbell is a great deal more than a nurse," Dr. Greene said with a smile. "She's also a grandmother currently suffering from empty-nest syndrome."

"I don't understand."

"Edith is a widow, who was practically running my office single-handedly when Chelsea, her three-year-old granddaughter, suffered a loss of hearing due to an acute case of tonsillitis five years ago. Since Edith's daughter, Angie, was a divorced single parent whose husband had disappeared, she couldn't afford to quit work to take Chelsea to the clinic.

"So, Edith quit her job here and moved in with her daughter and granddaughter, allowing Angie to stay on at Dean Witter. Things went along quite nicely until Angie married a broker from Merrill Lynch, who was transferred to Seattle to work in the Pacific Rim account department.

"Now Angie and her husband have taken Chelsea to Seattle, and Edith has asked for her old job back. Of course, I'd love to have her working here again—the children, by the way, all adored her—but I got the impression that she's incredibly lonely. And unfulfilled, now that she no longer has a little one to care for."

"And you think she'd be willing to come stay with Amy and me?"

"She'd love it," Dr. Greene said without hesitation. "Why don't I arrange a meeting between the two of you? I'm sure you'll get along famously. And believe me, dear, you couldn't find a better person to take care of your daughter. Not only is Edith warm and nurturing, she's also an expert when it comes to working with deaf children."

Not wanting to get her hopes up, Cassie agreed to meet this paragon. She wasn't at all disappointed. The sixty-something widow was intelligent, warm, and from the way she smiled and talked to Amy, who couldn't hear a word but smiled back in return, Cassie knew that Dr. Greene had not been exaggerating about Edith Campbell's love of children. What's more, she understood exactly how Cassie was feeling.

"It was a terrible shock for us, too," Edith told Cassie. "Chelsea had always been such a bright, vocal little girl, we couldn't imagine her suffering such a cruel fate. Of course, you'd think I would've taken it better, working for Dr. Greene, seeing deaf children every day, but I found myself feeling prejudices I'd never felt before. And feeling terribly guilty about them, too," she confided.

"And so, to make things easier, I began thinking of Chelsea as a normal child—a hearing child with a disability. Which was, of course, a horrendous mistake."

"Why?" Cassie didn't want to admit that she'd been trying to think of Amy the same way.

"Because after a time, I began to realize that I couldn't have been more wrong. Deafness isn't the same as having one leg a bit shorter than the other, or being blind in one eye.

"Unfortunately, in our society, deafness gives one a real sense of being different. It's a world apart, Ms. McBride, and it's our job to make certain that our deaf babies realize that the deaf world isn't populated by inarticulate, inferior beings.

"As unattractive as you might find the idea right now, Amy needs access to the deaf world as well as the hearing world. She needs to meet other deaf people who've achieved things in order to encourage a positive belief in herself as a deaf person. Along with her own ability to achieve."

"Amy is only one year old, Mrs. Campbell," Cassie felt obliged to point out.

"It's never too young to start building self-confidence." The woman patted Cassie's knee. "Don't worry, dear, you've lost a little time, but together we can make up for it."

Edith Campbell, Cassie soon discovered, was a female cross between Dale Carnegie and Norman Vincent Peale. She rattled on for another two hours, until the shortbread cookies were gone and the tea was cold, reciting sayings like: Deaf people can do anything the hearing can do . . . except hear. If your mind can conceive it and your heart can believe it, you can always achieve it. The slogans changed as the afternoon wore on, but the theme was always the same: Deaf Pride.

By the time Edith had finally stopped for breath, Cassie found herself, for the first time in six months, feeling wonderfully optimistic.

"How soon could you begin?" she asked.

"As soon as you need me."

"I needed you six months ago," Cassie admitted. "But as you said, together we'll just have to make up for lost time."

Cassie's optimism was stuck a near-fatal blow a week later after her appointment with the administrator of the clinic Dr. Greene had recommended.

The pediatric hearing and speech clinic was a bright, cheerful place with walls covered with murals painted by the children. There were dolls and toy race cars and jigsaw puzzles and small low tables painted in primary colors. During her meeting with the therapists, Cassie learned that in the beginning Amy would receive important one-on-one training that should be followed up at home. Later, she could be put in a group environment with children of her same age.

"It's a wonderful place," Cassie told Nina the following day, after describing the clinic in detail. "And the staff is professional but caring, and seem to honestly enjoy working with the kids."

"So why the glum expression?"

"Because it's horribly expensive and after spending most of yesterday afternoon trudging from one social service agency to the next, I discovered that I make too much money to qualify for assistance. But even if I found a second job, I'd never be able to afford the cost on my own."

"I have an idea about that," Nina said.

"No." Cassie shook her head. "You've already done too much as it is. I can't take any more money from you."

"Didn't anyone ever tell you that jumping to conclusions can lead to uncomfortable landings? As a matter of fact, I've been waiting for the right moment to spring my idea on you. Now that you've got your figure back"—she eyed Cassie's long, voluptuous frame with a professionally judicious eye—"it's time to think about launching you in the business."

"Sure," Cassie said. "Are you going to call *Vogue* and tell them I'm available, or shall I?"

"You'll need pictures first. I've already made you an appointment for nine o'clock tomorrow with Tommy Jones."

Cassie had worked at Grace Model Management long enough to know that Jones was one of the best in the business. Obviously, Nina had given this a lot of thought and was very, very serious.

"I have to think."

"Fine. You can think while we get your hair trimmed." She stood up and crossed the room to the door of the bathroom where Amy was having oatmeal washed out of her hair. "Edith," Nina addressed the woman who'd already become a fixture in Cassie's home, "I'm taking Cassie out for an overhaul. We should be back by six o'clock this evening. But it may be later."

"Don't worry about us," Edith said. "Amy and I will be just fine. You girls have a wonderful day on the town."

"After we get your hair into some semblance of a style, we have to do something about your nails," Nina said as she and Cassie shared the back seat of a taxi. "They're too short."

"You know I keep them short so I can change Amy's diapers."

"True," Nina said. "But that's going to be Edith's job now."

Something remarkably like jealousy coursed through Cassie. "I'm still going to be Amy's mother. Even if Edith is living with us."

"Well, of course you are," Nina said impatiently. "Christ, Cassie, you'd think you were handing your child over to the gypsies, not enabling her to have very expensive therapy and her own warm, grand-motherly private nurse."

Still bothered by the possibility of Amy calling Edith Mommy when she did learn to talk, Cassie didn't answer.

Three hours later, Cassie's hair had been turned into a flowing mane by Kenneth's magic scissors, a set of sculptured nails had been applied to the top of her own short ones, and Nina had given her a crash course in applying makeup.

"I feel like Eliza Doolittle," Cassie said as she watched Nina brush a sweep of vibrant color up her cheekbone.

"Good. You look terrific." Nina said.

It was dark by the time they returned to the apartment. Edith told Cassie that she'd put Amy to bed. Then, saying that the baby had been a delight, as always, she retired to her own room to watch "Dallas."

"I do so love that wicked J.R.," she revealed with a decidedly unma-tronly giggle.

"You're doing the right thing," Nina assured Cassie after she'd re-turned from checking her sleeping child. "You know," she said thought-fully, "meeting the way we did is turning out to be the best thing that ever happened to me. I didn't realize how much I needed a family."

"I know it's the best thing that ever happened to me," Cassie agreed. "Except for Amy."

"Of course it is," Nina agreed. "Just think, it could have been Ellen Lambert in the bathroom with you that day."

Ellen Lambert—a former Elite model—ran a rival agency and Cassie knew her to be more interested with the bottom line than her models' career choices.

"Ellen is like too many agents," Nina said scornfully, "in the business only to book models. But you know I take my girls' careers far more seriously than that. I'll create an image for you, Cassie. An image that'll make you one of the highest-paid models in the world."

She pulled a one-page agreement from her quilted Chanel bag. "All you have to do is sign on the dotted line and you'll be rich."

"Do you really think it's possible?" Cassie asked as she took a deep breath and signed her name to the brief agency agreement.

"Absolutely." Nina signed her own name on the line below Cassie's. "Now all we have to do is put together a portfolio. And change your name."

"Change my name? Why? What's wrong with my name?"

"Cassie McBride is a fine name for a little girl from Gallagher City, Oklahoma," Nina explained patiently. "But it isn't exotic enough for your new image. You're going to be a star and I've got just the name for you." She paused, letting the anticipation build. "Jade."

"Jade? What kind of name is that?"

"All the greats have only one name. And you're the one who told me that the Chinese call a beautiful woman a jade person."

Still entranced with the stone that entire civilizations had been built around, Cassie had read the description in a book she'd checked out of the library. She'd also learned that fragrant jade was the Chinese description for woman's skin and jade shattered referred to a beauty's death.

"I don't know if I could ever think of myself as Jade," Cassie argued.

"You'll get used to it in no time at all," Nina assured her. "Trust me, it's perfect. And besides being memorable, it makes everyone focus on your gorgeous green eyes. A woman with eyes like yours can rule the world."

"Yeah, I've been a real big success so far."

"You will be." Nina handed her a tulip-shaped glass. "To Jade. Fashion's newest celebrity."

Although it felt strange drinking a toast to herself, Cassie sipped her champagne and thanked whatever fates had brought Nina Grace into her life.

Cassie arrived at her photo shoot horribly nervous, but Tommy Jones remained remarkably patient, coaxing her with smiles and jokes that soon had her moving to the beat of the driving rock music booming from his stereo speakers.

"I thought he was going to shoot you in the studio," Nina said when the portfolio arrived by messenger from Tommy's Christopher Street studio.

"We did some shots there," Cassie said. "Then Tommy got all excited and said that he wanted to do something different from the same boring fashion layouts.

"Well, he certainly succeeded." Nina studied the mix of head and body shots designed to jar the senses: Cassie at a junkyard, clad in a black lace Oleg Cassini; leaning insolently against a marble column of the Metropolitan Opera House in a denim micro-miniskirt and studded leather jacket; in the paddock at the Meadowlands race track, wearing only a man's tuxedo jacket, black fedora, and skyscraper high heels.

"What do you know about Kenya?"

Cassie thought she must have misunderstood. "Kenya? As in Africa? Not a thing."

"Well, you will soon. One of my Paris-based girls was scheduled to do a shoot for French *Elle* in Kenya. Unfortunately, she made the mistake of falling asleep in the sun during a weekend in Monte Carlo, and according to the photographer, she's in the process of peeling through several layers of lobster red skin. He needs a model in ten days, I need to maintain my credibility with the French magazines, and you need a job." Nina grinned her satisfaction. "It's perfect."

After tearfully leaving Amy in Edith Campbell's care, Cassie walked her passport application through the inevitable red tape, and before she knew it, Jade, formerly Cassie McBride of Gallagher City, Oklahoma, found herself seated in the first-class section of a jetliner bound for Nairobi.

Africa was an amazing world apart. The raw and wild landscape was more powerful, more compelling, than Jade ever could have imagined. Even in the comparative safety of the luxurious safari tent, her adrenaline pulsed when the morning mist broke and she saw Mount Kilimanjaro filling the sky from neighboring Tanzania in almost theatrical splendor.

"It's incredible," she breathed, staring awestruck at the looming, snow-covered mountain.

"Not as incredible as you, *cherie,*" Stephan Riboud said. The photographer had not bothered to conceal his aggravation when he'd learned that Nina Grace had sent him a rank amateur. One look at Cassie and he appeared to change his mind. "You've definitely got it."

"It?" Jade asked absently, distracted by the sound of elephants out on the savanna.

*"Pulpeuse."*

"I'm sorry. I don't speak French."

Stephan lifted his shoulders in a distinctly Gallic shrug. "It's difficult to translate. Suzy Parker had it. So does Veruschka. And, on the rare occasion she allows a picture taken of herself with that *merveilleux* gap between her strong white teeth, Lauren Hutton.

"But you, *cherie,*" he said as he broke a bougainvillea blossom off a nearby branch and slipped it into her thick hair, "have it, as you Americans say, in spades."

Although she was in Africa for only eight days, to Cassie it seemed like a lifetime. Stephan set a relentless pace, moving them from the coffee and tea plantations, to the cedar forests and moors, to the jewellike lakes dotting the green Great Rift Valley floor, to the snow-dusted flanks of Mount Kenya. It was a land of infinite moods, a land that refused to be tamed.

While Stephan's camera clicked away, Cassie fed sugarcane to thick-skinned rhinos outside thatched huts built for the famous author and aviator Beryl Markham, raced with doe-eyed impalas across a polo field where electric wires had been strung to deter elephants, and swam in a lake where the shoreline had once been the site of leopard-drawn chariot races.

Nina had given her a copy of *Out of Africa* to read on the plane to Nairobi, so when Stephan decided to photograph her wearing a long, flowing white gauze dress, dining at a damask-draped table set with glittering crystal, Royal Worchester china, and sparkling silver, Cassie found it a simple task to imagine that she was a heroine in one of Isak Dinesen's works—a member of the so-called "White Tribe of Africa"—awaiting the arrival of her aristocratic lover. Behind her, gazelles and zebras were grazing peacefully.

The following day, she put on a man's white sleeveless T-shirt, khaki shorts, and lace-up leather boots to pose with a Masai warrior, her spear uplifted, a falcon perched on her leather-glove-clad arm.

*"Bon, bon,"* Stephan said approvingly, snapping away as she turned this way and that, her gaze absolutely ferocious. He had no way of knowing that the fierce look in Cassie's eyes came from her fantasy of driving her borrowed spear through Quinlan Gallagher's black heart.

On the final day in the country, Stephan took the crew to a private wildlife preserve along the Laikipia Escarpment. It was approaching dusk; a molten sun poured streamers of fiery colors down on them. Accustomed to humans, the zebras, giraffes, lions, and Cape buffalo ignored the woman in a minuscule fringed fake tiger-skin bikini lounging beside their watering hole.

"You're thinking of a man," Stephan demanded as he snapped away with his Nikon, trying to catch the light before it disappeared. "A dark, mysterious man. A man in shadows, a man with secrets. Secrets you yearn to know."

Although she thought she'd managed to exorcise Roarke Gallagher from both her mind and her heart, Stephan's words brought memories of that afternoon in the storm cellar flooding back. The afternoon Amy had been conceived.

Jade slowly lifted her arms and seductively combed her hands through her hair while looking at the camera from beneath heavy lashes. Desire, hot, dark, and dangerous, gleamed in her slanted, catlike eyes.

She was smiling in a secretive, feminine way. The invitation in that smile would make any male with blood still stirring in his veins be willing to follow her to hell and back. She was the kind of woman who could drive a man mad; she was the kind of woman a man would be eager to do anything for.

*"Magnifique,"* Stephan enthused. "You are melting my lens, Jade. Christ, if Eve looked anything like you do at this moment, I understand why Adam was not able to resist biting into that apple."

He continued to click away, even as he talked. "I fall in love with you, *cherie,* every time I look at you. Every time you look at me," he crooned encouragingly. "You are almost enough to make me wish I'd been born heterosexual, *ma chère,"* he said, giving Jade what she suspected was his ultimate compliment.

On her last night in Africa, while the rest of the crew partied on Stephan's stash of Colombian red, Jade sat alone by the campfire and contemplated how far she'd come in the last ten days. And not just in miles, although Kenya was admittedly miles and worlds away from Gallagher City, Oklahoma. Or even New York.

She was no longer that naive young girl who'd worshipped Roarke Gallagher. Neither was she the frightened young woman Quinlan Gallagher ran out of town. Her experiences had tested her, made her strong, encouraged her to take risks.

Staring up into the vast, star-strewn black sky, Jade decided that she liked the adventurous woman she'd become.

# *Ten*

*April 1983*

In a year, Jade's life had changed completely. The instant the French *Elle* hit the newsstands, she was declared the "New Face of the Decade." On a list that included British model-turned-actress Rachel Ward, *Harper's Bazaar* named her one of the most beautiful women in America.

Nina kept her booked months in advance; her hourly rate soared into the stratosphere.

Still, Jade lived frugally given her income, eschewing the drugs, clothes, and parties on which so many of her contemporaries frittered away their money. Models and photographers soon discovered that they could dine out for weeks on tales of Jade's thrift. One amusing anecdote had her hoarding miniature soap and shampoo bottles taken from hotel rooms. It was true.

Although the hungry days were behind her, Jade's dream of working at an auction house had gradually changed to the more ambitious goal of owning her own auction house.

"Don't you think that dream is a bit out of reach?" Nina had asked carefully when Jade told her of her plans.

"I'm not talking about a house on the scale of Sotheby's or Christie's, or even Bentley's," Jade had assured Nina. "What I had in mind was something more manageable, something along the lines of Bonhams in London, where I'd conduct perhaps eight or ten sales a year. Maybe only a sale every quarter in the beginning."

"Why not just open a gallery? Or an antiques business?"

Always pragmatic, Jade had already considered those businesses and had discarded the idea. "Too boring. I keep thinking back on the first auction I attended with Miss Lillian. Although the gemstones were incredible, it was the sale itself that excited me that day. I'll never forget the way all those powerful people had put themselves into the hands of the auctioneer. I knew that day I wanted to be the person holding the gavel, that I wanted to be the one in control."

She smiled self-deprecatingly. "I know that sounds arrogant, and more than a little bit impossible, but who would have thought that Cassie McBride, from the wrong side of the tracks, would someday be an international fashion model?"

The smile faded and Jade turned more thoughtful. "I know it's a long shot," she admitted. "But I have to try, Nina. Because if I don't, I'll end up dwelling bitterly on what might have been, like my mother did."

And so, she worked toward her illusive goal, earning more money than she ever would have dreamed possible. With the exception of time spent with her daughter, whom she adored, Jade lived in her own universe. A universe consisting solely of work. Soothing, predictable work.

Shortly after Amy's second birthday Ellen Walters, the therapist at Columbia, told Jade of a couple who, using their own techniques for teaching the deaf, were achieving remarkable results with children diagnosed as being far more hearing impaired than Amy.

"They run a group home," the therapist said. "In Brooklyn."

"I'm not putting Amy in a home," Jade repeated the vow she'd made so many times before.

"I'm not suggesting that she live with the Kings. However, if she were to spend a few hours each day there, the same way other children attend preschool, I believe that she'd benefit greatly from the social interaction with the other children. I happen to know the Kings have an opening," she said with an encouraging smile. "If you'd like, I could recommend they take Amy."

Telling the therapist that she would have to see the school herself first, Jade made the trip to nearby Brooklyn. The group home was on East Forty-second Street, a neat, tree-lined block with white picket fences. All the houses on the block were flying the American flag, giving it the festive look of the Fourth of July.

Jade knocked on the bright red door, causing a dog somewhere inside the house to bark. She could also hear the high, raised voices of children and the steady, driving beat of Michael Jackson's "Beat It."

The door was opened by an open-faced woman in her early fifties, casually clad in a pair of jeans and an oversize gray New York Yankees sweatshirt. "Hello, Jade," she said with a smile. "We've been expecting you. Please, come in."

Jade was wearing a red Oscar de la Renta suit and a white silk blouse she had unearthed in the back room at Loehmann's. The skirt brushed the top of her knees, the blouse had a high, ruffled neckline, and the jacket was fitted at the waist and squared off at the shoulders. Red-and-white spectator pumps completed the look. The minute she entered the house, she realized she was overdressed.

The dog Jade had heard barking was of indiscriminate parentage. It was also the size of a Buick. He took to her immediately, jumping up to leave muddy footprints on the front of Jade's skirt.

"Down, Rowdy!" Jeanne King grabbed the dog's collar.

A group of children raced into the room, tugging at the dog with filthy hands, scolding and laughing at the same time as they dragged him away.

"They're making mud pies in the backyard," Jeanne explained with an apologetic glance at Jade's skirt. "I'm afraid Rowdy has never learned he's not one of the kids. Let me get you a damp rag."

"Don't worry about it." Jade looked out the window at the backyard where children and dog were rolling on the lawn beneath a spreading elm tree. "I always wanted a dog."

"Terrific. You can have Rowdy. Cheap."

Jeanne King took Jade on a tour of the comfortably cluttered home. Handprints of all sizes smudged the woodwork. The carpeting was worn and spotted. "Winnie, our six-year-old, made grape Kool-Aid last week," Jeanne explained away one particularly vivid purple stain. "Unfortunately, she didn't quite make it outside with the pitcher."

Jade remembered when she'd been Winnie's age and had accidentally spilled milk while fixing Belle's breakfast. It had taken a week for the bruise on her cheek to fade.

Although the furnishings—none of which matched—were ancient enough to classify as relics, and toys and games were scattered all over the floor, Jeanne King had created a bright, airy atmosphere. Jade could imagine Amy eating breakfast in the cheerful yellow kitchen with crayon drawings covering the refrigerator door. She could see her playing with the colorful blocks piled high on one shelf of the homemade bookcase.

The other shelves were a confused hurly-burly of picture books, record albums, and stuffed animals.

What she refused to envision was her daughter sleeping in the cozy bedroom with the faded flower-sprigged wallpaper and the rainbow hand-painted across the ceiling. Fortunately, thanks to Edith, that wouldn't be necessary.

The woman had turned out to be a wonder—part nanny, part teacher, part housekeeper. She did all the shopping and cooking, took Amy to therapy, and practiced the audiology exercises with both mother and child. In the beginning Jade had argued that Edith was doing too much, but the grandmotherly woman had said that fussing over Amy and Jade gave renewed meaning to her life. And since she'd seemed absolutely sincere, Jade gave up protesting.

"You'll want to meet the kids," Jeanne said, taking Jade outside. In the corner of the yard, Jade saw they had planted a vegetable garden. Seed packets depicting radishes, carrots, and cherry tomatoes had been stapled to wooden stakes.

Jade had been apprehensive about coming. But now, as she was introduced to the six children, ranging in age from eighteen months to twelve years, Jade watched the sibling interchange going on between them and felt encouraged.

Most of them wore behind-the-ear aids; however, one little girl, who was obviously profoundly deaf, wore a black box strapped to the front of her brightly colored Big Bird T-shirt. Engaged in a spirited game of tag, the little girl seemed oblivious to the outward sign of her infliction.

The children's hands were flashing a mile a minute, and to Jade's surprise, some were talking amazingly well. No one seemed to mind that some of the others couldn't hear what they were saying. The little girl's heavy aid began to whistle shrilly; Jade watched a boy about seven, wearing dual aids and thick glasses, run over to her and casually turn down the volume.

"Some of them speak so well," Jade murmured, more to herself than to Mrs. King. "I hadn't expected that." In truth, over the past year of therapy, she'd come to the conclusion that Dr. Greene's diagnosis concerning Amy's eventual ability to communicate orally had been overly optimistic.

"All deaf children, like hearing children, are different," Jeanne King said. "And they achieve different things. That being the case, it's a mistake to expect them all to talk perfectly, which is why we use the TC approach here. Do you know anything about Total Communication?"

Many of the books Jade had read since Amy's diagnosis had argued for one or the other methods used in teaching the deaf: signed communication versus oralism. "I know that it's a philosophy that espouses the belief that sign is a perfectly acceptable support to oral skills."

"That's it exactly." Jeanne King's smile reminded Jade of the gold stars teachers used to reward perfect papers. "We total communicationalists believe—like the oralists—that a child must be able to learn language.

"However, since many deaf speakers admittedly have unintelligible speech, and others find lip reading difficult, we feel that sign language and finger spelling are natural adjuncts to lip reading, listening, and speaking.

"So, while we do strive for speaking skills, we believe that signing is also an acceptable way for the deaf to communicate," Jeanne assured Jade. Her hands moved in graceful harmony with her words. "In fact, if you agree to let Amy come here, you'll be expected to sign as well."

"I've learned some basic signs."

"Good. Then you've already got a head start."

"I've been trying to communicate with Amy," Jade admitted. "And some days I think she understands, but other days, I'm not so sure."

"It's difficult," Jeanne agreed with a compassionate smile. "And I'm sure your work, along with the therapy Amy has received, has given her a good foundation on which to start. But since our objective is to give the children the skills necessary to live in the hearing world, we'll also be spending a lot of time working on oral skills."

She put her arm around the oldest girl, twelve-year-old Jennifer. "As a matter of fact, the only reason we have room for Amy is that Jenny is transferring to a public school in the fall. Aren't you, sweetie?"

Jennifer's thin, freckled face, surrounded by a halo of carrot-orange hair, split into a broad grin. "Yes, I am."

Observing the obvious pride and excitement on the girl's face, Jade felt another faint flutter of hope.

She spent three hours at the house, meeting Jeanne's husband, David, a pediatrician who had abandoned his private practice in Manhattan to join his schoolteacher wife in running this extraordinary home, utilizing teaching methods they'd found effective with their own son, who'd been born profoundly deaf.

"Where is your son, now?" Jade asked politely.

"He's living in Manhattan," David said.

"He's in his final year at Columbia," Jeanne added with obvious maternal pride.

That alone would have been enough to impress Jade with the couple's credentials, but more important was their attitude. Although the Kings were interrupted innumerable times during her visit, they never displayed irritation or impatience. They were as warm and loving as if they were the children's parents. Even more loving than many, she decided, thinking back on her own childhood with Belle.

Jade arranged to have Amy begin attending the King's extraordinary school the following day. Within six months the two-year-old's progress was so remarkable that Jade allowed herself, for the first time since Amy's earth-shattering diagnosis, to feel truly positive about her daughter's chances to lead a fulfilling, normal life.

# Eleven

Jade was sitting in the library of The Asia Society on Park Avenue, trying to keep her mind on the paper she was writing on Taoist themes in Far Eastern art.

She was as nervous as a long-tailed cat in a roomful of rocking chairs. And even though she knew that the expression was something Cassie— never the chic Jade—would have used, she couldn't think of a better description of how she felt.

But she couldn't concentrate. Not today. Not when she'd finally been granted an interview with Reginald Bentley.

Her meeting with the auctioneer was not for almost an hour, but the slim gold minute hand of her watch seemed to be barely creeping around the rectangular face. When she realized that she'd read the same page for the last ten minutes without absorbing a single word of the essay contrasting Taoist and Buddhist themes during the Yuan dynasty, Jade gave up. She returned the leather-bound book to the shelf and headed for Bentley's.

Her heart was pounding as she approached the copper front door of the auction house, pounding so fast and so hard that she feared the doorman would be able to hear it. Her mouth was horribly dry; she licked her lips, a mistake, she realized, when she caught the doorman's gaze directed at her mouth. From the gleam of male appreciation in his eyes, she realized she'd been recognized.

She had dressed carefully for the interview, in a dramatic embroidered pink-and-black wool Geoffrey Beene suit that should have clashed with her wild mass of tawny hair, but didn't. Her earrings were gleaming drops of jet, reaching almost to her shoulders. Over the suit she was wearing a Russian sable coat and matching hat borrowed from Fendi. Her buttery suede gloves had been a Christmas gift from Nina.

Rather than trying to compete with the daughters of New York's Old Money, Jade had opted to look the part of the glamorous cover girl she suspected Reginald Bentley was dying to meet. She remembered from her days with Miss Lillian that the auctioneer had a weakness for celebrities.

The doorman opened the heavy door with a flourish. Jade entered the waiting room where she'd suffered such horrid humiliation. The current desk was a French veneer writing table from the mid-nineteenth century, *worth around four thousand dollars*, Jade estimated almost automatically. Although the desk and the woman behind it had changed, they both still exuded an unmistakable aura of Old Money.

"Good morning," Jade greeted the receptionist with a great deal more self-confidence than she had the last time she'd come here. "I have an appointment with Mr. Bentley. My name is—"

"Oh, I know who you are," the woman breathed. She was gazing up at Jade the same way Amy looked at a chocolate chip cookie. "Would you mind autographing this for me?"

She pulled that month's *Cosmopolitan* from the middle drawer of the desk. It was the third time Jade had graced the magazine's glossy cover, and for this issue the art director had gone for broke, dressing her in a sheer black lace bodysuit embroidered with beaded flowers. The look in Jade's eyes invited a man to mentally pick those flowers.

"Of course." She was surprised, but guessed even Old Money was occasionally tempted by sexy *Cosmo*.

She accepted the gold Waterman fountain pen the woman held out to her and wrote her name with a flourish. At that moment the inner door opened and Reginald Bentley rushed in.

"What on earth are you doing, Kimberly?" he snapped, clearly aghast. "You have no business harassing Jade this way."

His concern for her was amusing considering the way he'd treated her five years ago. Jade wondered if he even recognized her as that sorry, pregnant waif who'd begged him for a job and decided that he didn't. Her metamorphosis was too extreme.

"It's no bother, Mr. Bentley," she assured him with the smile that had become famous all over the world. Despite the smile, there was a cool distance to her, concealing what had once been shyness and was now reserve. "I'm flattered when someone recognizes me."

That was not exactly true, but having swallowed her pride to return for yet another attempt to land a job, Jade didn't want to get off on the wrong foot. She pulled an ivory envelope from her Fred Joaillier crocodile bag. She'd gotten the one-of-a-kind bag at a substantial discount after appearing in a Christmas advertisement for Fred's jewel-encrusted evening bags.

"I've brought a recommendation from Dennis Lyons." Jade had finally reenrolled at NYU. Dennis Lyons was the professor of Jade's antiques recognition class; he was also the man in charge of the student internship program. "He'll confirm that I'm very good at verifying provenances."

Since class had begun in September, Jade had spent every free moment in the fine arts section of the university library, locked away in the stacks, researching the past ownership of items Lyons had borrowed from their owners and brought to class.

Her dedication had paid off by landing her at the top of her class and earning the respect of her professor, who'd suggested the possibility of her interning at Bentley's in the first place.

"Oh, goodness, a formal letter of recommendation isn't necessary," the auctioneer insisted, even as he plucked the envelope from Jade's outstretched gloved hand. "Dennis described your many attributes over a lovely dinner of grilled partridge at the Knickerbocker Club last night." He was practically gushing. "I assured him that we'd certainly be able to find a position for a woman of your vast talents."

Personally, Jade thought that the only reason Bentley was hiring her was because of her admitted star appeal, but as Belle had always told her, beggars couldn't be choosers.

"Thank you, Mr. Bentley," she said silkily, flashing him another smile designed to bring a man to his knees. "I can't wait to see what you have in mind."

"I thought we'd put you in the estate acquisitions department," he said. When he began explaining his plan for her, Jade's spirits momentarily sagged. "Your duties will be to read the obituary columns," he said. "Then call up survivors and offer our services." He smiled encouragingly. "Of course, in your case, if you can manage to talk the survivor into a personal interview, I'm sure your fame and charm will help you close the deal."

"I don't want to offend you, Mr. Bentley," Jade said carefully, "and I'm certain that I must be mistaken, but it sounds as if you're hiring me to be a cutie."

Jade knew that the vast majority of good American antiques were brought onto the market by individuals known as pickers. A picker would cruise the countryside, looking for old houses. Often these pickers would hire *cuties*—attractive young women—to sweet-talk the owners of the houses into talking to their boss.

Jade's accusation caused a red flush to rise from the gallery owner's starched wing collar. "Of course that wasn't my intention," he said stiffly. "Still, you are a charming woman, Jade. There's no law that says you shouldn't take advantage of your God-given gifts. And then, after you've learned more about our business, we can reevaluate your position."

Jade was trying to decide what to do next to prove that she deserved a more responsible position than charming grieving individuals out of their inheritances when she noticed a transaction taking place across the room. A young man dressed in a Brooks Brothers suit was negotiating with a matron of indeterminable age about of piece of Mesoamerican jade the woman had brought in for consignment.

Jade realized that if she wanted Reginald Bentley to look beyond her glamorous image, she must first get his attention. She had learned that most Central American carvings coming to market were modern fakes, and that even most of the authentic old ones—by some estimates as many as eighty percent—were not actually jadeite. She decided the time was right to play a hunch.

"Excuse me, Mr. Bentley, I'll be right back." She walked over to the couple. "I apologize for interrupting," she said, "but I couldn't help noticing your magnificent Mayan mask." She gave the woman her dazzling smile.

From the way the irritated frown instantly disappeared from the woman's face, Jade knew she'd been recognized. "It's Copán, isn't it?" Jade asked.

"That's what the appraiser told my mother," the woman nodded. "My grandfather collected pre-Columbian art before it became fashionable. Personally, I've never seen the attraction, most of it's so primitive and ugly." She patted her ash blond hair. "Although I have always liked jade."

"So have I," Jade said. "I saw my first piece when I was still a girl and fell in love. Over the years, I've tried to learn all I could about the stone."

She ran her fingers over the intaglio of twisted snakes adorning the plaque. "And I do hope you won't be offended, but I don't believe this is jadeite."

The woman bristled visibly. "Of course it is! My grandfather bought it from a very reputable dealer." She named a century-old Madison Avenue gallery. "And it's been appraised twice since then."

Reginald Bentley, observing the woman's irritation from across the room, hurried over. "Is anything wrong, Mrs. Van Pelt?"

"I was just about to explain," Jade said, before the affronted matron could answer, "how archaeologists working in Central America have confused jade's worth by their introduction of the term *cultural jade* to describe any green stone carved by Mesoamericans.

"An inaccuracy that unfortunately has been reinforced by museum and gallery owners all over the world who decreed that the actual substance doesn't matter so long as the piece was authentic in terms of its date and origin, and was green. . . . Which makes you wonder why they don't just call all yellow metal gold."

She held the plaque in question up to the light. "This particular piece looks like albite."

"What makes you an expert?" the woman demanded, clearly shaken and just as clearly determined not to show it.

"I'm not an expert," Jade said. "At least not yet." She turned to Reginald Bentley. "There's a simple test to verify the stone," she said. "If you'd care to try it."

"I've never heard of any test that proves conclusively whether or not a stone is jadeite," he argued, his earlier unqualified admiration of Jade fading. She watched the dual desires—the man's unwillingness to insult a client and his equal unwillingness to purchase a fake—warring on his aristocratic features.

"It's not a well-known test," Jade conceded. "But since jadeite's specific gravity is three-point-two to three-point-four, if you put it in a mixture of methylene iodide, blended to a specific gravity of three-point-zero, it will sink. Nephrite, albite, serpentine, and chrysoprase, on the other hand, are lighter and will float."

"Even if that's true, wouldn't the chemicals harm the stone?" asked Reginald's dapper employee, who'd thus far remained silent during the exchange.

"It's perfectly harmless," Jade said. "And amazingly accurate. At least that's what I've read. Scientists at the Smithsonian analytical labs are the ones who devised the test. I'm sure they'd be more than willing to explain the process if you were to phone them."

Reginald Bentley rubbed his chin as he considered her words. "Mrs. Van Pelt—" he began carefully.

"I already know what you're about to suggest," the woman said, shooting a blistering glare Jade's way. "And although I should refuse on principle, since I have absolutely no doubt that the appraisers—the most respected in the business, I might add—are correct, I will permit you to test the plaque. To prove its authenticity.

"I must warn you, however, if anything at all should happen to my grandfather's treasure, you'll be hearing from my lawyer."

She gave Jade one last withering look, then stalked from the auction house.

"Well, now," Jade said after a long pause. She managed, with effort, not to reveal her own trepidations that the woman might be correct after all, which certainly wouldn't help her chances of gaining employment. "Where were we?"


Nina stopped by Jade's apartment after work. "Well," she said the minute Jade opened the door, "don't keep me in suspense."

Jade grinned. "I got it."

"Congratulations. Although I still can't figure out how on earth you're going to juggle a job with modeling and classes and making time for Amy." She tugged off her feather-trimmed suede gloves. "You're already burning the proverbial candle at both ends, Jade. Sometimes I find myself wondering how you fit in time to breathe."

"I'll manage." *Somehow,* Jade tacked on silently. As it was, she charged through life like a machine, never stopping to relax. She knew that she was becoming the kind of woman everyone admires and no one wants to be like.

"Well, if you're happy, I'm happy," Nina said. "Will you be conducting auctions?"

"Don't I wish. Bentley put me to work in the client services department which, while not what I was hoping for, is definitely better than working the ambulance brigade."

"The what?"

When Jade explained, Nina couldn't keep the shock from her face. "But that's—"

"Gruesome?" Jade supplied. "Macabre? Offensive? How about all of the above?" She shrugged. "The truth is that I probably would have been willing to do it, if it was the only way I could get my foot in the door. But then there was this little incident with a piece of alleged jadeite that made the man decide perhaps I knew something about the business, after all."

She went on to tell the story of Mrs. Van Pelt's pre-Columbian plaque. "Bentley called me just ten minutes ago and told me that the plaque floated, which meant I was right about it probably being albite. That's when he offered me the job in client services. He also hinted that after I graduate he might move me into appraisals."

"It really is terrific news," Nina said. "And now that you're going to be even busier than ever, why don't you let me give you the name of a good decorator. So you can finally do something with this apartment."

Nina and Jade were sitting in canvas directors chairs in the living room of the apartment Jade had bought five months earlier. The apartment had six rooms, a view of the East River, and a visible lack of furnishings.

Although Jade had decorated Amy's room, creating a flowered bower fit for a fairy-tale princess, and Edith's room was crammed nearly to the ceiling with the furniture and memorabilia collected in thirty-five years of marriage, the remainder of the apartment continued to look nearly the same as it had the day Jade moved in. The only additions were a few scattered folk art pieces collected in her travels.

Jade laughed. "One of these days I'm going to surprise you," she said. "You'll visit and discover the place draped in chintz."

"That's when I'll know the world is coming to an end. I'm serious, Jade, anyone would think you're a welfare case."

"I hadn't realized saving money was a sin."

"These are the Reagan eighties," Nina countered. "The years of wretched excess. You're supposed to be up to your gorgeous neck in debt. This place is depressing. It reminds me of a nun's cell."

A perfect analogy, Jade decided. It matched her sex life.

"Didn't I show you those posters I bought last week?"

"Antique circus posters for Amy's room don't count. You've got enough stuff in there for triplets."

"Much of it from Aunt Nina."

"I buy the kid stuff because I love an excuse to go into toy stores. You, on the other hand, are trying to ease your own misplaced guilt."

"It isn't exactly misplaced," Jade murmured.

"Don't tell me that you still believe you're responsible for Amy's deafness?"

"No," Jade said, not quite truthfully. "But I do feel guilty about spending so much time away from her. I know that all the experts say that quality time is what matters, and I can believe that in here"—she tapped her head—"but in my heart, I'm afraid that after she grows up, all Amy will remember of her mother is a lifetime of saying goodbye."

"Don't be ridiculous. I can't remember the last time you missed spending a Sunday with Amy. Why, just last month you raced back from that *Town and Country* swimsuit spread in Morocco."

"Children need their mothers when they're sick," Jade insisted, trying to recall one instance when her own mother had nursed her through an illness.

"She had chicken pox," Nina pointed out. "Surely Edith was capable of spreading calamine lotion on her tummy."

"It was my responsibility."

"Supermother lives," Nina muttered.

"Hardly."

Between the Kings' excellent teaching methods and Edith's coaching, Amy was progressing wonderfully. Her vocabulary was equal to that of many hearing four-year-olds, she was beginning to understand such abstract concepts as time, her ability to pick up and recognize sound was improving, and she was unmistakably happy. Still, Jade often experienced a painful tinge of jealousy whenever she saw Amy respond to Edith as a child would to a mother.

"How's school?" Nina asked in a not very subtle attempt to change the subject.

"The course on pre-Columbian art is a bear. And it doesn't help that the professor drones on and on. But, since that class helped me land my job today, I'm never going to complain again. Fortunately, not all my subjects are so dry. In fact, my Renaissance art history professor makes every class an event."

"Is the Renaissance professor a man or a woman?"

"A woman. She's an artist herself; you should see her work."

"Damn."

"What's wrong?"

"I was hoping some sexy artist had you all excited."

"You've been watching "Dynasty" again," Jade accused.

"Guilty. But these days, with my schedule, not to mention all the nasty diseases going around, watching Joan Collins bed all those gorgeous young studs is as close to a sex life as I get."

She sighed. "Maybe I ought to just sell the agency and establish an order of Episcopalian nuns." She looked around the room again. "And you can decorate the convent.

"By the way," Nina said, when she and Jade had stopped laughing, "did you happen to see the headline in yesterday's *Post?*"

"The one about me having a flaming affair with Mick Jagger?" Jade shook her head in disgust. "All I did was go to Jerry Hall's birthday party and immediately everyone thinks I'm trying to lure the man away from her."

"If that's what you had in mind, from the picture, you certainly were wearing the right bait," Nina said. "Where on earth did you find that skimpy gold lamé T-shirt dress?"

"Stephan Riboud's latest lover is a dress designer. He's opened a little boutique in Milan and I agreed to help give his career a boost by wearing one of his dresses to Jerry's party."

"All the speculation about who you're sleeping with is your own fault, you know," Nina pointed out. "The way you keep hiding out here with Amy and Edith when you're not working or going to school has everyone suspecting that your mysterious disappearances are trysts with a famous married lover. You're more elusive than Jackie O."

Jade stood up and walked over to the window, looking out at the Pepsi-Cola sign glowing across the river. "I have no intention of subjecting Amy to the press."

"I can understand that," Nina said. "But we both know that's not your only reason for keeping your child a secret."

Jade turned around, her stony expression sagging. "You're right, I don't want Roarke to know she exists. Amy's father didn't want her. So she's mine."

"I'm still amazed that no one from your home town has recognized you."

"The change was too drastic. Besides, no one in Gallagher City would ever expect Cassie McBride to end up with her picture on the cover of *Vogue.*"

In a subterfuge that had become a way of life, Jade always wore a blond wig—cut in a sedate chin-length bob—whenever she left the apartment with her daughter. She'd learned early on in her career that fame came with its own price, the foremost being a lack of privacy. Fortunately, her wild mane of fiery red hair was so much a part of her professional image that no one had ever connected the attractive young mother with the famous Jade.

"Still, considering your mother's condition—"

"My mother may be an alcoholic, but she's not stupid. I've already warned her that if she breathes so much as a word about my life to anyone, the gravy train stops."

Jade's tone was hard. And final. "Besides, like all drunks, my mother's universe has always revolved around herself. She'd die before admitting to anyone that her daughter had succeeded where she had failed."

Before Nina could comment, they were interrupted by a miniature whirlwind. "Aunt Nina!" Amy ran into the room, waving a piece of paper which she dropped into Nina's lap. "I colored a pitdure for you."

In her enthusiasm, her child's fingers rushed at the words, leaving one unfinished before hurrying on to the next. Once having discovered the power of language, Amy babbled away continually, proving Jade's earlier fears that she would never talk to be groundless. And although her speech was still filled with *dese* and *dis* and *dats,* Jade thought there was no sweeter sound in the world than that of her daughter's voice.

Nina picked up the paper, taking in the bright yellow elephant clad in a fluorescent pink Santa suit and carrying a blue bag filled with gaily wrapped presents. The sky above was a bright emerald green, the North Pole ice had been colored royal purple.

"It's beautiful." Nina moved her hand in a circle across her face.

"It Babar and Fadder Chritmad."

Nina nodded. "I see that. And thank you. I'll put it up on the wall in my office." She emphasized her words with her hands. Although Nina was not fluent in signing, between her lips and her hands, she was able to get her point across.

"I gonna be in a pway. At twool," Amy volunteered.

At the suggestion of Jeanne King, who'd observed Amy's love of dressing up and role-playing, Jade had enrolled her daughter in a newly established theater program for deaf children.

"I heard," Nina said. "Your mama tells me you're going to be a tree."

Amy nodded. "A bid twee. In de forest. And I got a codtume. With bwanches and Middus Campbell made me a bird nedt to put on one ob my bwanches." She lifted her arms like tree limbs and began swaying in an imaginary breeze.

"I can't wait to see it," Nina assured her with a smile.

"Amy." Jade tapped her on the shoulder, capturing her attention. She crouched down so she could be at eye level with her daughter. "Why don't you sit down on the rug? And color a picture for Mama?"

Jade had learned to speak in short sentences. She'd also learned that by exaggerating key words and by using longer words that were easier to lip-read, she could increase Amy's comprehension.

"Something pretty that Mommy can take to Greece."

"Oday." She was a beautiful child, with a mass of ebony curls which nearly hid her dual hearing aids and eyes the bright blue of the Mediterranean Sea. She was also sweet, undemanding, and amazingly sensitive to the moods of those around her. "I'll codor the Gwinch."

Jade smiled. "I'd love that."

Nina and Jade exchanged a warm look. "You're a lucky woman," Nina said.

"I know." Jade looked over at her daughter, seated cross-legged on the Berber rug, bent over her coloring book, a fat red crayon clutched in her fist. Her thick curtain of hair concealed her face, but the way she directed all her attention to her work made Jade's heart clench. Roarke had always tilted his head to the side like that when he was concentrating.

Jade shook the memory away. Her love for Roarke was dead. And like all deaths, it had been painful. But she'd survived.

"So," Nina said, dragging Jade from her unpleasant thoughts, "in a few days you'll be lounging around on Seriphos while the rest of us are slogging around in slush and snow."

"You're the one who booked the job," Jade reminded her. "So I can't see that you're in any position to complain. Besides, it'd be difficult to shoot a swimsuit layout here in the city."

"I know." Nina grimaced. "It's a dirty job—"

"But someone has to do it." They both laughed. As if sensing the hearty sound, Amy looked up from her coloring and laughed along with them. It was, Jade decided, a perfect moment. If only it were possible to freeze time.

Two nights later, Jade was doing some last-minute packing for her trip to Greece when the phone rang.

"It's about time you got home," the familiar voice came on the line. "What were you doing? Dancing at some fancy New York club with all your rich friends?"

Jade leaned against the wall, closed her eyes. "No, Mama. I had some last-minute things to buy for my trip."

"What trip? I don't remember you tellin' me about no trip."

"I'm flying to Greece tonight."

"Who would've thought that my little Cassie would turn out to be a real jet setter?'' Belle's words were slurred with alcohol. In the background Jade could hear the unmistakable sounds of a honky-tonk.

"Did you call for some special reason, Mama?" Jade asked.

"That bastard down at the bank says he has to hold your check until it clears. Somethin' about it being from out of state." Belle had to shout to be heard over the sound of the country and western band. "He didn't give a shit when I told him that if I don't get the money right now, I'm gonna get kicked out of my apartment."

Along with trying to save every spare cent from the day she got her first paycheck, Jade had sent regular checks to Belle. More than enough to pay the rent. Obviously, her mother had been on another binge.

"I'll wire you some money."

"Tonight?"

The only thing resembling cash she had in the apartment were the American Express traveler's checks she'd purchased for her trip. "I don't know if I can—"

"I'm not lyin', Cassie. That bastard landlord's gonna throw me out on the street at first light."

Jade glanced down at her watch and sighed. It was late, her plane left at midnight, and she still had to finish packing. "It'll be there in the next two hours. I'll stop at a Western Union on my way to the airport."

"That's my baby."

*Baby.* How old did a person have to be before they stopped being their mother's daughter? Jade wondered. She knew she'd done the right thing letting Belle think that she had an abortion. Because despite what she'd told Nina about Belle promising to keep quiet about her life in New York, Jade knew that as sure as God made little green apples her mother would get drunk one day and tell everyone within listening distance that her famous daughter had given birth to Roarke Gallagher's baby girl.

Jade didn't believe that the family would attempt to take custody of the child Quinlan had denied, but after the way Roarke betrayed her, she didn't want to give him the satisfaction of knowing he had a daughter. Nor did she want to risk Roarke deciding to fulfill his paternal responsibility. She didn't need Gallagher money to take care of her daughter. She and Amy were doing fine all by themselves. And although struggling to be an international sex symbol, student, mother, and breadwinner all at the same time was exhausting, Jade never, for a single moment, resented it. Amy was her pride and joy. The most exquisite of her private pleasures.

# Twelve

Jade was in love. In all her travels, she'd never experienced anything like the timeless beauty of the Greek isle of Seriphos. The climate, the natural beauty, the colors—the whitewashed houses and churches, the turquoise and navy blue of the Mediterranean, Ionian, and Aegean seas, the ocher of the earth—all had a way of paring life down to its simplest elements, offering a sense of relaxation. Or renewal.

At least it had been relaxing, until she saw that familiar tall male figure looking out over the water. Even from a distance, Jade recognized Roarke Gallagher immediately.

He was standing on the white cliff, his eyes hidden by the opaque lenses of his sunglasses, but his mouth was set in a firm, forbidding line that was a distinct contrast to the devastating smile she remembered so well.

Although she was looking at the camera, Jade could feel Roarke's intense gaze as she tried to obey the photographer's command.

Devlin dropped to his knees on the damp sand. "Come on, darlin', you can do better than that," he complained. "Think sex."

That was, unfortunately, all too easy. All Jade had to do was think of Roarke. And remember how his strong hands used to make her body come alive, how his mouth once warmed her flesh.

Jade struggled to follow Devlin's commands, but she knew that her actions were too stiff, her smile forced. When the rain finally cut the session short, Jade was relieved. Until she ran into Roarke on the way back to the hotel.

It had been a long day. Alone in her room, Jade was shivering from the rain and the unexpected encounter. She rubbed the slight ache in the small of her back as she called room service and ordered a pot of hot coffee. Then she went into the bathroom and began to vigorously rub her hair dry with a fluffy white towel.

A very few minutes later, she heard the room service waiter knock on her door. "That was certainly fast."

In Greece, she'd learned to expect excellent albeit leisurely service. The Greeks moved at a different pace than her own whirlwind. Her surprise turned to shock when she opened the door and saw Roarke standing on the other side.

"Go away."

Roarke caught hold of the edge of the door in midslam. "I just want to talk to you, Cassie."

"What are you doing here, Roarke?"

"On the island? Or here, at your door?"

"At my door."

"I don't know."

The honest answer caught her off guard. Part of Jade still wanted to slam the door in his face. But another part of her wanted to show him exactly how much she'd grown up. How far she'd come from that wide-eyed, adoring young girl he'd made love to. Then abandoned.

"I suppose you might as well come in," she said, opening the door the rest of the way.

She sat down on the sofa, crossed her long legs, and continued to rub her hair dry. "You're looking well."

Roarke chose a chair a few feet away. "So are you." There was a desperate yearning in his voice.

She shrugged and tossed the towel onto the bleached wooden table in front of her. "It's my job."

"You don't make it sound very glamorous."

"It isn't. Mostly it's uncomfortable—swimsuits in December, fur coats in July—and boring. But it pays the bills. And," she admitted, "it's the easiest money I've ever made."

A strained silence settled over them. "So, did you ever become an architect?" Jade asked casually, loath to have Roarke know that she'd devoured every word written about him. "Or did you go to work for your father?"

"I haven't been back to Gallagher City since that night."

The night he'd walked out of her life, leaving her pregnant. Jade averted her eyes to prevent him from seeing the pain he'd inflicted. "Your father must be very unhappy." The idea of high and mighty Quinlan Gallagher not getting everything he wanted was almost enough to make Jade smile.

"That's probably the understatement of the century."

"What are you doing on Seriphos?"

"I have my own architectural firm," he told her. "In San Francisco."

He was not telling her anything that she didn't already know. Last year, when she'd been there on location, Jade had looked up his address in the telephone directory.

She had stood outside Roarke's Montgomery Street building, watching the Americans and Japanese rushing in and out of it, clutching their stuffed briefcases and carrying folded editions of the *Wall Street Journal*. She had tried to imagine what she would do if Roarke suddenly walked out the bronze-tinted front door. But of course he hadn't, and after a while she returned to her hotel.

"Your own firm? You must be very successful. But I seem to remember you being determined to work in Europe."

"I've won some recognition," he said. "Although not nearly as much as you. As for the firm, I was lucky enough to get financial backing from Richard Hamilton, because I was willing to establish my office in San Francisco. Hamilton owns Hamilton Construction Company and as much as I wanted to stay in Europe, his offer was too good to turn down."

"I've heard of Hamilton Construction." Jade remembered the photo she'd seen of Roarke and Philippa Hamilton. "You still haven't told me what you're doing here."

"Hamilton's contracted to build an office complex on the island," Roarke said. "I'm looking over sites for him." Jade noticed that he didn't mentioned Hamilton's daughter.

"I see."

Another silence settled over the room, longer than the first. Roarke finally was the one to break it.

"I really am glad that you're doing well, Cassie—uh, Jade."

"Thank you."

"You've changed more than your name, haven't you?"

"What do you mean?" She expected him to say how sophisticated she'd become, but Roarke, as always, surprised her.

"You've built walls around yourself. Walls that weren't there before."

"I don't know what you're talking about," she lied. She'd worked damn hard to construct those walls and they'd done their job well, helping her to survive, keeping any man from ever hurting her again.

"Oh, I think you know exactly what I'm talking about," he countered. "There's just one thing I need to know."

A thousand thoughts raced through her head. Each one focusing directly on Amy. Was this when he finally asked about his child?

"If you really needed money that badly back then, why couldn't you have asked me? I knew about Belle, about how rough it was for you. I would've understood. Why did you feel you had to steal Aunt Lillian's ivory pieces?"

"What?" Jade leaped to her feet, her hands balled into fists on her hips. "After all we shared that summer, how could you have ever believed those vicious lies, Roarke? If you'd truly cared about me, even a little, you never would have believed them. Ever!

"Do you have any idea what it's like to be in jail? Can you even begin to comprehend the fear and degradation I felt? And if that wasn't bad enough, while I was all alone in that filthy cell, having to put up with Sheriff Lockley's obscene comments and dirty looks, I was forced to accept the unpalatable fact that I was just another sexual conquest for you."

"What sexual conquest? What the hell are you talking about?"

"I'm saying that the only reason I could think of for your having deserted me that was that you simply got bored with fucking the hired help."

"I didn't desert you!" Roarke was on his feet as well. "You knew all along that I had to go back to Paris, damnit!"

Anger was like a storm battering away inside her. Jade's body practically vibrated with it. "Of course I did. I just didn't expect you to take off in the middle of the night without saying goodbye."

"I said goodbye," he reminded her. "As for leaving, what did you expect me to do? Sit on my hands and let my father torpedo my work with Guimard? Christ, I left to try to salvage what was left of my career." He shot her a hot, angry look. "Is that why you stole those pieces? For spite?"

She tossed her head back. Their faces were inches apart. Their eyes locked. "Damnit, I never stole anything!" she raged. "And if you truly believe I did, Roarke Gallagher, then you're an even worse bastard than your damn father."

That did it. Comparing him with his brutal, autocratic father snapped the tenuous control Roarke had on his own temper.

"Goddamn you." He thrust his hands into her hair. Heat suffused her. Roarke's mouth crushed hers, demanding retribution, capitulation.

The kiss was a battle of wills, a contest for control. A war. Yet somewhere, deep inside, both knew that the battle had already been lost.

Her breath was knocked out of her as they fell onto the bed, locked in combat. She pressed her hands against his chest; he grasped her wrists and held them above her head.

Memories of Trace raping her on Shelby's bed came flooding back. She could almost smell his liquored breath; she could feel his tongue practically suffocating her as he thrust it down her throat. Fighting against both this man and painful memories of his brother, Jade scissored her bare legs; he shifted so that his body was pressed against hers, pushing her deeper into the soft mattress.

Jade wanted to hate him. She wanted to make love to him. The dual hungers tore through her body like a wildfire. Fury gave way to fear, fear to excitement, and excitement to passion.

Muscles bunched beneath his shirt as he countered every move. His mouth ravaged hers, his lips sped over her face, his teeth scraped the cord in her neck. The fingers of his free hand pressed against her throat. Her pulse beat wildly, fast and uneven.

Jade knew that he could feel her out-of-control heartbeat against his fingertips. "You wouldn't rape me."

"Oh no?" His hand moved slowly down her throat, across her collarbone. Against her will, her blood stirred.

"No." It was only a whisper. Her body had gone very still. Breathless, she stared up at him.

"You and I both know it won't be rape." He untied the robe with one hand and pushed away the thick material. When he buried his mouth in the soft golden flesh of her breast, Jade tried to recall why she shouldn't allow this to happen.

She tried to remember why it was wrong. But then his tongue grazed her taut nipple and needs too long suppressed swept her into a torrent of desire that left her gasping. As if sensing her surrender, Roarke released her hands.

Some small voice of sanity struggled to make itself heard inside her head. "Roarke. I can't."

"Of course you can." When his fingers trailed down her ribcage and over her stomach, she sighed. When his lips followed the trail his fingers had blazed, she trembled.

"Lord, you taste good," he murmured against her heated flesh. "Like coconut oil. And sunshine." His lips nibbled their way up the inside of first one thigh and then the other. "And sex."

Her fingers curled in his hair. Her body arched. She was melting. Like a candle that had been left out too long in the ripe Mediterranean sun. But even as her head spun, Jade reminded herself that she'd already allowed her heart to rule her head once where this man was concerned. To disastrous consequences. She would not—could not—risk making that same mistake again.

"Roarke." She pushed against his chest. "Really. I mean it. I don't want this."

He ran his palm down the axis of her body, smiling grimly when a soft, shuddering sound escaped her parted lips. Then, with a frustrated sigh, he levered himself off her body. "I've never forced a woman. And I'm sure as hell not going to begin with you."

Jade gathered the lapels of the robe together and left the bed. "I think you'd better go."

"Have dinner with me."

"I don't think that would be a very good idea."

It was obvious that Roarke had not gotten where he was today by giving up easily. "Even if I promise to be on my best behavior?"

"Now where have I heard that before?" Jade asked coolly. "Really, Roarke, I would have expected you to come up with a more original line."

Frustration was etched into every line on his face. "It's not a line, damnit."

"Give me one reason why I should trust you."

"You have got to be kidding." His gaze shifted significantly to the bed, reminding Jade of how close she'd come to surrendering. "Before we were lovers, we were friends. Can't we put the past behind us and share a civilized dinner?"

Lingering desire made her rash. "It would have to be an early evening. I have to be back on the beach at sunrise."

"I'll pick you up at six. That way, even allowing for the pace of Greek service, you'll be in bed by nine o'clock. In plenty of time to get your beauty sleep." He ran his knuckles down her cheek. "Not that you need it."

His smile reminded Jade of the Roarke she had once known. The Roarke she had fallen in love with. As he opened the door to leave, the room-service waiter arrived with Jade's coffee and a complimentary pastry.

After Roarke had gone, Jade sat in a rattan chair and sipped the strong brew while she stared at the rumpled bed. Well, she had stopped Roarke from making love to her. She had won the first round. So why did she feel so bad?

Jade soon discovered that there was no such thing as an unromantic dinner on Seriphos. The maitre d', sensing the vibrations between them, smiled knowingly and placed a flickering candle on the table. Her hair, illuminated by the candlelight, gleamed like fiery silk. The owner of the cafe sent over a bottle of wine and the violinist played a medley of seductive ballads, while the waiter serenaded them in a deep, rich bass voice.

"I know that I promised to keep this dinner civilized," Roarke said, when they were alone again. "But I can't sit here another minute without telling you that look like something from a midnight fantasy. That's a great dress!"

The dress, bought that afternoon in the village especially for the occasion, even as Jade had tried to convince herself that she wasn't really buying it for him, was a froth of tropical flowers that bared her sun-kissed shoulders.

Her fingers curled tightly around the stem of her wineglass. "Thank you."

"I suppose men tell you that all the time."

She wasn't about to let him know that her busy schedule, along with her unwillingness to hand over her hard-won control of her life to any man, had kept her away from all liaisons. If the gossip columns were even halfway accurate, Roarke certainly hadn't been living the life of a monk during the time they'd been apart. Jade was damned if she'd let him get the mistaken impression that she'd been saving herself for him.

"I get paid to create fantasies," she said instead.

"And from what I hear, it pays very well."

So he'd read about her, too. Jade rather liked that idea. "I'm doing all right."

The tension built throughout the meal as they tried to keep the conversation casual. But the pauses grew longer, the looks more heated.

By the time they returned to Jade's room, both knew how the evening was going to end.

"We have to talk about it," Roarke said with a definite lack of enthusiasm. "But not now."

His eyes were as deep and blue as the sea outside her french doors. Even as she warned herself against such folly, Jade fell into them. "No," she whispered. "Not now."

The soft admission was all that he needed.

Details blurred as Jade luxuriated in the pure pleasure of cloth being whisked over her warm skin. All the reasons why it wasn't wise for her to be with Roarke this way fled her mind, leaving her only with the need to touch. To be touched. To love. And be loved. If this was insanity, Jade welcomed it with open arms. She wrapped her arms around his neck and clung.

The moonlight wrapped the room in ribbons of silvery light while outside the open window the soft sound of the surf echoed a lover's sighs. The air was moist and heavy with the scent of heat-soaked flowers. Words were not necessary, desires were telegraphed by hands. By lips. By quiet sighs and low moans. He touched and her body burned. She tasted and his flesh flamed.

Lifting himself above her, Roarke looked down into flushed face. Her eyes were open and on his. Her shallow breath was coming in pants, his body was slick with sweat. The arousing scent of passion hung heavy in the room. They stared at one another for a long, charged moment.

Then she opened for him. Her mind, her heart, her body. And when he filled her, Jade wept.

A predawn light was painting the wide sky with fingers of pink and gold when Jade woke to find Roarke propped up on an elbow, looking down at her.

"I didn't truly realize until yesterday how much I'd missed you," he said, brushing a sleep-tousled curl away from her face with a heartbreakingly tender touch.

Jade knew that was her cue to tell him that she had missed him, too. But pride and a deep-seated sense of self-preservation made her keep that secret to herself. "It was your choice," she murmured.

"My choice?" he asked in a dangerous voice that reminded Jade uncomfortably of his father. "How the hell was it my choice?" He yanked on his jeans, left the bed, and began to pace. "Was it my choice you disappeared from Gallagher City without a damn word?"

He stood beside the bed, glaring down at her. "Was it my choice that you didn't answer any of my letters from Paris? Was it my choice that your continued silence left me thinking that all we'd shared that summer meant nothing more to you than a vacation fling?"

Furious, Jade threw back the sheets and leaped from the bed to stand in front of him. "I didn't disappear! I wrote you letters every day from the jail your father and brother put me in! So why didn't you answer?"

"What letters?" Roarke raked his fingers through the thick black hair he shared with his daughter. "I didn't get any goddamn letters."

Either he was the most accomplished liar she'd ever met, or he was telling the truth. "I sent them," she insisted. "And I waited and waited for you to come back and tell people that I wasn't a thief, but you never did."

"Oh, Christ." Roarke pulled her into his arms and held her close. "I never got any letters," he repeated against her hair. "Obviously, the sheriff took the ones you wrote from jail."

"On your father's orders." Jade wondered why she hadn't realized that in the beginning.

"I'd say that's a pretty good guess."

"But I wrote you another one," she said in a voice that was not nearly as strong as she would have liked. "From New York."

"I was moving around a lot that summer. Guimard had replaced me on the project, so I had to find another job." His arms tightened around her, his voice was rough. "But I swear, if I'd known what was happening to you, if I'd known my father had actually had you arrested, I would have said the hell with everything and come back to the States."

Jade wanted to believe him. "I didn't steal those figurines," she said quietly.

Roarke sighed. "I think, deep down, I always realized that," he admitted. "But then Shelby told me how you'd left town and she was so certain—"

"Shelby told you about what happened?" Jade interrupted. "When?"

Roarke thought back. "The end of August. I remember because she was visiting me in Paris and was furious that everything was closed because the French had all gone off on vacation."

Shelby had been in Paris, in August, when her letter would have arrived. "Did she stay with you?"

"Sure?" He glanced down at her, his expression curious. "Why do you—" Jade watched the comprehension dawn. "Surely you don't think she took your letter?"

That's exactly what she thought. But not wanting to ruin what had turned out to be a glorious reunion, Jade shrugged her bare shoulders. "I suppose whatever happened doesn't really matter now."

"No, it doesn't." He cupped her chin in his fingers, lowered his head, and kissed her. Jade heard herself moan as the kiss grew deeper, hotter. "Because we're together," he murmured against her tingling lips. "And that's all that matters."

But Jade knew that it was much more complicated than that. There were so many things still unsaid between them, so many past problems to resolve. And then, of course, there was Amy.

"What time do you have to get to work?" Roarke asked.

"The makeup man is supposed to be here at seven."

Roarke glanced over at the bedside clock. "That's not much time." He lifted her hand and pressed his lips against the inside of her palm. "All the more reason not to waste any more of it talking about things we can't change."

When had she become such a coward, Jade wondered. How could she possibly be afraid of the fragile touch of his lips against her skin? Myriad warnings raced through her mind, but she ignored them. Lifting her face for Roarke's kiss, Jade allowed herself to risk.

Later, still feeling the effects of their lovemaking, Jade lay back in the frothy surf. Although the makeup man had complained about the faint blue circles under her eyes, Brian was in seventh heaven. His camera clicked away, capturing the smoldering sexy look in her eyes.

"I'm surprised the fuckin' water isn't boiling," he said. "Whatever you're thinking of, darlin', for Christ's sake don't stop until I finish this roll."

Tossing her head back, Jade flashed him a seductive smile and thought of Roarke.

When the crew departed Seriphos for New York, Jade remained behind with Roarke. Together they explored the island, urban exiles delighting in the picture-postcard appeal. In the mornings they ate breakfast in hillside cafes where elderly men convened to gossip and argue, walked the winding white-painted streets, and swam in the warm ocean. Then they returned to their room where they closed out the sun with bright blue shutters and spent long lazy afternoons making love.

Evenings were spent in tavernas, laughing, dancing, and singing along with the mad violinists who frequented the island, amusing patrons with their inspired crooning. A moonlit stroll along the beach. Then back to the room where they'd make love again.

If every hour brought them nearer to the time when she would have to return to her world and Roarke to his, Jade refused to dwell on that unhappy thought. All her life she'd worked and planned toward the future. For this one halcyon week she was going to live one day, one hour, one glorious minute at a time.

When they weren't exploring the island, or making love, they talked, sharing bits and pieces of their lives during the five and a half years they'd been apart. To her amazement, when Roarke saw her books and learned that she was supposed to be studying for a test, he actually spent one lazy sunny afternoon quizzing her.

"Pi disk," he read from a text on Chinese art.

"One of six ritual jade pieces used in burial rites by the Chinese, who viewed the stone as a link between earth and heaven, a bridge between life and immortality. It was believed that emperors spoke to heaven through the pi disks," she answered promptly.

"Give the lady a Kewpie doll," Roarke said with a grin. "Now on to the lightning round. "Give me the dates of the Eastern Chou dynasty."

"Seven hundred seventy to two hundred twenty-one B.C."

"How about the Sung dynasty?"

"Nine hundred sixty to twelve hundred seventy-nine."

"Why is the Yurungkax River important?"

"That's easy. Translated to the White Jade River, it was the origin of Chinese jade, known as nephrite, which was at the center of Chinese tradition and civilization for more than five thousand years. The nephrite washed down from the Kunlun mountains, allowing jade pickers to collect the stone after the spring floods.

"Camel caravans on the Silk Road would stop on their way back from the Middle East and harvest huge jade boulders which were carried by camel more than two thousand miles to the emperor's workshops in Beijing." She took a breath. "It was at the Yurungkax in twelve hundred seventy-one that Marco Polo saw jade for the first time."

"Too easy, huh?" He thumbed through the heavy book, skimming over the portions Jade had highlighted in yellow. "Okay. What's the significance of seventeen hundred eighty-four in Chinese art history?"

"That was the date when, following a Burma trade treaty, the first Burmese jadeite arrived in Beijing. The bright green stone was decidedly flashier than Chinese nephrite and immediately displaced the native stone for jewelry and commerce. The Burmese continue to claim, to this day, that the jadeite taken from their land is the only true jade and the source of all Imperial jade, conveniently ignoring China's five-thousand-year legacy of subtle nephrite carvings.''

"I give up." Roarke shook his head in obvious amazement and closed the book. "I always knew you were gorgeous," he said, rewarding her with a kiss. "I didn't realize that you were also brilliant."

Reaching for another text, he picked up an all too familiar white booklet. Jade's blood froze.

"What's this?" he asked, thumbing through her thin manual communications book. Fluency in sign did not come easily, and as both Amy's oral and signing vocabularies increased, Jade had to work even harder to keep up with her daughter.

"It's a book on sign language."

"I can see that. What are you doing with it?"

"I've been doing some volunteer work with a school for physically challenged children," she improvised quickly. "Since a couple of the kids are deaf, I've been trying to learn to communicate with them."

"I'm impressed."

Jade shrugged, hating the way he was looking at her with admiration while she was telling him a lie designed to keep him from learning that he had a child.

"It isn't that big a deal," she murmured. "Can we just get back to work? There are still four more chapters to get through."

Jade was immensely relieved when Roarke discarded the sign language manual, picked up the proper book, and began quizzing her again. Later, they had dinner at the restaurant where they'd had eaten the first night.

After dinner, back in their room, Roarke told her that Trace had died after overturning his Ferrari. His brother had been drinking heavily the night of the accident and his companion, a married truck-stop waitress who'd been thrown free of the car, had suffered severe head injuries and a broken spine. Quinlan had paid the woman's family a hundred thousand dollars for their silence.

Trace had lingered for thirteen horrendous days in the Burn Unit of the Oklahoma City General Hospital before finally succumbing to infection. Having never forgiven Trace Gallagher either for the rape or for framing her by stealing his aunt's figurines, Jade had difficulty expressing sympathy for his suffering.

"What about Shelby?" she asked.

"She's living in Denver, married to the son of an oilman."

"Any children?"

"Are you kidding? My little sister is too busy spending the proceeds from that black gold to settle down and play mother."

Jade was secretly moved when Roarke went on to profess his desire for children. But she remained silent about Amy. If Roarke never received her letters, there was no way he could know that she'd had a child. Her breasts were high and firm, her flesh remained unmarred. There were no stretch marks, no telltale signs to give away her secret.

"Tell me about how you met Richard Hamilton," Jade asked. She really was interested in how he'd met Hamilton's daughter, but not wanting to ask outright about his involvement with Philippa Hamilton, Jade opted for a more subtle approach. "Is he the same Richard Hamilton that *Forbes* listed as one of the ten richest men in the world?"

"That's him. After I couldn't get my job back with Guimard, I interviewed with a bunch of firms in Europe—the ones that were impressed with my credentials offered me jobs that were little more than glorified draftsman positions, and those that offered me more autonomy weren't that prestigious."

"I remember you saying that you wanted to design important buildings," Cassie murmured.

Roarke took her hand and linked their fingers together on his bare chest. "I remember that night, too. And you're right about my not wanting to design ordinary buildings. Unfortunately, most of the European firms had all the geniuses they needed."

"You could have gone back to New York."

"I could have," he agreed. "But that would've been a step backward. Anyway, to answer your question, I was in London, interviewing with a British architectural firm. It had not been one of my more auspicious interviews. Within the first ten minutes it became obvious to both the overly stuffy firm and me that we were not an ideal match.

"I was running out of ideas when I heard that Hamilton was going to be in London, so I managed to finagle an interview. It was my lucky day. It turned out that his mood was every bit as black as mine. He had some problems with a hotel his company was going to build in Zurich. He knew there was something wrong with the plans, but he couldn't tell what."

"And you could?"

"As soon as I looked at the blueprints. Hamilton wanted to build a replica of the old grand hotels of Europe. Unfortunately, the thick squat building he'd ended up with was a parody of Greek revivalism."

"I remember you weren't really a fan of postmodernism."

"That's the understatement of the century," Roarke agreed. "Anyway, when I asked him if he'd be willing to scrap the idea for something more modern, he jutted out his chin like a bulldog and told me that it was supposed to look old, like the city." Roarke smiled, reminiscing. "In a lot of ways, he reminds me of my father, whenever he gets an idea into his stubborn head."

Jade did not want to talk about Quinlan Gallagher. "So what did you do?"

Roarke shrugged. "Not much. It took only a few quick strokes of the pen to eliminate half the columns, an ungainly trio of stoas, and a stone frieze that visually shortened the building."

Jade had read about the hotel in *Architectural Digest*. The magazine had described the building as something Aphrodite would have been proud to claim as her earthly home.

"So he hired you on the spot?"

"As a consultant, with backing to open up my own offices. As I told you, the only catch was that I'd have to come back to the States and move to San Francisco, but since European firms weren't exactly climbing all over one another to hire me, it wasn't that much of a sacrifice. I did make certain that I'd be free to do my own projects. I told you, Hamilton's a lot like Dad. And I spent too many years getting out from under my father's thumb to make that mistake again."

"I've seen pictures of his daughter," Jade said carefully. "She's very beautiful." Philippa Hamilton had always reminded Jade of the other women who worked at Bentley's, the type who had made her feel so gauche that horrible afternoon after she'd first arrived in the city. Like them, Richard Hamilton's daughter was impossibly slim and unbelievably blond. And very, very chic.

"I suppose she is," Roarke agreed easily. "But she's not as beautiful as you."

He shouldn't be able to make her this happy, Jade told herself as he gathered her into his arms. His touch was strong, yet gentle at the same time. A warmth that began somewhere in her lower regions was spreading thickly outward. When his tongue tempted, Jade surrendered. With a soft moan she twined her arms around his neck. Her mind emptied.

Even though it felt incredibly right to be with Roarke again, Jade knew that the past could not be so easily overlooked. She was certainly not the same person she once was and neither was Roarke. They needed time. Time to see if these feelings were more than the product of a moon-spangled, romantic island.

Despite her lofty dreams, Jade was a pragmatist. Life with Belle had taught her at an early age that people who made the mistake of dreaming about happily-ever-afters only ended up being disappointed. Until now, until this magical second chance with Roarke, Jade had never known how seductive happiness could be. And it terrified her.

"Lord, I really do hate to go," Roarke said as he and Jade lay in bed, their limbs tangled and their fingers linked.

Jade had secretly been relieved when Roarke first mentioned that he needed to return to San Francisco. She'd been dreading their parting, but Amy's play was only a few days away and she had no intention of missing her daughter's theatrical debut.

"You can't ignore your work."

"I should have everything wrapped up by next week. Ten days at the most," Roarke said. "Then I'm coming to New York to settle some personal business."

Even as Jade basked in the warmth of Roarke's smile, she had a premonition of something awful lurking in the shadows, some monster in the tunnel of love. Shaking off the disturbing feeling, she lifted her face to his kiss and allowed herself to dream.

He was gone the following morning. Watching his plane soar over the brilliant blue sea, Jade made an important decision: When Roarke came to New York, she was going to tell him about Amy. Because whatever the future held for them, Roarke deserved to know his daughter.

# Thirteen

The Children's Theater of the Deaf's performance of Little Red Riding Hood was held in Soho, in the loft of a massive Greene Street building. Originally a warehouse, the nineteenth-century building, which now housed an avant-garde gallery on the first floor, boasted an exterior facade of Corinthian columns that at first glance appeared to be stone, but was actually cast iron.

The audience consisted solely of family and friends, and the youthful players were poignantly disarming. They seemed so innocent and unaware of the cruelty of the world outside, Jade found herself worrying about their survival if and when they attempted to leave the safety, acceptance, and security of this isolated world of the deaf.

Although two more children had left the Kings' for mainstreaming into the hearing world since Amy's arrival, Jade couldn't help wondering how well they were really faring in a society that was not known to greet the deaf with open arms.

Blinking lights—red, yellow, and white—were used as stage cues and, when necessary, prodding from the teachers on the sideline. While far from professional, the young actors were very enthusiastic.

Amy was too young to have been given a big role. But that didn't stop her from garnering attention. Jade was torn between pride and embarrassment when her daughter, dressed as a tree in a brown leotard and towering green headdress, stole the show.

Rather than remain quietly treelike, Amy's expressive face had revealed an amazing number of emotions: trembling fear when the wolf appeared, exaggerated horror when he ate Little Red Riding Hood's grandma, suspicion when her classmate, clad in a bright red cotton hood, professed doubt about the wolf's appearance, and joy when woodcutter arrived to save the day.

As the boy with the ax chased the wolf from Grandma's house, Amy, carried away with unbridled enthusiasm, abandoned the script and energetically tackled the boy playing the wolf, making it appear that the villainous carnivore had been done in by a falling tree.

"You were wonderful!" Jade said to Amy, when she joined the cast and other parents for punch and cookies. Her fingers flashed with heartfelt enthusiasm. "I'm so proud of you!"

Amy's face was flushed with happiness, her eyes shone like sapphires. "Did you dee everybody cwapping?" Although she still had trouble with her "s" and "l" sounds, her speech therapist had assured Jade that Amy was making amazing progress.

"I did."

"I like thid," Amy decided. "A lot. When I growed up, I gonna be an actredth. And people will cwap for me. Won't dey?"

Amy's vivid imagination had already taken her places she'd never been before, giving her a kind of freedom and opening to worlds not always experienced by the deaf.

Now, as Jade looked down into her daughter's proud and shining face, she knew that just as she had escaped the poverty and meanness of her existence with Belle in Gallagher City, Amy, despite the challenge of her deafness, would succeed at whatever she decided to do.

"Of course they will clap," she answered. She put her hands together and clapped loudly. "And clap and clap and clap—"

Amy took her hand. "Dat's enough cwapping," she said. "The odder kidth will feel bad if I get more 'tention than dem."

Amy was a thoughtful child, intuitively attuned to others' needs and remarkably kind. Just last week Jeanne King had told Jade how they'd taken the children out for ice cream and when they came out of the store, Amy had seen a woman crouched inside a cardboard box across the street.

The woman had started shouting obscenities at the group, but unable to hear, Amy raced across the street and held out her strawberry ice cream cone to the obviously dumbfounded woman, who first fell silent, then began rummaging around in a tattered Bloomingdale's shopping bag. A moment later Amy had returned, a dazzling smile of satisfaction on her face, the bottlecap the woman had given her in exchange for the ice cream clutched in her small hand.

As she sat with her daughter at one of the Lilliputian tables, eating the shortbread cookies one of the mothers had baked and drinking the overly sweet pink punch, Jade thought about Roarke, and bringing him to meet Amy. She knew Roarke would fall in love with his daughter at first sight.

"You look marvelous," Nina said the day after the play. "Greece must have really agreed with you."

Jade's smile spoke wonders. "It did."

"Is there some sexy Greek fisherman I should know about?"

"What did you think of the play?" Jade asked, deliberately changing the subject.

"I told you yesterday—sorry I had to forgo the postplay goodies and dash off to that meeting—but it was terrific. Of course, Amy is always a delight. And growing like a weed. Not to mention the fact that the way she interjected a little improvisation into the play was absolutely inspired. . . . Don't try to dodge the question. Who's the man?"

"She is growing, isn't she?" Jade agreed with a proud smile. "She told me after the play that she wants to be an actress when she grows up."

"Is that possible?" Nina asked, momentarily sidetracked.

"Her teacher told me that there are some deaf theater groups in the country." Jade laughed. "But even if there weren't, Amy would probably just start one of her own."

"She's got her mother's stubbornness," Nina said.

Jade laughed again. "I prefer to think of it as tenacity. She refilled their tea cups. "I saw Roarke."

Nina nearly dropped her cup. "In Greece?"

"In Greece," Jade confirmed.

"Well, that explains why you've been smiling like the Mona Lisa ever since you got back. I take it things went well?"

"Better than well. It was wonderful." Jade grinned. "What would you say if I told you I think I'm in love?"

"I'd say it's about time. So, tell me everything. What did Roarke say when he found out he was a father?"

A guilty flush colored Jade's cheeks. "I didn't tell him."

"What?" Nina leaned forward, about to argue, when the doorman rang.

"Yes, Martin?" Jade answered.

"There's a Mr. Gallagher here in the lobby."

Roarke. Obviously he'd finished up his business sooner than scheduled. "Please send Mr. Gallagher up, Martin."

"Oh, don't go," Jade said when Nina rose to leave. "I want you to meet Roarke." Even the way she said his name, with such pleasure, was an act of love.

Jade flung open the door at the first knock. "Oh." Her heart clenched when she saw Quinlan Gallagher. How did he find her? What did he want? "It's you."

Ignoring Jade's obvious distaste and lack of hospitality, Quinlan glanced past her into the room. "Aren't you going to invite me in, Cassie? After I've come all this way to see you?"

Wanting to slam the door in his face, but needing to know exactly what Quinlan wanted, and whether he'd found out about Amy, she stepped aside.

"What are you doing here, Quinlan?"

Nina sensed the tension in the room. In Jade's voice. "I can stay."

"No." Her expression was as grim as Nina had ever seen it. "Everything's fine."

Nina looked at the man's cruel rugged face and hesitated.

"Really," Jade insisted in a voice that sounded nothing like her own usually strong one.

"If you need anything," Nina murmured as she hugged Jade good-bye, "just call."

"I'll be fine," Jade repeated. Even as she heard herself say the words, she wondered who she was trying to convince. Nina? Or herself?

The moment they were alone, Jade spun on Quinlan. "What the hell do you want?"

Quinlan had never been one to beat around the bush. "I saw your picture on the cover of *Sports Illustrated* a while back, Cassie, and from the way you were flaunting your nipples in that wet white bikini for any Tom, Dick, or Harry down at the barbershop, I knew that you may be rich and famous now, but inside, you're no different from your mama. Which is why, when I heard about you and Roarke playin' house down in the Greek islands, I couldn't believe that a kid of mine would be so stupid twice in one lifetime."

So Quinlan had recognized her. Jade wondered who else knew about her resurrected life. She'd worked so hard to keep the past a secret. Not for her sake, she told herself now. But for Amy's.

Jade glanced down at her watch. Fortunately, Edith had taken Amy to therapy shortly after Nina's arrival; they weren't due to return for another hour.

"What I was doing and who I was doing it with is none of your damn business."

"Isn't it?" Quinlan began wandering around the room. "Funny how Roarke doesn't seem to agree."

"What are you talking about?"

"Why, didn't I mention that he's the one who told me about bein' with you?"

Jade felt the color leave her face. "I don't believe Roarke told you! I don't think he even speaks to you!"

"He's changed his mind about not talkin' to me now that he's working for me."

"He's not working for you. He has his own architectural firm. In San Francisco." She couldn't, wouldn't, believe that he had lied to her.

Quinlan smiled agreeably and asked, "Didn't he tell you about doing consulting work for Richard Hamilton?"

"Of course, but—"

"I signed a deal with the Greek government to drill for oil beneath the Aegean. Since the contract runs for five years, I figured it'd make sense to have my own headquarters. . . . Hamilton's building it." He gave her a cold smile. "And Roarke's the architect."

"I don't believe that," Jade insisted. She caught sight of a picture of Cookie Monster Amy had drawn and surreptitiously shoved it under a stack of magazines. "Roarke was furious when he found out you cost him that job with Guimard. He'd never work for you."

"Now that's where you're wrong, missy," he said. "You see, Roarke and me fought for a whole lot of years about his going into architecture instead of comin' back home to work for the family business. Now that he's got his own company, he feels like he's in the catbird seat. I figure that's why he couldn't resist a chance to show his old man exactly how good he is by designing a world-class building for Gallagher Gas and Oil."

As much as she hated to admit it, that made some measure of sense. Quinlan had always been vocal about his objections to Roarke's career choice; competition between father and son being what it was, Jade supposed Roarke would welcome the opportunity to strut his stuff.

"You want more than just a building."

"You always were a bright girl, Cassie," he allowed. "And if Roarke and I get along well enough while we're working together on my office complex, well, who's to say that he won't decide to set up shop back in Oklahoma, where he belongs."

"Where you can control him, you mean," Jade accused.

Quinlan's only answer was to shrug his shoulders. He began wandering around the room.

"Nice place." He stood, arms crossed, observing a Maori warrior mask on the wall. "Not much furniture, but you should be used to that. Some of the places you and your mama lived."

He picked up a kachina figure she'd bought at a trading post in Arizona. "You know, I always figured you were just tryin' to trap Roarke into marrying you, but I suppose there might have been an outside chance that it was his kid. You bein' so available, and all. And boys bein' what they are."

He exchanged the kachina for a Guatemalan clay fertility figure. "It's just as well you got rid of that baby."

"Afraid a bastard might have polluted the precious Gallagher blood lines?" Jade asked acidly.

"Probably wouldn't be the first time," he answered candidly. "Padraic was supposed to be one helluva stud."

Jade was getting sick and tired of playing cat and mouse. Worried that he was might wander into Amy's room, she grabbed the Indian figure out of his hand. "Either you get to the point, or get the hell out of my home."

"All right. Since you and my boy seem to be gettin' close again—"

"Roarke is not a boy."

Quinlan was not used to being interrupted. Or corrected. He looked as if he'd love to wring her neck. "Since you and *Roarke*," he corrected impatiently, "are sleepin' together, I guess it's up to me to fill you in on a little family secret that your mama probably should have told you about a long time ago."

Jade remembered the premonition she'd had the last night on the island with Roarke. Here was the demon, she realized. The monster in the tunnel of love. Her heart picked up a rapid flutter. "What secret?"

"About me bein' your natural daddy." Quinlan paused to allow his words to sink in. "Like I said, it's a good thing you had that abortion. With you and Roarke sharin' the same blood, there's no tellin' what kinda kid you could've had."

Jade felt a cold, crushing sensation, like a two-ton block of ice pressing against her chest. "You're lying."

"If you don't believe me, ask your mama."

"That's exactly what I'm going to do. As soon as you get out of my apartment."

"I was just leaving." He turned in the doorway. "There's just one more thing."

"What now?"

"I wouldn't advise you tellin' Roarke about my little fling with your mama. I don't want anythin' comin' between my boy and me, just when we're starting to put bygones behind us."

She lifted her chin. "You don't control me, Quinlan. I'll tell Roarke whatever I want."

"Even if your career would take a nose dive, people find out that the famous Jade is an ex-jailbird?"

"You never know," Jade bluffed, "it just might give me a certain cachet."

She could tell he was furious at the way she'd stood up to him and was struggling not to show it. "You got guts, girl," he allowed. "Too bad your mama's not as strong as you turned out to be."

"Are you threatening my mother?"

"You want me to make things real tough on Belle," Quinlan said, "go ahead and put me to the test. But believe me, Cassie, what happened to you, gettin' locked away in jail and all, ain't nothin' compared to what might happen to your mama if you don't keep that pretty mouth shut."

His smile was as cold as a witch's heart. "You give it some thought," he advised. And then he was gone.

Jade didn't want to discuss anything so important and personal over the telephone. Besides, Belle was a journeyman liar; Jade wanted to be able to look her in the eye when she asked if Quinlan's hateful accusation was true.

She made up an excuse about a last-minute photo shoot, which Amy accepted, but Jade suspected Edith didn't quite buy. Nevertheless, a few hours after Quinlan Gallagher's departure, Jade was on a plane, bound for Oklahoma.

Her mind whirled with a range of complex emotions. Her rediscovered love for Roarke, her fierce protective instincts concerning her daughter, her fear that Quinlan wasn't lying. And, if he was telling the truth, her anger toward Belle for having kept such a potentially dangerous secret from her all these years.

The rental car booths were all in a row, populated by uniformly cheery women dressed in red, yellow, or green. Stopping at the first booth, Jade rented a car to take her to Gallagher City.

Jade's heart sank when Belle answered the door. Her mother had been drinking again. Experience had taught her that her mother was horribly unreliable when she'd been drinking. So Jade pretended to listen to Belle's numerous complaints about her life, but her mind was on her mission and she didn't hear a word. When Belle finally ran down, Jade told her about Quinlan's accusation, praying that her mother would deny everything.

To Jade's horror, that didn't happen. "Shit," Belle said, lighting a cigarette with shaking fingers. "I don't know why he couldn't have let sleepin' dogs lie."

"Then it's true?"

"Yeah. Me and him had a little fling back then."

"But how do you know that he's my father?" Jade had never known Belle to be monogamous.

"Quinlan's a jealous man, Cassie," Belle said. "And I don't have to tell you that he can be one mean son of a bitch. Hell, I didn't have the guts to sleep with any other guy when I was with him."

Belle inhaled and blew a long stream of smoke out her nose. "Quinlan Gallagher's your daddy, all right. Ain't no question about it."

"But you always said that my father was an oil-rig worker."

"Well, I couldn't exactly go around tellin' everyone in Gallagher County that Gallagher knocked me up, could I?" Belle answered with patient logic. "Besides, him and me worked out a deal."

"What kind of deal?"

"The usual. He gave me money and I kept my mouth shut."

The world wavered, grew faint. Jade closed her eyes against the sudden vertigo. "I still can't believe it."

"Hell, girl," Belle complained, "for a smart kid, sometimes you don't have the brains God gave a mule. Why do you think they treated you so good up there in Quinlan Gallagher's fancy house? Until you messed up a cushy deal by swipin' Miz Lillian's fancy knickknacks."

"I didn't steal anything!"

Belle shrugged. "Whatever. The truth is, Cassie, that you are as much Quinlan Gallagher's flesh and blood as Shelby is. Or Roarke."

The next day, as she was driving back to the Oklahoma City airport, the shakes hit Jade so badly, she had to pull off the road. She sat there, trying to regain her equilibrium. Her mind was numb, but her senses were not so dulled that she couldn't feel the yawning hole Quinlan Gallagher had punched into the center of her life.

Jade felt as if she had a stiletto of ice buried in her heart. She spent the flight back to New York trying to convince herself that Belle was lying. But for what purpose? She hadn't told her mother about her reconciliation with Roarke. Nor had she told her about Amy. As far as Belle was concerned, Jade and Roarke were old news.

When Jade had continued to express disbelief, Belle, displaying a clarity of thought she hadn't demonstrated for a very long time, had come up with remarkably detailed specifics of her trysts with Quinlan.

As the plane made its descent into Kennedy Airport, Jade came to the reluctant conclusion that there wasn't any reason for Belle to lie. Quinlan Gallagher was her father. She tried to think what that meant; how it made her feel to know that by blood ties, at least, she was just as much a Gallagher as Shelby.

Jade decided that it didn't matter. She'd grown used to not having a father a very long time ago. And Quinlan Gallagher had certainly never played a paternal role. All he'd done was supply the sperm, and in that respect he was no different from a randy tomcat prowling neighborhood back fences. Her feeling toward the man was revulsion. And a lingering hatred that made her wish she had the power to hurt him as he'd hurt her. And Amy.

The jet's tires had just thubbed against the runway when the fact of Amy's deafness came crashing down on Jade. The doctors had never been able to give her a satisfactory reason for her daughter's condition; now Jade felt that she knew the truth. Sweet, beautiful Amy had been forced into a world of silence because her mother and father were sister and brother. The shattering thought was almost too much to bear.

# Fourteen

"Mama! Guess what I made at school today!" Amy's face glowed like the noonday sun, her hands moved with youthful grace.

Usually just the sight of her daughter could lift Jade's spirits. Today, as she looked into her daughter's smiling face, Jade saw her sin staring back at her.

"Mama!" Impatient, Amy pulled on Jade's skirt to get her attention.

"I'm sorry, sweetheart. What did you make?"

Her fingers shook, her sign was vague, and her face failed to give the necessary emphasis to her words, but Amy, filled with the glory of new knowledge, didn't notice. "I made the world. Wait dere. I go ged id."

She ran to her bedroom, returning with a rather lopsided sphere created from Play-Doh. "See," she said, pointing to a silver star she'd pressed into the bright blue surface, "thid ith New York. Where we lib."

Kneeling down, Jade took the globe in her own hands and traced an imaginary line from New York to Oklahoma. On this miniature world, it was only inches away. In reality, Gallagher City, and all it represented, might well have been on another planet.

"It's lovely, darling," she said with an encouraging smile, though there was ice forming inside her.

"Id for your cowection."

"Collection," Jade corrected absently. She tapped her tongue against the roof of her mouth.

"Collection," Amy repeated. "Do you like id?"

"I love it." She said the words slowly, carefully, allowing Amy to read her lips.

"Did you know the world ith round?"

The way she tipped her head was so like Roarke that Jade had to bite her lips to keep from crying. "Yes. I did."

"And it spinth around and around. Like a merry-go-round."

Unable to speak, Jade nodded.

Amy's bright eyes turned quizzical. "Then how come we don't get dizzy?"

Who said we don't? Ever since Belle had confirmed Quinlan's deadly bombshell, Jade had felt as if the Earth had tilted precariously and was about to spin off its axis.

"I don't know, honey."

"Mama?" Amy tipped her head back. "Why don't you wear a hearing aid? Like me?"

Because my mother, as irresponsible as she was, never did anything bad enough to cause me to be born deaf, Jade thought. "Because it makes sounds too loud," she said instead.

"Johnny mudder wear a hearing aid," Amy persisted.

She'd entered into an inquisitive stage that Jade usually found exciting, albeit exhausting. This newest batch of questions, however, hit too painfully close to home.

"Johnny's mother is deaf," Jade answered, bringing her right index finger to her ear, then lowering it beside her left hand.

Jade had reluctantly begun to use the dreaded word when Amy's speech therapist suggested that it would be preferable for Amy to hear it first in a loving environment before encountering it from someone less thoughtful.

"Like me," Amy said.

Jade nodded. "Like you."

Amy considered that for a long, drawn-out minute. "Do you like me deaf?"

"I love you. Just the way you are."

Another long pause as Amy thought about this new idea. "I wish you were deaf, Mama. Then we could be the same."

Drawing her daughter close, Jade pressed her trembling lips against the shiny cap of black hair.

Jade's guilt was relentless, it tore at her day and night. Unable to escape it, she spent long and lonely days staring up at the ceiling where accusing faces—Roarke's, Quinlan's, Belle's, and worst of all Amy's—stared back at her from the swirls of white plaster.

"You look terrible," Nina complained. It had been two weeks since Quinlan Gallagher's unexpected visit and Jade seemed unwilling, or unable, to shake herself out of her malaise.

"That's not so surprising, since I feel terrible." Jade rubbed the back of her neck. "I think I must be coming down with the flu."

It was the same thing she'd told Reginald Bentley when she'd called in sick. Although she'd won a hard-earned promotion to acquisitions, for some reason Jade was afraid to think about, her heart was no longer in her work. She'd even risked getting a reputation for being unreliable by having Nina get her out of a very lucrative shot she'd been scheduled to do in Australia.

"I think you've got a bad case of the I'm-missing-my-man blues," Nina contradicted. "I thought Roarke was due to come to New York last week."

"He got tied up in San Francisco. Something about problems with a building inspection."

"Then you two aren't having problems?" Nina probed carefully.

"Of course not," Jade said. "And you're right, I'm turning into a slug." She dragged her hand through her hair. "I need a new job. Any new job."

"Funny you should mention that," Nina said, pulling a manila file from a desk drawer. "Have you ever heard of Sam Southerland?"

"Sam Southerland," Jade repeated thoughtfully. "Isn't he some maverick West Coast corporate raider?"

"That's him. He recently gained control of Donaldson Enterprises," Nina confirmed, naming a large publishing, newspaper, and television empire. "After what was reported to be a brutal proxy fight."

"So? What does a publishing company have to do with me?"

"It seems that among Donaldson Enterprises' assets is a perfume company created solely to market a scent called Everlasting by a designer who had the bad timing to die before the perfume could ever be marketed. So the whole idea was just put on the shelf and forgotten.

"So, here's where you come in. Apparently Southerland was planning to scuttle the dormant company. Until he saw a larger-than-life portrait of you sprawled seductively across the side of a San Francisco cable car. You know, the one where you're pushing liquor."

"I know which one." When the advertisement featuring her wearing that sexy black velvet halter dress began appearing on buses and billboards all over the city, Jade hadn't been able to go anywhere without hearing wolf whistles.

"He called and asked if you were available. When I told him that you were booked through the end of the year, he offered to pay ten times your hourly rate. Naturally that got my attention, so I shipped your portfolio to his San Francisco office right away. I got off the phone with him just before you arrived. He'll be in town tomorrow and wants to meet you."

Jade arched a tawny brow. "Just like that?" Sam Southerland sounded like another Quinlan Gallagher. Jade disliked him already.

"Just like that," Nina agreed. "I told him you'd meet with him in his suite at the Waldorf at three. Which gives you approximately twenty-four hours to get yourself back in shape. You need your hair and nails done, and a facial. Oh, and stop by the Chanel counter at Saks and get some of that stuff to get rid of the shadows under your eyes. You really do look like death warmed over."

"Thanks for the vote of confidence."

"It's your job to look terrific, Jade. And if Southerland thinks you're the girl for his perfume campaign, he's willing to pay for exclusive rights."

"What if I don't want to work with him?" Jade asks.

"You're not getting any younger," Nina reminded her.

At twenty-three, Jade was far from ancient. But she was all too aware of the fact that fifteen-year-old Brooke Shields's ubiquitous spots for Calvin Klein jeans six years ago—the ones that had been blamed for creating the "year of the leer" in advertising—had established the belief that in modeling, the younger the better.

"If I were you," Nina continued, "and there was a client willing to set me up for life, I'd agree to work with the devil himself."

"That's exactly what I'm afraid of," Jade muttered.

"He doesn't sound that bad," Nina assured her. "Here, I dug up a little background." She handed Jade the file. "I thought you might be interested."

Nina was wrong. Jade wasn't interested, not even a little bit. She'd had her fill of rich, powerful, egocentric men. Even as she continued to remind herself of that all-important fact, that night, as she soaked in the bathtub, waiting for the clarifying mask to set, Jade found herself reading the clippings Nina had given her.

From what she could tell, Sam Southerland was rough-hewn, outspoken, and single-minded—the quintessential self-made man. He'd begun his financial empire thirty years earlier, at the relatively young age of twenty-five, by convincing a group of fellow loggers to purchase a northern California timber company. After suffering financial reversals, the company was going to close down and lay off all the loggers, Sam included.

The *Wall Street Journal* had quoted him as saying that going broke as the owner of a lumber company was a "hell of a lot better than going broke on unemployment."

Under his management, the company turned around and began to show a profit within eighteen months. Within three years he'd bought out the other owners, who'd never been interested in managing the business in the first place, and signed a multimillion-dollar trade deal with the Japanese.

Over the years, he'd expanded into computers, chemical companies, airlines, and anything else that struck his fancy.

"Well, if he thinks he can buy me," Jade muttered, "the man's in for a very rude awakening."

Sam Southerland was tall and muscular, and although there wasn't an ounce of fat on his body, his wide shoulders and broad chest reminded Jade of a bull. His chestnut hair was liberally streaked with gray and his rugged face had the kind of five o'clock shadow that resisted shaving.

He was wearing a pair of expensive gray dress slacks and a crisp white shirt; the collar was unbuttoned and the sleeves were rolled up nearly to the elbows, exposing strong forearms. He was, Jade thought, a man who would look at ease in a lumberjack bar or an elegant drawing room. When he shook her hand, she felt the row of callouses on his palm.

"After studying your portfolio, I thought I was prepared for you," he said, his dark eyes filled with masculine appreciation. "But your photos don't begin to do you justice. Damned if you aren't prettier than a speckled pup."

"I'd thought I'd heard every line there was," Jade responded with the protective reserve she wore like a second skin around men. "Apparently I was mistaken."

"Hell, that isn't a damn line," he countered gruffly. "If we're going to do business together, you should know right off the bat that I'm tough, but I'm a straight shooter. I'll never tell you anything but the out-and-out truth."

"You've no idea how that relieves my mind," she said coolly. "But you've overlooked one small fact, Mr. Southerland. I haven't yet decided whether we'll be doing business together." Her message was clear: he, not she, was the one being looked over.

If he was put out by her less than cordial attitude, he didn't reveal it. "Call me Sam."

He walked over to the desk where black-and-white glossies of Jade in a number of poses were scattered over the polished surface. "I doubt that you could take a bad picture, but when I saw these, I knew that you were a woman who could sell antifreeze to the Arabs."

He held up one of the powerfully sensual photos of her Kenya layout. In it her oiled skin glowed like polished copper. When the photos had first appeared in the French *Elle*, rumor had it that Grace Mirabella, never one to compliment a rival publication, had been overheard saying that these provocative photos made Jade look more like the prototype for some divine superrace than a mortal woman.

"Thank you," she murmured.

"Hell, you don't have to thank me for telling the truth." Opening a bottle of Everlasting, he stuck it under her nose. "Tell me the first thing that comes to mind."

The lushly romantic perfume was a tribute to orange blossoms. "Weddings," she said. "Brides in lacy white dresses."

"Virgins," Sam supplied.

If she was surprised by his bluntness, Jade was more impressed by how precisely he'd described the scent. "Exactly."

"Which makes it all wrong for you."

"Should I be insulted?"

"Of course not. You're a beautiful woman, Jade, but the image you project is definitely not that of a blushing virgin bride." Uncapping another bottle, he said, "Now try this. It's the scent those damn fools who were running Donaldson Enterprises passed up in favor of Everlasting."

"Oh," she said, breathing in the exotic musk and amber notes, "it reminds me of Kenya."

"Bingo! That's exactly what it's supposed to make you think of. I want to ride the wave of popularity created by Streep's performance in *Out of Africa*. Ever since that movie came out, all the women on both coasts have taken to wearing khaki. I took a walk down Madison Avenue this morning and it looked like an explosion at Banana Republic. . . .

"I'm calling this new perfume—drum roll, please, maestro," he said, slapping his hands on the desktop—"Tigress."

"But Africa doesn't have any tigers," Jade felt obliged to point out. Having come here prepared to hate him, Jade was finding Sam Southerland fascinating.

"Creative license," he said, waving her words away with an impatient hand. He had nice hands, Jade noticed irrelevantly. Broad and dark with long tapering fingers. "I've got the scent, I've got the concept, now all I need is for you to agree to be my Tigress woman."

With an absolutely straight face he went on to offer her a three-year figure that made her current billable hours look like minimum wage. "I assume Nina told you that I'll want you to sign an exclusive contract," he said.

"Are you serious?"

"I'm always serious about business. So, what's it going to be, Jade? Yes? Or no?"

"You'll have to discuss it with my agent."

"Then my lawyers will get together with Nina and hash out the details. But since the agreement will ultimately be between us, Jade, I want to hear your answer for myself."

Jade realized that this man had just agreed to fund her dream. "I'd love to be the Tigress woman."

"Good." Sam rubbed his hands together with satisfaction.

Revealing that he'd expected no other outcome, he reached into the bar refrigerator, pulled out a bottle of champagne, and drew the cork. Her gaze once again drawn to his strong hands, Jade watched as he deftly poured the sparkling gold wine and set the bottle aside.

"To us," Sam said, handing her one of the crystal flutes. "And our successful partnership."

His enthusiasm was contagious. Jade lifted her glass, smiling for the first time since Quinlan Gallagher had arrived at her door two weeks ago and dropped his devastating bombshell.

"To us."

Jade soon discovered that Sam Southerland had no patience with slackers. He believed in working at a whirlwind pace and a mere five days after their meeting in the suite, she found herself on a vast advertising soundstage in Brooklyn, clad in a minuscule suede tiger skin bikini and a barbaric necklace of feathers and bones, surrounded by live tigers while Tommy Jones clicked away with his camera.

"That's terrific, sweetheart," Tommy coaxed as Jade tossed her head, causing her hair to fly out in a fiery arc. "Now, give me that famous come-hither look."

The klieg lights warmed her flesh in a room that was too cold for her scant apparel; the automatic motor drive on the photographer's Nikon whirred. Changing her position with a smooth, feline grace, Jade lowered her eyes and smiled at the camera lens through her thick lashes.

"Christ that's sexy," Tommy all but growled. "That face, those tits, legs that don't end. I've seen 'em all, but you're the best, baby."

Jade had worked with Tommy Jones enough times to know that he said that to all the girls. But somehow, when the lights were turned on and his camera was clicking away, he had the ability to make a woman believe that she was truly the most beautiful woman in the world.

With his deep, cigarette-roughened voice and hands that were always touching—arranging hair, playing with a strap, lingeringly unprofessionally over a thigh—Tommy could make a woman look and feel more than beautiful, he made her feel sexy.

"Jesus, you've got me hot," he crooned as he walked over to her and tugged the bandeau bikini top scandalously lower.

When his fingers brushed over her flesh, Jade felt an automatic jolt of something that almost resembled desire. Something she knew would dissipate like morning fog the minute the lights were turned off and Tommy's camera was put away.

"Annie," he called to his assistant, "rice powder."

Tommy took the silver-handled sable brush and dipped it into the powder, then drew it ever so slowly over the crest of Jade's breasts, creating a shimmering copper gleam reminiscent of burnished wood.

"You look," he murmured, looking deep into Jade's eyes, "good enough to eat."

He played with the bikini top a bit more, making no attempt to conceal the outline of the mammoth erection pressing against the front of his black jeans.

That too, was part of his success. Unlike so many other photographers Jade had worked with, Tommy Jones was one hundred percent heterosexual. He owed a great deal of both his fame and his fortune to the fact that he'd understood at a very young age that the relationship between a photographer and a model should be intimate, sensual, even erotic. And although Jade was one of the few women in the business who hadn't slept with him, she wasn't entirely immune to his technique.

And now, as she let herself pretend to be the irresistibly desirable woman Tommy was telling her she was—a woman capable of bringing the strongest man to his knees—Jade was almost able to forget that she was working with a pair of wild animals. And that Sam Southerland was standing in the shadows, watching with those bold, direct eyes she suspected never missed a thing.

Just as she was almost—but not quite—able to forget that Roarke had finally arrived in New York.

When he'd called from Kennedy that morning, inviting her to breakfast, she'd begged off, telling him she had to work, and no, it wasn't something she could reschedule. His obvious irritation at her refusal rankled; his work had kept him in San Francisco and now that he was finally free, he expected her to drop everything to be with him.

When she'd told him about working for Sam Southerland, Jade hadn't been surprised to learn that the two men were acquainted. After all, they both lived in the same city.

When she'd asked him where he would be staying, the lengthy pause told Jade that Roarke had assumed he would be staying with her. But he'd recovered quickly and said that he would probably book a suite at the Plaza.

That's when Jade had suggested that they get together for a drink in the Oak Bar. Complaining that after all these weeks apart he didn't want to share their reunion with strangers, Roarke insisted that they meet in his suite. Something Jade was not looking forward to.

"Okay, sweetie," Tommy called out, bringing Jade out of her thoughts with a jolt, "now pat the kitty's head."

"You're kidding." Jade's incredulous gaze went from the enormous animal to Tommy and back again.

"It's all right, Miss," the trainer said with a Texas twang that reminded Jade uncomfortably of Oklahoma. "You don't have to worry about a thing. Old Punjab's as gentle as a house cat. He'd never bite."

"That's what they all say," she muttered. Taking a deep breath, she reached out and tentatively put her hand on the wide orange-and-black head. To her surprise, the male tiger began to purr.

"That's terrific," Tommy called out, snapping away. "God, I think you just made another conquest, babe," he said when the tiger, apparently enraptured by her gentle stroking, began nuzzling her thigh. "Okay, that's it."

Tommy took one last shot and began rewinding the film. "You were, as always, Jade, remarkable. How about cracking open a bottle of bubbly to celebrate yet another dazzlingly successful collaboration?"

Jade had to give the man credit for tenacity. After four years of rejections, he refused to stop trying. "Sorry, but I have plans for this evening."

"Next time, then." It was the same thing he always said.

Jade smiled. "Perhaps." It was the same thing she always said.

She was on her way to change clothes when Sam caught up with her. "That was some dynamite work."

"Thank you."

"I was going to ask you out to dinner so we could discuss the next phase of the campaign, but I heard you tell Jones that you've already made plans."

"Yes. I have."

He would have had to be as dull as a stone not to perceive the sudden chill in the air. "I guess this is where you tell me that you never mix business and pleasure."

Jade wasn't surprised that he was quick. What did surprise her was the way she felt something dangerously close to regret that he was apparently willing to give up so easily.

"I don't want to offend you, Mr. Southerland—"

"Sam," he reminded her.

"Sam," she agreed. "But it's just that—"

"Hey, you don't have to apologize, Jade. As a matter of fact, I've always had the same rule." His grin was open and slightly embarrassed. "I guess I just kinda got carried away by the Tigress woman."

His broad hand reached out, as if to touch her hair, but he pulled it back. "Funny, since I'm the one who created the idea in the first place. But today just proved I was right. You are absolutely perfect for the part."

"Thank you." It was more than the flattery—she heard that all the time. It was something else in his voice, something warm yet at the same time nonthreatening, that elicited from her an honest smile in return.

She looked down at her watch. The shoot had run overtime, and she was already an hour late meeting Roarke.

"I'm sorry," Sam said, noticing her not so subtle glance. "You have someplace you're supposed to be and I'm standing here yammering." He pulled a sheaf of papers from the inside pocket of his jacket. "You can study these tonight. We'll begin shooting tomorrow morning."

"Shooting?"

"The television spots," he reminded her. "This is the script."

"You certainly don't waste any time, do you?"

"Not when it's something I want," Sam agreed.

"I've never done any television."

"Don't worry, something tells me you're a natural actress."

His tone made Jade look sharply up at him, but his expression remained steadfastly neutral.

"Have a good evening," he said, reaching out again, this time allowing himself to ruffle her hair. "I'll see you back here again, tomorrow morning, seven o'clock sharp."

"Seven o'clock?"

"That's when we've scheduled the crew. Do you have a problem with that?"

Jade's first thought was that Sam Southerland was unbelievably bossy. Her second thought was that for what the man was paying her, if he'd wanted her to show up on the Brooklyn Bridge at 4:00 A.M., she'd have no right to complain.

"Seven's fine."

"Good." His grin suggested that he'd expected that to be her answer. "I'll bring the coffee."

With that he turned, leaving her to watch him walk away with a long, confident stride. She also noticed that Annie, Tommy's twenty-something assistant, practically swooned when he stopped to say something to her. Which wasn't all that surprising, Jade decided. Since Sam was a very attractive, vital man. He was also undeniably sexy.

That thought brought her mind crashing back to Roarke. Tonight was going to be one of the hardest nights of her life. Because she was going to have to tell the man she loved that she could never see him again.

"Do you have any idea how much I've missed you?" Roarke's eyes held the warmth of a physical caress as they moved over her face.

Breaking free of his welcoming arms, Jade walked over to the window, pulled aside the crewel draperies, and looked out over Central Park. "How did the problems with your building inspections turn out?"

Roarke shrugged. "Okay. Once I managed to convince the inspector that I wasn't going to pay for a green tag."

"Pay? You mean like in bribery?"

"It's a way of life in the construction business, Jade. But not one I'd ever subscribe to." He crossed the room to stand behind her. "Why are we talking about work when we've been apart for almost four miserable weeks?"

He took hold of her arm, turned her around, tilted his head, and touched her forehead with his own. Her eyelids drifted shut. "Four weeks," he murmured. "It seemed an eternity."

They stood that way, foreheads touching, eyes closed. Jade listened to the clip clop of hooves on the street below, heard the whinny of the carriage horses, and remembered a magical night when Roarke had taken her for a carriage ride through the park.

She shivered.

"Cold?" When Roarke ran his hands up and down her arms, Jade pulled away.

"I'm fine," she insisted, burrowing deeper and deeper inside herself.

"Something's wrong."

"Why should anything be wrong?"

"You're not acting like yourself."

"I'm just tired." That much, at least, was the truth. "The shoot was only supposed to last four hours, but Tommy didn't realize that the tigers had to be walked around the set every forty-five minutes, so they don't get stressed out. You've no idea how horrid tigers smell, by the way. Of course, if consumers knew the truth they'd never buy Sam's perfume, but fortunately—"

"Honey." He took hold of her shoulders. "You're rambling."

"Yes, well." She took a deep breath. "I was just trying to explain why I'm not my usual cheery self. I'm sorry, Roarke, I suppose you're accustomed to women entertaining you."

"I certainly don't expect you to entertain me, Jade."

"Good." She flashed him a brilliantly false smile. "Because I'm afraid I left my tap shoes at home."

He ran a hand through his dark hair and looked into her face, as if testing the emotional weather brewing there. "I don't understand. Are you angry at me?"

"Why should I be angry?"

"Well, I know I was held in up in San Francisco longer than I'd planned, but you knew it was business."

"Yes. That's what you said."

"You sound as if you don't believe me."

She shrugged. "You can't blame me for wondering if Philippa Hamilton had anything to do with your not rushing to New York."

"Are you jealous? Of Philippa?"

"Of course not."

"Good. And for the record, I haven't been with another woman since Greece."

"Your life is your own, Roarke. I certainly don't have any say in it. Just as you don't have any say in mine."

Obviously frustrated, he caught her chin in his hand and when she would have looked away, held her unwilling gaze to his.

"What the hell has happened? I thought we'd made a commitment on Seriphos."

"A commitment?" She raised her eyebrows. This was even more difficult than she'd expected. Jade felt as if she was making her way through a bizarre new landscape without a map. "Is that what you thought?"

"Yes. As a matter of fact, that's exactly what I thought," Roarke ground out.

"Well. I guess you thought wrong." The bitter lie on her tongue trailed down her throat like the taste of dissolved aspirin.

Even as she watched Roarke react, Jade felt nothing. It was as if she'd taken a deep whiff of anesthesia before undergoing traumatic heart surgery.

"I don't believe you. Damnit, what we shared on that island was a helluva lot more than a holiday fling, Cassie."

She knew that his slip back to her old name was proof of his exasperation. Even as it killed her to hurt him, Jade knew that she had no choice. Because if she told him the truth about her mother and his father, he'd be bound to confront Quinlan, which would only end up hurting Belle, who had been hurt enough. What Jade couldn't admit, even to herself, was that after a lifetime of lying to protect her mother, old habits didn't die just because she might want them to.

Quinlan Gallagher had left her no choice. No options. And now, if she allowed herself to succumb to Roarke's obvious shock and anger, her nerve would falter.

"You're right." She put her hand on his chest and felt the beat of his heart. "What we shared on Seriphos was something very special and I'll never forget it. But it wasn't real, Roarke. It was simply an illusion created by the sun and the sea and the fact that we were miles from anyone who knew us. For that one glorious week we could have been the only people on earth and I'll always cherish the memories of our time together."

She turned away, unable to look at him any longer. "But now we're back in the real world and it's time to get on with our lives."

"I was hoping I could convince you that our lives could be joined."

"With you in San Francisco and me in New York?"

"Commuter marriages are all the rage, Jade," Roarke said with a coaxing smile that suggested he was not yet prepared to throw in the towel.

An icy chill shivered through her. "Are you asking me to marry you?"

For so many years she would have given everything she had to have this man propose. And now that he had, the truth of her parentage made it impossible for her to accept.

"I love you, Jade," he said. "Looking back on it, I think I loved you even when you were Cassie, but I was too caught up in my war with my father that summer to realize that you were probably the best thing that ever happened to me.

"And although I'd planned to do it right, with champagne and candlelight, now that it's come up, yes, I am asking you to be my wife."

Those long-awaited words made her ache inside.

"Speaking of your father," she said with studied offhandedness, "why didn't you tell me that you were working with him?"

A guilty flush darkened his cheeks. "I'm not working *with* my father. He asked me to design a building for Gallagher Gas and Oil."

"It's rather the same thing, isn't it?" Jade asked. "Since the company is privately owned and all control is in your father's hands. After all, everyone knows that Quinlan Gallagher is G. G. and O."

"All right." His shoulders slumped. "The reason I didn't tell you was because after we finally got a chance to talk about that summer, and I realized that my father had treated you so abominably, I knew you'd hate the idea of me having any kind of relationship—even one that was strictly professional—with the man who'd caused you so much grief."

If you only knew exactly how much grief, Jade considered.

"How did you find out?" he asked.

Jade shrugged. "It's not important."

"I was going to tell you."

"Oh? When? Before or after we were married?"

He dragged his hand down his face. When he dropped it to his side, she could see the frustration etched into every line of his handsome features, saw it swirling in his dark blue eyes.

"Look, you've had a long day," he said. "Why don't I call down for dinner while you take a long, hot, soothing bath, and we can talk about this when you're feeling more rested."

She folded her arms over her chest. "When I'm more agreeable, you mean."

He stared at her as if he'd never seen her before. Which was, Jade considered, pretty much the truth. She'd always been so acquiescent where this man was concerned, before. Now she could not afford to give so much as an inch.

"When you're rested," he repeated. When he came toward her, Jade moved away. "How about it, Jade?" he cajoled. "We'll have a nice dinner, then spend the rest of the night getting to know each other again."

That was precisely what she couldn't allow. "I can't."

"Can't?" He arched a dark, forbidding brow. "Or won't?"

She absolutely refused to be baited. If they got into a fight, emotions could escalate the same way they had on Seriphos and before she knew it, she'd be back in bed with him, committing the sin of incest.

"I have to study my lines." As if to prove her words, she reached into her bag and pulled out the sheaf of papers Sam had given her. "We're shooting the television commercial tomorrow and I don't know a thing about when to pause, or what words to stress, or any of the other tricks of the trade. I really have to study, Roarke."

"We can study them together after dinner," he suggested. "I'll help you learn your lines."

It was so, so tempting. Tell him, a little voice in the far reaches of her brain cried out. Tell him what Quinlan and Belle told you, then he can deny it and give you some proof—any proof—that they lied and you'll have no reason not to stay here with him. Where you belong. Forever.

"I don't think that's a very good idea," she said instead. An anniversary clock on a nearby table chimed the hour. "It's getting late. I really should be going."

"I can't believe this," Roarke muttered under his breath, but loud enough for Jade to hear him. "Okay. How about breakfast tomorrow morning?"

"I never eat before a shoot."

"Coffee, then. Black, no cream, no sugar, guaranteed not to add an ounce."

"I already told Sam I'd have coffee with him." It was only partly the truth, but from the shock that moved in violent waves across Roarke's face, Jade knew she'd scored a direct hit.

"You're having breakfast with Sam Southerland?"

"Not breakfast. Coffee."

"Breakfast, coffee, what the hell you're eating or drinking doesn't matter." Roarke brushed her words away with an angry flick of the wrist.

"What matters is that you're spending time with him that you could be spending with me."

"He's my boss."

"So you said. He's also old enough to be your father."

That he was jealous was obvious. Jade reluctantly realized that such emotion could work in her favor. "He's not that old."

"I happen to know that the man is fifty-five years old, Jade. You're twenty-three." He folded his arms over his chest again and glared down at her. "Unless my arithmetic is totally off the mark, that makes him old enough to be your father."

She shrugged. "I told you, Sam is simply my boss. There's nothing going on between us."

"Not yet. But the man has a reputation. He's known for using all his millions to buy whatever he wants."

She stiffened her spine. "Are you suggesting that I'm for sale?" Jade did not have to feign her irritation.

"I'm saying that it seems very strange that when we were together on the island, you led me to believe that I was important to you, that there was a place for me in your life. And now, less than four weeks later, you're working for Sam Southerland and I can't even get you to agree to take time from your busy schedule to have a damn cup of coffee with me!"

"I'm sorry you feel that way," Jade said. "I'm sorry you don't trust me enough not to sleep with my employer. I'm sorry you don't trust me enough to tell me that you're working with your father again and I'm sorry that you've come all this way for nothing."

She raised a hand that trembled only slightly to his cheek and felt the muscle tense beneath her fingertips. "I'm sorry about everything, Roarke," she said in something close to a whisper. "But two things I'll never be sorry for—that summer we first made love and our time together in Greece."

"Yeah, we'll always have Seriphos," he muttered. "You're actually serious about this, aren't you?"

Jade swallowed. "Yes. There are too many things working against us, Roarke. I'd much rather end it now, before we wind up making each other miserable."

"That wouldn't happen, damnit."

She bit her lip to keep from crying. "I'm afraid that's where you're wrong." She brushed a last, soft kiss against his stony, frowning lips. "Goodbye, Roarke."

And then, with a heavy heart, she left, closing the door behind her, shutting him out of her life with a cold, decisive click.

Roarke spent the next three days trying to get through to Jade. But she'd instructed her doorman to tell him that she was out of town. Finally, frustrated in his attempts to talk to her in person, he left a blistering farewell on her answering machine.

"Okay, Jade," growled the familiar deep voice, "you win. I've finally gotten it through my hard Okie head that you're really not going to give us a chance." Jade could tell that he was furious.

"You can tell your doorman that I won't be bothering him again. Because I'm going back to San Francisco. Where the women don't carry concealed weapons."

Jade rewound the tape with trembling fingers, then spent the rest of the evening sitting alone in the dark, silent tears streaming down her face.

Three months later, images of Jade surrounded by tigers were everywhere. The public demand for the perfume was phenomenal, making Sam even richer and Jade the hottest property in the business.

Six months after the successful launch of the Tigress campaign, Jade graduated from NYU. Nina was on hand to cheer for her. As was Sam, who surprised her by flying in from San Francisco. It hadn't been easy, but she'd finally achieved the first part of her goal. Unfortunately, to Jade's dismay, Reginald Bentley displayed a convenient lapse of memory.

"What do you mean, you can't offer me a full-time position?" she demanded. "You promised to promote me to the floor."

"Yes . . . well," he stammered, running his finger inside his starched white spread collar, "you must understand, Jade dear, that our buyers are, as a rule, very conservative. I'm not certain they could accept your new image."

"But it's only a modeling job," Jade countered. "You've never complained before."

He had also never complained about all the extra hours she'd worked in the storeroom, uncrating merchandise. Nor had he complained when she'd agreed to appear, without pay, at several white-tie auctions; for some reason even she couldn't quite discern, prices always rose dramatically when Jade was on hand to provide window dressing.

"Before, your advertisements were in good taste," he argued. "But these latest. . . . A person can't pass a billboard or a bus stop, open a magazine, or turn on the television without seeing you sprawled amid all those tigers." He shook his head. "No, even if the buyers could accept you, which I doubt, I'm afraid that the Tigress woman would detract from the merchandise."

"Are you telling me that so long as I'm spokeswoman for Tigress perfume I can't work here?"

"I'm afraid so."

"But my contract with Southerland Enterprises still has two and a half years to go."

"I'm sorry. There really is no way we can possibly consider allowing you to conduct auctions. However," he said, brightening somewhat, "if you wish to stay on in customer relations—"

"Don't put yourself out," Jade snapped. "I quit."

Undaunted, she walked out the copper door and marched over to Sotheby's and Christie's. The story was the same all over the city. The Tigress woman, it seemed, was pure poison.

"It isn't fair," she complained to Sam over dinner. "I've spent years preparing for this, I'm more knowledgeable than most of the people working at any of the houses. Including that prissy prig, Reggie Bentley. But I might as well be right back where I was when I first got to town."

"You shouldn't let those society snobs get you down," Sam advised.

"I know." Jade's shoulders sagged dejectedly. "I've told myself that at least a hundred times a day this past week. But it doesn't really help."

"They're just a bunch of hot-house orchids, rooted in depleted soil. Hell, they've intermarried so damn much they've weakened the strain." Sam looked at her thoughtfully. "You know, now that you mention it, I realize I've always figured you to be a native New Yorker. You never talk about your past."

"There isn't that much to tell." Jade fell back on the vague, unverifiable biography she had concocted. "I was born in India, but I don't remember anything about it. My parents traveled a lot. They were missionaries."

"Were? Are they retired?"

Having grown up in an alcoholic household, Jade had learned to lie well. In the beginning, she'd lied to protect her mother. Later, she lied to protect herself, to keep people from knowing what went on behind the drawn drapes of the McBride home. Despite the fact that she thought Sam might be the one person who could understand how hard a climb she had made from the bottom rung of the ladder, Jade found it easier to stick to her story.

Unable to look at him, she began toying with her cutlery. "My parents are both dead. They died in a train wreck. In Bangladesh."

"I'm sorry."

"It was a long time ago. They had a wonderful marriage," she said. "They loved each other very much."

"I'll bet they loved you a bunch, too."

"Yes. They did." His expression was so warm, so caring, that for the first time in her life, the facility with which the lies came from her lips made Jade ashamed.

# Fifteen

Five days after her dinner with Sam, Jade received a letter from Remington's, a famed San Francisco auction house, offering her a job. Knowing immediately who had prompted the generous offer, she called Sam at his San Francisco office.

"You used your clout to get me a job," she said.

"Now don't go getting your back up," he said over the hiss of the long-distance wires. "You told me you were qualified to do the work."

"I am, but—"

"And didn't you specialize in oriental art?"

"You know I did, but—"

"Since San Francisco is up to its armpits in ebony, ivory, mother-of-pearl, and jade, you're perfect for the job. So what's wrong with accepting a little help from your friends?"

Jade was tempted. But there was Amy to consider. "I appreciate what you've done, Sam," she said, "but I'm going to have to turn the offer down."

There was a long pause. Just when Jade thought the line had gone dead, Sam said, "How about doing me one little favor?"

"What?"

"Wait twenty-four hours."

"I'm not going to change my mind."

"Honey," Sam said with a low chuckle, "if there's one thing that life's taught me, it's *never* to say never. Promise?"

There was no arguing with him when he was this way. "I promise."

"That's my girl."

Eight hours later, the night doorman woke Jade with the news that she had a visitor.

"We need to talk," he said when she opened the door.

"It's the middle of the night." Jade stepped aside, allowing him into her apartment.

"That's not my fault. You only agreed to twenty-four hours." He glanced significantly at his wide-banded gold watch. "We're already at sixteen hours and counting."

Without waiting for an invitation, he sat down on the sofa. "You really are the most gorgeous woman I've ever seen. Even wearing that god-awful nightshirt."

Jade folded her arms across her chest. "Got something against Garfield?"

"Not on you. How does a man get a drink around here?"

"There's a piano bar down the street," she suggested sweetly.

"Cute, Jade. Real cute."

Admitting she was licked, Jade went into the kitchen and brought out the bottle of brandy. She poured Sam a glass and, handing it to him, sat down beside him.

"Aren't you having one?" he asked.

"If I'm going to get into an argument with you, I'd better keep my mind clear," Jade countered.

"Suit yourself."

"I truly appreciate your trying to help, Sam. But I'm not going to change my mind about the job."

He took a drink. "Fine."

Jade looked at him in surprise. She didn't trust his sudden, uncharacteristic acquiescence. "Really? That's it? After flying all the way across the country, you're not going to try to get me to back down?"

"Of course not. You're a grown woman, Jade. Smart as a whip, too. And from the smart way you've handled your career, I trust your judgment implicitly."

"Then why are you here?"

"To hear the real reason why you can't move to San Francisco."

"It's a long story."

He stretched his arm out along the back of the couch. "I'm not going anywhere."

There was something in his expression that made Jade decide that Sam deserved the truth. Taking a deep breath, she plunged into the dangerous conversational waters.

"A long time ago, when I younger, I thought I was in love. I'd had a crush on the guy for years, and then, finally, I made the mistake of believing he felt the same way about me, and we became lovers."

"And now this guy lives in San Francisco? What's the matter? Is he married?"

"No, he's not married. And he doesn't live in San Francisco," she lied, not wanting him to start wondering if he knew the man in question, which, of course, he did. "But that's beside the point. Even if he did, that wouldn't stop me from moving there."

"So what's the problem?"

"I have a daughter."

To Sam's credit, he didn't blink an eye. "What's her name?"

"Amy. She's nearly six."

"I'd like to meet her."

Jade was not as surprised as she might have once been by Sam's immediate acceptance of Amy's existence. Sam Southerland was a warm, gregarious, loving man.

"I think I'd like that, too," she said honestly. "But there's more." She took a deep breath. "She's deaf."

Sam looked deep into his brandy as he digested that for a moment. "Is there anything that can be done to help her? Jade, if you need money tell me . . ."

"Money won't help." Giving him a wobbly smile, she said, "If it did, I wouldn't have let anything stop me from helping her. The doctors think that her deafness was probably caused by antibiotics I took during my first trimester of pregnancy."

It was the truth, so far as it went. What Jade didn't tell him was that she had her own horrifying idea about why her child was forced to a life of silence. "They also told me it's irreversible."

"But there are other doctors," Sam argued. "They're making medical advances every day, Jade. Let me bring Amy to California; we'll get her the best specialists money can buy."

"She's been to specialists," Jade said. "And they all end up with the same diagnosis. It's irreversible nerve damage."

Knowing firsthand how Sam refused to admit defeat, Jade knew how frustrating he must find her answers. "But she's not like some character out of Dickens. She has a marvelous nanny, Mrs. Campbell, who's like a grandmother to her, she goes to a marvelous school in Brooklyn, and is a budding young star in the Children's Theater for the Deaf.

"Which is why I can't go to San Francisco. Amy's happy here, Sam. I couldn't possibly uproot her."

"Since you're being so agreeable, can I ask for one more favor?"

"What?"

"Come back to San Francisco with me. For just a few days."

"But—"

His fingers curled around her chin, holding her distressed gaze to his. "I think I have the answer to your problem. There's a school in the Napa Valley renowned for its work with the deaf—"

"The Valley of the Moon Academy." She'd learned of it while investigating schools years ago. "But the waiting list is over two years long."

"No problem. As a hefty contributor, I'm on the board. Your little girl could start next week."

"It wouldn't be fair," she said reluctantly.

"Life's not fair," he argued. "Damnit, Jade, all these years you've carried the burden by yourself." His knuckles moved up her cheek, soothing, encouraging. "Let me help you just this once."

"You've already done so much."

"Helping you makes me happy," he said simply. "I'll make you a deal. Let me bump Amy to the front of the line and I'll give the school a contribution to cover the cost of six additional scholarship students."

What had she ever done right in her life that she would meet such a marvelous man? Perhaps it was simply God's way of evening things up a little. Jade made up her mind. "Thank you."

"You're welcome." He tossed off the rest of the brandy. "You'd better get packed," he said. "I filed a flight plan that has our plane taking off in two hours."

"Our plane? You expected me to run off to San Francisco with you, just like that?" Jade didn't know whether to be furious at the man or to admire his self-confidence.

"You don't have to get that gorgeous back up. I wasn't planning to hogtie you and throw you on board," Sam said. "If you'd refused to come with me, I simply would have flown back alone."

"Why don't I believe that?"

"Beats me," he said, reaching out to ruffle her sleep-tousled hair with a friendly hand. "Need any help packing?"

\* \* \*

Jade flew out to San Francisco, visited Remington's, and found it ideal. She also visited the Valley of the Moon Academy, which was located only fifty minutes away from San Francisco. The proximity to the city would allow Amy to make weekend visits home. The campus was beautiful. Set amid the rolling green hills of California wine country, the grounds boasted lots of trees and gardens. In the distance, the volcanic blue cone of Mount Helena seemed to be standing guard over the valley. There was, she noticed, also a football field, a basketball court, a baseball diamond, and an Olympic-size pool.

"You have a sports program here?" she asked the director, who surprisingly was a woman in her early thirties.

"We don't believe in setting up limits to what our kids can achieve," Lisa Palmer said. "Our basketball team is actually quite good, and our swimming team is going to be great." She smiled up at Sam, who'd accompanied Jade to the school. "Thanks to Sam. He put up the money for the pool last year."

It was yet another surprise in a day of surprises. The first had been when a group of children had come running up to Sam as if he were a long-lost uncle and he'd greeted them by signing fluently.

The more Jade saw of the school, the higher her approval of its program soared. The dormitory rooms looked more like bedrooms in private homes and the lunch the kitchen served was far from the standard institutional fare.

"The students take an active part in the running of the Valley of the Moon," Lisa told Jade after she'd commented on the appealing food. "They plan the menus, help prepare the meals, serve them, as you see, and work on the cleanup detail. If Amy comes here," she warned, "she'll be assigned to a weekly work detail."

"She's not six years yet," Jade protested. She couldn't believe that she was expected to pay the costly tuition for her daughter to be put to work.

"That's old enough for simple chores." Lisa gave Jade an understanding smile. "We have to be more than a school here," she explained. "We try our best to provide a homelike atmosphere. Surely you have Amy set the table, pick up her clothes, things like that at home."

"She sets the table," Jade allowed.

"There, you see," Lisa said comfortingly. "It's for her own good. The one thing I'm sure you don't want is for Amy to get the impression that she's some sort of invalid."

"No," Jade agreed. "I certainly don't want that."

"Why don't we show Jade the theater," Sam suggested. "Amy will definitely love the drama program." He had remained uncharacteristically quiet during most of the tour, allowing Jade to gather her own impressions. Knowing that Sam was a man who preferred to control everything in his environment, Jade appreciated this hands-off attitude. She realized it did not come easily to him and was grateful for his consideration.

The theater was a real one, with a full stage, curtains, and light and sound controls that would not have looked out of place on Broadway. "Good heavens," Jade said, as she sat down in one of the red velvet seats, "This is quite impressive."

"It was a donation from Maggie Newman," the director named an actress who'd recently broken new ground for the deaf by winning an Academy Award for Best Actress. "She was a student here and once a year she returns to teach a workshop. The kids love her."

The school, especially the drama program, was perfect. And thanks to her workaholic practices, Jade could easily afford the tuition. There was still one obstacle to overcome.

"Although you may find it to be a contradiction, considering what a public life I live," Jade said when they were back in the director's office, "I'm a very private person. I've managed to keep people from knowing about Amy, not because I'm ashamed of her," she was quick to insist, "but because I don't want her subjected to the press. I've seen what's happened to other children of so-called celebrities. I want to protect her from the glare of the spotlight."

"I can understand your feelings." Lisa Palmer folded her hands on her desk and gave Jade a reassuring smile. "Amy won't be the only child enrolled at Valley of the Moon with famous parents," she said. "And for the record, we are every bit as protective of our children as you are.

"In time, when she acquires all the skills necessary to live in the hearing world, she will have to learn to deal with the same things the rest of us do. Including the publicity that comes with being the daughter of a famous model. But for now, I can assure you that Amy's privacy will be maintained."

It was what Jade had been hoping—praying—to hear. She decided to go ahead and make arrangements for Amy's enrollment, then drove back to San Francisco with Sam.

"May I ask you a personal question?" Jade turned to Sam.

"Sure."

"How do you know sign?"

"Oh, that." Sam shrugged his wide shoulders. "My father went deaf in an accident at the mill before I was born. I guess it was quite a horrible adjustment, but he got some help from the Academy's adult living program. I guess you can say I'm sort of bilingual. When I was growing up, sign was my second language."

"Why didn't you ever say anything?"

He glanced over at her, surprised. "In the first place, I never considered it any big deal. I mean, I usually don't go up to people and say, 'Hi, I'm Sam Southerland, I intend to buy your company, and by the way, my father was deaf.' Also," he pointed out, "I didn't even know you had a child until a few days ago. Let alone one with a hearing loss."

He had her there, Jade decided. And although Sam was very nonchalant about everything, she knew it couldn't have been as easy as he was saying. It was not the first time since she'd met him that Jade was forced to consider Sam Southerland a remarkable man.

One remaining thing had concerned Jade about the move to California. And that was Edith Campbell. But she needn't have worried. After she'd explained the situation, Edith had simply asked, "So when do we move?"

With that problem out of the way, it was time to broach the subject with Amy. Jade was grateful when Sam asked to be there with her.

"Hello." Kneeling down in front of her, he spoke and signed at the same time. "I'm Sam. I'm a friend of your mother's."

Amy looked from Sam to Jade, then back to Sam again. "Are you married?" Her words were getting clearer, Jade noticed with a burst of motherly pride. In the beginning, only Jade and Edith, then Nina, had been able to understand her. Now, although she still dropped her consonants from time to time, anyone could make out what Amy was saying.

"No."

"My best friend Cathy's mother just got married," Amy informed him. "When they come back from their honeymoon, she's going to leave here and go live with them."

"I guess you're going to miss her a lot, huh?"

"Yes." Amy bobbed her head. "But she's lucky because she's going to get to live with her mommy and her new daddy." She gave Jade a pointed look that was mature beyond her youthful years. "I wish my mommy would get married so she could stay home with me all the time."

"Your mommy would love to be with you all the time too, sweetheart," Sam said. "And maybe someday that'll happen, but right now, your mother has to work."

"That's all she does," Amy complained, her tight signs revealing a resentment Jade had not been aware that she'd been feeling. "Work." Her small hands, as they crossed in front of her for the work sign, were clenched so tightly together her knuckles were white.

Sam exchanged a brief, reassuring glance with Jade, who looked as if her world had just crumbled beneath her feet. She'd worked so hard to make certain that Amy didn't lack anything. And although she knew that she couldn't expect a child to understand the demands of the adult world, Jade felt both guilt and a slight resentment that her daughter would even feel, let alone reveal such personal disapproval to a total stranger.

"Work is something grown-ups have to do," Sam told Amy. His expression became grave, his sign more formal to denote the seriousness of his words. "But she came here with a surprise for you."

"What kind of surprise?" Amy looked at her mother expectantly.

"How would you like to go to California?" Jade asked. Amy's accusation had definitely hit home. As Jade asked, her hands trembled slightly.

"For a . . . ," Amy's smooth brow furrowed as she tried to recall the proper sign. Sam and Jade both waited patiently. "Visit?" she finally asked.

"Not a visit," Jade answered. "To live."

Amy's eyes grew wide and suddenly filled with tears. "Leave here? Go away from here?" The hot tears overflowed her eyes to run down her distressed face. "Away from my friends?"

"Your mommy and Mrs. Campbell will be going to California with you," Sam quickly assured the pale little girl. "Your mommy's found this wonderful school where you can swim and ride horses and be in lots of plays."

Amy scrubbed at the moisture on her cheeks with the back of her hands. "Be in plays?"

"Lots of plays," Jade assured her. She dabbed at her daughter's tears with a tissue. "It's a wonderful school, Amy. And we'll still get to be together every weekend."

Amy considered that for a long silent time. "Are you going, too?" she finally asked Sam.

"I live in California," Sam said. "We'll see each other a lot."

Another long drawn out silence. "Okay," Amy decided. "I'll go."

At that, Jade let out a deep breath she'd been unaware of holding.

*   *   *

"I'm going to miss you," Nina said over their good-bye lunch at the Plaza's Palm Court.

"Not as much as I'm going to miss you." Jade's eyes were dry, but inside she was sad. "As soon as I get settled, you're going to have to come to visit us in California."

"You won't be able to keep me away," Nina agreed. "I've been thinking of establishing a West Coast agency for years. San Francisco sounds like just the place to do it."

Nina and Jade's smiles were brittle. Although they continued to swear that no distance, not even a continent, could keep them from remaining as close as ever, both knew that their lives, which had been entwined for so many years, were moving apart. It was a wrenching feeling.

Two days later, Jade, Amy, and Edith were aboard the Southerland company jet, winging their way across the country to a new life.

Jade knew Sam was wealthy, but exactly how much money he possessed had never really sunk in. Until she stepped aboard his Boeing Statesman. Larger than the Cessna Citation, the single-pilot jet Sam had told her he liked to fly himself, the Statesman was capable of carrying twenty-four passengers nearly four thousand miles, nonstop. It was also the ultimate in personal transportation.

Glove-soft leather, sculpted wool, and inlaid hardwood floors adorned the main lounge; Irish crystal and English china contributed to the luxurious dining room ambiance. The bedroom, home to a queen-size bed, was equipped with state-of-the-art sound and video systems; the adjoining bathroom boasted an Italian marble vanity and gold fixtures.

"I like airplanes," Amy said, bouncing up and down in her leather seat. "A lot."

"Don't get used to this," Jade warned as she buckled her daughter's seat belt. Edith was across the aisle, her nose already buried in one of the historical romance novels she was addicted to.

"If you married Sam, we could fly all the time," Amy said.

Jade was relieved that the pilot chose that moment to start the engines. The loud whining sound forestalled a reply and soon Amy, engrossed in the picture books Sam had instructed be put on board for her, appeared to put the matter of Sam's relationship with her mother out of her mind.

Sam was off on business in Amsterdam when Jade, Amy, and Edith arrived in San Francisco. But that didn't stop him from ensuring that everything about their trip went smoothly. They were met at the airport by Joan Peterson, one of Sam's administrative assistants—a tall young blonde wearing a severely tailored gray suit—who took them by waiting limousine to the Fairmont Hotel.

After seeing that they were comfortably settled into their penthouse suite, Joan Peterson promised to return the following morning to take them on a red-carpet tour of the city.

"I'm afraid we don't have time for that," Jade said. "I'd planned to begin looking for a house tomorrow."

"That's all taken care of," the woman assured her briskly. "You have two days allotted for sightseeing, then the real estate agent who handles Mr. Southerland's various California property acquisitions is prepared to show you several available town houses and homes. I believe they all possess the features Mr. Southerland has specified you'll be needing."

"Mr. Southerland seems to have thought of everything."

Jade's dry tone went right over the woman's head. "He always does," she said.

The next months passed in a blur as Jade settled Amy into her new school and moved into a spacious Queen Anne Victorian home on tree-lined Sacramento Street. Along with her modeling work for Tigress perfume, she took on the task of organizing an auction of oriental art for her new employers at Remington's.

She was happier and more fulfilled than she'd ever been. But she couldn't relax because experience had taught her that if there was one thing those hellfire-and-brimstone preachers in Oklahoma were right about, it was that the devil always got his due. Anything good was automatically followed by something bad. That was the way the world worked.

Which was why Jade wasn't surprised when one afternoon she received a call from an Oklahoma doctor telling her that her mother had been hospitalized. Although she'd sworn never to return to Oklahoma, she took the first available flight to Oklahoma City.

Jade had hoped that the doctor had been exaggerating her mother's condition. Now, as she stood beside her sleeping mother's hospital bed and took in Belle's hollow cheekbones and emaciated frame, Jade realized that his description had been charitable.

"Is she going to die?" she asked when she met with the doctor in his office.

"I'm not gonna beat around the bush with you, Miz McBride," he said in a deep Oklahoma drawl. "Your mama's in bad shape. She's sufferin' from pneumonia and acute malnutrition."

"But surely those things can be cured? Money's no problem," Jade added quickly, afraid he might judge her ability to pay by Belle's meager living conditions.

Jade had been stunned by Belle's apartment; there was no reason for her mother to be living in such a grim, dangerous place. Unless she was drinking up most of the money Jade sent her every month, which she appeared to have been doing.

"So long as she responds to the antibiotics, we can lick the pneumonia. And if we keep her here long enough, we can probably put a little meat on her bones." He gave her a long, direct look. "But you and I both know that isn't gonna solve your mama's problem."

Yes. Jade knew that. When she'd first arrived at the hospital that morning, Belle had been screaming her head off, shouting about some soap opera vixen named Erica seducing Merle Haggard and Johnny Cash and turning them into communists. The nurse explained that the delusion was a result of her mother's alcoholic dementia.

When Belle struggled to get out of bed in order to warn the country and western stars about the villainous plot, the resident on duty ordered a sedative. That had been four long hours ago and her mother was still dead to the world.

"What do you suggest, Doctor?"

"There's a detoxification sanitarium in Norman," he said. "The staff doesn't claim to work miracles, but given enough time, they should be able to clean your mother up and get her back on her feet."

So she could go out and start the cycle all over again. The words remained unsaid, but the doctor's expression told Jade that they were thinking the same thing.

"How long is enough time?"

"Two months, minimum. We can get the paperwork started right away. That way, as soon as Belle's lungs are clear, we'll transfer her to the sanitarium."

Without giving her an opportunity to fall back off the wagon, Jade tacked on mentally. She thought back on her time in jail, when all her freedom had been taken away from her. It was the most frightening, humiliating time in her life. Was committing her mother to a sanitarium all that different from putting her in jail?

"Miz McBride?" the doctor asked.

Jade briefly closed her eyes. There was, she reminded herself, no other choice. She made her decision. "Where do I sign?"

As if the devil were determined to make up for lost time, her first night back in San Francisco, Sam unwittingly dropped another bomb.

They'd returned to her house after a luxurious dinner at the Empress of China, the garden restaurant high atop the China Trade Center. Amy was at school, Edith was visiting her daughter, son-in-law, and grandchildren in Seattle, and they had the house all to themselves.

"What are you doing next Saturday evening?" Sam asked. He'd built a fire and they were sitting together on the sofa, close enough to be companionable, without any overt romantic overtones.

"Probably sewing sequins on Amy's princess costume," she replied. "She's determined to be the most glittery Cinderella in history."

Sam chuckled. "She's a firecracker, that daughter of yours," he agreed. "But do you think you can take a few hours away from your domestic duties to attend a wedding with me?"

"I suppose I could get away for a few hours," Jade answered. "Who's getting married? Anyone I know?"

"I don't think so. She's the daughter of a business associate, Richard Hamilton."

"Philippa Hamilton?" Jade could barely say the name.

"That's her." Sam glanced down at her curiously. "I didn't realize you'd met."

"We haven't. But I couldn't miss seeing her picture all over the society pages."

"The woman does get a lot of ink," Sam agreed.

"Who's the groom?" Jade asked with studied calm, dreading the answer she knew was coming.

"Roarke Gallagher."

"The architect."

"That's him," Sam agreed easily. "And although I usually hate any society affair that makes me dress like a headwaiter, if I don't show, I'm afraid Hamilton will take it as a slight." He ran his hand down her arm, linking her cold fingers with his. "But having the most beautiful woman in San Francisco on my arm will make the evening almost bearable."

"The bride's supposed to be the most beautiful woman at her wedding," Jade felt obliged to point out.

"Most weddings," Sam said. "But since Philippa Hamilton can't hold

a candle to you, I guess she'll just have to be content with second place."
He bent his head and kissed her.

"You know," he said thoughtfully, "as much as I hate to jinx their chances by saying anything, I really can't see those two making it."

"Why not?"

"Because this'll be Philippa's third marriage and her usual groom is the kind of society dandy who looks good in black tie and escorts her to all the important functions, while letting her have her way about everything." He shook his head. "Gallagher's always struck me as a maverick. The man's too independent to let his wife have the whip hand."

"Perhaps she's looking for a different type of man this time."

"That's a possibility. If she isn't," Sam predicted, "I don't give the marriage a year."

Roarke and Philippa's wedding was the social event of the season. The guest list of nearly four hundred ran the gamut from old San Francisco society represented by a great number of Spreckels and Crockers to new-money rich like Sam and Jade.

The ceremony was held in the garden of the bride's parents' expansive estate, and Jade decided that the gardeners must have worked overtime to ensure that every rose bush on the grounds would be in full bloom, perfuming the summer air with their sweet fragrance. A white bridge covered with white orchids had been erected over the pond, and adding a decidedly theatrical touch, a pair of snowy swans floated serenely on the still blue water.

A chamber group made up of members of the San Francisco Philharmonic Orchestra, clad in white dinner jackets, began playing something classical Jade recognized but could not name. A moment later, a parade of uniformly chic women moved solemnly over the bridge, their airy flowered chiffon tea-length dresses seeming to float around their calves as they walked. The attendants' white-gloved hands rested on the arms of equally handsome men who were formally dressed in silver gray cutaways.

A white satin runner laid between the rows of satin-covered folding chairs created an aisle leading up where Roarke stood, his hands clasped behind his back. Accustomed to seeing him in faded work jeans on the ranch, or casual wear in Greece, Jade thought he looked strangely alien and decidedly uncomfortable in stiff, formal white tie. He'd also never looked more inaccessible.

A pause in the music drew everyone's attention. And then, the strings began the familiar opening strains of the *Lohengrin* wedding march. Everyone gasped in delight as Philippa Hamilton appeared in a cloud of antique Brussels Duchesse lace. The billowy white Givenchy confection was so heavily beaded it crossed Jade's mind that an entire village of women in India must have gone blind sewing all those pearls onto the lace. The glowing bride carried a nosegay of white roses and lily of the valley that showered the air with their fragrance as the she glided past the wedding guests.

Forced to sit quietly and watch Philippa Hamilton exchange wedding vows with the man she'd once loved, Jade mused that it would probably be a great deal less masochistic to leave San Francisco and move to a place where the people practiced self-flagellation.

Blessedly, the rest of the wedding passed by in a blur. Jade vaguely remembered taking her place with Sam in the long line of guests offering best wishes to the happy couple. Roarke's blue eyes narrowed dangerously when Sam introduced her, but his response was fleeting and he gave no sign that they'd met before.

His coolly polite greeting both relieved and hurt Jade, even as she tried to tell herself that she didn't care what he thought of her. But that was another lie. Because try as she might to shut her heart to this man, she did care. Too much.

Rather than dwell on what might have been, Jade threw herself into her work with renewed vengeance.

Every so often Sam would suggest that she slow down and try to enjoy life for a change. There were times when Jade secretly admitted to herself that she might be trying to do a bit too much, but she also knew that she loved every frantic minute.

As Jade sat at her Queen Anne desk on Sunday mornings, while Amy was still asleep upstairs, adding up the column of figures in her various deposit books and money market accounts, Jade felt a slow deep pleasure that was almost sexual.

Their first Christmas in San Francisco was, Jade decided, a storybook holiday season. She and Sam attended Amy's play where, moved by the little girl's enthusiastic portrayal of the Ghost of Christmas Future, Sam's dark eyes grew suspiciously moist. After a celebration of eggnog and red-and-green-sprinkled sugar cookies, they'd taken Amy back to the city to spend the holidays.

Two days before Christmas, Jade and Sam attended a performance of Handel's *Messiah* at the War Memorial Opera House.

Throwing caution to the winds, Jade had splurged for the first time in her life and bought a ridiculously expensive dress for the occasion. When she opened her front door and saw the look of stunned male appreciation in Sam's eyes, she decided the gown, fashioned from a beaded cognac-colored velvet that brought out the bronze tones in her hair, was worth its extravagant price.

"Since I pay you a helluva lot of money to look terrific, I should know, more than anyone, exactly how beautiful you are," he greeted her. "But tonight, you've outdone yourself."

"I'm glad you approve." Smiling, Jade twirled like Amy showing off a new party dress.

"Approve doesn't even begin to cover it. I'm going to be the envy of every man in San Francisco when I walk into the opera house with you on my arm."

"Funny, I was thinking how every woman will be envying me." Jade's laughing green eyes looked Sam up and down. "You're looking very distinguished tonight, Mr. Southerland." She'd always considered Sam an attractive man, but she was more than a little surprised at the ease with which he wore his formal attire. "I think you were born to wear tails."

He laughed at that. "Are you saying people won't realize that I'm just a lumberjack who's been luckier than some?"

"You make your own luck," Jade said firmly. "And if you're a typical lumberjack, I'm amazed the woods aren't overrun with women looking to catch one of their own."

"That's what I like about you, Jade," Sam said with a bold, swash-buckling grin, "you lie so damn well." He reached out to ruffle her hair in his familiar gesture, stopping when he realized the damage he'd do to her upsweep.

After saying goodbye to Amy, who was in the kitchen with Edith, happily making pans of peanut-butter fudge, they drove to the opera house.

While Sam stood in line to check their coats, Jade was content to remain on the edge of the action and observe the elegantly dressed crowd. The women had definitely pulled out all the stops for this holiday season. Jade couldn't remember the last time she'd seen so much beading and so many jewels in one place.

Her gaze swept the room, pausing at the enormous tree decorated in white lights, tinsel, and silver and crystal balls. Beside the tree, dressed in a silver dress that shimmered like tinsel and made her look like an ornament, stood Philippa Hamilton Gallagher.

Her expression was definitely at odds with the warmth of the season. As she glared up at Roarke, Philippa's face was twisted into an angry grimace worlds different from the cool smile Jade had seen in so many newspaper photographs.

"I don't understand," she complained loudly enough for Jade to hear. "You work so well with my father, why did you turn down such a generous offer?"

"I've told you," Roarke answered with ill-concealed frustration. "If I sign that exclusivity agreement with your father, I won't be able to put in a bid for the new federal courthouse."

"Why on earth would you want to design a silly old courthouse?"

"I've never designed a courthouse."

Philippa shook her blond head in frustration. "You've never designed an outhouse, either," she said acidly. "I suppose that will be next on your wish list?"

"If I could do it my way, it might be a challenge."

"You are, as usual, absolutely impossible!" If looks could kill, Jade considered, Roarke would be six feet under. Muttering a pungent curse under her breath, Philippa spun on her silver stiletto heels and marched away. Heaving a long, weary sigh, Roarke followed.

Jade was still staring after them when a deep voice sounded at her ear. "Champagne for the prettiest woman in the place," Sam said. The smile on his face faded. "Jade? Are you all right?"

"Of course." She shook off the lingering, destructive feelings of regret and flashed him her most dazzling smile. "I was just thinking of something."

"Must've been pretty unpleasant."

He was looking at her with those intense eyes that never missed a thing. Averting her gaze, Jade took a calming sip of the champagne he'd handed her. "Isn't that a beautiful tree?" she asked with feigned brightness.

His fingers curved around her arm. "Jade?"

Saved by the bell. Jade could have wept with relief when she heard the discreet bell summoning everyone to their seats.

"We'd better go."

His fingers tightened. "This isn't New York, Jade. People tend to take their own sweet time."

He was right about that. With the exception of a clutch of little blue-haired ladies wearing fox stoles and their best jewels, no one else had budged.

"I'm sorry," she said, putting down her glass. "But you know I'm a horribly punctual person."

Sam's frustrated look suggested that he knew that she was purposely evading his question, but he didn't want to ruin the evening by arguing. "Whatever you want, Jade." Putting his hand against her back, he ushered her up the stairs to their box.

Although the performance was excellent, Jade's mind wasn't on Handel's music. Try as she might, she couldn't stop thinking about Roarke, and Greece, and the love they'd shared on the island for that one magical week. She'd told herself time and time again that she'd gotten over the pain of discovering that Roarke was her half brother.

She had even made herself believe that his marriage to Philippa Hamilton didn't bother her. But now, as she sat beside Sam in the darkened opera house, listening to the glorious chorus, Jade realized that she'd been lying to herself. Because it did still hurt. Much more than she realized.

By the following day, she'd managed, with her usual self-discipline, to put thoughts of Roarke and his new wife behind her. Professing that it had been years since he'd had a visit from Santa Claus, Sam invited Jade and Amy to spend Christmas Eve night at his Pacific Heights home. Edith was in Seattle, visiting her family. A towering silvery blue spruce claimed a large part of the front parlor; beneath it Sam had piled mountains of gaily wrapped presents.

While Amy sat cross-legged on the faded Aubusson rug in front of the fire, eating her fill of the holiday treats Sam's cook had prepared and stringing popcorn for the giant tree, Jade read aloud from *A Child's Christmas in Wales*. Sam accompanied her narrative with the elegant combination of signs and spelling he'd learned as a youngster. Dylan Thomas's lush words swung in strong curves, hung on the air, full and rich and heavy with vowels, as beautiful as the author had intended.

It was a miracle, Jade thought, wondering what kind of fool she'd been to let last night get her down. Her life was filled with so much joy and love that entire days went by without her fearing the usual inevitable crash.

On Christmas morning the parlor looked as if a tornado had blown through it.

"A small, blue-eyed tornado," Sam said with a grin. His gaze circled the discarded piles of gift wrap and ribbons strewn over the carpet. It looked as if it had been snowing peppermint-striped paper inside the room. "Either that or a hoard of Huns."

Amy, clad in the Grinch pajamas Sam had given her the night before, looked up from where she was dressing one of the three new dolls Santa had brought her. Sam had this particular doll custom-made in Germany with Amy's face. The red velvet dress with its wide lace collar the doll wore was a duplicate of the Christmas dress Jade had bought for her daughter at the Emporium. She'd found a marvelous dressmaker willing to copy it for a reasonable fee.

"Sam?" Amy asked.

"Yes, darling?"

Her eyes were wide and as brightly blue as they'd been the day she was born. Only Jade knew that they were replicas of Roarke's. "Are you gonna be my daddy?"

While Jade blushed at her daughter's forthright question, Sam's response was to throw back his head and laugh. "I don't know, sweetheart," he said. "But now that you bring it up, it sure sounds like a pretty good idea to me."

Jade looked at him quickly, unable to tell if he was serious or not. But Sam's friendly face was giving nothing away.

As the days went by, Amy's unexpected introduction of the topic altered their relationship. For the first time since she had met Sam, Jade began looking at him not only as a boss and a friend but as a potential lover. There was a heightened awareness that hadn't existed before. An awareness that let Sam know his uncharacteristic patience hadn't been in vain.

# Sixteen

Jade's first auction for Remington's drew both old money and new. She didn't know if the turnout was because people were curious to see the Tigress woman in person or because the items offered for sale were genuinely inviting. Whatever the reason, Jade was extremely grateful and relieved.

If there was one moment when she thought her nerves would get the best of her, it was when she stepped up to the podium and saw Roarke and Philippa sitting in the third row. When Roarke's eyes met hers and held for a long, suspended moment, her hands began to shake and her heart picked up a rapid beat. Jade reminded herself that she'd worked toward this moment for years. She couldn't let this ghost from her past ruin things.

"Good afternoon, ladies and gentlemen," she said in a smooth, controlled tone that belied the giant condors flapping their wings inside her stomach. "It's a lovely day for a sale. Shall we begin?"

She turned to her right, where instead of the usual draped display table a beautiful Eurasian model stood, clad in a strapless black sheath. Gleaming against her porcelain skin was a pearl necklace. Sighs of appreciation rippled across the room.

"This exquisite piece consists of fifty-five perfectly matched pearls and weighs a total of eight hundred fifty-one grams. It was given by a Japanese nobleman to the emperor Mutsuhito upon the restoration of his ruling power in eighteen sixty-seven. It took divers ten years to find natural pearls perfect enough to meet the daimio's rigid specifications. One shudders to think how many pearls were discarded in the search for perfection." Again an appreciative murmurer moved through the assembly.

"The emperor named this necklace Serene Moonlight, which, as you can see, was an inspired choice. I will open the bidding at fifty thousand dollars."

Jade did not allow the pace to lag, urging the bidding from fifty thousand to sixty, seventy, eighty, and higher still. All the time, she remained controlled, her voice did not betray the excitement she was feeling.

"I have one hundred and fifty thousand from the gentleman in the back of the room," she said. "The bid is one hundred and fifty thousand dollars." She paused, looking around the room, her calm green gaze settling on one prosperous-looking Japanese gentleman in the front row who, seemingly oblivious to the fever around him, was studying his glossy catalogue with a magnifying glass. "One hundred and fifty thousand dollars," she repeated.

With the barest movement, he lowered the glass and met her gaze. "I have one hundred and sixty thousand," she said, drawing a gasp from onlookers who had assumed the top price had been met. "One hundred and sixty thousand dollars."

And then they were off again, invisible bids flying at her from two men, one in the back of the room, the other in the front, both of whom appeared to have contracted a near-fatal case of auction fever. Abandoning all limits, they dueled savagely, each determined to win at any cost. Jade remained an absolute paragon of calm.

"Two hundred and fifty thousand," Jade said. "Two hundred and sixty thousand. Seventy. I have two hundred and seventy thousand. . . . The bid is two hundred and seventy thousand dollars." She paused and then, accepting the inevitable, hit the mahogany podium with her ivory gavel. "Sold for two hundred and seventy thousand dollars."

The necklace had gone for more than double the reserve. Still caught up in the excitement, the assembled bidders stood, applauding Jade's courage.

The auction picked up speed. A three-color, glazed pottery quatrefoil dish from the Chinese Liao dynasty sold for seventy thousand dollars; a Japanese sword, signed and dated in the sixth month of Showa went for one hundred and fifty thousand; a twelfth-century wood carving of the

Chinese goddess of mercy Guan Yin sold for two hundred thousand, and in a feverish round of bidding, a sixteen-inch high Sancai glazed pottery figure of a court lady from the Tang dynasty sold for three hundred thousand dollars to the man who'd lost out on the pearls.

"You were amazing!" Sam couldn't stop staring at Jade. "I've never seen energy like that in one human."

They were back at Sam's house. Jade had kicked off her black alligator pumps and was resting her feet on his coffee table. Nina, who had come west to give Jade moral support at her first auction, was with them.

Jade was physically exhausted. But her mind was still whirling with numbers. "I was lucky that things went so well."

"It wasn't luck," Sam said. "You did it, sweetheart. *You* whipped those bidders into a feeding frenzy."

"I've never seen anything like it," Nina agreed. "I thought you'd made a mistake when you kept the bidding going on that necklace."

It had been a calculated risk. Jade knew that if she had pushed and had not managed to move the price up, she would have been perceived as failing, regardless of the fact that she'd already received a bid well over the reserve.

"Thanks to Sam, I knew they'd fight it out to the end," Jade said.

"Me?" Sam appeared genuinely surprised. "I don't know a damn thing about jewelry. Except that it's expensive and Freud called the collecting mania a substitute for the sex drive."

Jade wasn't about to touch that analogy. "Remember when you told me that the Carson Department Store chain was up for sale?"

"Sure. I was thinking of buying it myself, but I decided the price would leave me too leveraged."

"Do you happen to recall who did buy it?"

"Eisaku Shoda."

Jade grinned. "Who was sitting in the back of the room."

"I don't suppose you sent a catalogue to Tanaka?"

"I thought he might be interested in acquiring some lovely oriental pieces," Jade said innocently.

"Who's Tanaka?" Nina asked.

"He's the Tokyo investor Shoda beat out on the department store deal," Sam divulged.

"He was also the one bidding against Shoda for the necklace," Jade revealed.

Sam laughed. "You are one helluva smart woman."

Jade smiled. Life couldn't get more perfect than this.

* * *

The following morning, after seeing Nina's plane off, Jade dropped by Sam's house. "I feel like I've been rode hard and put away wet," she muttered, staring glumly into her coffee.

"I haven't heard that expression in years," Sam said, looking at Jade with a slight measure of surprise.

Still exhausted from the emotional strain of conducting her first auction, Jade had unconsciously slipped back into her Oklahoma twang. "I picked it up from a makeup woman," she said, knowing that she was sounding unreasonably defensive, but unable to stop herself. "She grew up in Texas. Or Oklahoma, I forget which."

"Well, I'm not surprised that you're wrung out," Sam said. "You've been working too hard. One of these days I'm going teach you to relax."

It was, Jade considered, a perfect morning for it. The fog had yet to burn off and the house was wrapped in a soft silvery blanket. Seated there in the cozy comfort of his kitchen, Jade found herself wishing that she could freeze things just as they were. Sam was so good to her; never in her life had she ever had anyone care for her as much as he did.

"Sam?"

"Yeah, honey?"

"Would you do me a favor?"

"Anything."

And he would, Jade realized. Without question. "Let's make love."

"Sweetheart," he said, pushing his chair back, "I thought you'd never ask."

They walked hand in hand up the stairs to his bedroom. The mattress sighed when Jade, more nervous than she'd ever been, sat down on it.

Sam stood beside the bed, looking down at her, an expression Jade had never seen before on his face. "What's wrong?"

"Nothing." He shook his head, as if coming out of a fog. "I was simply thinking how damn lovely your are, and how sweet, and smart and accomplished, and yet strangely vulnerable, and wondering how the hell I'd gotten so lucky at this late stage in my life."

"I'm the lucky one." Jade was shaken by the extent of feeling in his dark eyes. They warmed her everywhere they touched. "Please," she whispered, holding her arms out to him.

Sam sat down on the edge of the bed and began to unbutton the tiny pearl buttons running the length of her cream sweater, folding back the cashmere with extreme care, as if he were unwrapping the most exquisite of gifts. His fingers skimmed her torso, doing unbelievable things to her nervous system. When he kissed a trail along the scalloped lace edge of her ivory camisole, Jade shivered.

"You are so soft." His breath warmed the satin covering her breast; Jade bit her lip to keep from crying out.

"No." He returned his mouth to hers, his tongue soothing the tender skin of her lip. "Don't do that." He slipped first one strap of the camisole over her shoulder, then the other. "I don't want you ever to hold anything back." He tugged the satin down to her waist. "I want to know what you like." His mouth on her breast drew out sensation after exquisite sensation. "I want to know what gives you pleasure."

"You do," she whispered, her voice a ragged thread of sound.

It was all he needed to hear. He continued to undress her with agonizing slowness, treating each new bit of flesh to the same prolonged exploration. He left her only long enough to undress himself, but to Jade it seemed an eternity. His hands tempted, his lips seduced. His tongue, as it breached her parted lips, promised.

"Oh yes," she breathed when he joined her on the bed. Her pliant body moved like quicksilver in his arms and Jade knew that if she were capable of coherent speech, she would have been begging him to take her now. But he continued to torment her, touching, kissing, licking, discovering points of pleasure that left her shuddering in his wake. Her skin, gleaming with a pearly luminescence in the silvery light, grew feverishly hot, arousing them both.

Jade's breathing grew heavy. The soft sounds she made when his mouth loitered at the inside of her thigh caused a fire to burn in his loins, but still Sam waited. His fingers drew slow, tantalizing circles through the copper curls between her legs, causing her to arch her body in a bow of utter abandonment.

"I've wanted you from the start," he said thickly. "Every night I dream of you. And every damn morning I wake up alone."

"I've wanted you, too." She gasped at the feel of his long, gently probing fingers. "I just didn't want to admit it. Not even to myself."

Sam savored her soft admission as much as he savored her warm, moist readiness. He watched the need rise in her eyes as he caressed her.

It was torment. Torment mixed with a shimmering pleasure that made her weak. "Sam . . . Oh God . . . Please . . ." Her voice drifted off, her mind emptied, every nerve ending in her body concentrated on one quivering spot.

When his teeth grazed the sensitive nub, her passion shattered into a thousand crystalline pieces. As she shuddered to climax, Sam thrust into her.

Each time he withdrew, his need to fill her grew greater; each time he surged back into her velvet warmth, he felt as if he'd explode. Then, finally, unable to hold back any longer, he was spilling his seed into her warm loins.

Their lovemaking moved their relationship to a whole other plane and when, two weeks after first making love, Sam invited Jade to meet his children, she didn't hesitate to accept.

Jade's first dinner with Sam's children was a strained and unbearably lengthy affair. It began inauspiciously when Jade arrived at Sam's home an hour and a half late. She'd spent the day in the Napa Valley, appraising the estate of one of California's wealthiest vintners. Every auction house in the country had been salivating over the robust, native Italian's treasures since his unexpected death of a heart attack six weeks earlier. When the widow ultimately contacted Jade, the resulting tremors shot through the art world like a series of aftershocks along the San Andreas fault.

The man's extensive ivory collection was everything it had been rumored to be. Enthralled, Jade nearly forgot about Sam's dinner party. Fortunately, she remembered just in time, and although she knew she was cutting it close, if she pushed the speed limit by about ten miles an hour and didn't run into any traffic, she could make the trip from Sonoma to San Francisco with time to spare. Unfortunately, she hadn't planned on a freak accident blocking the southbound lanes of Highway 121.

Although Sam seemed to find Jade's tale about an overturned truck-load of table grapes outrageously funny, his children were clearly not amused. At first glance, Sam's eldest son, Adam, bore a striking resemblance to his father. Closer scrutiny revealed a softness of spirit, a lack of the gritty integrity that defined Sam Southerland.

"That's quite an amusing story," Adam said in a polite but cool tone that hinted he didn't believe a word.

"Well, I'm still sorry. You've no idea how much I've been looking forward to meeting all of you," Jade said with a smile.

"And we've been looking forward to this dinner as well," Michael, the other son, responded, eyeing Jade over the rim of his martini glass. "We don't usually have an opportunity to meet father's"—he paused—"friends."

Friends meaning playmates, Jade concluded. She felt her smile slipping.

Unlike her two brothers, Sam's daughter, Monica, back in San Francisco after her third divorce—from an Italian painter—didn't bother to
hide her animosity behind strained politeness.

"Tell me, Jade," Monica asked, "is it true that foreign photo shoots
are one long, drug-induced orgy?" From that enlightened remark, conversation had gone downhill.

Having grown up with alcoholism, Jade immediately recognized it in
Sam's youngest son. When Michael Southerland put his tanned hand on
her knee, she thought of Trace Gallagher. Not wanting to cause a scene,
Jade merely brushed his hand away, reining in the desire to jab the tines
of her fork into the back of it.

"What did you think of my offspring?" Sam asked, once he and Jade
were finally, mercifully, alone. They had made love, and were sitting in
the kitchen, fixing a midnight snack of sandwiches and an herbal tea Jade
had discovered in Chinatown.

"I don't think they liked me very much." That, Jade considered, was
an understatement. It was more than a little obvious that they saw her
as a rival for not only their father's attention but, worse yet, his fortune.

"I think you're right," Sam agreed easily. He was slicing the roast
chicken into thick slices. "Not that it matters since I don't give a damn
what they think."

"You don't?"

Sam looked as surprised as she did. He put down the knife. "Of
course not."

"Then what was this dinner all about?"

He stared at her for a long, drawn-out second. Then he threw back
his head and laughed that deep booming laugh she had come to love.
"You can't have thought that this was some sort of elaborate test to see
if my children would accept you."

Actually, that was precisely what Jade had thought. It was also why
she'd been a nervous wreck. For the first time in her life, she'd almost
understood Belle's use of alcohol as a tranquilizer. "Wasn't it?"

"Hell no. I just figured that since I have every intention of asking you
to be my wife, I owed you an insider's look, however unpleasant, at the
family you'd be marrying into."

He frowned. "I suppose its partly my fault they're so unpleasant," he
conceded. "I was so damn busy building an empire that I left them to

their mother, who spoiled them rotten. But I promise not to make the same mistakes with Amy."

"You want me to marry you?"

"After the way we've spent the past fourteen days, I figure that the least I can do is make an honest woman of you." His tone was casual, but the question in his eyes was not.

"I don't know what to say."

Sam, who had grown up on the Monterey coast, in the migratory path of the brilliant Monarch butterfly, had learned at an early age that if you want to hold a butterfly, you must keep your hand open and relaxed. Grip too hard and you'll crush it.

"You don't have to say anything except that you agree to think about it. But you'd better not take too long to accept, darlin', because I'm definitely not getting any younger."

"You're not old at all."

He brushed his lips against hers, enjoying the sweet taste. "Sweetheart, I've got socks older than you."

He had never brought up the difference in their ages until after they'd become lovers. Now, Jade realized, he mentioned it at least once a day. Wanting to reassure him that age would have nothing to do with her decision, she gave him a slow, seductive smile more suited to the Tigress woman than the sophisticated businesswoman she'd become.

"You're not old," she repeated. "And I can prove it."

Dropping to her knees, she unzipped his jeans. His penis, revived from their earlier lovemaking, sprang free. Jade cradled it in her palms, warming it with her touch. Her fingers traced the stony thickness of his cock, and when she slipped her lips over him, Sam leaned back against the counter, shoved his hands into her wild mane of hair and decided that perhaps he wasn't such an old codger after all.

# Seventeen

By early 1989, Jade's reputation in the art auction world was beginning to flourish. Just as satisfying was her relationship with Sam, which grew stronger with each passing day. And if there were occasions when he warned her about pushing herself too hard, he never once belittled her goal.

The only cloud on Jade's horizon was her mother, who was sliding deeper and deeper into the abyss of alcoholism. Belle, who would dry out and then quickly slip back, suffered all the symptoms of her disease: hepatitis, heart palpitations, high blood pressure, malnutrition. Along with the suicide attempts, fires from smoking in bed, accidental poisonings, and car crashes. There were times when Jade felt as if she spent half her life on planes rushing to her mother's bedside.

Jade still hadn't accepted Sam's proposal. Thoughts of her mother and her own childhood had kept her from doing so. Marriage meant sharing everything. Being totally open. Unfortunately, Jade had made a second career of concealing her emotions. But now she was struck with the icy fear that she could eventually end up just like Belle. Alone.

"To the Tigress woman." Sam lifted his glass in a toast. "May she enjoy her retirement."

They were alone in Sam's den, sitting on the leather sofa, drinking champagne. It was the final day of her contract with Sam's perfume company and although Jade was grateful for the money she'd earned as the perfume's model, she was relieved when Sam didn't attempt to talk her into renewing the contract. Instead, he'd opted to go for a variety of different looks intended to show that any woman with spirit could be a Tigress woman.

"Three years," Jade said. "Sometimes it seems as if we've known each other forever."

"And every day's been a delight." Sam put a fingertip under her chin, tilting Jade's head, and kissed her. "Why don't I take you out for a ridiculously expensive dinner to celebrate?"

"Oh, Sam, I'd love that, truly I would. But I'm afraid I've made other plans."

"Oh." If she hadn't been watching his face so carefully, Jade would have missed the fleeting look of disappointment that came and went in his eyes.

"Actually," she said, running her fingernail up the front of his shirt, "I took a chance that you'd be free and booked the Cliff House for the weekend."

The Cliff House was one of the most charming inns on California's central coast. Set high on a cliff, as its name suggested, the quaint Victorian inn boasted six bedrooms, a deluxe suite with its own sitting room and bath on the top floor, and a sweeping vista of the ocean.

"What a great idea. Which room?"

When she didn't answer, he said, "Don't tell me you managed to get the Redwood Suite. That's booked months in advance."

"Actually, I booked all the rooms."

She would have guessed it impossible to surprise Sam. But she'd managed. "You booked the entire inn? For us?"

"I wanted you all to myself," she answered, looking up at him through her lashes in a coy manner that was clearly not her way, which made it all the more seductive. "All weekend."

In response, Sam kissed her again. "Have I ever told you," he said against her smiling mouth, "that I love your style?"

"Hundreds of times." Jade began unbuttoning his shirt. "But I certainly wouldn't mind hearing it again."

They undressed each other slowly. In the silence their eyes met and held as they savored the moment for a long, suspended time.

Then, with a soft laugh, Jade wrapped her arms around Sam's neck and pulled him to her.

\* \* \*

The coastal drive from San Francisco to the Monterey Peninsula is one of the most spectacular displays of scenery in the world. Rugged, eroding cliffs thrust upward from a whitecapped sea; on the east side of the winding two-lane highway, silvery wisps of fog nestled in the hollows of the pine-forested slopes of the Santa Lucia mountains. Offshore, crab boats strained at their anchors as they were tossed like playthings on the dark roiling waves.

They stopped for lunch in Monterey, where their window table offered an incredible panorama of the bay and yacht harbor. After lunch, they continued driving down the coast. As the narrow road wound through the stone ramparts of Big Sur country, the gray clouds that had been hovering overhead all morning opened up. A stiff wind drove the water against the windshield.

All the elements were here in this rugged country—waves, wind, thunder, lightning, rain, floods, fire, all clashing with a ferocity that added a dimension of cruelty and terror to the devastating beauty of the scenery. Watching Sam nonchalantly maneuver the car around the slick curves, Jade realized that he was definitely attuned to this untamed environment.

He turned off the highway, heading up the mountain on a steep, twisting, knuckle-whitening gravel road. Finally, the road came to an abrupt end.

The Victorian house seemed to defy gravity; it clung to a rock escarpment overlooking the swirling walls of surf that crashed against enormous boulders below. The sea air had weathered the clapboard exterior to a pewter gray only shades lighter than the angry sky behind it.

The rain was heavy. "We're going to have to run for it," Sam said.

Jade put the hood up on her slick red raincoat. "I've got the key."

"Okay." He opened the door. "Let's go."

The house was every bit as wonderful as Jade remembered. The antiques, including English brass beds, Tiffany lamps, and claw-foot tubs, were original.

Dispensing with their usual rule of providing only breakfast, the absent owners—a mother and daughter—had left a cold supper consisting of smoked pheasant, crusty french bread, various fresh fruits and cheeses in the refrigerator, and a bottle of sherry on the sideboard, and had gone to the trouble of laying a fire in the stone fireplace of the upstairs suite.

Jade and Sam took their supper upstairs to eat in front of the crackling fire. Outside, the storm continued. Inside they were warm and secure.

"There's something I want to ask you," Jade said when Sam returned to the suite after taking the empty plates back downstairs to the kitchen. She was sitting in front of the fire, clad in an emerald silk robe.

"Is this where you tell me what's been bothering you all day?" He sat down beside her on the rug and stretched his long legs out in front of him.

Jade could hear the sharp staccato of the raindrops on the roof; thunder rumbled in the fog surrounding the house. "How did you know I have something on my mind?"

He shrugged. "I always know when you're upset, Jade. Most of the time I just can't figure out why."

She knew he was talking about the way she had always behaved after her mysterious visits to her mother. Someday, she would have to tell Sam the truth about Belle. But not right now. Tonight was the most important night of her life; she refused to let her mother spoil it.

"I'm not really upset," she said. "It's just that I want to ask you something and I'm having trouble thinking of the right words."

"Anything you want, Jade," Sam answered without hesitation, "anything at all, it's yours. All you have to do is ask."

Taking his strong, kind, wonderful face between her palms, she said: "If you haven't changed your mind, or gotten tired of waiting for me, I can't think of anything I'd rather do than spend the rest of my life with you."

"Are you talking about living together, or—"

"I want us to be married," Jade said with a burst of passion. She was infused with a warmth that had nothing to do with the flicking orange flames in the fireplace. "I want to be your wife, Sam Southerland. If you'll still have me."

"If I'll still have you? Christ, Jade, I've been waiting three years to hear you say those words." His fingers cupped her chin as he looked deep into her eyes. "But why now? After all this time?"

She didn't know how to explain about her mother and how on her last trip to Oklahoma, she'd realized how very close she was to spending her life alone, too. Sam was a patient man, but she suspected that even he wouldn't wait forever.

And then there was Roarke. Although she hated to admit it, even to herself, Jade knew that part of her had avoided making a commitment to Sam because of lingering feelings for the man she'd once dreamed of building a life with. But it was time for her to face facts: Roarke was married, and even if he weren't, there could never be a future for them.

Since Jade couldn't reveal any of that to Sam, she told him what truth she could. "It wouldn't have felt right to marry you while I was still under contract as the Tigress woman. But now I no longer work for you and I came to realize that my life wouldn't be the same without you in it. So—" she took a breath "—I'd like to negotiate a new contract. A lifetime one."

He pulled her into his arms, nearly crushing her, but caught up in her own urgency, Jade didn't complain.

Wanting came in a flash. Icy rain lashed at the windows; neither of them heard it. The wind moaned; it was ignored. A tree branch scraped against the side of the house; it went unnoticed.

Sam and Jade lost themselves in a passion-filled storm of their own making.

Two weeks after her romantic weekend with Sam at Big Sur, Jade was called to the Montgomery Street office of Kaplan, Kaplan, Huntington, and Norris, attorneys at law. At first curious about why she'd been summoned, Jade was thrilled to discover that the heirs of Mary Harrington, an elderly Pacific Heights matron who'd recently died, had chosen her to conduct the estate auction of their mother's prized possessions.

"There's just one catch," Jade told Sam later that night. "Mrs. Harrington specifically insisted that Remington's not be given the commission."

"Mary Harrington and Jason Remington had an ongoing feud for as long as anyone can remember," Sam explained. "I think it had something to do with a falsified provenance on a painting Mary bought back in the fifties, but I'd suspect even the two of them had forgotten the specifics."

"I don't know if I can accept," Jade said.

"Why not?"

"Because I'd have to quit my job at Remington's."

"So? You've been saying for years that you wanted your own auction house. It seems to me the commission you'd make on this sale would give you one helluva start."

"I don't have any place to conduct an auction."

"I've already taken care of that. The manager of the Fairmont assured me that he'd be more than happy to have you hold the sale in his ballroom."

"You knew?"

"Mary told me what she planned to do six months ago, after she was diagnosed with inoperable liver cancer. I promised not to say a word to you, but I did agree that she was doing the right thing. As you know, over the past few years she's focused solely on Eastern art, and for my money—and for hers, too, apparently—you're the best in that field."

He smiled down at her. "So, when she died last week, I called the Fairmont and booked the ballroom."

Jade flung her arms around his neck. "I love you, Sam Southerland."

Although she'd met Mary Harrington on several occasions and had been invited to her mansion to view the woman's vast collection of oriental art, this time Jade was looking at the items with an auctioneer's eye.

Entering the magnificent entry hall was a bit like stepping inside of a Fabergé egg, one fashioned by an artisan who had been Asian rather than Russian. Crowded together atop a black lacquered table inlaid with mother of pearl was a bronze urn with dragon handles, a grouping of jade tomb figures designed to provide eternal companionship for the deceased, a glazed pottery watchdog, a carved red lacquer box adorned with gold butterflies, a jade Chinese tripod censer, and a Korean celadon water dropper in the form of a duck.

On the walls were Japanese scroll paintings of waves dating to the 1700s, another depicting the gods of thunder and wind she recognized as having been painted by Sotatsu, the leading Japanese painter of the Edo period. A portrait of Ch'ien-lung, the fourth emperor of the Ch'ing Manchu dynasty in full Manchu ceremonial regalia, painted on silk by Castiglione, a European missionary living at the court, shared space with a Tawaraya fan painting depicting court ladies.

Nearby was a landscape screen of the four seasons, painted by Sesshu, a Japanese painter renowned for adapting Chinese models to the Japanese ideals and aesthetic sensibilities. The screen bore Sesshu's seal and signature and an inscription attesting that it had been painted in the artist's seventy-second year, 1492. The same year Columbus had set off for the new world.

Mary Harrington's furnishings were as magnificent as her choice in art. A purple sandalwood table sat beside a straight-backed bamboo seated armchair. Obviously designed for a senior member of the Chinese patriarchal family, the curved legs were stylized imitations of elephant trunks.

In her bedroom, set on a riser, dominating the room, was a magnificent four-poster bed in the Chinese style. Rising from the four posters was a red lacquered pagoda, topped by a bronze dragon holding a pearl in its claw.

There were more museum pieces in this house than Jade had ever seen in one place in her life; the quantity and quality made her lightheaded, like Alice after she'd fallen down the rabbit hole.

"This is all so amazing," she breathed as she examined an exquisite fierce celadon lion. The pale, bluish-green cast was luminous and slightly opaque, revealing it to be the famed Longquan glaze from the Southern Sung period, 1127–1279, which Jade had learned was a deliberate attempt to copy the more treasured and costly jade.

Although the green glazeware dated back more than three thousand years and was an essential step in the process leading to porcelain, many experts, Jade included, considered celadon to have a beauty all its own.

Indeed, Xu Yin, a ninth-century poet had described a set of Imperial teacups made of what he called celestial celadon to be like curling disks of thinnest ice filled with green clouds, and like bright moons cunningly carved and colored by spring water.

Celadon had traveled the high seas, sharing the holds of tall-masted ships with silk and musk and copper coins. Due to the Muslims' belief that celadon glazeware changed color when poisoned food was offered on it, it became particularly popular during the time the Mongols had ruled Peking during the Yuan dynasty. By the fourteen century, celadon's days of triumph had ended as porcelain overtook it in popularity.

But now, as Jade ran her fingers over the pale bluish-green snarling lion, she considered that its cool, aesthetic effect was soothing and very Chinese.

"The old girl was quite the collector," exclaimed Aaron Kaplan, the attorney escorting her through rooms that could have doubled as a pirate's treasure trove.

Now that, Jade decided, taking in a blue satin Imperial dragon robe embroidered with silk and metallic thread hanging on the wall in front of her, had to be the understatement of the millennium.

"Mary's attorney told me that her family always figured that her love of beautiful things was a fairly harmless addiction," Jade told Sam after her inspection of the house. They were having lunch on the glassed-in terrace of an Embarcadero restaurant.

"I suppose it was, considering some of the others she could have taken up," Sam said.

Thinking of her mother's addiction to alcohol, Jade silently agreed.

Sam glanced down at his watch. "I've got a meeting with some bankers at three, but how would you feel about taking a short walk along the waterfront? There's a building I want to show you."

Ten minutes later Jade was touring a waterfront building located near the Embarcadero.

"I'm going to buy this lot and raze the building," Sam said, gazing around the dilapidated brick factory with satisfaction. "And in its place, I'm going to build the biggest, most elegant auction house the art world has ever seen."

And he would, Jade knew. He had proven over the past three years that he would do anything for her, including take the world apart and put it back together in a way that pleased her. He was the most generous, loving man she'd ever met.

She put her hand on his arm. The five-karat diamond solitaire on the ring finger of her left hand sparkled in the noonday sun. "I can't let you do that."

"Why not?"

"It's too expensive."

"Damnit, Jade, quit being so stubborn. I've got money I haven't even counted yet. You won't let me buy you the kind of jewels most women want. And you refuse to wear fur anymore. So would you at least let me give you this as a wedding present?" He ran his palms up and down her arms. "I've never asked you for very much," he reminded her. "But I'm asking you to let me do this for you."

Sam was so genuinely nice that Jade often forgot that he was one of the richest men in the world. "All right," she said, "but on one condition."

"What's that?" Suspicion furrowed his broad brow.

"That you rein in your impulse for always having the biggest and best and simply build the most beautiful auction house in California. We can tackle the world later."

He laughed, the big, booming laugh she'd come to love. "Sweetheart, you've got yourself a deal." Sam grinned, his earlier irritation disintegrating like morning fog. "And now that we're agreed, we need to get started on the specifics. Will you let me help with the design?"

"Considering how many office towers you've built all over the globe, I'd be crazy not to." Jade looked out over the bay, admiring the breathtaking view and trying to decide how to use it to enhance her sales.

"You've no idea how glad I am to hear you say that, sweetheart," he said. "Because I've already invited Roarke Gallagher to dinner."

"Roarke Gallagher?"

"Word about town is that he's gotten antsy working with his father-in-law," Sam told her. "The gossip must be fairly accurate because he jumped at the opportunity to talk shop. And he's good, Jade. Better than good, he's terrific. His buildings are bold and innovative and best of all, original. Just like a certain gorgeous lady I'm crazy about. I think, when you have a chance to discuss your design ideas with him, you'll agree."

Her thoughts in a turmoil, Jade managed to mutter a vague agreement.

# Eighteen

Something was definitely wrong. As the evening dragged on, Sam sensed undercurrents that he hadn't expected. Dinner was decidedly strained with Roarke icily polite and Jade uncharacteristically remote.

"I hear through the grapevine that you're considering taking over Hamilton Construction," Sam said to Roarke.

Roarke's fingers tightened around the stem of his wineglass. His father-in-law, who had professed a desire to retire, had brought up the idea of Roarke abandoning his architectural firm in order to take over the reins of Hamilton Construction.

When Roarke turned down the offer, Philippa had been furious, insisting that he reconsider. Didn't he understand that she'd been raised to be the wife of a powerful man? With that single statement, his wife had managed to denigrate not only his work but his entire life. She'd also dealt a near death blow to an already shaky marriage.

"The grapevine's wrong. I'm an architect. Not a developer."

"Well, I can't deny that I'm relieved," Sam said. "I'd hate to have to start looking around for another architect to design my fiancée's auction house."

"I'm looking forward to the challenge," Roarke answered tightly.

He was furious at the way Jade had beguiled Sam Southerland into giving her whatever her black heart desired. Obviously, she had been holding out for a richer man than he had been three years ago, and although he was now a wealthy man in his own right, Roarke knew that his bank account wouldn't even amount to Sam's daily interest.

Roarke didn't know how he could work closely with Jade. But neither did he want to turn Sam down. Not only did he like and respect the older man, but since his business relationship with his father-in-law was strained, Roarke couldn't afford to offend a potential client.

If Roarke was reluctant to work with Jade, she was even less eager. But Sam was so enthusiastic about the project—like a little boy anticipating Christmas morning—she knew that she couldn't refuse to let Roarke design her building without explaining her aversion.

Midway through the meal, Sam excused himself to take a phone call. Left alone, Jade and Roarke dropped the pretense.

"Nice sugar daddy you've latched onto," he ground out as he refilled his wineglass. He'd already polished off nearly a bottle single-handedly, making Jade wonder if he'd developed a drinking problem.

"Don't criticize what you could never understand."

"Oh, I understand, *Cassie,*" he said. "Only too well."

He took another long drink of the crisp dry Sauvignon Blanc. It was Sam's label; he had bought a Napa Valley winery recently for no other reason than that he'd tasted the wine and liked it.

"I suppose congratulations are in order," Roarke said. "Or is it best wishes for the bride?"

"It doesn't really matter," Jade said, "since you wouldn't mean either."

"Hey, you want to sell your body to the highest bidder, that's your business."

"That's not what I'm doing."

"Isn't it?" His eyes were chips of blue ice. "You can call it what you want, Cassie. But your behavior would make a Borgia proud." The disgust in his voice was painful to hear.

"Speaking of selling yourself to the highest bidder," she murmured, not wanting him to escape unscathed, "how did that office building in Greece turn out for your father?"

His expression turned even stonier. "I've no idea. Since I didn't end up designing it, after all."

"Too bad," she murmured, but she didn't mean it. She was curious about exactly what had happened between Roarke and his father, and it pleased her to know that Quinlan couldn't always control everything or everyone.

An uncomfortable silence settled over the table. Roarke finally broke it. "So what do we do now?"

Jade forced an uncaring shrug. She'd played this charade before. "Sam says that you're very good at your work."

"I'm damn good."

Like Sam, Roarke displayed a confidence and a pride in his achievements that would have made a lesser man appear smug. Reminding herself of all the reasons she shouldn't feel anything about him, Jade stayed remote.

"Well, since I want the best, I suggest we plan a building." Her voice was thick with pain she was too proud to shed as tears.

Roarke failed to notice Jade's distress. Instead, he wondered when had she gotten so damn cold. "You do realize that planning a building will entail a great deal of close contact."

Jade took a sip of wine and eyed Roarke calmly over the crystal rim of her glass. Inside, her nerves were screaming. Outside, her expression remained flawlessly neutral.

"I certainly won't have any trouble with that," she lied.

Roarke looked as if he was about to question that statement, but Sam chose that moment to return, and Jade felt like a condemned prisoner who'd just received a reprieve.

As the evening dragged on, Jade took pride in her ability to act as if everything were normal. And why shouldn't she? she wondered bitterly. After all, she'd had a lifetime of practice.


Jade felt like a circus performer, juggling flaming torches while dancing on a high wire, as she prepared for the auction of Mary Harrington's treasures, consulted with Roarke on building plans, and tried to make time for Amy on weekends. Sometimes it seemed as if there was never enough hours in the day to get things done. Fortunately, Sam had agreed to put off their wedding until after the auction.

Making things increasingly more difficult was Jade's unrelenting desire for Roarke. She couldn't help herself.

He would be sketching something she wanted changed on the blueprint when Jade's mind would drift and she would remember the feel of those strong hands on her body. And despite her deep love for Sam, despite the realization that her desire for Roarke was wrong, despite everything, she wanted him.

Jade wished that Sam's business interests didn't keep him away so much of the time. If he were only there to run interference, she and Roarke wouldn't be forced to spend so much time alone.

One bright spot on the horizon was that Nina had, as she'd been promising to do for years, arrived to open a West Coast agency in the Embarcadero complex. Her plan, she'd told Jade over the phone, was to spend approximately one week each month in the city.

Jade was waiting at the gate when Nina's flight arrived. "I've missed you."

"Not as much as I've missed you." Nina returned Jade's hug.

"You're welcome to stay with me for as long as you want," Jade said as they left the airport. "With Amy away at school all week, and Edith volunteering every afternoon at the homeless shelter, the house gets lonely."

Nina leaned back in the soft leather passenger seat of Jade's Mercedes. "You're paying Edith to volunteer?"

"She takes care of the house, but with Amy gone all week, it leaves her with a lot of extra time. Besides, you know how good she is with children. The kids at the shelter love her."

"Perhaps you ought to consider bringing Amy home full-time."

Jade shot her a disbelieving look. "After what I told you about Roarke? My God, what if Sam invited him to our house or worse yet, he stopped by some day with architectural changes? What if he and Amy ran into one another?"

"What if they did? Perhaps it's time you got over your paranoia about the Gallaghers stealing your daughter. Besides, even if Roarke did try anything like that, Sam would stop him."

"I don't want to talk about Roarke," Jade insisted. "And it's a moot point because Amy loves her school."

That much was the truth. What Jade didn't mention was that Amy was doing so well that her teachers had suggested mainstreaming her into the San Francisco school system. Something that Jade had, thus far, managed to put off. Not that she didn't feel guilty.

"Besides," Jade said, "along with preparing for the auction, I've been trying to acquire a decent inventory for Jade's, which involves a lot of travel. I've decided to specialize in oriental art, specifically jade."

"What a good idea. It will make a perfect promotional tie-in with your famous name."

"That's what Sam said. And I suppose it's true, but you know I've always had a special fondness for jade, so it makes sense. Especially here in San Francisco, where Gumps and other dealers have already established a strong market for the stone. However, in the beginning I can't afford to be all that choosy. Thanks to Mary Harrington naming me in her will, I've received some commissions for traditional European paintings, so I leased space for a gallery in Cow Hollow and hired a couple of European experts to work there."

Her recent actions had generated a rumble of irritation from a great many dealers in the city. Those who shared her oriental focus resented her using her fame as an international model to gain publicity for her fledgling enterprise while she cut into their acquisitions. Other dealers felt she should stick to the Eastern market and refer those interested in either buying or selling European art to them.

Fortunately, since she'd always been upfront and had told Jason Remington of her dreams of someday owning her own house, he hadn't said a negative word about her resignation. In fact, he'd even wished her well. But that was before two of his best employees deserted him to work for her, Jade admitted.

"Maybe as more people start coming to you, you'll be able to cut down on your traveling," Nina suggested carefully.

"Don't I wish. But I can't see that happening any time soon. So, since I've been spending almost as much time in China, Japan, and Hong Kong as I do in the city, Amy's much better off at school."

"I seem to recall a time when you believed she was better off at home," Nina pointed out.

Jade didn't answer what she knew to be all too true. What was also true was that her daughter had become very temperamental. Recently, several of Amy's little friends had left the Valley of the Moon school to live at home and attend local public schools. It was not surprising that Amy now wanted to live with her mother in San Francisco.

Jade repeatedly tried to explain about her busy life, saying it was impossible for a child to share. But Amy, who wasn't in the mood to accept any excuses, spent most of their weekend visits sulking.

"I brought you a present," Jade said on one particularly unpleasant Saturday afternoon. Since her first trip to Kenya, Jade had always returned from her travels with some little gift for her daughter. In the beginning, the gifts had been simple things—a pink shell from a glittering beach, a coconut carved to look like a monkey's face, a plastic statue of King Kong climbing the Empire State Building. These days the presents were a great deal more costly, and if there were times a little voice in the back of her mind pointed out that she was trying to buy her daughter's love and affection, Jade steadfastly ignored it.

Amy unwrapped the gilt package and lifted the Madame Alexander doll from its bed of white tissue paper. The doll was dressed like a Russian czarina, in a red velvet cape and ermine hood from which glossy black curls—so like Amy's—tumbled free. Tiny black leather boots graced her feet, and her hands were tucked inside a fluffy white muff. It was the most beautiful doll Jade had ever seen, and although it was an outrageously expensive gift for a little girl, she hadn't been able to resist.

"I wanted a new Barbie," Amy said, discarding the exquisite doll without so much as a second look.

"But this doll is so much better," Jade insisted. "Look at those beautiful blue eyes, they look just as real as yours, and her eyelashes—"

"She boring. She doesn't do anything."

"She can do anything you want. It's called using your imagination." Jade was quickly losing patience. On the flight home from JFK, she had held the box in her lap, unwilling to allow anything to happen to it. She couldn't wait to see Amy's thrilled expression.

"I told you, Mama, astronaut Barbie comes with a real flag and a space suit and a walkie-talkie."

With a pout, she turned her back, refusing to look at her mother. Jade sighed, knowing that the argument was not about dolls at all, but about Amy's increasing insistence that she live at home. Jade realized that somehow, the person she loved most in the entire world had become a victim of her subterfuge.

Making matters worse was the call about her mother, who had been back in a sanitarium and had now vanished from the grounds. The director assured Jade that the police were looking in all the usual spots; it was only a matter of time. It was not uncharacteristic for Belle to behave like a recalcitrant juvenile delinquent; she ran away from treatment centers with predictable regularity. But each occasion forced Jade to live with the fear that this would be the time the police would find her mother dead.

More and more Jade felt as if the tidy tapestry she'd woven of her life was in danger of becoming unraveled. All it would take would be for some unseen hand to tug too hard on one of the delicate strands, and everything she'd worked so hard for would disintegrate in front of her eyes. Whenever she began to feel overwhelmed, she would immerse herself even more deeply in her work. It was the one aspect—the only aspect—of her life where she felt in control.

* * *

"Tony DiAngelo agreed to take the photos for the catalogues," Jade told Sam. DiAngelo was a coup; the famed photographer was renowned for his portraits of the rich and famous. The same people Jade was inviting to the auction.

"Catalogues? Plural?"

"Didn't I tell you? I've decided that the only way to manage things is to have three separate sales on three days—the first for furniture, another for paintings, the third for collectibles."

"I suppose that makes sense."

"It's either that or try to conduct a thirty-six-hour marathon. After all, it took eight curators a month to catalogue everything. Thank God for computers. I've talked to the hotel, and they'll give me the ballroom for three days, and I've booked a block of rooms for out-of-town buyers."

"Good idea. That gives you a captive audience." He frowned thoughtfully. "You'll need extra security. I'll arrange to have some of my people there for the entire week."

"That isn't necessary. I've contacted the firm we used at Remington's. They're expensive, but well worth the cost."

"Sounds as if you're right on top of things."

His dry, slightly resentful tone flew right over Jade's head. "I hope so. I keep waking up in the middle of the night with lists of things I've almost forgotten. Which reminds me," she said, "did I tell you we were videotaping Mary's house?"

"No. Why?"

"It was Tony's idea. He thought that along with the regular glossy catalogues, we should make a videotape of each of the rooms to show exactly how amazing the sale is. Of course, the items themselves are exquisite, but seeing them the way I first did, all crammed together, piled atop tables and covering the walls, should generate a lot of excitement."

"And greed."

Jade grinned. "Exactly."

"Did anyone ever tell you that you're beautiful when you're talking about money?"

"Actually, no one's told me that I am beautiful in a very long time," Jade said with a sad little sigh. "My lover has been away a lot lately. On business."

He brushed his lips against her hair, breathing in its clean scent. "The man must be a damned fool."

Just as he lowered his head to kiss her, the phone rang. And rang.

"Ignore it," he said, nibbling enticingly at her neck. But Jade had stiffened in his arms.

"I'd better see who it is. Things have been so hectic lately, I don't dare miss a call." Jade didn't add that she'd been on pins and needles, awaiting word of Belle.

"Hello?" Her shoulders sagged. "Of course," she agreed flatly. "Thank you for calling. Yes, I'll be there first thing tomorrow morning."

When she turned back to him, Jade pressed her forehead against the firm line of his shoulder and allowed his strength to flow into her.

The news that Belle was back in the hospital was both good and bad. Good that her mother had been found alive; bad that she was undergoing surgery for injuries received after running her car into a ditch.

"Sam, you're going to hate me, but—"

"You're canceling our weekend in the mountains."

Reminding himself that he'd fallen in love with all the intriguing aspects of Jade, including the workaholic, Sam bit back his frustration.

He had put aside important merger negotiations and flown three thousand miles for two rare, uninterrupted days with Jade. But Sam wasn't particularly surprised; it wasn't the first time their plans had been interrupted by her mysterious trips. Trips that Jade had never been willing to discuss.

Sometimes, her explanation was merely a "need to get away." Other times it was "personal business." And there were occasions when she wouldn't even bother to offer one of her flimsy excuses. Still, Sam assured himself that someday Jade would trust him enough to share her secret.

Jade saw the disappointment in his eyes and touched his cheek, which was pleasantly scratchy from his hours spent in flight. "I promise, as soon as this sale is over, I'll make it up to you."

He wanted to shout at her. To demand to know what—or who—it was that was more important than he was. He wanted to ask her, Where the hell are you going? And why? But he'd learned that it didn't work with Jade; you couldn't ask a thing right out or she'd back away.

Loving her in spite of his aggravation, Sam put his arms around her. "Do we have time for dinner?"

"Actually," Jade said softly, "I'm not very hungry. How about you?"

Of all the Jades he'd fallen in love with—the loving mother, the hard-driving businesswoman, the breathtakingly beautiful model—it was this one, the reluctantly vulnerable, soft one, who had first claimed his heart. Her eyes were inviting him to bed, but Sam had the feeling that she didn't just want to make love, she needed to.

Without a word, he scooped her up in his arms and carried her into the bedroom where he managed, for a short time, to exorcise whatever ghosts and demons were haunting her.

The day before the auction, Jade had taken a break and was trying to work off some of her anxiety by repotting geraniums. She was out on the wide back porch of her Queen Anne house, when Edith appeared in the doorway.

"You have a visitor," Edith announced with obvious surprise. Other than Sam or Nina, no one had ever been invited to the house.

Jade, who was wearing a pair of skintight cutoffs and one of Sam's T-shirts, wiped her hands on her shorts, and asked, "Who is it, Edith?"

"Me," the familiar voice offered as Roarke appeared behind Edith.

Jade's first reaction was to turn pale. Her second was to cast a quick, involuntary look at the second-floor window of Amy's bedroom. Fortunately, it was Thursday and her daughter was away at school.

"Would you like me to bring some ice tea out for you and your guest?" Edith asked, her concerned gaze sweeping Jade's face in a way that told Jade she hadn't missed her reaction to Roarke's appearance.

"No, thank you, Edith," Jade managed, through lips that had gone unbearably dry. "Mr. Gallagher won't be staying very long." When Edith had retreated back into the house, Jade turned and forced herself to look directly at him. "This is a surprise."

"I'm sorry to bother you at home," he said. "But I needed your approval to change the stairs. Fire ordinances." He explained that when he discovered she wasn't in the temporary office she'd leased in one of Sam's downtown buildings, or at her Cow Hollow gallery, he had tracked her down at home. "The enclosed stairway you wanted was too narrow to pass code. But I think you'll like the change I've come up with."

She took the plans he offered, spreading them out on a glass-topped table. The rich loamy potting soil still clung to her hands as she examined the blueprints.

"They're cantilevered now?"

"Red steel," he went on. "The cantilevered stairs will open up more space."

"I suppose you're right. But red?"

"Why don't you withhold judgment until you see them in place," he suggested. "If you don't like the color, we can repaint."

"I suppose that makes sense." She continued studying the blueprints.

"So, tomorrow's the big day."

"Excuse me?" When she glanced up from the plans, Jade saw Roarke looking at her in that familiar, throat-catching way.

"I was referring to the auction."

"Oh." An extraordinary amount of tension emanated from her body; as hard as she tried, Jade could not drag her gaze away from his lips. "Yes. It begins tomorrow."

"Nervous?"

"Horribly." They were talking about business, but their eyes were speaking a remembered language all their own.

"You'll be terrific, as always." Then he suddenly switched gears. "How the hell long do you think you can keep this act up?"

"What act?" She forced the words through her tightened throat. "I don't know what you mean."

Feeling a sudden need to escape Roarke's intense look, she stood up and walked to the end of the porch. The afternoon sun made her hair gleam like molten copper laced with strands of gleaming gold. "The changes are fine. And the more I think about it, the more I like the idea of the red stairs."

"The hell with the damn stairs." Roarke came up behind her and put his hands on her shoulders. "You know what I'm talking about," he ground out, turning her to face him. "The way you pretend that what we had never existed."

"Roarke, please. You're married."

"I know."

But not for long, he thought to himself. His marriage was on the skids. Although he'd known from the beginning that Philippa was devoted to her father, he'd never suspected that her feelings were as strong as they were. The unpalatable truth was that Philippa would always put Richard Hamilton before anyone. Even her husband. These days, especially her husband.

"But that doesn't stop me from wanting you. Or you from wanting me."

"I don't." Jade was trembling from his nearness and her own reckless desire.

"Don't you?" He spread his hand over her back and let it glide familiarly down to the soft curve of her hip. "Do you look at him the way you look at me?" he demanded quietly.

"I don't look at you in any way. I don't want you."

In the lengthy silence that followed her assertion, Jade found herself waiting for a bolt of lightning to strike her for telling such an outrageous lie.

"Really?" Roarke's lips curved in a faint smile. "Let's just test that, shall we?"

Jade's mouth went dry. Words deserted her.

As Roarke slowly lowered his head, Jade saw the purposeful gleam in his eyes and knew that she didn't have a chance of fighting him. What was even worse, she didn't want to.

She stood there, rooted to the spot, unable to resist. She told herself to remain passive, to prove to him that this stolen kiss didn't mean anything to her. That he didn't mean anything.

But Jade was not prepared for the explosion that rocketed through her as his mouth met hers. Her hands, which should have been pushing him away, refused to obey her mental commands; her fingers curved into his broad shoulders.

Roarke's hands slipped beneath the T-shirt and moved up her back, caressing her warm flesh with a confident, practiced touch. "Christ, you feel good."

When he pulled her against him, Jade felt the unexpected hardness of alien muscle against her breasts, her stomach, her thighs. Hunger rose, hot and primitive. He had lured her to the brink and she knew it would take only the gentlest shove before she went toppling over the edge.

Imagined fantasies flashed before her mind's eye—erotic, vivid, demanding. She was alive—vibrantly, brilliantly alive. Every nerve ending reached for his touch; every pore sought relief from a passion too long denied. It was frightening. And it was wonderful.

Roarke buried his hands in her hair, sifting it through his fingers like grains of burning sand. Her scent swam in his head, passion battered away inside him, threatening to do away with any vestiges of propriety.

He wanted to feel her hot and naked beneath him; he needed to feel her flesh like flaming satin against his skin; he longed to hear the soft little cries she made when he took her over the top; he wanted her hands to stroke his body as he would caress hers until all control had disintegrated. Roarke ached for Jade with every fiber of his being.

"Goddamnit, I want you," he groaned against her lips. "Here. Now. Before one of us comes to our senses."

He yanked down the zipper on the shorts and thrust his hand inside the silk of her bikini panties. She was warm and moist and ready for him.

*Before one of us comes our senses.* Roarke's words sent reality crashing down on top of Jade.

"No." Frantic, she pushed at his shoulders, breaking the heated contact. Before he could stop her, she'd spun away from him. Her fingers shook as she tried to rezip her shorts. "You have to leave."

"What the hell is the matter now?" Roarke asked incredulously. "You can deny it all you want, Jade, but what we had—what we still have—is real. And it isn't going to go away simply because you want it to. I want you. And you want me. So what's the problem?"

"Wanting's not enough." She combed her shaking fingers through her tumbled mass of hair. "Besides, I already told you, Roarke, you're married."

"You weren't thinking about my wife a minute ago."

"You're right." Jade took a deep breath. "I allowed things to get out of hand," she admitted. "But it was only physical. Just sex. Nothing more."

His only response was to lift a disbelieving eyebrow.

Just sex? As he took in the sight of her stricken face, Roarke wondered if she knew exactly how wrong she was. Sex was the only thing he and Philippa had ever shared. No laughter, no tears. No emotion. And certainly not love. It was fucking: hot, abandoned, even debauched— sometimes Roarke, who considered himself reasonably sophisticated, was shocked at the things Philippa had encouraged him to do—but it was still only lust. Even that excitement was wearing thin; the last few times they'd had sex had made frighteningly little impact on his senses. Unlike what he'd just shared with Jade.

"Really," Jade insisted. "Even if it was more than that—which it wasn't—I'd never leave Sam."

"His money means that much to you? Even after you've become wealthy in your own right? Christ, Jade, how much money do you need to wash Gallagher City out of your blood?"

"I don't care about Sam's money," Jade flared. "I love him. And I'd never hurt him."

Roarke folded his arms over his chest. "I seem to remember a time when you said you loved me."

"I thought I did. But that was a very long time ago. When I didn't understand the difference between loving and wanting. I love Sam," she repeated. "In a way that I could never love you."

That much was true. With Sam, Jade felt safe and secure. While her relationship with Roarke was like a roller coaster ride to hell.

Roarke couldn't decide which he wanted more—to wring her gorgeous neck or drag her down onto the flagstone and make love to her until they were both too exhausted and satiated to move. He suspected either would be eminently satisfying.

Not trusting himself to speak, Roarke turned on his heel and left her alone. And trembling.

# Nineteen

Interest in Mary Harrington's bounty lured buyers from all corners of the globe. They arrived in chauffeured limousines, taxis, private cars, or simply walked down the Fairmont Hotel's sweeping gilt stairway from the rooms Jade had booked for them, converging on the enormous ballroom in time for the elaborate buffet dinner the evening before the three-day sale began.

These were the heavy hitters, individuals willing to pay dearly for the privilege of getting the first glimpse of what was reported to be the world's largest oriental treasure trove. The crowd was as eclectic as Mary Southerland's collection: movie stars shared tables with European princesses and princes, oil-wealthy Arabs traded shop talk with Texas billionaires, Japanese industrialists discussed New York property values with Wall Street bond traders.

In all, five hundred prospective bidders dropped one thousand dollars a plate, contributing a cool half a million dollars to the establishment of a summer camp for physically challenged children. The charity dinner had been Sam's idea; Jade, knowing that his interest stemmed from his love for Amy, had been moved beyond words when he'd first suggested it.

Jade couldn't sleep. Finally, she gave up even trying and went to the hotel, where she spent the predawn hours amid the fabulous treasures, committing her fastidious script to memory.

The tension was palpable at the public viewing before the auction. For three hours, rivals nodded with feigned cordiality as they examined the exquisite works of art, compared the actual items to the photographs in Tony DiAngelo's glossy catalogues, made notations in the margins, and inevitably fell in love with at least one of the many unique pieces. Few spoke, although some acquaintances exchanged cheek kisses, then separated immediately and returned to barely acknowledging one another.

At last, the oversize double doors opened, and the polite manners that had been drilled into many of the participants since birth were discarded. As if reacting to the sharp report of a starter's pistol, bidders scrambled for their seats.

Jade did a quick crowd count as she walked toward the podium. The spacious grand ballroom was packed; all the chairs had filled quickly, leaving latecomers to stand along the side and back walls. There were more people in this room than in all of Gallagher City. That thought, more than anything, made Jade realize exactly how far she had come.

The low murmur of conversation ceased the moment she stepped up to the mahogany podium. Anticipation was etched on every face; the tension in the room was so electric that Jade could practically hear it crackling around her.

"Good afternoon, ladies and gentlemen," she began, and launched into a brief history of Mary Harrington and her love of beautiful things. Then, as her green eyes moved slowly over the crowd: "Shall we begin?"

Jade kept the pace moving at an explosive speed; invisible bids flew from all corners of the room. Predicting a large turnout, Jade had hired double the usual number of bid spotters. Her foresight paid off as the young women dressed in gray smocks kept track of those bidders Jade might otherwise have missed.

During a blazing afternoon, one hundred pieces of furniture were sold, among them a dazzling scarlet lacquer armoire that had once belonged to Consuelo Vanderbilt, the duchess of Marlborough; a pair of boxlike Chinese cupboards with a large decorative painting of storks and mountains spread across their entire surface, the interior painted in different colors and secured with a prismatically designed padlock; and an altar table inlaid with jade and shimmering mother-of-pearl.

After a brief refreshment break of finger sandwiches, champagne, and tea, the bidding began again, continuing into the night. It seemed to Jade as if her head had barely hit the pillow when it was time to begin the second day of auction.

Spurred on by excitement of previous day, the assembled bidders gave a new meaning to the term *auction fever*, fighting with the ferocity of pit bulls over ancient Chinese scroll paintings and Japanese screens.

By the third and final day, prices soared into the stratosphere as the participants bid on an eight-hundred-year-old Korean celadon bottle from the Koryo dynasty, one-of-a-kind carved jade belt hooks, a charming collection of nineteenth-century carved ivory puppies known as puppies netsuke, and an eighteenth-century porcelain carp dish hand-painted with gold.

"The carp," Jade informed the bidders as she pointed to a new item that had gone on display—a Japanese metallic-embroidered silk robe depicting golden carp leaping through swirling waves in a dynamic, shimmering design—"is a symbol of strength, courage, and perseverance in the East."

Tempers flared as old feuds, fired by three days of competition, grew more heated. Two fist fights broke out on the floor (the pugilists were politely, but swiftly, removed by uniformed guards), and one disgruntled bidder stalked from the room in a fit of pique after losing out on a blue-and-white Yuan dynasty porcelain temple vase with elephant-head handles.

A lacquer jewelry chest inlaid with mother-of-pearl and painted with dragons sold for eight thousand dollars, a red and gilt lacquer Chinese playing card box went for thirty-five hundred dollars, a Ming lacquer bowl with a silver lining cost the Japanese buyer twelve thousand dollars, and a breathtaking six-foot-tall bronze pagoda, bearing the crest of Tokugawa, a leading shogun family of the Edo period, closed out at two hundred and seventy-five thousand dollars. The price was more than twice what Mary Harrington had paid for the pagoda ten years earlier and nearly fifty thousand dollars over the reserve.

By the time the last item—a Ming dynasty court figure, intricately carved from a superb piece of clear green jadeite—was sold to an anonymous telephone bidder, Jade was exhausted.

"I can't believe it's finally over," she sighed. Kicking off her pumps, she curled up in a corner of the sofa. She'd been working at a feverish pitch, and as grateful as she was that the sale was a success, Jade felt strangely depressed.

Sam sat down beside her, put her stocking feet in his lap, and began massaging them. "Feeling a little letdown?"

Jade put her head against the back of the sofa and closed her eyes. "Mmm, that feels good. And yes, actually I am." She opened one eye. "How did you know?"

Sam shrugged. "I always feel the same way after closing a big deal. It's only natural."

"I suppose so," Jade agreed. His fingers were doing wonderful things to her aching arches.

"You know, of course, that you were terrific. As usual."

Jade smiled. She had the feeling that she could have fallen flat on her face and Sam would have said the same thing. But, this time, she knew he was telling the truth. She had been good. Better than good, she'd been damn wonderful. Even the late edition of the *Chronicle* had referred to the sale of the pagoda as "the rap heard 'round the world."

But better yet, several of the bidders had approached her about consigning a few of their own possessions. Since acquisition was the lifeblood of business, that was particularly satisfying. She'd also received several résumés from people currently employed at the finest auction houses in the world, seeking an opportunity to come to San Francisco and work at Jade's.

Life was perfect. So what was wrong? "It's strange," she murmured. "I feel as if I'm drifting."

"If you feel the need for an anchor, I'd be more than happy to volunteer."

"Anchors tie you down. I've never thought of you that way." On the contrary, Sam encouraged her to test her wings, to soar.

"How do you think of me?"

"As a husband," Jade answered without hesitation. "Now that Mary Harrington's auction is behind us, I intend to put all my creative energies into planning our wedding."

"I don't understand," Sam complained a week later. "Amy was thrilled at the idea of our marriage. And she'd be a beautiful flower girl. So why do you want us to elope like a couple of love-sick teenagers?"

"Amy deserves her privacy. Just because my modeling made me a public figure is no reason for her to suffer. I don't want her exposed to the press," Jade insisted.

In truth, she was terrified by the idea of her daughter and Roarke together in the same room. Amy looked more and more like her father with each passing day. She had the same ebony curls, the same blue eyes, even many of the same mannerisms.

Someone—Sam, or worse yet, Roarke—would be bound to notice. Small lies had led to bigger ones and now Jade found herself enmeshed in the sticky web of her own deceptions.

"But she was heartbroken when you told her that she couldn't attend the wedding."

"She'll get over it." Jade knew firsthand what a hardy organ the heart could be.

Her sharp answer made Sam look at her curiously. He'd never known Jade to deny her daughter anything. Except, he considered thoughtfully, the opportunity to live in a real home and attend a neighborhood school like other kids. Was it possible that Jade found having a deaf child an embarrassment?

No. Keeping secrets was just Jade's way, Sam reminded himself. She was an intensely private person. The most private he'd ever met. Perhaps her only motive was her desire to protect Amy. But as much as he wanted to believe that, the needle on Sam's built-in bullshit detector was going off the scale.

Whatever her reasons, Sam realized that Jade was unlikely to change her mind. "How about a compromise?"

Jade looked at him warily. "What kind of compromise?"

"We have a small, private wedding. Just you, me, and Amy. And Nina, since she's your best friend and is kind of responsible for bringing us together, and Edith, of course. And if you wouldn't mind, I'd like to invite Warren."

Warren Bingham was not only vice president at Southerland Enterprises, he'd been Sam's best friend since grade school. More reserved than Sam but intelligent and kind, Warren was someone Jade had liked from moment she'd first met him.

It sounded wonderful. Jade immediately agreed.

"Any premarital jitters?" Nina asked Jade one evening a week before the wedding. They were having a rare girl's night out together: dinner at L'Etoile, to be followed by a gallery opening in North Beach.

"A million."

"Because of Roarke?"

"Of course not," Jade said, not quite truthfully. "Our little affair was over a long time ago."

"I don't see how you can consider any relationship that resulted in a child to be a little affair." When Jade didn't respond, she asked, "Does Roarke know it's over?"

"Yes." When would she stop lying? Jade wondered miserably. Sometimes it seemed as if her entire life was based on nothing but a flimsy tapestry of fabrication. "Besides, it doesn't really matter because he's married."

"From what I hear, not for long."

"I haven't heard any rumors about a divorce."

"That's because you're too busy working to bother with idle gossip. I do some of my best business over the smoked duck salad at the Garden Court. I also hear the latest dirt, and according to the ladies who lunch, Roarke is straining at the leash and Philippa, who has never allowed marriage to interfere with pleasure, is sleeping with some third-generation Romanian count."

"Gossip," Jade said dismissively.

"Sometimes gossip turns out to be true," Nina pointed out. "Anyway, would it matter? If Roarke were single again?"

"No." Jade's answer was quick and emphatic. It was also the truth.

"Are you sure you're doing the right thing?" Nina asked.

"Positive. I love Sam. And he loves me. He even wants to adopt Amy. It's time we became a family."

North Beach began as a bustling village boasting the largest concentration of Italians west of Chicago. Italian was the language of the streets, bocci ball was the sport of choice, and cannoli were more common than Tootsie Rolls.

After World War II, the works of such men as Allen Ginsberg and Jack Kerouac encouraged a generation of disaffected and iconoclastic souls to move to the neighborhood. Bearded bards haunted the City Lights Bookstore, read their poetry in coffee houses, listened to cool jazz, and smoked dope.

During the sixties and seventies, North Beach became a sort of Barbary Coast—San Francisco's answer to Times Square. Beneath the surrealistic glow of neon, strip joints, massage parlors, topless bars, transsexual reviews, and X-rated movie houses catered to prurient interests.

The gallery they were looking for was on upper Grant Street, in the heart of the old beatnik stomping grounds. Although the street was still a major artery in the city's Italian enclave, the oriental script adorning many of the shops stood as mute evidence of the city's ever-changing face.

The one-man show featured Gabriel Deveraux, a sculptor from Louisiana's bayou country. Waiters carried trays of Cajun Bloody Marys, befitting the artist's heritage, instead of the usual cheap champagne.

The wooden sculptures were larger than life. They were also blatantly erotic. When Jade came upon a sculpture depicting a couple making love, she felt a sudden jolt of desire. The woman was seated astride the man, his hands grasping her broad hips. Her spine was arched and her head was thrown back, making it appear as if she were in the throes of orgasm.

"Amazing, isn't it?" Nina murmured under her breath.

"They're certainly realistic," Jade agreed. Plucking a glass from the tray of a passing waiter, she took a long drink. The bartender had not stinted on the Tabasco sauce; fire flamed to the roots of her hair, contributing to her discomfort.

Two hours later, after dropping Nina off at the Mark Hopkins, where she kept a suite, Jade still had sex on her mind. Unfortunately, Sam was in Zurich. Needing to unwind, she drove down to the waterfront.

San Francisco wore its evening gray coat of fog. It moved through the streets in thick runners, making ordinary things—street lights, fire hydrants, coin telephones—into objects of mystery as Jade stopped by her building site. The old warehouse had been razed, the rubble cleared away, and concrete footings poured, revealing the shape of the building to come.

She walked around the lot, letting her imagination run free, picturing her auction house as Roarke had designed it. From the outside, the building would appear starkly utilitarian, a modernist linear arrangement of cubes covered with stucco, subtly shaded in gray, soft aqua, and white. The stark lines allowed the building to appear larger than it actually was.

To break up the soft colors and hint at the drama within, Roarke planned to add horizontal bands of crayon-bright colors—tomato red, sunshine yellow, and royal purple. Oversize doors would sit between glass blocks, which echoed the glass on the waterfront side of the building. The idea was to let in the sun without allowing the dramatic view to detract from the art.

Inside, Jade had selected black marble flooring and creamy white walls. The unexpected touches of brightness planned for the interior—a grape-colored railing and the red cantilevered staircase—had been Roarke's idea.

"It's going to work." The fog's odd acoustic quality made the deep male voice sound as if it was coming from right behind her.

Startled, Jade spun around to see Roarke slowly emerge from the filmy gray shadows, as silent as a cat on a carpet. "I didn't expect to see you here."

"I didn't expect to see you, either. I figured you'd be home getting ready for your wedding."

"I had dinner with Nina. I suppose I should have gone straight home, but something drew me here."

"I know the feeling."

"Do you come here often?"

"It's my job, remember? But yeah, I usually stop by on my way home."

"I was imagining it all finished," Jade admitted softly.

"Your stage."

She remembered describing it that way during the early planning stages. "I realize that sounds incredibly egotistical, but—"

"No. It's exactly what it should be," he said quietly. "Don't forget, I've seen you in action, Jade. Put a gavel in your hand and you become one helluv'an actress."

With or without a gavel, she was one helluv'an actress, Jade considered grimly. After all, hadn't she managed to convince Roarke that she didn't love him?

"It's going to be a wonderful building. Sam was right—you're very good at your work."

He shrugged. "You were an easy client because you knew exactly what you wanted."

"I recall a time you didn't find that a plus."

They had argued over her belief that bay-facing windows would detract from the art. The glass block had been a compromise. He stuck his hands into the pockets of his trench coat and gazed out over the vacant lot.

"You can be frustrating. But despite everything that's happened, I like the idea of us working together on something that's so much a part of both of us."

Guilty thoughts of Amy flooded her mind. Jade tried to push them away and failed. Out over the icy waters of the bay, gulls dove for fish, their querulous cries echoing in the fog.

Dropping her eyes, she said, "I'd better get home."

"Can't keep the bridegroom waiting." His voice was roughened with emotions she didn't dare contemplate. The night breeze sent a few strands of hair across her cheek. Roarke reached out and brushed them away. "May I ask you a personal question?"

She lifted her eyes to his. Distressed, they widened, dominating her face even more than usual. "I don't think—"

"Are you happy? With Sam?"

"Yes." It was little more than a whisper, but it was the truth. "Yes, I am," she repeated, stronger this time.

He let out a long breath. "I'm glad."

"Are you really?"

"You sound surprised."

It was Jade's turn to shrug. Turning away, she pretended a sudden interest in the lighted buoys guiding the ships out into the bay. *If only there were buoys in life*, she mused sadly. *Showing the way.*

"I thought you were angry with me. Because—" She couldn't make herself say the words.

"Because you love Sam and not me?"

Unable to answer past the lump building in her throat, she nodded.

"I was angry," Roarke admitted. "And bitter at the way things turned out between us and frustrated because I never could understand what the hell happened to change your feelings during those weeks between Seriphos and when I saw you again in New York. But just because my marriage has turned out to be a disaster doesn't mean I'd ever wish such unhappiness on you."

A poignant silence fell between them. Reaching out once more, Roarke ran the back of his hand up the side of her face.

"I hope Sam realizes that he's a very lucky man," he murmured. She hadn't heard such sincere warmth in his voice since their time together in Greece.

He slipped his hand back into his pocket and stepped back. As Jade returned to her car, she could feel his eyes on her every step of the way.

She drove home through the fog-bound streets, telling herself over and over again that she should be relieved that she and Roarke had made amends. After all these years, they were finally free of one another.

Unfortunately, she'd never anticipated such an overwhelming sense of loss.

Sam and Jade's honeymoon—spent in a white stucco villa overgrown with crimson and violet bougainvillea in Positano, on Italy's Amalfi Coast—was the kind of which most couples could only dream. They took long, moonlit strolls along the shore, and laughed and frolicked in the warm water like carefree children.

They talked long into the night, and they made love wherever and whenever they wanted—on their private terrace under the stars, in the villa's sparkling blue pool, on the yacht Sam had hired for the occasion, in the hand-carved bed, drenched in warm, buttery sunshine.

And if there were times when the rocky coastline reminded Jade of Seriphos—and Roarke—she pushed those thoughts away.

The day before their return to San Francisco, they were having lunch on the terrace, surrounded by lemon trees and dark green vines. The lush scent of the flowering plants overspilling the terra-cotta urns mingled enticingly with the salt air. Looking out over the wrought-iron balustrade, Jade could see the yacht bobbing on the cerulean sea, its crisp white sails fluttering in the breeze.

"Happy?" Sam reached across the table and took her hand.

Jade smiled. "You must be a mind reader. I was just trying to remember when I'd ever felt so fulfilled."

Enjoying the warmth of the sun, Jade stretched her legs out onto a adjoining chair and admired her tan. Although her skin was now a soft golden color, she was still pale compared to the Concorde set who inhabited the hillside during the summer.

In Positano, no one seemed to worry about such unpleasantries as wrinkles or melanomas. Indeed, nude was the preferred dress code, while mahogany appeared to be the color of choice. Aging European aristocracy wore their leathery skin and crow's-feet proudly; at night, in gowns by Valentino and Oscar de la Renta, they distracted the eye from their wrinkles with glittering jewels.

And such jewels they were! With an auctioneer's expert eye, Jade had quickly decided that the collection of serious gems and baubles worn at a single dinner party could probably feed the entire third world well into the twenty-first century.

"I could stay here forever," she said.

"We could, you know."

She looked up at him curiously, surprised to find no trace of humor on his rugged face. "I was only fantasizing, Sam. We have so many responsibilities back in the world. Amy—"

"Amy'd love it here."

True enough, Jade admitted. "What about your work?"

"I could run the companies just as well from here. Or, hell, I could sell them all and settle into comfortable retirement with my beautiful wife and child."

He was serious, Jade realized. "But I couldn't do my work from here."

He shrugged. "With all the money floating around this place, you could easily relocate."

That was also true. Along with the European industrialists, creative talents such as Franco Zeffirelli and Gore Vidal regularly held court on the coast. And just last night, Jade had seen Jacqueline Kennedy Onassis dining with friends at a beachfront bistro.

"But we've spent so much money on the Embarcadero site—"

"And that's all it is, Jade," Sam said. "Money. Believe it or not, darlin', it can't buy happiness."

No, Jade thought silently, but it could damn well make life a lot easier. "It's a wonderful fantasy," she agreed. "I think we'd better just leave it at that."

Sam had never met a woman as driven as Jade. While dropping out of the rat race in order to spend his days making love to his wife and playing with Amy sounded eminently satisfying to him, he knew that Jade could never be happy with such a life. How much money did she need? How much wealth and success did she have to accumulate before she stopped running from whatever demons were pursuing her?

He wanted to take her in his arms and assure her that he would always protect her. But, knowing that such a declaration would only make her uncomfortable, he did the next best thing.

"How badly did you want to go sailing this afternoon?"

Jade read the desire in his eyes; a desire she knew was mirrored in her own. "I think," she said with a slow, seductive smile, "that I'd rather take a nap."

They walked hand in hand to the bedroom, where they spent the rest of the long, sun-filled afternoon making love.

Much, much later, savoring the tranquillity that always followed their lovemaking, Jade was struck with the dazzling realization that somehow, when she wasn't looking, she had fallen madly and wonderfully in love with her husband.

# Twenty

Although Jade had hoped to keep everything about her wedding low-key, she was not at all that surprised when she returned to San Francisco and discovered that Nina and Sam had conspired to throw a party to celebrate the private nuptials in style.

"You could have at least kept things simple," Jade complained to Nina as she watched the tuxedo-clad waiter circling the room, filling crystal flutes with peach champagne.

"Believe me, Jade," Nina said, "your idea of simple and your husband's definitely don't jibe. You know the string quartet playing in the parlor?"

"That's exactly what I mean—"

"Sam's original instructions were to hire the San Francisco Symphony Orchestra. You've no idea what it took to cut him down to just those four musicians.

"And if Gloria Steinem had overheard how much feminine wheedling I forced myself to do to convince your husband that a fountain spewing champagne in the backyard garden was overkill, she would've canceled my subscription to *Ms.*"

Jade glanced across the room where her new husband was holding court. He was, she realized, having a wonderful time.

"Thank you for not inviting Roarke," she murmured, after glancing around to make certain no one was standing nearby to overhear.

"I can't take the credit for that. He was on Sam's list, but his secretary told me he was in Brazil. Seems he's hoping to design a hotel in Rio de Janeiro."

Whatever the reason, Jade was grateful for his absence. Although she'd honestly put her volatile feelings for Roarke behind her, she wasn't certain she was prepared to deal with him on anything other than a strictly business basis.

After greeting what seemed to be just about everyone in San Francisco, Jade's smile began to feel frozen on her face. She'd escaped for a moment's solitude into the library when a manila folder Sam had left on the desk caught her attention.

The name on the file was frighteningly familiar. After all, hadn't she grown up seeing it on nearly every building in town? She reached out to pick it up just as Sam appeared in the doorway.

"There you are," he said. "I missed you."

"I've only been gone a minute, darling."

"Really? It seemed an eternity." His smile faded and his gaze turned concerned as he viewed Jade's pallor. "What's wrong?"

"Nothing." She saw her hands were trembling.

"You're not mad at me, are you, Jade? For going behind your back with Nina like this?"

The honest concern etched onto his rugged face caused her heart to do a little flip in spite of her distress. "Of course not." She toyed with the file. "Gallagher Gas and Oil," she pretended to read for the first time. "I hadn't realized you were in the oil business."

Sam appeared surprised at her sudden change in subject. "I'm not. Are you certain you're not angry?"

"Not at all. Are you thinking of going into the energy business?"

"I wasn't. But Warren found this Oklahoma-based company that's currently overextended and looking for some additional financing. He thought I might be interested."

"Do you think that's wise? What with all the environmental problems oil companies are having?"

"I hadn't planned to create an oil slick in the bay, Jade."

He was looking at her. Looking close, looking hard. Jade struggled for a casual tone. "Well, still," she murmured, "I can't believe it would be a very good public-relations move."

Even as she said it, she knew she was behaving strangely in Sam's eyes. Not once, in all their years together, had she offered any suggestion about the way he ran his companies. On those occasions when they had discussed business, it was either the Tigress campaign or her own financial plans.

"Are you asking me not to buy into G. G. and O?"

"Of course not," she said quickly. "That isn't my place. I was only suggesting that you might want to give it more thought."

His gaze sharpened even more, moving over her face, searching for clues to her thoughts, but Jade managed, with effort, to keep her expression calmly composed.

"Hell," he decided with a shrug, "I was never all that wild about the idea, anyway."

When he tossed the file into a desk drawer, Jade could have wept with relief. "About the party . . . " she said, twining her arms around his neck.

"Damn." Sam's own hands settled on her hips. "I knew you were angry."

"That's not what I was going to say." She went up on her toes and gave him a long, heartfelt kiss. "I was the one who was wrong," she said after they came up for air. "I should have realized how important our wedding is to your business."

"Is that what you think this party is all about?" His hands were on her hips and he put her a little away from him. "I don't give a damn about making any more business contacts, Jade. I'm just so happy about being married to you that I wanted a chance to share my terrific fortune with our friends."

An open, gregarious man, Sam made friends easily and often. Jade, on the other hand, had many business acquaintances, but with the exception of Nina and, of course, Edith, she couldn't honestly claim any of the people crowding into the house as her friends.

"Well, whatever the reason, I'm still glad you and Nina went behind my back," she said.

"Why don't you tell me that after I tell you who just arrived?"

The sympathy in his eyes gave Jade the answer. "Your children?"

He gave her a quick squeeze. "In person. And anxious to give their best wishes to their new stepmother."

"If I know Monica, she's already calling me step-mommy dearest," Jade said with a sigh.

Since their first inauspicious meeting, Jade and Sam's three grown children's paths had crossed half a dozen times. None of those occasions had been the least bit pleasant.

"One of these days," Sam said, as they left the library, "they're going to realize what a gem you are."

"Don't hold your breath."

Conversation ceased the minute Jade walked into the parlor. Avid eyes moved back and forth between the newlyweds and the unholy trio standing in the center of the room, their scowls at direct odds with the festivities of the evening.

"Monica," Jade said, flashing them one of her most brilliant, most professional smiles, "and Adam. And Michael! What a wonderful surprise."

A collective sigh of relief swept over the room as Jade embraced her new stepdaughter, refusing to acknowledge the fact that Monica remained as stiff as a rod of cold steel. And every bit as unbending, Jade was to discover later that evening.

She had slipped away from the guests to compliment the caterer on the hors d'oeuvres, when Monica cornered her in the kitchen.

"I suppose you think you've won the battle," Sam's daughter snapped. She was holding a cigarette in one hand, a glass of champagne in the other. It was obviously not her first drink; as she swayed unsteadily toward Jade, champagne sloshed over the top of the glass and spilled down the front of her dress.

The waiters and catering kitchen staff watched while pretending to go about their duties.

"I wasn't aware we were battling."

Monica glared at her for a long moment, then blatantly dropped the cigarette onto the brick floor and ground it out with the heel of her shoe. "So now you're a liar. As well as a slut."

Jade reminded herself that this woman was her husband's daughter. His drunk daughter, she tacked on as Monica grabbed an open bottle of champagne from the counter and refilled her glass. More wine splashed over her chic black Bill Blass dress.

"Don't you think you've had enough?" Jade asked quietly.

"I've had enough of you." Monica pointed the bottle in Jade's direction. "Adam and Michael kept telling me that you were just another one of our father's passing fancies. But I knew differently. I could tell the first time I met you that you were nothing but a gold digger who intended to get your hooks into him."

"I love your father—"

Monica cut her off with a drunken wave of a perfectly manicured hand. "The only thing you love is money. And don't bother denying it because everyone knows that the famous Jade is motivated first and foremost by the almighty dollar."

"That's not true!"

"Isn't it?" Monica's face was inches from Jade's; her breath smelled of tobacco and alcohol. The heavy scent of Poison filled the room like an oppressive cloud. "Tell me, Jade, would you have married my father if he was still some dirt-poor logger?"

"That's irrelevant," Jade argued. "Because he's not. He'd already made millions before I met him."

"Point made." Monica gave her a sly, dangerous smile. "The ugly truth is that you're only interested in his bank account."

Tilting her head, she polished off the champagne. "You know it. I know it. It seems everyone in San Francisco knows what you're after. Except my father. Which just goes to show what happens when an old fool starts behaving like a horny old goat."

Her cold gaze turned on Jade again. "Tell me, Jade, what do you do when you're forced to have sex with my father? Close your eyes and compound your daily interest until it's over?"

A sound like a gunshot rang out as Jade's hand slapped Monica's cheek.

"If that's your best shot," Monica said, "then you're in trouble. Because you may have won the battle, Jade, but you're damn well not going to win this war."

Turning on her heel, she staggered out of the kitchen, leaving Jade to wonder what on earth she was going to tell Sam.

But it appeared that as much as they disliked Jade, none of Sam's children, his daughter included, were all that eager to tangle with their father. Days passed with no sign that Monica had mentioned their altercation to Sam.

Hoping that her stepdaughter's threat had only been the champagne speaking, Jade said nothing.

"I don't believe it!"

Jade stared up at Peter Spenser, a Carmel gallery owner she'd dealt with several times in the past. A couple of weeks before Christmas, Jade had purchased a magnificent Renoir from a private collector for her Cow Hollow gallery, which she had subsequently sold to Spenser. Now he was back, accusing her of selling him a forgery.

"It can't be a fake!" she insisted. "The provenance was impeccable!"

"Provenances can be forged," he reminded her.

"I know that. And whenever I have doubts, I sell the item 'as bought.' And I always make it a rule to test paintings, however solid the provenance. In the case of the Renoir, I had it checked at the best laboratory—the chromatography, the spectroscopy, the X-rays, everything checked out."

"Perhaps you should investigate your testing laboratory," he suggested silkily, handing Jade a typewritten report from another lab. As she scanned the few lines, Jade's blood ran cold.

"Well, there certainly seems to be a discrepancy," Jade admitted in a voice that was amazingly calm, considering that she felt as if she were having a heart attack. She reached into the drawer of the Regency mahogany writing table she'd unearthed at an antiques shop in Monterey and pulled out her checkbook.

"Of course I intend to get to the truth about this," Jade said. "But so you aren't penalized in the meantime, I'm prepared to reimburse your purchase price, along with the cost of your tests."

"I'm afraid that won't do."

She glanced up at him, her silver Monte Blanc pen poised over the embossed check. "What do you mean, it won't do?"

He studied his highly buffed nails for a long-suspended moment. "I believe that my silence about this fraud should be worth at least a quarter million."

"Two hundred and fifty thousand dollars? That's blackmail!"

"Perhaps." His smile was edged with malice. "But if you're going to dump forgeries on the market," he hinted darkly, "you're going to have to learn to pay the price, darling."

Furious, Jade realized that he was not bluffing. Having no choice but to meet his price, she wrote out a check for the amount he was demanding, silently swearing never to permit the horrid man to attend another one of her auctions as long as she lived.

After he left, Jade buried her head in her hands, wondering how she could have let herself be duped that way.

"Not that I was the first," she insisted to Sam later, over dinner. "Even the Metropolitan was caught red-handed when they discovered that their fabulous Rospigliosi Cup, the same one they'd displayed for years as an example of the pagan splendor of the Renaissance, wasn't the work of Benvenuto Cellini at all. It was really made by Reinhold Vasters in the nineteenth century.

"Of course Vasters was a wonderful goldsmith, as well as a master forger," she allowed. "And his works are worth quite a lot these days. But that still doesn't take away the fact that the Met was duped.

"And everyone knows that the British Museum left a phony sixth-century tomb on display for years—just because the Louvre had one and they were jealous. They knew it was a fake the first year after they bought it." She didn't pause for a breath. "And, you've heard about Hans van Meegeren, that Dutch forger who spent World War II turning out phony Vermeers. He—"

"Jade, darling." Sam caught her hands in midair. "I believe you. So who are you trying to convince? Me, or yourself?"

"Myself, I suppose," Jade admitted in a soft rippling sigh.

When the new test results confirmed Spenser's findings, Jade was horribly depressed. But she was also angry.

Unaccustomed to giving up without a fight, she hired a private investigator who specialized in art theft and fraud for insurance companies. Although he was reputed to be the best, his office located above a pawn shop in the Mission District—a neighborhood where bright murals vied with graffiti-scrawled walls—was less than encouraging.

Mickey McLaughlin had red hair, a pug nose, and so many freckles Jade could hardly see any skin between them. He obviously found time to lift weights; his upper arms swelled against his rumpled shirt sleeves. He was wearing faded blue jeans and sneakers, and try as she might to picture him in the art world, Jade found such a mental leap impossible.

She perched on the edge of the rickety chair, clutching her purse in her lap as if she thought this red-haired giant might suddenly leap across the scarred old desk and snatch it from her.

"I know," he said easily, as if reading her mind, "I don't look the part. But believe me, you get one helluva big bang for your buck when you hire Mickey McLaughlin."

"I heard you're good. And I know firsthand how deceiving appearances can be," Jade allowed.

Mickey leaned back in his chair, put his elbows on the arms, and studied her over linked fingers. "So, why don't you tell me what you're doing here."

After Jade related everything that had happened with the Renoir, Mickey said: "Now who would hate you enough to set you up like this?"

"I thought I made myself quite clear," she said stiffly. "It's obvious that Peter Spenser's involved in a forgery-and-blackmail scam. I'm hiring you to find proof of that."

"I know Spenser," Mickey said, "and trust me, sweetheart, he isn't smart enough to fake a picture of a dog playing poker. So, we're back to the first question." As he poured her a glass of water from a plastic pitcher on the credenza behind him, he asked her again, "Who hates you?"

Quinlan Gallagher was the first name that came to mind, but Jade knew this was not Quinlan's style. He didn't mind killing, but he wanted to be on hand to see his victim's blood.

Jade took a sip of water. "I don't know."

Mickey shrugged. "Well, someone sure as hell does," he said. "But don't worry, the art world's an incestuous place. It won't take long to track down your forger."

Despite Jade's misgivings, Mickey McLaughlin proved to be as good as his reputation. Only two weeks after she'd written out her retainer check, Jade was back in the Mission District, sitting in a cozy booth in the St. Francis Fountain, reading through his report.

"I can't believe this," she said finally. She leaned back and stared up at the pink ceiling, trying to corral her wildly racing thoughts. "The woman I bought the painting from went to college with Monica Southerland? How on earth did you find that out?"

He shrugged. "I have my sources. And they all say that Southerland broad wouldn't mind even a little bit if one Sunday morning you fell off the ferry and ended up as shark bait." He drew loudly on his straw, sucking up the last of his banana shake.

"And since even she wouldn't hire a professional killer," Jade mused, "she did the next best thing." Jade couldn't even begin to imagine what a complicated scheme Monica had hatched in her hatred. "But how did she pull it off?"

"Actually, it wasn't that difficult," Mickey said. "Her ex-husband, that Italian, is a painter."

"Unsuccessful," Jade recalled.

"He's a bust at selling his own stuff," the investigator agreed. "But that didn't stop the guy from figuring out a way to make a buck in the art business. According to my sources at Customs and Interpol, Nick Branzino has a nice little racket going turning out copies."

"You're kidding!" Monica's former husband an art forger? Jade wondered if Sam knew and decided he must not.

"Afraid not. Authorities keep trying to snare him, but he's too slippery. Word is that he's got some help from local authorities who tip him off whenever anyone gets too close."

"But the painting passed so many tests," Jade argued, still unwilling to believe that even Monica could hatch such a devious scheme.

"One of the reasons Branzino is so successful is that he's supposed to have developed a method of aging canvas and paint that not all of the testing places have caught on to yet. Then, after he finishes the painting, he forges provenances by making up names or using names of dead people and finally, to give the provenances some authenticity, he tosses in the names of impoverished European aristocrats who are willing to go along with the scheme for a cut of the sale price."

"Monica really does hate me," Jade murmured as it all sank in.

"Sure looks like it," Mickey agreed cheerfully. When he saw her stricken look, his expression changed to one of sympathy. "I hope this isn't going to cause you problems in your marriage."

Jade gazed across the street to the park where dazzling murals had been painted by neighborhood artists—a lively mix of Mexican, Colombian, Guatemalan, Nicaraguan, and Salvadoran people.

"It won't." Her voice was soft, but firm. "Because Sam isn't going to find out."

That afternoon, Jade drove to Monica's house on Russian Hill. The Salvadoran houseboy told Jade that his employer was out in the garden. If she would wait in the front parlor, he would tell her that she had a visitor.

"Oh, it's you," Monica greeted Jade, with a deliberate lack of enthusiasm. "I can't believe you have nerve to come here, after what you did."

"What I did?" Jade asked in disbelief. "If you're talking about marrying your father—"

"I'm talking about running to him with the outrageous lie that I conspired with Peter Spenser to sell you a forgery, then blackmail you." Monica began pacing furiously, her high heels making staccato tapping sounds on the marble floor.

"What are you talking about? I have no intention of telling Sam what you've done. The only reason I came here today is to tell you that if you don't call off this vendetta, you'll find that I'm a lot tougher than I look."

Monica folded her arms over her silk-clad breasts and glared at Jade. "You're a liar as well as a conniving slut," she spat out. "You couldn't wait to tell my father. And you'll undoubtedly be pleased to know that he was here this morning, threatening to cut me out of his damn will if I ever did anything to harm his precious wife again!"

Jade realized that somehow, Sam had found out about Monica's subterfuge even before she had. Which wasn't surprising. He'd been furious when he'd learned about Peter Spenser's blackmail scheme. He had obviously hired his own detective and uncovered the same damning facts Mickey McLaughlin had found.

"I just found out myself a few minutes ago," Jade insisted. "I had every intention of keeping this between us."

"And I'm Catherine the Great," Monica said, her voice dripping with sarcasm. "Now that you've done your gloating, why don't you get the hell out of my house. Before I have you thrown out."

Jade didn't bother to deny Monica's charges again. It was obvious that Monica hated her so much that she'd never believe her.

That night, as she and Sam lay side by side in the antique bed she'd bought from the Mary Harrington house, Jade broached the subject of Monica's behavior.

"I love you, Sam Southerland," she said after she'd told him about the two meetings, first with Mickey, then with Monica. "And I love the way you care about me. But you have to let me fight my own battles."

He lifted a thick strand of hair from her shoulder and wrapped it absently around his hand. "Have I ever told you how much I love your hair?" he murmured, as if he hadn't heard a word of her plea.

"Yes, you have, and I never tire of hearing it. But you're dodging the issue."

"I'm not dodging anything, Jade," Sam corrected. "I'm simply trying to get used to the idea that you don't need me."

"That's not true at all. Of course I need you. I need your love and your strength and your support and—"

"But you want me to love you enough to back off and let you enter the fray alone."

"Never alone." Jade lifted her eyes to his wounded ones. "Because I know that you're always behind me."

Sam considered that for a long, silent moment. "I guess I can be accused of being chauvinistic from time to time, sweetheart. And although I'm really trying to be a modern, sensitive, understanding guy, deep down inside, I can't quite shake the feeling that women are the gentler sex."

Gentler meaning weaker, Jade considered. But she loved Sam enough to understand that he didn't mean to belittle all she had accomplished. "I know you feel that way, Sam, but—"

"I still can't see where it's so wrong," he interrupted in a burst of male aggravation, "wanting to protect my wife—whom I adore—from some of life's more unpleasant aspects." He ran his hands up and down her back, warming the sea green silk of her nightgown beneath his strong wide palms. "But I'll try not to be so overbearing."

She brushed her lips against his frowning ones. "Thank you, darling."

He pulled her closer, his hand moving down to cup her buttocks, molding her body to his, allowing her to feel the full extent of his arousal. "I have just one last question."

The way he was nibbling on her neck was causing coherent thought to desert her. "What's that?"

"Does this mean that I have to cancel the purchase of Spenser's Carmel property?"

His quiet question immediately cut through her lassitude. "You're buying the gallery? But why?"

"The land's prime beachfront property. Carmel Beach is right at the foot of Spenser's Ocean Avenue site."

"I realize that. But I didn't know it was for sale."

Sam shrugged, but his eyes were dancing with impish devils she'd witnessed before. "Seems Spenser went into foreclosure," he said mildly. "Golden Gate Bank called his note yesterday. He's been having financial difficulties lately. I guess his share of the quarter million you gave him wasn't enough to bail him out."

Since Sam was on the board of Golden Gate Bank, Jade had a very good idea how and why the gallery owner's financial problems finally caught up with him. She also knew that she should resent Sam's employing such heavy-handed tactics on her behalf, but as she succumbed to her husband's seductive touch, Jade could only shake her head with wonder at being so loved by this gentle, powerful man.

# Twenty-one

Sam was out of town again, leaving Jade feeling strangely at loose ends. No longer accustomed to spending her evenings alone, she was pleased that Nina was working at her West Coast agency this week.

"God, you look gorgeous," Nina said, looking Jade up and down after they'd returned from dinner and a movie. "If marriage can make a woman look this good, maybe I should consider giving it another shot."

"You should," Jade agreed with a grin. "These days I want everyone to get married so they can be as happy as I am."

"That's because you're one of the lucky ones. So, how's Jade's coming along? I drove by the building this morning. It looks nearly done."

"There's still a lot of work to do inside," Jade said. "But I'm pleased with how it's going. If you have time, I'll take you down there tomorrow and show you the recent changes Roarke has made."

"Speaking of Roarke, how are you two getting along?"

"Fine, what little I see of him. We do most of our communicating through secretaries, which is fine with me."

"You can't keep avoiding the man forever, Jade."

"I know, but it's still so awkward."

"I don't understand why," Nina pressed. "Lots of women can still have feelings for their first love without falling apart when they're in the same room." She frowned. "Unless you're still in love with him."

"No," Jade said quickly. "I love Sam." Not wanting to dwell on the subject, she said, "Come look what I just bought for my next auction."

Nina followed her into an adjoining room and watched as she moved aside a Georgia O'Keeffe flower painting to reveal a wall safe.

"This is an inro," she said, handing a set of stacked four-inch-long Japanese lacquer boxes to Nina. "They were worn suspended from the sash of a kimono and used to store medicines. Since there used to be strictly proscribed laws regarding the amounts of valuable materials—lacquers, jade, and gold—a person could own, the inro was one of the ways wealthy Japanese could exhibit their taste and prosperity without drawing the wrath of jealous shoguns."

"It feels like satin," Nina murmured, running her fingers over the lacquer.

"Lustrous to the eye and satisfying to the fingers," Jade answered, paraphrasing some long-forgotten Eastern philosopher. "It's hard to tell, but this particular piece has more than forty different shades of gold incorporated in the design."

Nina looked closer at the golden rabbits sitting in the golden grass, looking up at a round, golden moon. "It's truly incredible. How much do you plan to sell it for?"

"The reserve is seventy-five thousand," Jade said.

Nina slipped the set of boxes back into the satin-lined velvet case. "At nearly nineteen thousand dollars an inch, it's definitely a bargain," she said dryly.

Jade laughed. "Wait until you see what else I've been hoarding."

"Oh, I like that," Nina said, pointing to a beaded necklace.

"It's a Yamato necklace," Jade said. "The canoe-shaped carnelian beads symbolize high rank or shamanistic ritual powers. The round beads are lapis lazuli, and of course the cylinder-shaped beads are jadeite."

"Your specialty," Nina said with a smile.

"Yes, but now that the Chinese have begun doing so much excavating, I think there's going to be strong market for celadon, for all those people who'd rather have a good piece of glazeware than an inferior-quality jade, so I've been buying as much of it as I can. . . .

"And now, for the *pièce de résistance*—" she took out a pale green basin, its bottom decorated with a design of four carp. "This is a jadeite spurting basin, from the Ming Dynasty," she said, filling the basin from a pitcher of water she'd brought into the room earlier. "Watch."

She began rubbing the handles of the basin, causing vibrations that in turn caused spouts of water to erupt from the mouth of the fish.

"Isn't that fun?" she asked, grinning broadly. "I can't wait until this weekend when I make the fish spit for Amy."

"Just what every little girl needs, a priceless plaything," Nina said.

They were laughing at that when the phone rang. A moment later, Edith appeared in the doorway. "I'm sorry to disturb you ladies, but there's a phone call for you, Jade."

Jade's face brightened. "Is it Sam?"

"No, he didn't give his name."

Thinking it might be Roarke, Jade said, "Would you please take a message, Edith? I'll call the gentleman back."

Edith left only to return a moment later. "I'm sorry, but he says it's important. He said he was with the police."

Exchanging a look with Nina, Jade walked over to the desk and picked up the receiver. "Hello? What? Who? You're with the *Chronicle*? But my housekeeper said . . . No, I didn't hear anything about . . ." Her voice drifted off. Jade went numb; the receiver fell to the persian carpet.

Nina scooped it up. "Hello? Who is this? . . . His what? Oh, my God. No, Mrs. Southerland has no statement to make." She slammed the receiver down. "There has to be a mistake," she assured Jade, who, standing nearby, was porcelain pale.

Three phone calls later, Nina had confirmed the reporter's claim. Sam's Cessna Citation had gone down during a freak snowstorm over the Sierra Nevada mountains. Sam, the pilot, was in critical condition.

For two weeks Sam remained in critical condition, slipping in and out of consciousness. Jade stayed stubbornly by his side, as if she could keep him alive by the sheer strength of her will. Her unfailing devotion did not go unnoticed by Roarke, who was surprised to discover how deeply Jade cared for her husband.

Roarke, who had called several times, now found her pacing the waiting-room floor. "How is he?"

Jade stopped pacing and turned to look at him. Any other time, his presence would have stimulated some vital emotion. At the moment, she was too exhausted to feel anything.

"He was conscious this afternoon. But then . . ." Her voice cracked and she turned away. "Oh God, what will I do if he dies?"

Roarke was shocked by her appearance. Her once voluptuous body was all angles; a stiff wind would blow her away. Grief and lack of sleep had etched dark shadows beneath her eyes.

"You'll go on," Roarke predicted. "Like you have in the past. But he's not going to die."

Jade slumped into a green plastic contour chair. "I've tried praying," she said flatly. "They have a chapel here, and I go in and get down on my knees and ask God to give me my husband back." Her gaze, as she looked up at Roarke, was heartbreakingly bleak. "But all the time I'm praying, I can't believe that it's doing any good. So then I'm terrified that God's going to punish me for my doubts by taking Sam away."

"It doesn't work that way."

"How do you know?" Her still-remarkable eyes seemed to be begging for reassurance.

"Because if there is a God running the show, he's too busy keeping the planets from spinning into one another to punish us for having doubts. Doubts he allowed by making us human in the first place."

"I hope you're right." She lowered her face to her hands for a long time.

Roarke waited. "I've heard rumors about your wasting away," he said after a time, "so I thought I'd buy you some lunch."

Jade's gaze finally focused on Roarke. "Thank you. But I'm not hungry."

Roarke didn't argue. "Fine. Then you can keep me company while I eat." He took her gently by the arm and led her out of the hospital.

After a meal at a nearby Chinese restaurant, Roarke pointed out, "You were hungry. That's what comes from not eating for days."

"Nina sent you, didn't she?"

"No." At her disbelieving look, he said, "All right, I knew you and Nina Grace were close so I stopped by her office to see how you were holding up. She's concerned about you, Jade. So am I. So, for that matter, is your housekeeper."

"You talked to Edith?"

"I dropped by the house to see how you—and, of course, Sam—were doing. She told me where you were, after going on at great lengths about how you refused to eat properly and how worried she was." He smiled. "She sounded as if she's been with you a long time."

"More than eight years," Jade said. "And from the very first day she's always seemed more like family than an employee."

"I could see that. Anyway, we decided that since neither she nor Nina Grace has had any luck getting you to listen to reason, I thought I might give it the old college try."

"What made you think you'd have any more luck?"

"Simple." He winked at her, reminding her of the bold young man she'd once been in love with. "I'm stronger. If I needed to, I was ready to throw you over my back and drag you kicking and screaming to the restaurant." His teasing gaze, as it took in her too-thin body, turned serious. "You're not helping Sam by not taking care of yourself, Cassie."

"I know. But it just doesn't seem right . . ."

"For you to be going about your life while Sam may be dying in there?"

"Yes." It was the first time she'd acknowledged those feelings, even to herself.

Roarke took her hand, enveloping it in his own. "Sam loves you, Cassie. He wouldn't want you to suffer, too."

"I keep telling myself that. But it doesn't help."

Roarke held out the plate of fortune cookies. "Here. You haven't had dessert."

Jade shook her head. "Really, I couldn't eat another thing."

"It's not a proper Chinese dinner without a fortune cookie."

Jade didn't have the strength to argue. She plucked a crisp cookie from the plate, broke it open, and extracted the slender slip of paper.

"What does it say?"

It doesn't mean anything, Jade told herself. They print these things up by the hundreds. The thousands. It was only a coincidence. "You first."

Roarke looked at her curiously, then broke his cookie and read: "He who hesitates is not only lost, but miles from the last exit. . . . That's an ancient Chinese saying?"

"I suppose even fortune cookies have to keep up with the times."

"I guess. So what does yours say?"

"It's foolish."

"They always are. That's the idea. Now you've got me curious." He plucked the paper from her nerveless fingers. "To fear love is to fear life."

"I don't think that's even Chinese," Jade protested.

"It's not. Actually, it's Bertrand Russell. Want to hear the rest?"

"I don't think—"

"To fear love is to fear life, and those who fear life are already three parts dead."

Jade turned away, unable to meet his suddenly warm gaze. "You shouldn't be talking this way. Not now."

"You're right." He'd come here today with the sole purpose of comforting her. Now Roarke realized that by wanting more, he was getting into dangerous waters. "I was out of line. And I'm sorry if I upset you."

"It's not just you. Damnit, this shouldn't be happening." She hit her hand on the table. "Not to Sam. He's the kindest, most wonderful person I've ever known. Why can't I be in there, instead of him?"

Roarke forced down the hurt to his ego her words caused. "I don't know."

"It's not fair." Jade swiped at the free-falling tears with the backs of her hands. Sam was going to die without ever knowing the truth about who and what she was. He'd fallen in love with a liar. A deceiver. Her guilt was more than she could bear.

"Cassie. Jade." Unable to bear her grief, Roarke put his hands on her shoulders. Jade moved away.

"Thank you for lunch," she said raggedly, "but I need to be alone."

"Whatever you say." He pulled out his pen and wrote a pair of numbers on the back of her fortunes. "Here's my office number and my number at the hotel. I've moved out of the house," he answered her questioning glance. "Call me any time you need me. Day or night."

Her heart breaking, Jade was unable to accept the comfort he was offering. "Thank you."

Six hours later, after she had resumed her vigil beside Sam's bed, she sat telling his unresponsive figure about Amy. The fact that he was unconscious hadn't stopped her from talking nearly nonstop, on the outside chance he could hear her.

"Amy got the part of Tigger in her new play," she said. "That's the good news. The bad news is that I'm expected to come up with a tiger costume." She squeezed his fingers and forced herself to smile. "How good are you at basting a seam?"

"Probably better than you," he mumbled.

Jade almost knocked the glass of water off the side table. "Sam? Oh, my God, Sam, you can talk." Lowering the rail, she sat on the bed beside him.

He opened his eyes and looked up at her. "I could if you'd shut up long enough to let me get a word in edgewise."

He was going to make it. Hope was a hummingbird, flapping its delicate wings inside Jade's breast. "Whatever you say, darling."

"I know." He took a deep breath. "About Amy."

Jade's heart clenched. "What about Amy?"

"We don't have time to play twenty questions, sweetheart. I was coming back from Oklahoma when the plane crashed. I talked to people there, Jade. I know everything. About your mother, and Roarke. I put things together and figured out that Amy's his child."

"Oh, my God." She began to tremble. How could he have suspected she'd lied about her past? How could he have known where to look?

"I understand." His fingers tightened on her ice-cold ones. "I understand why you felt you had to lie, but . . ." He began to cough. Jade, panicky, reached for the call button, but he stopped her with a faint wave of his hand. "No. I'm okay."

She brushed his gray hair back from his forehead. "We can talk about this some other time."

"I don't have a lot of time, sweetheart."

"Don't say that!" Jade shook her head. "You're going to be fine. All you need is a little rest, and some tender loving care and—"

"Jade." He reached up and pressed his fingers against her lips. "I've given this a lot of thought and I want you to hear me out. Please?"

Her lips had turned to stone. Jade could only nod.

"You've got to tell Roarke," Sam insisted. "He's a good man. He'll take care of Amy. And you."

"No," Jade protested with a sob. "We don't need Roarke to take care of us. We have you. Don't you see, Sam, you're going to get better and Amy'll come live with us all the time, just like you wanted and we'll be a real family and—"

"Jade?"

"Yes?" Tears were flowing in wet ribbons down her cheeks.

"I love you. Always." His fingers, strong again for this brief, fleeting moment, tightened on hers. Then relaxed.

"Always," Jade whispered.

The monitor above his head began making a high-pitched wail. Seconds later, Jade was pushed aside by a team of white-clad doctors and nurses. Standing by the door, alone and brokenhearted, she watched the code team's futile attempt to save her husband's life.

Numb with grief as she was, Jade found telling Amy that Sam would not be coming back to be the hardest thing she had ever done. Since it was the middle of the week, Amy was in school. Wanting—needing to be alone with her daughter—Jade drove to the Valley of the Moon Academy, found her on the soccer field, and took her back to her room.

"Amy, darling, I'm afraid I have bad news."

The small face paled to the cold gray color of a January sky. "About Sam?"

"Yes." Jade took a deep breath and blinked back the tears stinging at the back of her eyelids. "The doctors really tried to save him, sweetheart, but he was too badly hurt."

"Sam died?"

"Yes. I'm so sorry, and I hate to have to hurt you this way, but I'm afraid he did." Jade's hands shook; the words broke stutteringly through her fingers.

Amy's lips quivered. Her eyes glistened. "But Sam loved me. He wouldn't die!"

Jade tried again. "Of course he loved you. In fact, that's one of the last things he told me, before—"

"No!" Amy tore her hearing aid from her ears, threw them to the floor, and screamed out her pain. "You're a liar! I hate you. And I hate Sam for dying and leaving us all alone. Again!"

The air was alive with Amy's anger and grief. Her delicate hands shot out her disbelief, words trembled and broke to pieces, until finally, she jerked out of Jade's arms and began kicking the wall and slamming her door, needing to hear, to feel, the noise of her pain.

Finally exhausted, the little girl collapsed on her bed, her thin body racked with sobs. Lying down beside her, Jade spent the night, the two of them, mother and daughter, wrapped in each other's arms, seeking comfort from their closeness.

Although it was difficult, as soon as she returned to the city with her daughter, Jade put on a properly businesslike, gray and black Armani suit and drove to Sam's Montgomery Street office.

Everyone, from the garage attendant, to the elevator operator, to the chic woman seated at the desk outside Sam's penthouse office, offered condolences. The expression on each face told Jade that Sam's employees honestly shared her loss.

But she couldn't miss the worry she viewed on their faces as well. Which was why she'd dragged herself down there when she would much rather have stayed home with Amy, eating the chocolate chip cookies Edith had been mixing up when she'd left the house.

After packing Sam's personal possessions into the cardboard boxes his secretary had left on the floor by his desk, Jade escaped into the ladies' room, washed her face, dried her red-rimmed eyes, then reapplied her makeup with a trembling hand.

She knew she looked like hell, but fortunately her life no longer depended on her looks, so she only gave her reflection one last cursory glance before heading down to the office of Warren Bingham, Sam's vice-president and longtime right arm.

"Jade." Warren rose immediately, his handsome face filled with sadness and sympathy. "It's good to see you," he said, greeting her as if it had been months rather than days since they'd last sat together, attempting to offer each other comfort, outside Sam's room.

A friend of Sam's since boyhood, Warren had been there when Sam had first begun Southerland Enterprises. And he'd remained there until the end.

"Please, sit down." He gestured toward the cordovan red leather sofa. "Can I have Mona bring you anything? Tea? Coffee, mineral water?" His brow furrowed. "Or, if you'd prefer something stronger—"

Jade managed a weak smile. "Don't worry, Warren, I haven't started drinking at ten in the morning. At least not yet." Rather than take a seat on the sofa, she chose a visitor's chair on the visitor's side of the desk. "And no, I don't really care for anything, thank you. I've come here on business."

Taking his cue from her, he returned to his own high-backed leather chair behind the glossy expanse of polished mahogany.

"Whatever you want, Jade," he said easily. "Sam always said you had an excellent head on your shoulders, which is readily apparent from the success you've already made of Jade's. If you intend to take Sam's place at Southerland Enterprises, I can get you up to speed in no time at all."

"Actually, the idea of running Southerland Enterprises is the furthest thing from my mind," Jade said. "But, since Sam left me as sole executor of his estate, I realized this morning that as appealing at the idea was, I couldn't hide away at home and feel sorry for myself. Not when so many other people are involved."

"There have been a great many rumors circulating," Warren revealed.

"I'm sure there have been. And I should have anticipated that the employees would be concerned about their futures, but all the time Sam was in the hospital, I was too worried about him to fully comprehend what a vast empire he'd created.

"I also managed to overlook the fact that such an enormous machine, even one as well oiled as the one you and Sam have created, doesn't keep running by itself forever. So . . ."

She took a deep breath, made a mental apology to Sam in the event he might not approve of what she was about to do, and said, "I'd like you to begin selling off the companies."

Jade gave him credit for the way he managed to conceal his shock. "All of them?"

"Every last one," she confirmed. "But there's no need to rush. Anyone who wants to stay on during the transition is free to, and I want you to ensure that people won't be laid off when the companies change hands."

"I feel obliged to tell you that you'll definitely lessen your bargaining position if you insist on that particular clause."

"Fine." She waved away his warning. "Sam always said he had more money than he could count. If we have to spend some of it to remain loyal to those people who remained loyal to him, then we'll do it."

This time her smile was a little more natural. "But thank you for pointing it out to me. Sam always said you were honest to a fault. That's why I know I can count on you."

"May I ask what you intend to do with the profits?" he asked. "They're going to be considerable; you should probably have a plan."

"I do. But a lot depends on you."

"On me?" An eyebrow climbed above the horn-rimmed glasses.

"I'd like you to stay on, Warren," she said. "My plan—Sam's plan, originally—is to create a foundation that will build camps for physically challenged children in every state."

He whistled softly. "That's no small order."

"That's why I need you."

He folded his hands and looked out the vast expanse of bronze-tinted glass to where the sun-gilded orange towers of the Golden Gate Bridge rose high above the bay.

"Sam always thrived on new challenges," he mused aloud. "We always laughed that I was the conservative one."

"I think you both loved challenges," she argued. "Otherwise the two of you would have kept working in sawmills. I also believe that you were forced to play the role of a conservative devil's advocate to keep things in balance whenever Sam's enthusiasm started to run away with him."

"I think you might be right," he admitted. He leaned back in his chair and toyed with the antique Waterman pen. Jade knew that the lacquer pen was a Christmas gift from Sam; she'd found it in a neighboring Cow Hollow shop.

"Camps for physically challenged kids, huh?" His lips curved in a slow smile. "I've always liked kids. You've got yourself an administrator, Jade."

Jade felt the burdensome weight of sole responsibility that had settled on her shoulders lightening. "You've no idea how pleased I am to hear you say that." she said. "If you'd draw up the papers, I'd appreciate it." When she named a suggested salary, he didn't bother to conceal his surprise.

"But that's a great deal more than I'm currently making. Even with annual bonuses."

"I know. I also know that you're going to earn every penny, Warren." She stood up, and when he came around the desk to see her out, pressed a light kiss on his cheek. "Thank you," she said softly. "For everything."

Matters settled to her satisfaction, Jade left the office, pausing several times on her way out of the building to accept condolences from Sam's employees.

It was only after she was in the privacy of her car, headed back home, that she allowed herself to weep.

Grief was relentless. Jade became obsessed with images of Sam's gleaming red plane crashing into snowy mountains. The pictures flashed unceasingly in her mind during the day, they tormented her sleep at night. The bed where she'd experienced such bliss became a sterile and barren desert.

She couldn't accept the fact that Sam was gone. He'd always been so strong. So invincible. She moved through the rooms like a sleepwalker. She sat in his chair, she wore his shirts, she slept on his side of the bed, and tucked his unwashed pajamas beneath the pillow so she'd wake up to his scent as she had on so many other mornings.

She'd drive up the coast, park her car, and walk along the cold and fogbound beaches, weeping and railing at Sam for leaving her, at God for taking him away, at herself for the lie that had led him to be in that plane in the first place, and at the unrelenting loneliness. But nothing could fill the enormous hole her husband's death had left in her heart.

The F.A.A. investigators had retrieved Sam's personal things from the wreckage. When she saw the familiar journal, Jade's tears began again. He'd written so many things on the lined pages that he hadn't shared with her. His knowledge that she wasn't being honest with him, hope that someday she'd trust him enough to share whatever secrets she was hiding.

The last page was the one that broke her heart.

*I wonder if Roarke knows he has a daughter,* Sam had written in his bold dark script. *Probably not. Gallagher isn't the kind of man to relinquish responsibility for his own flesh and blood.*

Sam had gone on to guess why Jade kept Amy a secret. All those complaints about the press and Amy's privacy were nothing but bullshit—he had always known that. For some reason, Jade had made the conscious decision never to tell Roarke that he was Amy's father. Sam's discovery also explained why Jade had been stalling on the matter of Amy's adoption.

For two pages of the journal he vacillated between keeping his trip a secret and telling his wife the truth. Finally, Jade read, he had made his decision.

*I'll just have to convince Jade that it doesn't matter whose daughter Amy is,* Sam finished up with his own inimitable self-confidence.

Through tear-blurred eyes Jade read Sam's declaration that he couldn't have loved her daughter more if she had been his own and that he'd only been waiting for the right time to insist that Jade allow him to adopt Amy.

*Looks like the time is now.*

But there hadn't been time. Because on the way back his plane had crashed.

Having always believed in extravagance in life, Sam did not change his style in death. His instructions, left with his attorney, were quite specific: There was to be no funeral. No memorial service. Indeed, Jade was to throw, in Sam's own words, "the biggest, most raucous damn party this town has ever seen."

Unable to ignore her husband's last wishes, Jade opened their Pacific Heights house to all his friends, ignoring the gossips and society columnists who expressed indignation about the impropriety of such an event.

"I can't believe the way the press is acting," Jade said to Nina shortly before the guests were due to arrive.

"It's Monica," Nina revealed. "The bitch is trying to make you look like a heartless gold digger."

"Well, she's certainly doing a good job of that."

"Anyone who knew Sam knows that you're doing the right thing. As for the others, just ignore them. You know what Cole Porter said when he was criticized for using thirty thousand candles at one of his parties?"

"I don't think so."

"He said that he was simply employing thirty thousand candlemakers."

Knowing that Nina was trying to cheer her up, Jade attempted a smile. But the effort proved too difficult.

Later, she managed to gather the strength to address the gathered group of more than two hundred. "I've invited you all here tonight because you're Sam's friends. We've done our grieving in private, and now we've come together to celebrate a remarkable man's even more remarkable life. Sam was never one to stint on having a good time. So please, eat, drink, and make my husband proud."

Champagne flowed like the Niagara, damask-draped tables groaned with food. A Motown group played dance music in the front parlor, while out on the back terrace, a jazz combo entertained the overflow from the packed house.

Roarke found Jade there. After her brave words, she'd retreated back into the cold, lonely shell of her grief.

"Quite a bash," he greeted her. "Sam would have loved it."

Startled, Jade realized that she'd drifted into a daze again. Ever since Sam's death, she would wander aimlessly into a room and find herself still standing there, motionless, minutes later.

"I only wish we'd had time for more parties while he was alive. He asked me, again and again, to cut back on my work, to take time to smell the flowers, but—"

"Don't." Roarke touched her cheek with his fingertips. "No recriminations. You were the best thing that ever happened to Sam Southerland, Jade."

"You're only saying that to make me feel better."

"No. I'm saying that because it's what Sam told me."

"And he was the best thing that ever happened to me."

Roarke pushed down the stab of envy. What kind of bastard could be envious of a dead man?

"By the way," Jade said, "I've been meaning to call and thank you."

"Thank me for what?"

"For lunch that afternoon, for one thing. And for bumping the story of Sam's death from headline news to below-the-fold." Roarke's public accusations of kickbacks at Hamilton Construction had caused a government inquiry into his father-in-law's business. That revelation, along with Roarke's subsequent divorce, was the talk of the town. "By the way, you were very brave to risk professional fallout going public about Hamilton's troubles."

"They used inferior steel on that building, and it was clear that the next tremor could have knocked it down like a house of cards, taking a lot of innocent people with it. I'm not a hero—the papers are wrong. I simply didn't have a choice."

"That's the same thing Sam would have said." She sighed. "You know he was always proud to be your friend."

"Not as proud as I was to be his. Sam Southerland was one of a kind."

Jade felt a few of the chains loosening around her heart. She smiled. "He certainly was."

One week after the party, Jade was confronted by Monica, Adam, and Michael Southerland. With the exception of small cash bequests to his children, Sam had left everything to Jade.

"Let me get this straight," Jade said. "If I don't give up all claims to Sam's estate, you'll reveal the truth about my background." Jade knew that her husband's lawyer had told Sam's disgruntled children that the will was airtight.

"That's it in a nutshell," Monica agreed. From the moment the unholy trio had entered her home, Sam's daughter had acted as spokesperson.

Jade looked out the window at the garden she and Sam had planted together. For some reason, the bright red rhododendron gave her both strength and comfort. "I'm still not sure why I should care."

Monica's smooth forehead was deeply furrowed. She puffed viciously on her cigarette. "Because if the truth of your less-than-spotless past gets out, it'll destroy the business you've worked so hard to establish."

Her mouth drew into a hard line. "How many of San Francisco's good citizens would continue opening their doors to the illegitimate daughter of an alcoholic prostitute? How do you think people would react if they learned you've been convicted of theft?"

As stricken as she was by their knowledge of her secret past, Jade was weary of living a lie. She was tired of keeping her daughter a secret. She was tired of worrying that she'd run into someone who knew her in her past life. She was tired. Period.

She met Monica's blistering glare head-on. "You're the one who told Sam, aren't you?" she said. "You're the reason he flew to Oklahoma." *And you're the reason he died.* The accusation went unspoken, but it hovered over them.

"If he'd just taken my word about your unsavory past," Monica answered defensively, "he wouldn't have had to go to that godforsaken place." She ground her cigarette out in a Baccarat ashtray and immediately lit another one.

"May I ask a question?" Jade asked.

"What?"

"How did you find out?"

"I was in Paris for the collections," Monica revealed, "when I ran into an old friend of yours." When Jade refused to give her the pleasure of asking who, she asked, "Does the name Shelby Gallagher mean anything to you?"

The idea that Shelby, who had stolen her letters to Roarke, would be the one to reveal the secret of her past made Jade wonder if life was nothing but a series of intersecting lines of hateful coincidences.

"I loved your father." Jade said quietly. "And although I doubt that you'll believe me, I did not marry him for his money."

Adam's utterance was something between an oath and a cough.

"It's true," Jade insisted quietly. "But it's also a moot point because all I'm keeping is this house and Sam's place on the coast. Sam loved both places and they have a sentimental meaning for me."

"What are you going to do with the rest?" Michael Southerland asked. Avarice burned in his watery blue eyes. She could smell the Scotch from where she stood.

"I'm setting up a foundation to administer a nationwide network of camps for physically challenged children."

Monica was on her feet. "We'll challenge the will. My father would never have agreed to that."

Jade stood up as well. "As a matter of fact, it was his idea. Now, if you don't mind, I'm sure you can find your own way out. I have work to do."

Instead of feeling guilty about ordering his children out of the house in which she and Sam had shared so much love, Jade believed that she could almost hear her husband applauding.

# *Twenty-two*

Always a workaholic, Jade worked around the clock now that Sam was gone. Work became a comfort, a retreat, a lover, as she threw herself into planning upcoming auctions and writing a monthly newsletter she'd begun for catalogue subscribers. In addition, she continued to make buying trips to the Orient.

And if that weren't enough, there was always her auction house to keep her mind from dwelling on her grief. As construction continued on the building, Jade and Roarke worked well together. If there were times when Jade seemed to be feeling the chemistry that was always lurking beneath the surface, Roarke allowed her to back away without comment.

Although she'd eschewed social events after Sam's memorial party, finally, three months after she'd cleaned out her husband's desk, Jade allowed herself to be talked into attending a showing of Tony DiAngelo's photographs at the Museum of Modern Art.

As she dressed for the evening, Jade realized that it would be the first time she had gone out since she'd been widowed. She wanted to crawl into bed and pull the covers over her head. But, reminding herself that the purpose of the evening was to raise much-needed funds for an AIDS hospice, she forced herself down the stairs and out the door.

The series of photographs was titled simply: Western Women. Taking a less-is-more approach, Tony had abandoned the society portraits that had garnered him both fame and fortune and filmed his subjects in black-and-white against a stark white background, stripping away the nonessential.

She paused in front of the furrowed, grittily determined face of a Colorado gold miner.

"What's the inflationary price of a thought these days?" a voice asked in her ear.

She turned and looked up at Roarke. "I was just thinking that I've never met that woman, yet I feel I know her. In a strange way, it's like looking into a mirror." Indeed, Jade had been shocked to recognize herself in the eyes of these strangers. She saw their visions, anxieties, and hopes.

A tear slid down her cheek. She shook her head. "I'm sorry."

Roarke brushed it away. "Mourning takes time."

"That's what I keep telling myself. But some days are harder than others."

"You and Sam made some good memories together. Memories to cherish. He was a lucky man, Jade. And he knew it."

"I recall a time when you thought differently."

"I was wrong. What are you doing after you leave here?"

Jade moved on to a photo of a young woman singing at a Wyoming rodeo. The woman's face, while alive with the sheer pleasure of performing to an audience, also betrayed both the hope and the despair inevitable in such a life-style. The woman reminded Jade of Belle. She didn't bother to answer Roarke, hoping he wouldn't push it.

"I've been craving pizza all day. But I hate to eat alone," he insisted, flashing his most winning smile. "What do you say?"

"Pizza's fattening," she said automatically, a holdover response from her modeling days.

His gaze swept over her. She was wearing a soft swirl of flowered silk georgette. The romantic dress was totally unlike the faded jeans he remembered her wearing around the ranch.

"All the better. You're too skinny."

"Thanks for the compliment."

"You could never be anything but beautiful to me," he said easily. "But you've lost a lot of weight since Sam died. As his friend, I know he'd want me to see that you're eating properly."

"Is that why you've been hovering over me like some overprotective German shepherd?"

"Who, me?"

"Everywhere I go, there you are."

"San Francisco's a small town."

"True. But that doesn't explain what you were doing on the same beach at Big Sur last Sunday."

"I was jogging."

Jade eyed him suspiciously. For the past weeks, she would have suspected that Roarke was stalking her, were it not for his take-it-or-leave-it attitude whenever they were together. Indeed, he'd been a perfect gentleman.

"Let me say good-bye to Tony," she decided. "And we'll leave."

Entering the Kearny Street restaurant was like stepping down into a grotto. It was dark, steamy, and filled with mouthwatering aromas. The pizza, baked in an oak-fired oven, was the best Jade had ever tasted. Or perhaps, she was willing to admit, it was the company.

"How are you, really?" Roarke asked, looking deep into her eyes.

"I've been better." Jade shrugged. "It's the little things," she admitted. "Just when I think I'm getting over Sam's . . ." She couldn't say the word *death*. ". . . I'll open a drawer and run across his lucky softball socks or the antique pen I bought him for our anniversary. It just tears away the scar tissue and I start to hurt all over again."

Tears welled in her eyes; she dabbed at them with a paper napkin. "I'm sorry."

"Don't be ridiculous. I've read that talking about a loss like you've had is important for healing." He reached across the table and took hold of her hand.

A private person by nature, Jade couldn't imagine rattling on about such intimate things as the feelings she'd been experiencing. She hadn't even been able to be honest with her own husband, Jade considered bleakly, as the guilt that was never far away since Sam's death swept over her.

"I know it's hard," Roarke coaxed gently, "but why don't you at least try talking to me."

He meant it, Jade realized. And although she knew that encouraging any intimacy between them was folly, she heard herself saying, "Sometimes I'm so mad at him. For dying, and leaving me all alone."

"I think that's probably pretty natural."

"Do you? Do you really?"

"Sure. It's nothing to feel guilty about."

"But I do. Every time I find myself wallowing in anger and self-pity,

I feel terrible, because Sam's the one I should be feeling sorry for. He's the one who died.

"But you're the one who was left all alone," Roarke pointed out.

She digested that for a long minute. "There are all these little ambushes of grief," she related. "Ordinary things I never expected, like the pen, or the socks. Yesterday, I was in Saks, at Union Square, and I saw a man on the escalator who looked so much like Sam. My first thought was, Look, there's Sam. Then I told myself, Don't be stupid, Sam's dead."

Roarke's fingers tightened reassuringly around hers. "It happens."

"But you don't understand. My next thought was that I had to go home and tell Sam what a foolish mistake I'd made." A sob rose painfully in her throat. "It all happened within seconds. And it happens all the time."

"I can see how that must be painful," Roarke allowed thoughtfully. "But I think it's probably part of the process of healing.

"I certainly didn't suffer a loss like yours, Cassie," he said, slipping again into using the name he'd known—and loved—her by. "But, in its own way, divorce carries its own legacy of pain and guilt."

"I'm sorry about your marriage breaking up," Jade said softly. She was dying to ask if the rumors of his wife's infidelities were true, but didn't.

As if he were reading her mind, Roarke said, "I always suspected she'd been with other men. My wife needed a great deal of attention, more than I could give her. But there was one man I could never compete with. When I found out about the kickbacks on Hamilton's building, push finally came to shove and Philippa ended up right in the middle. I wasn't all that surprised when she chose her father."

"But it must have hurt."

"It hurt my pride," Roarke agreed. "And my male ego. And you know how I hate failing at anything. But, I guess in the long run, I mostly felt relief."

Not knowing what to say to that, Jade remained silent.

"Enough about me," he said, releasing her hand and sitting back in the booth. "This was supposed to be your therapy session, not mine."

"I've already gotten a lot off my chest," she said. "How about we find something a bit more upbeat to discuss?"

The conversation flowed easily, moving from Bay area sports to the weather, unpredictable as always, to the last-minute changes made when they'd learned that the flooring planned for her auction house had become unavailable.

"Speaking of business, there's something I've been meaning to ask you," Jade said.

"About the auction house? Is something wrong?"

She had moved in two months earlier, and other than a few minor problems she had worked out with the contractor, the building was as perfect as she and Roarke had envisioned.

"No. I love my building and I can't wait to hold my first auction on that marvelous revolving stage. But this is something else."

Leaning forward, she told him about her planned camps, pleased when he appeared to be honestly interested.

"I'd like you to seriously consider designing the buildings," she finished up.

Instead of answering immediately, he began doodling on a red paper napkin. Jade watched the series of circles turn to squares, then parallelograms. "It sounds like the type of challenge I enjoy," he answered finally. "But why do I hear a *but* in your offer?"

"These would be camps," she pointed out carefully. "A place where children could go horseback riding, swimming, roast marshmallows over a campfire."

"I was a Boy Scout, Jade," Roarke reminded her. "I'm well aware of what a camp is." Jade watched the comprehension slowly dawn on his face. Rather than being offended, as she'd feared, he threw back his head and laughed. The bold masculine sound pulled an unwilling chord deep inside her.

"You were afraid I'd want to replace the kids' cabins with some sleek, modern, streamlined steel-beamed buildings, weren't you?" he accused, his smile taking all the bite from his words.

"Well," Jade began, tearing her own napkin into little pieces, "I know you've always preferred modern architecture, but—"

"Jade, Jade," he said on a deep sigh. Reaching across the table, he covered her nervous hand with his once again. "You must have been reading my mind."

"What do you mean?"

"To tell you the truth, lately I've been forced to wonder if I haven't gotten myself into a rut. It seems that because I've made a name for myself designing modern buildings, the only clients who come to me are ones who want the same type of construction. Believe me, cabins would be a refreshing change."

Caught up in their shared enthusiasm for the project, they talked late into the night, until the manager finally reluctantly told them that it was past time to close the restaurant.

Jade's pain gradually diminished over the following months. Belatedly realizing how badly she had neglected Amy for her work, she began to cut back on her hours in order to spend more time with her daughter, who'd become even more contentious since the crash.

To Jade's surprise, her work continued to flourish even as her relationship with Amy, who was finally beginning to recover from Sam's death, blossomed anew. And there was always Nina, who, insisting she could run both agencies just as well from the West Coast, had stayed in San Francisco to offer Jade much-needed moral support.

Her life was nearly complete. It was missing only one person. One man. Roarke.

"I don't understand," Nina said one night when she and Jade had gotten together for a Katharine Hepburn double-feature video festival. "Roarke's a good man. He's successful, responsible, kind. And his feelings for you certainly aren't any secret."

"We're friends," Jade hedged, pushing the rewind for *The African Queen*. Now there was a romantic movie. No nudity, no sex to speak of, but passion had sizzled on every fame. They just didn't make movies, or men, like that anymore. She decided that Humphrey Bogart reminded her a lot of Sam. "That's all."

"Sure. That's why there's a lusty gleam in his eyes whenever he looks at you. You can't tell me you don't want him, Jade. We've been friends for too long for me not to recognize desire when I see it."

"All right," Jade said, as she inserted *The Philadelphia Story* into the VCR.

"I'll admit it. I want Roarke. No. It's more than want. I love him. In fact, if you want to know the truth, except when I was married to Sam, I never stopped thinking about him. Now are you satisfied?"

"Not really," Nina said. "Since you still haven't told me why you've been keeping the guy at arm's length. It's been nearly a year since Sam died, Jade. It's time to get on with your life."

Jade had kept her secret for so many years that it was tearing a ragged hole in her heart. "There's something I didn't tell you," she said quietly. "Something about Amy."

"I know Roarke's her father."

"It isn't that. Well, it is. But . . ." Jade was twisting her hands together in her lap. "It's my fault that Amy's deaf."

"Damnit, Jade," Nina complained dismissively, "we've been all through that. The doctors could never give you a definitive answer. Those things happen."

"Yes," Jade agreed bitterly. "Those things happen. Especially when you father a child with your own brother."

"What?" Nina stared at her. "But you don't have a brother. You told me that you were an only child."

"I was. Actually, I suppose it would be more accurate to say my half brother." Taking a deep breath, she told Nina the story Quinlan Gallagher had told her and Belle had confirmed.

"I don't believe it," Nina insisted. "There's not the slightest resemblance between you and Roarke." She reached out and took both Jade's hands in her own.

"Obviously Roarke's father had his own reason for lying, and as for your mother, well, honestly, Jade, you can't consider her a reliable source. You owe it to yourself, not to mention Amy and Roarke, to discover the truth. Even if it means confronting Belle and Quinlan again."

Three days later, Jade flew to Oklahoma.

Once again she was shocked by her mother's appearance; Belle was so emaciated that she seemed almost unable to move properly. "Hello, Mama," she said. "You're looking well."

"You always were a damn liar, Cassie," Belle said. "I suppose that was one of the few things we had in common."

"Yes." Jade took a deep breath. "That's what I've come to talk to you about."

Belle gave her a long appraising look. "Well, since you've come all this way, you might as well sit down."

Jade sat down on the orange vinyl couch. Her nerves were so on edge, she barely noticed the broken spring. "It's about Roarke."

Guilt flashed across Belle's face. "What about him?" She lit a cigarette.

"I want to know if he's really my half brother."

"Of course he is," Belle said on a stream of exhaled smoke. "Why would I lie about a thing like that?"

"Perhaps because Quinlan made you?" Jade ventured carefully.

Belle was silent. "I never asked to be a mother," she said finally.

Jade had heard that assertion before. More times than she cared to count. "I know," she said softly, forcing herself to be patient, to let her mother tell her story her way.

"I just wanted to be loved." Belle took a long drag on the cigarette. "For a long time I blamed you when no guy'd ever stick around. After all, what man would want to put up with some other guy's kid?"

What man, indeed? Jade considered, thinking of Sam, with a flash of pain at the bittersweet memory.

"I was jealous of you," Belle said. "Livin' the good life up in the Gallagher mansion while I struggled for every dime."

"I gave you what money I could, Mama."

Belle appeared not to hear her. She was on a roll. "Oh, I knew you were embarrassed havin' a drunk for a mother. Every damn time you had me committed to one of those fuckin' sanitariums, I figured it was your way of paying me back for all the years I was such a rotten mother. Do you think I planned to be an alcoholic?" she demanded, looking Jade straight in the eye.

Jade shook her head. "No."

Belle jabbed the cigarette into the air. A gray scattering of ashes fell to the soiled carpet. "You're damn right I didn't. There wasn't one time, when I was little, when I said, when I grow up, I think I'll be an alcoholic. I just drink to escape my life."

"Mama?"

"Yeah?"

"You haven't answered my question. About whether or not Quinlan Gallagher is my father."

Belle's hands shook as she lit another cigarette from the end of the first. "He's not. The whole thing was a lie. To keep you away from Roarke."

Jade closed her eyes, praying for strength. "Why?" she whispered. "Why did you go along with him?"

"Because he blackmailed me, damnit," Belle flared.

"He blackmailed you? How?"

"He set me up to be arrested for prostitution and was goin' to send me off to the County Work Farm. What was I supposed to do?"

Jade thought of Amy. No one would ever be able to force her to hurt her daughter the way Belle had hurt her.

"You gotta understand how it happened," Belle said. "It was a long time ago, after I got out of that hell of a treatment center you sent me to in Dallas."

"That treatment center was very famous." *And very expensive,* Jade remembered.

"It was hell," Belle repeated. "The roughest damn one ever. Every day this muscle-bound nurse gave me an injection to make me allergic to alcohol, then I had to sit in this puny closet of a room where they forced me to drink. Well, let me tell you, pretty soon even the smell of whiskey was enough to make me toss my cookies."

"But you stopped drinking."

"I was on the wagon for two long, dry months," Belle agreed. "And despite what you think, I really tried. I even went to AA meetings every day. Then one day, I was sittin' on a metal folding chair in the basement of the Gallagher City Holy Spirit Pentecostal Church, looking around at all the posters and platitudes hangin' on the walls, when this soft noise started up buzzin' in my head.

"I didn't really need a drink," she assured Jade. "It was only an experiment to see if I could keep the liquor down. And I had to get rid of that buzzing."

"I went to this really tacky joint," she said, causing Jade to remember all the places she'd dragged her mother out of over the years, places where cigarette smoke hovered over the room like a pall and sawdust littered the floor. "But I gotta tell you, I liked it a helluva lot better than that stuffy old church basement."

Belle explained how she had perched on a stool and taken a tentative sip of the white wine the bartender poured from a gallon jug (after first wiping the dust off) beneath the bar. She waited. When she didn't immediately throw up, she took another longer sip. Again, nothing happened.

"But you know you can't drink, mama," Jade protested as the familiar frustration built up inside her. One drink always led to another. Then a whole lot more.

"Wine ain't really drinking," Belle argued. "Anyway, to get back to the story you said you were so all-fired anxious to hear, I'd just finished the second glass of wine and was waitin' for it to smooth out the rough edges when the door opened and this man came in. He smiled at me, so I smiled back."

Three glasses later, the bartender placed a creamy brandy Alexander in front of her.

"When I told him I didn't order that, he told me it was from the gentleman at the end of the bar," Belle explained. "Well, I certainly didn't want to be rude, and besides, a brandy Alexander is more like a dessert than a proper drink."

Jade was not at all surprised to hear that Belle and the man had moved to a back booth. Innumerable brandy Alexanders later, the man suggested they take the party somewhere else.

"You gotta understand, Jade," Belle insisted. "It'd been a long time since I'd been with a man. So damn long. And not one minute of it had been any fun at all."

"I still don't understand how going to bed with a strange man ended up with Quinlan blackmailing you."

"I guess it was the money."

"The money," Jade repeated on a dull tone.

"When he asked how much I charged, I was gonna tell him that I might have been down and out in my day, but I'd never exchanged sex for money. But then I started figgering, since I'd already decided to go to bed with him, what harm was there in accepting a little token of his appreciation? After all, he'd already paid for the drinks. How different could a little cash be?"

How different indeed. Jade rubbed her hand across her eyes.

"When I told him one hundred dollars, he didn't blink an eye," Belle confided. "Which made me feel pretty good, you know, 'cause that's a right expensive price."

When Jade didn't dare answer, Belle went on to relate how the stranger took her to the Rose Rock Motel, where he turned out to be such a dynamite kisser she'd forgotten about the money. Until he counted five crisp twenty-dollar bills into her palm.

"Right after that, the bastard reached into those tight jeans and pulled out his badge, and said I was under arrest," Belle said. "For prostitution."

"Gallagher set you up," Jade said flatly, seeing the oilman's fingerprints all over Belle's arrest.

"I figgered that out for myself when the old bastard showed up at the jail and told me that he was the only thing standing between me and the County Work Farm, and how if I tried to escape, the guards would shoot me."

"He threatened to kill you?" Just to keep his son away from me? Jade wondered. She'd known Quinlan was brutal, but she hadn't realized that he was crazy.

"I was a little buzzy, but I was still thinkin' clear enough to know he meant every damn word. If I live to a hundred, I'll never forget that man's eyes." Belle shuddered at the memory. "They reminded me of a rattlesnake's."

Jade had seen those eyes before and knew that Belle, for once, was exactly right. Quinlan Gallagher's eyes were like a rattlesnake's—cold and flat and venomous.

"I wanted to tell him to go to hell, but I've played enough poker to know when the other guy is holding the winning cards," Belle said. "And Quinlan Gallagher was holding all aces.

"Besides," she insisted with a flash of her old defiant attitude, "when I told you that lie, it was over between you and Roarke for years. It didn't seem like it'd do any harm."

Not do any harm. Jade tried not to hate Belle for all the pain and lost years she had caused. Years that she and Roarke could have been together. Years that Amy could have known her father. Relief and regret swept over her in waves. Then another blinding thought occurred to her. If Roarke wasn't really her brother, the doctors were right. She wasn't to blame for Amy's deafness, after all.

"But why would he tell such an incredible lie?" she asked. "And, why would he go to so much trouble to frame you, and make you back him up?"

Belle shrugged. "You'll have to ask the old bastard himself," she advised. "Quinlan didn't fill me in on the particulars why he was havin' me run in for soliciting."

Jade had every intention of doing exactly that. And a great deal more. But first there was one more lie—a lie of omission—to deal with.

"There's something I have to tell you," Jade said. "Something I realize I should have told you years ago."

Slowly, stutteringly, Jade told her mother all about Roarke. And more important, about Amy.

"Are you telling me that I'm a grandmother?" Belle asked, obviously shocked by Jade's revelation.

"Yes. Does that bother you?" Jade knew how her mother dreaded the thought of getting old.

"I don't know. I need some time to think about it." Without another word, Belle got up and walked outside. Jade watched her walk down to the end of the dirt road and back again. She was smoking the entire time.

"Do I get to meet her?" Belle asked upon returning to the apartment.

"Of course."

"Is she gonna call me Grandma? Or Belle?"

"She'll call you whatever you like."

Belle mulled that one over as she lit yet another cigarette. "I never thought I'd hear myself sayin' it, but *grandma* does have kind nice ring to it," she decided. "Loretta Lynn's a grandmother."

Jade nodded, suppressing her smile. Apparently, what was good enough for Loretta was good enough for Belle.

"I got another question," Belle said.

"What?"

"Do you still have the brochure for that new clinic you've been pushing? That one all the movie stars go to?"

Perhaps she was tired of being a drunk. Or perhaps she realized that they both had suffered enough pain. Perhaps, Jade considered, Amy represented the new chance her mother had been looking for.

Whatever her reasons for wanting to try again, Jade allowed herself a glimmer of hope that after a lifetime of failure, this time Belle would have the strength to face the facts of her alcoholism. And exorcise the demons that had been haunting her for so long.

# Twenty-three

The first thing Jade did after she returned to San Francisco from Oklahoma was to arrange a meeting with Warren Bingham.

After a brief time spent being brought up to date on how the divestiture was going, as well as the funding for her foundation, she said, "There's one more thing I'd like you to do."

"Anything," he said promptly, reminding her of Sam.

"I want you to ask around and see if Gallagher Gas and Oil is still in financial trouble. If it is, I want you to buy up every bit of paper on the company."

Jade would have had to have been blind to have missed the strange expression that appeared briefly on his face. "What's wrong?"

"Nothing, really," he said. "It's just strange."

"I know I've asked you to sell off all the other companies, but—"

"No, that's not what I was referring to at all." He folded his hands atop his desk and looked thoughtful. "The day Sam died, he called me from Oklahoma, from the Gallagher City airstrip, actually, right before he took off."

"And?" Jade thought she could guess the rest.

"He gave me the very same instructions. But, then, before I could make a move, he'd crashed and I certainly didn't want to bring it up with you while he was in the hospital, so I waited, but then you came in here and instructed me to divest of everything, so I assumed that Sam's orders were moot."

"They were, at the time. But things have changed."

She was relieved when he didn't ask any questions. "I'll get on it right away," he said instead.

"If I were you, I would have gone straight over to that old bastard's house and told him exactly what I thought of him," Nina said when she heard about Jade's trip.

"I thought about it," Jade confessed. "But when I called the house, Miss Lillian told me that he was in New York. Besides," she admitted, "at the moment, I'm not sure I could have been in the same room with Quinlan Gallagher without doing something drastic."

"Well," Nina decided, "I can certainly understand that. So where do things stand with you and Roarke?"

"I don't know." Jade had been trying to decide what to do about Roarke. Should she tell him about Amy? Should she ask his forgiveness for having kept his daughter from him? Should she try to make up for all those lost years?

"He's in Washington state, on the peninsula right now, looking over a possible camp site. And then he's scheduled to go to Idaho. When he gets back, I'm going to have to do something." She studied her hands. "I just haven't decided what.

"But," she said, "Quinlan is another matter entirely. Warren tells me that due to the continuing oil bust, he's dangerously overextended. By this time next week, you'll be looking at the controlling owner of Gallagher Gas and Oil."

The old saying was right after all, Jade decided seven days later, as she accepted the sheaf of papers from Warren Bingham: Revenge was a much sweeter dish when served cold.

### June 1991

Dark, threatening clouds hung over the land as Jade drove her rental car out to the Gallagher estate. She wanted to get the confrontation over with as soon as possible. Her stomach had been tied up in knots for the past twenty-four hours.

The mansion, once a gleaming white, had faded to a dull gray that matched the lowering sky. It had been a long time since anyone had worked in the garden, Jade determined. The once dazzling rose bushes bent with the weight of dead blossoms.

Jade was surprised when Quinlan himself opened the door. He appeared no less surprised to see her standing on his doorstep.

"Well, if it isn't Cassie McBride," he greeted her with a decided lack of cordiality. "I didn't think you'd ever have the nerve to show your face around these parts again."

Ignoring his pointed reference to the last time she'd been at this house, Jade glanced past him. "Aren't you going to invite me in, Quinlan?"

"Don't know why I should," he drawled.

"Perhaps the name Bay City Trust Company will ring a bell."

"Well, it damn well doesn't."

"Oh dear, I see you haven't been notified, yet. I suppose that leaves me to explain that Bay City Trust recently purchased all your outstanding notes from Oklahoma City National Bank and Tulsa Savings and Loan."

A muscle jerked in his cheek. "You might as well come in," he said, stepping aside. "Seein' as how you've come all this way, Cassie."

"Please," she said, entering the foyer that had once seemed so vast, "call me Mrs. Southerland." She gave him a cool smile. "Oh, but perhaps you didn't know," she said with feigned sweetness. "I'm Sam Southerland's widow."

"Seems I heard somethin' about that," he muttered.

"Did you also hear that I was administrator of his estate?" she asked. "And that I established Bay City Trust Company specifically to handle such funds?"

The color drained from the oilman's ruddy face. "I don't think I heard that," he said in a voice a great deal less robust than the one she was accustomed to hearing. "Why don't you sit down and make yourself at home," he suggested. "I'll have Miss Lillian get us some refreshments."

He was gone—in order to compose himself and plot a new diabolical course, Jade suspected—before she could answer.

Despite her distaste at the idea of being in the home of a brutal man who had once tried to crush her, Jade could not resist the lure of the house's exquisite objects. The rooms were not as well kept as they'd once been. In fact, the gloomy aura brought to mind Miss Havisham's home in *Great Expectations*.

An elderly Miss Lillian, ever the lady, greeted Jade in the parlor with a Royal Dalton plate of ladyfingers. "I made the tea myself," she said, pouring from a Russian samovar that had belonged to an Imperial Russian household. Her behavior did not suggest that there was anything unusual about serving tea to a woman who had once been her housemaid. Nor did she indicate how many years had passed since the last time Jade had been in this room. "I do hope it's all right." Her voice, once strong, was as thin as spun glass.

The backs of the woman's hands were marred with dark age spots; her once elegant fingers, now gnarled with arthritis, looked every bit as fragile as the bone china she carried. It was as if Miss Havisham herself had stepped from the pages of the Dickens novel. All that was missing was the ancient, yellowed wedding gown.

Jade could not find it in her heart to be angry at this frail wisp of a woman. She took a sip of the English Breakfast tea. "It's fine," she said kindly. In truth, her tension gave the tea an unpleasant metallic taste.

Miss Lillian gave her a grateful smile, cast a quick, nervous glance toward her brother, then scurried from the room.

"Well," Quinlan demanded, once they were alone again, "why don't you say what you've come here to say, then we can get down to brass tacks and talk about how we're going to work together."

"I don't believe I've agreed to work with you," Jade said mildly.

"Gallagher Gas and Oil is my company."

"Actually," Jade said, taking the papers from her alligator bag, "I believe that since I'm holding notes equaling more than eighty-five percent of the company's current worth, Gallagher Gas and Oil is now my company."

If she'd expected him to cave in immediately, Jade was to be disappointed. "Look here, Mrs. Southerland," he said, mocking her married name, "perhaps you've forgotten the way things work out here in the oil patch. One hand washes another. There's no reason you and I can't work out a reasonable deal."

"Such as?"

"I hear you've got yourself a real nice little auction business goin' for yourself. So, here's my offer—you take Miss Lillian's collection and I'll keep my mouth shut about your past. A past that you sure as hell wouldn't want all those fancy city types to know about."

Amazing how remarkably like Sam's children Quinlan sounded. Unable to sit still, she began to walk around the room, picking up various treasures, some of which she could remember helping to purchase.

"That sounds vaguely familiar," she murmured. As she examined a piece of Waterford crystal, her mind flashed back to a long ago day when Miss Lillian had told her about Ireland, and the castle Gallagher.

Jade shook off the distant memory. "This isn't the first time you've resorted to blackmail to get what you wanted," she accused softly. "Is it?"

Quinlan astonished her by throwing back his leonine head and laughing. "I wondered how long it'd be before you found out about that little trick."

"A little trick." Jade's head was spinning. How could he remain so blasé about such treachery? "To keep me from Roarke."

"What the hell did you expect me to do, sit by and let some round-heel's little slut take my son away? Just when it was beginnin' to look like I was gonna get him back home again, running the company and the ranch, where he belonged? Hell, Cassie, or Jade, or Mrs. Southerland, whatever you're callin' yourself these days, if you want to get ahead in this world, you'd better learn to play hardball. Or get out of the game."

To Jade's amazement, he actually smiled. "But that's all water under the bridge. I'm a pragmatic man, Cassie. I've had to be. We can still do business, whatever little problems we've had in the past."

Little problems? Quinlan's revelation cut across Jade's thoughts like broken glass. She didn't realize that her fingers had snapped the fragile stem of the wineglass until she felt the warm flow of blood trailing down the inside of her wrist.

"Goddamn it," Quinlan cursed. Pulling a white handkerchief from his pocket, he wrapped it around her hand. Just the touch of his hand on hers made Jade tremble.

She pulled her hand away. "I can't believe you think I'd actually be willing to do business with you. After all you've done."

Even if Quinlan Gallagher had represented her last opportunity, Jade could never work with the very man who had caused so much devastation in her life. She picked up an antique Colt .45 Peacemaker from an open case on a nearby table.

"Be careful with that," Quinlan warned. "It's loaded."

"Oh?" She ran her fingers over the silver barrel. "Isn't it dangerous to keep a loaded gun around the house?"

"I was at the gun club this morning with a guy who said he might be interested in buyin' it and wanted to make sure it was in working condition. I'd just got back when you showed up."

Without a word, Jade lifted the gun and aimed it directly at him.

"Would you put that damn thing down?" His complexion had turned an ashen gray and Jade could see fear building in his eyes.

"In a minute." She glanced up at the oil painting of Quinlan over the fireplace. It was enormous and hung in a vulgar gold frame. Although

Quinlan had been a young man when the painting was commissioned, cruelty had already etched harsh lines into his face. She had always hated that painting. . . .

"Cassie, the gun . . ." Quinlan moved forward an inch.

"It would be so easy," she murmured, more to herself than to him. "All I'd have to do is pull the trigger. And poof. You'd be gone. Unable to hurt anyone again."

"Hell, girl, you don't have the guts to kill anyone. You always were too much of a softie."

"I've gotten a lot tougher. Thanks to you."

He reached out a hand. Jade found herself enjoying the way it trembled. "Cassie, you don't want to do this," he coaxed, in a voice that had lost its arrogance. "Look, we can work out a deal. You can have every antique and painting in the house. I never liked the damn dust collectors anyway. I only bought them to keep Miss Lillian happy. But I remember her telling me how much you loved her treasures. Well, now they'll all be yours. And the proceeds should pay off my loans. How about it, Cassie?"

"I'm already a rich woman, Quinlan. Besides, there isn't any amount of money that could make up for what you've done. As for your outstanding loans, has it ever occurred to you that your arrogance is ultimately going to prove to be your downfall?

"Your almighty ego kept you from taking Gallagher Gas and Oil public, even when the oil bust hit and you desperately needed a fresh infusion of capital. But you couldn't give up absolute control, could you, Quinlan? Not even to save the company all those Gallagher ancestors whose portraits are hanging in the upstairs hallway worked so hard to build. And now, here you are, mortgaged up to your red neck. And as I'm sure you'll recall, those notes were due on demand."

"Cassie . . ."

"So, you can take this as official notification that I'm calling them all due, Quinlan. Now."

Taking a deep, steadying breath, Jade closed her eyes and pulled the trigger.

# Twenty-four

As Jade raced from the house, lightning split the sky and cast her in stark relief. Her suede pumps flew across the wide, columned portico and down the curving driveway, over the red brick paving stones. With nerveless fingers, she rooted through her handbag, searching desperately for her car keys; her cream toque hat, airborne by a sudden gust of wind, landed amid a trio of pudgy cherubs frolicking in the center of the algae-filled fountain. Jade didn't notice.

Fumbling blindly to unlock the door, she dropped the keys onto the ground. It took a total of three tries before she was able to get the door open and two additional attempts to coax the engine to turn over.

"Damn, damn, damn," she cried in frustration. Pushing the gas pedal to the floor, Jade slammed her left hand against the steering wheel and twisted the key yet again with her right. It finally caught, and with a mighty roar of the car motor, she tore down the driveway, leaving behind a trail of black rubber.

It was dusk. Heavy black thunderheads, pregnant with rain, throbbed overhead; gray shadows yawned across the wide-open Oklahoma landscape. Wondering what had possessed her to embark on this dark pilgrimage, Jade pushed her foot down on the accelerator and sped past the forest of "For Sale" signs on her way back to the Rose Rock Motel.

The signs, the graffiti sprayed across the red brick front of the Sears catalogue store, the boarded-up windows of the Kleen Kloze laundromat, and the abandoned Winn-Dixie market were all proof that Gallagher City, Oklahoma, was on the skids. The windows of the Ranchers' Trust Bank had been soaped opaque; some of the broken ones had been replaced with sheets of plywood. Some hadn't. Caught up in her thoughts, Jade didn't spend time considering the obvious signs of economic recession.

*Fool,* a voice screamed out in her mind. *What made you come back?*

"To settle things," Jade muttered. Her knuckles whitened as her fingers tightened on the steering wheel. "Once and for all." The first scattered drops of rain began splattering against the windshield. It was almost as if fate had decreed that she and Quinlan Gallagher would meet again.

The rain turned to hail, hammering on the roof of the car. Lightning washed the town in a brief stuttering light. When she turned the rental car into the potholed parking lot, a crack of thunder sent involuntary shivers up her spine. She had to get out of there. Leave Gallagher City and never look back.

She parked beneath a flashing red and blue neon sign: ROSE ROCK MOTEL, BARGAIN PRICES, TV, TRUCK AND U-HAUL PARKING IN THE REAR. A "For Sale" sign flapped forlornly in the wind; weeds grew halfheartedly through the cracks in the asphalt.

Opening the car door, she made a dash for the bungalow. Thunder exploded, not above her but around her. Lightning flashed so brightly that she could taste the electricity in the air. Nearby—too close for comfort—a bolt of lightning split a cottonwood tree in two. A moment later, Jade was safe inside her room, leaning against the locked door, her heart pounding so fast she could no longer distinguish the individual thuds.

On the way into the bathroom to retrieve her cosmetic case, Jade paused in front of the cloudy full-length mirror attached to the back of the door. She was, to put it charitably, a wreck. Her hair looked as if she'd taken an eggbeater to it, her face was pale, she'd bitten off all her lipstick and damn . . . an ugly bloodstain spread across the damp front of her skirt.

The alabaster wool suit was nearly new and Jade hated the idea of it being ruined. Old habits, like youthful obsessions, died hard, and although she was now an extremely wealthy woman, she hated to lose such an expensive suit. She was desperate to get out of Gallagher City before the events of the past few hours came crashing down on her, but she knew that if she didn't make an attempt to get the blood out before it set, it might be too late by the time she got back to San Francisco. She changed to the emerald green silk kimono she'd purchased on her last trip to Hong Kong and began scrubbing away at the spot with cold water.

The storm was stalled directly overhead. Electricity ignited the sky; thunder rumbled like cannon fire. Wind gusted, rattling the windows. That, along with a sudden, unexpected hammering on the door, made Jade jump.

"Oh, hell. What now?"

Leaving the skirt, Jade returned to the other room. As she peered through a wide crack in the shutters, her blood turned to ice. Standing on the narrow bungalow porch was Walter Lockley, Gallagher County's sheriff. Taking a deep breath that was meant to calm, but didn't, she opened the door.

"What can I do for you, Sheriff?" Jade's voice held a cool composure she didn't feel. The sight of the man's ruddy scowling face brought back a flood of memories, none of them pleasant.

Sheriff Lockley was tall and paunchy; his belly strained against the shirt of his rumpled khaki uniform. He was wearing a handgun in a holster, the Sam Browne belt slung low on his ample hips, as if to emulate some gunfighter he'd seen on the late, late show. But he still looked like the aging playground bully Jade knew him to be.

Lockley pushed back his gray Stetson and eyed Jade with something that resembled amusement. "Well, damned if the gossip mill wasn't well greased this time," he drawled. He was smiling, but it was not a pleasant smile. It was cold, cynical, and typically cruel. "When Virgil Taylor told me little ole Cassie McBride had come back to Gallagher City, I accused him of drinking too much of that white lightnin' he'd brung back from his cousin Ernest's Tennessee still. But here you are. In the flesh."

His gray eyes raked her lewdly from head to foot. Jade gathered the collar of the kimono closer together. "In case you hadn't heard, I'm Jade Southerland now."

The sheriff shrugged. "Well, now, missy, I've always believed that a leopard never changes his spots. And the way I see it, a McBride is still poor white trash, no matter what fancy name and city clothes she puts on."

"Did you come for some particular reason, Sheriff?" Ice coated each word. "Or have you taken over Miss Minnie Hogue's old job as Gallagher City's welcome wagon lady?"

The only signs of Lockley's anger were the bright red spots on his cheeks. "Still got that smartass mouth, don't you, gal?"

"So they say." Jade's initial fear gave way to irritation. "So why don't you just state your business, Sheriff, before the rain ruins that pretty new cowboy hat?"

The red spots on his cheeks deepened, like a fever starting to spread. His eyes locked onto hers and held.

"Miz Cassie McBride, alias Jade Southerland," he announced, shouting to be heard over the violent thunderclap that almost drowned him out, "you are under arrest. For the murder of Quinlan Gallagher."

Appearances were damning. The stain on Jade's skirt, soaking in the bathroom sink of her motel room, was presumed to be Quinlan Gallagher's blood, as was the blood on the monogrammed handkerchief found on the front seat of her rental car.

"Your fingerprints match those on the Peacemaker you used to kill him," Lockley announced. "You want to try to explain that?"

"Quinlan wanted me to take his collection on consignment." It was the truth as far as it went. Jade saw no reason to volunteer the fact that she'd turned him down. "I had to examine the gun in order to determine its value."

He didn't even attempt to conceal his disbelief. "What about the powder burns on your fingers?"

Her shoulders slumped. "All right," she admitted, "I shot the damn gun. But not at Quinlan." She took a deep breath. "You have to understand, I was angry. So I shot that damn portrait of him."

"Yeah, we spotted the hole right off," the sheriff agreed. "Helluva thing to do to an expensive piece of art. But the way I figure it, your first shot went wild. It was the second that killed Gallagher."

"The second?"

"You know as well as I do that you fired two shots from that revolver."

"I don't know any such thing. I didn't kill the bastard!"

"How do you explain the witnesses?"

Jade blanched. "Witnesses?"

"I've got two ranch hands who saw you drivin' away from the house after they heard the shots. I also have witnesses who remember you swearing that you'd get even with Gallagher if it took you the rest of your life."

"There was only one shot! And as for getting even—that was a long time ago," Jade protested. "I was young. And upset."

His grin reminded her of a rattler. "Tell that to the jury."

When she was finally allowed to use the telephone, Jade called Nina.

"Don't worry about a thing," Nina said. "I'll find you the best criminal attorney in the country."

To Jade, who'd been expecting someone along the lines of Perry Mason, Margaret Brown was a revelation. She had come directly to the jail from the airport, and dressed in traveling clothes of jeans and a "Save the Whales" T-shirt, with a wild halo of curly brown hair surrounding her elfin face, she could have passed for a teenager. One look at the attorney made Jade's heart sink.

"I appreciate you coming all this way," she said, choosing her words with extreme care. "But may I ask how old you are?"

Margaret Brown arched a shaggy brown eyebrow. "I hadn't realized age was a primary concern to someone facing a murder charge."

Jade blushed. "It's just that I wondered if you—"

"Were old enough to have much of a track record?" Margaret finished up for her. "Let me put it this way: I am, in certain lofty law circles, referred to as a bit of a prodigy. I graduated *cum laude* from Sarah Lawrence at nineteen, was on the Law Review at Stanford. I joined the firm of Daley, Hartwell, Kaplan, and Steinberg, of which you've undoubtedly heard."

The firm Sam had used for his business dealings. Jade nodded. "Of course."

"I made partner two years ago. Over the past ten years I've earned a ninety percent success rate in my courtroom cases, which would have been higher if all my clients had been as honest with me as I expect you to be. I'm also ridiculously expensive, but since you're loaded, that shouldn't present a problem." She sat back in the hard wooden chair and folded her hands on the scarred oak table. "Any more questions?"

"Only one," Jade said. "When can you start?"

Margaret grinned. "I already have."

Under Margaret's relentless probing, Jade confessed everything, including her long-held belief that Roarke Gallagher, Amy's father, was her half brother.

"Which would have made Quinlan Gallagher your father," Margaret pointed out, not ceasing her constant scribbling on the yellow legal pad. "Betrayal is a time-honored motive. I would assume, after all you've told me about your relationship with the deceased, that there was a time when you had contemplated murder. Especially when you found out how he'd blackmailed your mother into telling you a lie that kept you from being with the man you loved."

"When I was younger, after I got out of jail, I hated Quinlan. There was even a time I wished him dead," Jade admitted. "I even fantasized about killing him myself. But wishes and fantasies aren't actions. I never would have done anything about it."

"Wouldn't you?"

"No."

Margaret made a notation on her pad. "What about later?"

"Later I became too caught up in my own life—Amy, my job, Sam—to give him any more than a passing thought. In a way, I suppose I should be grateful to him."

"Grateful?"

"If he hadn't run me out of town, I wouldn't be where I am today."

"So you didn't kill him."

"No," Jade repeated emphatically, "I didn't kill him."

Margaret gave her a long, probing look. Finally, she put her pad away in her briefcase and said, "I'll be back."

"Where are you going?"

"The first thing I'm going to do is to get you out of here."

"Before the trial? Can you do that?"

"I'm going to do my damndest," Margaret promised. "Hang in there. And don't say anything to anyone."

Unfortunately, Quinlan Gallagher's power seemed to extend beyond the grave. "The damn judge refused to grant bail," Margaret fumed. "Muttered something about the possibility of you fleeing the state."

Jade wasn't surprised. "Now what?"

"Now we roll up our sleeves and get to work. Oh, by the way, there are some friends of yours outside who are dying to see you."

Jade had never been so happy to see anyone in her life as she was Nina at that moment. "Whatever you need," Nina said after giving Jade a hug. "Moral support, financial support. Anything. Everything. And look who I brought with me."

Jade glanced over Nina's shoulders at Mickey McLaughlin.

"Before I got the cushy art gig, I worked for the D.A.," he answered her unspoken question with a grin. "Don't worry, we'll have you out of here in no time."

"I don't know how to thank you."

"Hey," he said with a shrug, "you know better than anyone that I don't come cheap. But you also know that you get what you pay for. Besides," he said with a bold wink, "it sure as hell doesn't hurt my business having such a classy broad for a client."

Jade was feeling lucky for having such good friends when Margaret said, "There's someone else waiting to see you."

"Belle?"

"Better," Nina said softly.

Margaret left the room. Moments later, she returned with Roarke.

"Oh, Roarke." Love blazed in Jade's unguarded face, but was immediately replaced by despair. Obviously he had come back to Gallagher City to bury his father.

"Mickey and I still have to check into the motel, such as it is," Nina said. She bent down and gave Jade another hug. "Everything's going to be all right," she whispered. "You'll see."

Mickey said his good-byes, but Jade didn't hear. Nor was she aware of Margaret professing a sudden need to call the state police labs and get the report on the bloodstains on Quinlan's handkerchief. Their words were nothing but a vague buzz in Jade's ears as she waited for Roarke's reaction.

Roarke tried not to show how upset he was by Jade's appearance. Her hair was pulled back from her too-thin face; purplish shadows darkened the pale skin beneath her eyes, eyes that were filled with alarm. He wanted to take her in his arms, to make love to her until this nightmare went away. Instead, he crouched beside her chair.

"They certainly were in a hurry to leave us alone. I didn't realize it was that obvious."

Jade looked at him blankly, readying herself for anything.

"How much I love you," he explained.

The unexpected declaration reverberated inside her head. "What?"

"I love you." His hands on her face kept her from turning away. Their eyes met, his warm and reassuring, hers wary and uncertain. "I always have. Even when I was trying my damndest to hate you."

Jade's shoulders slumped with relief that he didn't hate her and regret that she'd cost them so much pain. "Oh, Roarke . . . I didn't kill him."

"I know."

"Really?"

"Of course."

"Why are you here?"

"To be with you. And to help Margaret and McLaughlin prove your innocence."

Jade knew that however this nightmare turned out, she would be grateful for this one wonderful moment.

"Oh, Roarke," she whispered, sounding like an echo, but unable to express her feelings in words.

The wealth of emotion in her eyes told him everything. Roarke kissed her, and she moaned his name as his mouth covered hers. Pleasure flowed into her like fine wine, warming her blood, blurring her senses.

Jade's eyes were closed; her lips parted. Desire overwhelmed caution. She pressed her hand against his chest and felt the powerful beat of his heart, its rapid rhythm echoing her own. If they had been anywhere else. . . . If they had been alone. . . . But they were in the attorney's room at the Gallagher City jail.

"We can't do this." She pulled away, breaking the blissful contact.

"Not here," Roarke agreed. "And not now. But soon."

"No." Jade jumped to her feet and began pacing, like a caged animal. "I can't think about us." She wrapped her arms around herself, as if trying to hold in check all the turbulent emotions churning around inside her. "Not now."

Puzzled by her sudden emotional swing, Roarke reminded himself that she'd been through a helluva lot. She was entitled to be upset.

"Then we won't." He caught up with her in midstride. His hands were on her waist, turning her to face him. "For now we'll concentrate on getting you out of here."

Jade lowered her forehead to his shoulder and allowed his strength to flow from him into her. The warm sensation of his kiss still lingered on her lips, taunting her with memories of other days. Other kisses. And although she wanted desperately to believe that Roarke would understand about the lies she had told him, she was terrified that he would never forgive her for keeping his daughter from him all these years.

Margaret's expression the following day was grim. "We've got a problem."

"So tell me something I don't know," Jade said dryly.

"Your skirt has disappeared."

"What?"

"The one with the blood. It never made it to the state lab."

"What happened to it?"

"That's open to conjecture. But I'll bet that wherever it is, Quinlan Gallagher's handkerchief is with it."

"The handkerchief's missing too?"

"Yeah." Margaret shook her head in disgust. "Isn't that an amazing coincidence?"

"But without them . . ."

"We're going to have a helluva time proving that you're telling the truth when you say that the stains were caused by your blood," Margaret said. "But on the other hand, without the physical evidence, the prosecutor won't be able to bring them up in the first place."

"But there's still the revolver."

"Yeah." The attorney's expression was less than encouraging. They both knew that considering the past feud with Gallagher, her fingerprints on the trigger of the Peacemaker would undoubtedly damn her in the eyes of the jury.

"I'm still working on the change of venue," Margaret said. "Plus, Mickey's got something up his sleeve."

"What?"

Margaret closed her notebook. "I'll tell you if it works out. Meanwhile, keep your chin up. This will all be over before you know it."

As she returned to her cell, Jade wished that she could feel as optimistic.

The following day, Jade was on her way out to the ranch. Pulling strings that went beyond Gallagher City to the governor, Margaret had gotten Jade out of jail on a three-hour pass.

"It's just a hunch," Mickey explained as he drove Roarke, Margaret, and Jade out to the ranch. "But seventeen years in the business have taught me to trust my instincts. And those instincts are telling me that Roarke's aunt knows more about her brother's death than she's saying."

From the fear on Miss Lillian's face when she opened the door, Jade decided that Mickey McLaughlin's professional instincts were right on target.

"Why, Roarke," Miss Lillian said, obviously flustered. "This is a surprise." Her expression closed as she turned to Jade. "And Jade. I hadn't realized they let you out of jail."

"Hello, Miss Lillian," Jade said. "I was given a pass to come talk with you." She took a deep breath. "I wanted to tell you that I wasn't the one who killed Quinlan."

The elderly woman stood there for a long time, staring up at Jade.

"Well, please, come in," she said finally. "I'll make a pot of tea and we'll visit."

Jade almost laughed. Even in the midst of a murder investigation, the woman was prepared to make tea. Jade also noticed that Roarke's aunt had pointedly failed to respond to her profession of innocence.

"I'm sorry, Aunt Lillian," Roarke said, "but—"

"Tea sounds perfect," Mickey broke in, giving Roarke a warning glance. "It'll cut the dust."

Miss Lillian smiled up at the detective. "That's what Quinlan always used to say." Her smile faded to a frown. "Of course he was referring to bourbon. My brother," she said in an aside to Margaret, "was not a tea drinker."

They waited in the parlor while Miss Lillian busied herself in the kitchen. Margaret offered to help, but the elderly woman refused, insisting that she was more than capable of taking care of things. After all, hadn't she been running this house all her life?

"Quite a museum your aunt has here," Mickey commented, glancing around the antiques-filled room, his expert eye appraising Miss Lillian's treasures.

"If collecting were a religion," Roarke said, "Aunt Lillian would be its patron saint." He picked up a small Meissen porcelain shepherdess from the table beside his Sheraton chair. "That was always one of the things she loved about Cassie—Jade," he corrected himself with a smile Jade's way.

"Oh?" Margaret asked.

"Jade was the only person who ever understood my aunt's obsession with beautiful things." He put the porcelain back on the table.

Miss Lillian's arrival in the doorway forestalled further conversation. The mood was definitely strained as the frail woman poured the tea. Jade was amazed once again at how old she looked.

"I've thought about you, Miss Lillian," Jade offered into the strained silence, "quite a lot over the years."

Something flashed in her pale eyes. Something that looked a lot like fear. "You have?"

"Of course. You opened up an entire world for me. I wouldn't be where I am today if you hadn't taken me in and taught me so many things. I've always been sorry that I never had the opportunity to thank you."

"You always were a quick learner," Miss Lillian said. "Cassie had the gift, you know," she said to the others. "Not many people do." She picked up a Baccarat swan.

"The gift?" Margaret asked gently.

Miss Lillian traced the exquisitely carved wing with her fingertips. "It's a different world," she said dreamily. "With its own secret language. Cassie was born to speak that language." She walked across the room and held the swan up to the window. The crystal caught the sunlight and broke it into rainbows that danced on the walls. "Needless to say, Quinlan was not."

"What makes you say that?" Roarke kept his voice low. "He certainly never complained about the money."

"So long as he had it," Miss Lillian snapped. Her spine stiffened, her mouth hardened into a tight line. "But the minute he gets into a little trouble, what's the first thing he does?"

A look of dread appeared in Roarke's eyes. Seeing it, Jade reached out and put her hand on his arm. "Sell his collection?" Jade asked.

"Not *his* collection." Miss Lillian spun around, with a deadly look in her eye. *"My* collection." She hit her fist against her thin breast. "It was all mine. It may have been his money, but I was the one who discovered all these wonderful things. I was the one who brought them here and turned Quinlan's house into a proper, beautiful home. A home he could be proud of."

"You must have been very angry when he told you that he was going to take it all away," Mickey suggested.

"He didn't tell me," she raged. "He went behind my back. When I heard him arranging with Cassie to sell everything off, leaving me with nothing, I realized I had no choice."

"You had to kill him," Roarke said flatly.

"Yes." Miss Lillian's eyes blazed with the fury of a zealot. "I had no choice, you see. He was going to take them all away. All my lovely things."

Even though he realized that his aunt's confession would free Jade, Roarke's eyes filled with tears.

Three hours later, Jade stood on the courthouse steps, breathing in the fresh exhilarating scent of freedom. "You will take her case, won't you?" she asked Margaret.

"If you really want me to," the attorney said. "From what I've seen of Miss Lillian, it shouldn't be that difficult to prove diminished mental faculties. Although why you'd want to help her after all that family has put you through—"

"She's Roarke's aunt and she *was* good to me."

Margaret had already discovered Jade's stubborn streak. "Hey, it's your money. So, what are you going to do now?"

"I have to talk to Roarke."

Margaret reached out and squeezed Jade's hand. "Good luck."

# Twenty-five

Jade stared around the motel room in disbelief. Fragrant white candles bathed the room in a warm, flickering light. White roses bloomed everywhere, on the dresser, on top of the television, on the floor surrounding the bed. The bed had been turned down; the mended muslin sheets had disappeared. Rose petals, looking like snowflakes in the muted, glowing light, had been scattered over peach satin sheets.

"It's not the honeymoon suite at the Ritz," Roarke said. He traced the line of her cheek with his finger, surprised to find that his hands were not steady. "But it'll have to do, for now." His mouth was a whisper away from hers. "Because I can't wait for you any longer."

When he kissed her, there was an instantaneous flash of heat. Startled, Jade tried to back away, but his arms tightened around her waist, holding her close.

"Don't you think we've played this game long enough? I love you. I loved you when you were Cassie and I love you now." His hands tugged her blouse loose and slipped under the hem. "And I want you." His fingers slid up her ribcage, his slow, seductive touch seeming to melt the ivory lace covering her breasts. When he plucked at her lace-covered nipples, Jade felt a deep, answering pull between her legs.

Encouraged by her trembling, Roarke inserted his hand between her legs. "I want to be there," he said, pressing his palm against her mound. "I want to be inside you, Jade. We've waited so damn long I think I'll go mad if I can't make love to you. Now."

A row of gleaming gold buttons ran down the front of her silk blouse. Slowly, one by one, he unfastened them and savored what he saw. "You are so beautiful." He lowered his head and took one aching breast into his mouth. "Absolutely exquisite."

The sweet scent of roses swirled in Jade's head. Ribbons of desire, like streams of flowing golden light, ran through her veins. "Oh, Roarke."

"I like to hear you say my name." He unzipped her skirt; it fell to the floor. "Say it again."

"Roarke." Without breaking the exhilarating contact between them, Jade stepped out of the skirt. Her legs, encased to the top of her thigh in ivory silk, gleamed like pearls.

He drew her to the bed. "Again."

"Roarke."

The rose petals caressed her flesh. Roarke lay down beside her and kissed her ears, her eyelids, her jaw, her hair. He lifted one slender leg in the air and kissed her ankle, behind her knee, the warm soft place on her thigh where the stocking ended. Then he slid her bikini briefs down her legs.

When she felt desire rising, Jade slid free of his embrace. "My turn."

Unbuttoning his shirt, she pushed it off his shoulders. Next she unfastened his belt, ridding him of the faded denim jeans and cotton briefs. Dressed, Roarke was a remarkably handsome man. Nude, as he was now, he was magnificent. Jade touched him everywhere, loving the feel of his taut muscles beneath her wandering hand.

The brush of a fingernail against his dark nipple inflamed, the caress of her lips against his belly aroused. She moved her body sinuously against his, like a cat, and he burned. Her sultry laugh shimmered over his moist flesh as her mouth nibbled his hip.

Jade curved her fingers around the width of his erect penis and stroked it lovingly. When she took him in her mouth, embracing him with her tongue, Roarke thought he'd explode.

"I've always enjoyed playing with fire," he said, tangling his hands in her hair and lifting her head for a long, soulful kiss. "But let's not put it out too soon."

He pressed her back onto the bed and pulled a pillow beneath her hips, slanting her pelvis toward him. He sat back on his haunches and drank in the sight of her. Her eyes were glowing but there was nothing resembling submission in their catlike depths. She looked wild. And wanton.

"If you'd looked like this back in the days of witch hunts," Roarke murmured huskily, "you would have been burned at the stake."

As his lips created an urgency that was almost painful, every inch of Jade's body tingled, every nerve ending screamed out with desire. Her back arched off the bed. And then the expanded moment shattered. Jade turned her head, muffling her ragged cry into the pillow. Spent, she lay there, long legs still spread, her body flushed pink with orgasm.

Fired by the provocative sight, Roarke moved into her. Relinquishing the final vestiges of control to the primitive forces that had taken over his body, each thrust was deeper, harder, hotter. She came again and again, the soft cries that accompanied her orgasms exciting him until finally, he poured into her, calling out her name as he filled her with his seed.

"You are incredible," Roarke said when he could talk again.

Jade smiled. "You're not so bad yourself."

"It certainly took you long enough to realize that."

A shadow moved across her face. "I need to explain. About Seriphos. And why I lied to you about my feelings afterward." She closed her eyes against the pain that long-ago memory caused. "About a lot of things."

"We have a lifetime to talk. Right now there's only one thing I want to know."

"What's that?"

"You are going to marry me, aren't you?"

Jade sat up and pulled the sheet up to cover her breasts. "There's something you need to know before I give you my answer."

"There's nothing you can say that would change my feelings."

Love was shining in his eyes. Engulfed in an icy wave of guilt, Jade bit her lip and looked away. "Perhaps you ought to wait until you hear the truth." She rose from the bed, took her robe from her suitcase, and put it on.

Afraid that Roarke would not be able to forgive her for keeping his daughter's existence a secret all these years, Jade began stutteringly to explain that she hadn't pretended about her feelings on Seriphos. That she had fallen in love with him all over again—if she had ever fallen out of love.

"I knew you weren't faking."

"I wasn't. Not then. But then . . ." She sighed. "Oh, God, this is so hard." She took a deep, shuddering breath. "Your father visited me shortly after I got back to New York."

"My father?"

Sinking to a vinyl armchair, Jade told him all about his father's accusations, going on to reveal her trip to Gallagher City, where Belle had confirmed the hateful story.

"So the old man pulled one of his Machiavellian stunts on you. That finally explains everything." Roarke's mouth drew into a harsh line. "I'm sorry that he caused you so much grief."

Jade managed a shrug. "It's all over now."

"Yes." Roarke knew they were both thinking of his father's death. "If only you'd said something. I could have told you that we were living in Iran the year before you were born, while my father negotiated oil leases, and there was no way you and I could have been brother and sister."

Roarke frowned. "I suspected when you refused my proposal that he'd been the one to tell you about my designing his building. I also had the distinct feeling that he'd done something else to make you change your mind about us," he muttered. "But you wouldn't tell me the truth, and when I came down here and asked what the hell was going on, he denied even having seen you since you left town after the arrest."

He sighed and shook his head. "I couldn't prove a damn thing, but I also knew right then and there that there was no way I was ever going to work with him."

"So you ended up doing exactly what he had been trying to stop in the first place," Jade murmured.

"You should have told me," Roarke repeated quietly. "My father's damn lies cost us so many years."

Some of those lost years Jade could not regret. Because of Sam. And if her husband—a husband she'd truly, deeply loved—hadn't died, she wouldn't be having this conversation now. But Sam had died, and now it was past time to tell Roarke the truth.

"I couldn't tell you," she said in a voice that was little more than a whisper. "Because I felt so guilty."

"Guilty?"

She bit her lip so hard that she broke the skin. "Because of Amy."

"Amy?"

She closed her eyes. "Amy's your daughter."

"But I don't have a . . ." Comprehension hit like a thunderbolt, and he stared at her. "You had a child? My child?"

As frightened as she was, Jade felt a sense of relief to finally have her closely guarded secret out in the open. "Yes."

"When? After Seriphos?"

"No. Amy was born nine months after that first time we made love in the storm cellar." She'd always known the day her daughter was conceived; the afternoon of the tornado had been the only time that summer Roarke had forgone protection.

"That time?" he said disbelievingly, his mind engaged in rapid calculation. "But that would make her—"

"Ten," Jade said softly.

"Ten? Ten years old?" His hand curled into an unconscious fist. "You kept my daughter a secret from me for ten years? Why?"

All the reasons that had once seemed to make so much sense now seemed to hold as much substance as San Francisco fog. "It's complicated."

"The hell it is." Roarke enjoyed the rush of pure fury running through his veins. At least it cleared the clouds from his brain.

He was towering over the chair; Jade shrank back from him. "I didn't think you'd want her." Outside the window an unearthly orange glow hovered over the landscape as the sun prepared to dip beneath the horizon. "After all, you never answered my letters."

Roarke remembered something from their conversation on Seriphos. "The letters you wrote me from jail."

"Yes."

"But I told you, I never got any damn letters."

"I know." She looked away, unable to meet his furious gaze.

Roarke slammed his hand onto the dresser. "Look at me when I'm talking to you, damnit!"

Jade slowly turned around and lifted her chin. "I know what I did was wrong. Perhaps it was even unconscionable. But I can't go back and do things differently, Roarke. As much as I'd love to."

"Ten years old. Christ." Her glared at her. "Who else knew? Belle. My father?"

Jade shook her head.

"That, at least is something. Does Nina know?"

"Of course. I lived with her when Amy was born. We wouldn't have survived without Nina's help."

"Remind me to thank her," he said dryly. "What about Sam? Surely even you couldn't keep a growing daughter a secret from your husband?"

"Of course not. Sam knew all about Amy," Jade said flatly. "He loved her. He wanted to adopt her."

Some dark force forked through him. "You were going to let another man adopt my child? Without a word to me?"

"It seemed like the right thing to do at the time. But I realize that I was wrong." Jade's voice caught on a sob. "One of the last things Sam said to me, before he died, was that I should tell you the truth."

"Sam knew I was Amy's father?" Such treachery from a man he'd thought to be a friend hurt nearly as badly as Jade's deception.

"Not until the end."

"Poor bastard." Roarke's voice was flat. Empty. "He loved you more than life itself. And you lied to him, too?"

Jade didn't answer. The silence stretched between them like a fuse. Finally, Roarke scooped up his clothing from the floor and got dressed. "You'll be hearing from my attorney."

"What?"

He pinned her with a cold glare. "You've had the first ten years of my daughter's life. I'm sure I can find a judge to grant me the next ten years."

He was going to walk out of her life, Jade realized with a shock of awareness. And try to take Amy with him.

"Roarke." She held out her hand. "Please, darling—"

"Don't call me that!" He shot one last blistering look at her, then marched out the door. Leaving her alone to face the consequences of a lifetime of lies.

After a sleepless night, Jade was sitting in the terminal waiting for a flight back to San Francisco.

"I'll call Jonas Reeves the minute we get back to town," Margaret assured her. After arranging to have Miss Lillian temporarily committed to a Tulsa mental health hospital, she was returning to San Francisco to tie up some loose ends on a previous case before preparing the elderly woman's defense. "He's the best custody attorney in the state."

"Roarke's right," Jade said flatly. "I kept his daughter from him for years. I know I owe him. But not sole custody!"

"Roarke is a reasonable man, Jade. He'll settle for visitation rights. Or joint custody," Nina said.

Jade raised her eyes to Mickey's impassive face. "If you discovered that a woman you'd once loved had kept your child a secret, wouldn't you want revenge?"

"I'd want to hurt her, at first," Mickey agreed roughly. "The male ego's a delicate thing, Jade. No man likes to feel he's been made a fool of."

Jade gave Nina an "I told you so" look.

"But," Mickey continued, "after I cooled down, I'd realize that two wrongs didn't make a right. And taking a child away from a mother who loves her is a pretty powerful wrong."

"Mickey's right," Nina insisted. "After he's had time to think, Roarke will listen to reason."

"And if he doesn't," Margaret tacked on as their flight was called, "Jonas Reeves will see that he does."

Jade was in line to board when Roarke appeared. "We have to talk."

His sober expression, along with the memory of the violent words he'd thrown at her, made Jade cautious. "Our plane's about to take off."

He put his hand under her elbow and drew her out of the line. "You can take a later one."

Mickey stopped and turned back toward her. "Is everything all right?"

Before Jade could open her mouth, Roarke answered for her. "Look, Mickey, I appreciate everything you and Nina and Margaret have done. But now I need a few hours alone with Jade so I can apologize for going off half-cocked the way I did yesterday. And then, if she does forgive me, I'm going to need even more time to figure out how to propose to this lady."

Turning to her and ignoring the interested glances of passersby, he said, "If I were to beg you most humbly to marry me, do you suppose there's even the faintest chance that you might possibly say yes?"

Jade heard the love in his husky voice; she saw it in his dark eyes. Flinging her arms around his neck, she went joyfully into his arms. "Oh, yes," she said in a half laugh, half sob. "Yes, yes, yes."

The sky was a vast blue bowl overhead as Jade and Roarke drove through the vineyards of Napa Valley. "I can't remember the last time I was this scared," Roarke admitted.

"She's going to love you."

"God, I hope so." He pulled the car up in front of the large rambling Valley of the Moon Academy.

"Relax." Jade patted his knee. "Our daughter is not only brilliant, she inherited her mother's excellent taste in men."

"I just wish Berlitz had a crash course in sign language." So much to learn, Roarke thought. So many years to make up for.

"Don't worry. Everyone speaks a bit differently, so things might go a bit slow in the beginning, but once Amy learns to read your lips, you can probably skip learning sign all together."

"I have no intention of forgoing anything that'll help me communicate fully with my daughter."

"Fine. So for now, you talk, then I'll translate in sign. That way Amy won't miss anything."

"It's a deal."

They found Amy in the theater, absorbed in a dress rehearsal for an upcoming performance of *Peter Pan*. Standing at the back of the darkened theater, Jade and Roarke stood hand in hand and watched their daughter, wearing gossamer fairy wings, soar above the stage.

After Wendy, John, and Michael had waved a fond farewell to Peter and Tinkerbell, the house lights went up and Jade moved toward the stage, Roarke following behind her.

"Mama!" Ignoring her trailing wings, Amy ran up the aisle toward Jade. "I was *sooo* worried that you wouldn't get back from your trip in time to see my play."

Jade had refused to allow anyone to tell her daughter the truth about what was happening in Oklahoma. As far as Amy knew, her mother was simply away on another buying trip. If she'd been found guilty . . . well, Jade hadn't allowed herself to consider that possibility.

"You know I'd never miss one of your performances," Jade said now.

"Did you see me fly?"

"I saw you," Jade confirmed. "And it scared me to death, seeing you up there so high."

"You always worry too much," Amy complained with a wide grin. "I'm hooked onto a wire. I won't fall."

Thanks in part to Sam, Amy's speech was now nearly as understandable as a hearing child's. Before he'd died, Sam had donated specially programmed computers to the school that took the phonetic sounds of speech and reproduced them in colorful waves onto the monitor, allowing the students to match their spoken words to the changing patterns on the screen. The subsequent improvement in the children's speech had been nothing short of remarkable.

Amy's gaze slid from Jade to Roarke. "Hello."

Roarke found it disconcerting to see the same face he viewed in the mirror every morning on this little girl. "Hi."

"Amy, this is Roarke Gallagher," Jade said. "He's a friend of mine."

Amy looked at Roarke with renewed interest. "Like Nina?"

"More like Sam."

Amy considered that. "Did you know Sam?"

"Yes." Roarke had to restrain himself to keep from touching her. "He was a friend of mine."

"He was my friend, too. After he and Mama got married, he was going to adopt me. But then he died."

"I know."

"So now I still don't have a dad." Amy, always the actress, gave a long, dramatic sigh. Then she tilted her head and looked up at him. "I'm Tinkerbell."

"I can see that," Roarke said. "You fly very well."

"I know." Amy bobbed her head. "I wanted to be Peter Pan, but Mrs. Daniels, she's my teacher, said I was still too young. So they gave the part to Brenda Dawson. She's twelve years old and in the sixth grade."

"Personally, Tinkerbell's always been my favorite character," Roarke divulged. Reminding himself that patience was a virtue, he waited until Jade repeated his words.

"When I was a boy," he continued, after Jade's hands had stopped, "my aunt took me to New York to see the play on Broadway. Ever since then I've been a firm believer in fairies."

"I believe in them, too," Amy agreed. "Did you clap when Tinkerbell was dying?"

"Until my hands were sore."

"Good. I hope people clap tomorrow night."

"They will," Roarke assured her.

Amy gave Roarke another long, intense look. "Are you coming to the play?"

"You bet. And I have every intention of clapping until my hands are sore again."

"That's nice. Now I won't have to worry so much." Amy exchanged a look with Jade. "I like him," she announced.

"I knew you would," Jade said with a smile. "And now, why don't you run backstage and change out of your costume. Roarke and I want to discuss something with you."

The bright blue eyes went from Jade to Roarke and back to Jade again. "What?"

The original idea had been to break the news gently over a leisurely picnic lunch in the meadow. But Roarke found he'd run out of patience.

"With your permission, I'd like to marry your mother, Amy," he said. "I've loved her for a very long time and I want to spend the rest of my life with her."

Then, surprising Jade, who didn't suspect that he'd planned such a thing, Roarke went down on his right knee and took a blue velvet box from his pocket. "And I'd also be very happy if you would do me the honor of becoming my daughter."

"Oh, it's pretty!" Amy examined the small pearl ring. "Thank you." She thrust the box toward Jade. "See?"

Jade's eyes filled with tears. "It's lovely." Her whispered words were directed to Roarke, which kept Amy, who was busy trying the ring on her finger, from hearing them.

"It fits," Amy announced, holding out her hand. "I want to show Heather." She ran back down the aisle, gilt wings bobbing, to where a trio of pirates and a dark-haired girl dressed in a long white Victorian nightgown were sitting cross-legged on the stage, engaged in a spirited game of Go, Fish.

"Heather's her best friend." Jade turned to Roarke. "Have I told you how much I love you?"

"Several times in the past three days. But I wouldn't mind hearing it one more time." He lowered his head to kiss her when Amy came running back up the aisle.

"Heather's jealous," she announced. "She only has that stupid ring she won at the carnival last month. . . . Do you really love my mother?"

Roarke was still trying to get used to the idea that this beautiful, spirited girl was his daughter. "With my whole heart and soul." This time he did not need Jade to translate. "We also want you to come to San Francisco and live with us."

"And go to a real school? Like other kids?"

"That's the plan."

Amy looked up at Jade. "I think we should say yes."

Jade's smile bloomed so wide she felt as if her face were going to crack. "I think so, too."

Jade and Roarke were married in a small Napa Valley chapel, exchanging vows that they'd written themselves. The bride was beautiful in a cream silk dinner suit studded with pearls, the groom handsome in a navy suit. Amy, wearing a pink organza dress that a fairy-tale princess would have envied, scattered white rose petals from a woven basket; Nina and Belle served as witnesses.

Belle had made the trip from the halfway house in Oakland where she was living while attending counseling classes at U.C. Berkeley. She had arrived at Jade's house the day before the wedding, clad in a Camp Betty

T-shirt and jeans. She had gained a much needed ten pounds and her hair, tinted a subdued blond and cut in a stylish bob, had regained its youthful sheen. For the first time in a very long while, Jade allowed herself to believe that her mother was truly on the road to recovery.

As she and Roarke left the chapel in a shower of birdseed (Amy's "ecologically correct" contribution), Jade was floating on air.

Seriphos was everything Jade remembered it to be. The sun was warm and golden, the air was perfumed with the heady scent of bougainvillea, and music floated on the soft Mediterranean breeze.

"Happy?" Roarke was watching Jade brush her love-tangled hair into a semblance of order. They were getting ready to go out.

Jade put down the silver-backed brush. "Deliriously."

When she went to put on her earrings, Roarke caught her hand. "Wait."

"Oh, Roarke." Jade's breath caught in her throat as he replaced the coral studs with a pair of flawless emeralds. "They're magnificent." She turned, reveling in their brilliance.

"Not as magnificent as the lady wearing them. I knew it," he murmured as he nuzzled her neck.

"What?"

"That they'd match your eyes."

Green eyes met with stormy blue in the mirror. Together they watched his hands skim over her ivory silk sheathe. Roarke had a sudden urge to see Jade naked, wearing only his sparkling emeralds in her ears.

"What are you doing for the rest of the night?"

"Making love to you?"

"I knew I'd married a clever woman." He unzipped her dress. It skimmed over her hips and landed in a silken pool at her feet. She was wearing a lacy teddy that clung enticingly to her curves and her flesh carried the intoxicating scent of jasmine and sandalwood. "So what are you doing for the rest of your life?"

Jade's answering laugh was low and sultry. Smiling up at her husband, she tilted her head back for his kiss. "Making love to you."

1262 4440

FIC
ROSS

Ross, JoAnn.

Private pleasures.

$19.95

| DATE | | | |
|---|---|---|---|
| | | | |
| | | | |
| | | | |
| | | | |
| | | | |
| | | | |
| | | | |
| | | | |
| | | | |
| | | | |
| | | | |
| | | | |
| | | | |